OX 3/2013

11/12 PW,SW,BL

C'R

D0057040

The Seven Tales of Trinket

The Seven Tales of Trinket

Shelley Moore Thomas

Pictures by Dan Craig

FARRAR STRAUS GIROUX / *New York*

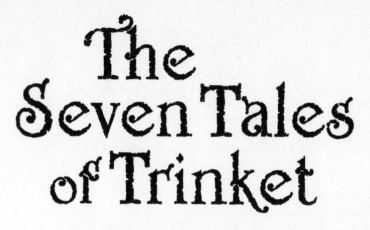

Farrar Straus Giroux Books for Young Readers
175 Fifth Avenue, New York 10010

Text copyright © 2012 by Shelley Moore Thomas
Pictures copyright © 2012 by Daniel Craig
All rights reserved
Distributed in Canada by D&M Publishers, Inc.
Printed in the United States of America by
RR Donnelley & Sons Company, Harrisonburg, Virginia
Designed by Anne Diebel
First edition, 2012
1   3   5   7   9   10   8   6   4   2

mackids.com

Library of Congress Cataloging-in-Publication Data
Thomas, Shelley Moore.
   The seven tales of Trinket / Shelley Moore Thomas. — 1st ed.
      p.   cm.
   Summary: "Guided by a tattered map, accompanied by Thomas the Pig
Boy, and inspired by the storyteller's blood that thrums through her
veins, eleven-year-old Trinket searches for the seven stories she needs
to become a bard like her father, who disappeared years before."—
Provided by publisher.
   ISBN 978-0-374-36745-9 (hardcover)
   ISBN 978-0-374-36744-2 (e-book)
   [1. Storytellers—Fiction.   2. Fantasy.]   I. Title.

PZ7.T369453Se 2012
[Fic]—dc23
                                                            2011050075

To Sean

CONTENTS

Isle of the Selkies

Conelmar

Crossmaglin

Banshee's Tower

Ringford

Agadhoe

The
Seven Tales
of Trinket

A Story Begins

MY FATHER WAS A TELLER OF TALES. *It runs in the blood, I think, for never have I loved anything so much as a story.*

Except for my mother, of course.

I loved her well.

Her death was the worst thing I've ever known. Worse even than when my father left and never came back, for that has been almost five years past and that pain is now but a dull, empty ache.

My mother's last breaths begin this story, for each story has a beginning. That is the first thing a storyteller must learn.

THE BARD'S MAP

The night was cold and the wind whispered softly, rustling leaves and occasionally rattling the shutters of our small cottage. But the sky was so clear I could see every star, even the tiny ones. Despite the chill, I spent a lot of time outside looking at the sky. It was better than being inside our cottage, which held nothing but memories of happier times, and looking at my mother, sick with the wasting. Once she had been pretty, and even as she faced death, her eyes still held a twinkle.

" 'Twas what your father first noticed about me: my eyes," she had told me many times. "Lovely Mairi-Blue-Eyes, he called me." Large they were, like sapphires, except that I had never seen a real sapphire, so I had to take her word.

I felt a hand on my shoulder. It was Thomas, the Pig Boy. "Old Mrs. Pinkett says to come in. She says . . ."

He did not finish the sentence.

Somehow, we both knew this night would be my mother's last. There was so little left of her. Thomas squeezed my shoulder as I rose to go inside. I entered as quietly as I could, though the door creaked as a light wind rushed in beside me. Old Mrs. Pinkett nodded over at the bed where my mother lay. Her once soft arms now felt of brittle bone. But her eyes were more alive than ever.

"Sing for me, Trinket," she whispered. So I sang for her the songs that we had made up in the years since my father left. They were not as beautiful as his, but we tried our best. For my mother always said that a house without music would be a lonely house indeed. When I finished, she raised a frail hand to my cheek.

"I've much to tell you, Trinket, and so little time," she said.

"First, tell me, once more, tell me the beginning," I said.

She drew a breath and began. "Once, a handsome story-teller whisked a fair maiden off her feet with his silvery words and amazing tales. He promised her a story each night and during the whole of their time together, he was true to his word. He carried her off with his words to places far away. And when she finally agreed to marry him, he took her to a little cottage by the sea where they were most joyfully happy.

"Their happiness was complete upon the birth of their babe. *Our precious child*, they called her, *our delightful trinket*, and that became her name. *Your* name: Trinket. The bard's daughter."

I smiled when she said my name.

Then she coughed. I turned to pour her some water, but there was Thomas, cup already in hand. I wanted to thank him but he disappeared as quickly as he'd come. My mother coughed again, this time even more harshly. I gave her water, but she had trouble swallowing. She tried to speak, but her voice rasped, sounding small and choked.

I took over the telling, willing my own voice to be strong.

"The traveling bard left one day when the girl was six, off on one of his storytelling, story-collecting adventures, for that was the life of a bard. He traveled from castles to villages, from coasts to mountains to valleys, telling the stories that were his own.

"He kissed the top of the child's downy head," I went on. My mother smiled, for I had added the *downy* part since the last time. "And called from the top of the hill, *I shall see you with the season's change.*"

I hesitated, then continued.

"But he never came back."

In a whisper, my mother took over the tale, adding the parts where perhaps he was kidnapped by pirates and forced to stay aboard a ship until he'd told ten thousand tales, or perhaps he had defeated a fierce dragon by putting it to sleep with a bedtime tale and had to tame all the dragons in the land with his stories.

Yes, she had told me time after time, *that is why he could never come back.*

My mother waited for his return. It took a long time for her heart to break completely. And when the illness came last winter, she had no fight left in her. A mended heart could have stood strong against the rampage of the fever and the wasting that followed. But a heart in little pieces had no chance.

She coughed and pulled me closer. "Trinket, my sweet girl. You have choices to make, you know."

"I know."

I could live with Old Mrs. Pinkett and learn the healing arts, but as much as I liked her, I did not feel the call in my bones to heal others. That is what Mrs. Pinkett said I should feel if I were to learn from her. My bones felt only empty.

I could live with Thomas the Pig Boy and his mother and learn the care and keeping of pigs and the occasional sheep, but the smell was too much. And though Thomas and I had spent most of our lives together, playing and getting into trouble, I'd no wish to be daughter to his mother. She was a rough woman with a sharp tongue that hurt far worse than getting a smack. How Thomas put up with it, I did not know.

My mother would want to know the direction I would take, Old Mrs. Pinkett had told me. It would help to ease her passing if she knew what my future might hold. But I was not so ready for my mother to leave. Not ready at all.

She looked at me, seeing more than I wished for her to. Her sapphire blue eyes squinted slightly. "I know what you are thinking."

"I am not even thinking in this moment. You must be mistaken." My lie sounded false, even to my own ears. The wind whispered and hissed through the cracks in the shutters as if doubting my words as well.

"You are thinking of him."

"Him who?" Though we both knew exactly who *him* was. My father.

"You want to go and find him."

Did I? I had never spoken these words, but in her last moments, my mother knew the questions I had been too afraid to ever ask.

"There is a map, Trinket. A map in the old chest . . ." She coughed again and this one rattled throughout the room. A gust blew open one of the shutters and it creaked back and forth whilst the wind whistled around us, secretive and chilling.

There was no time to dally, so I asked, "What *really* happened to him, do you think?"

She was quiet and her breath did not come for a moment, causing me to think that perhaps she was gone, but then she sighed and closed her eyes. The flurry in the room calmed to a gentle breeze.

"I wish I knew."

Those were her last words.

———

I cried for a whole week after she passed. I cried until the tears would come no more and my soul was empty.

"'Tis the way of things, lass," said Old Mrs. Pinkett. "Death is but the other side of life."

Thomas cried, too, after I assured him it was not unseemly for a boy to do so. He'd spent most of his life, when not with his pigs, skulking around our cottage. Eventually, we'd set a place for him at our table each night. I think my mother thought of him as a son. A messy, wild son.

She was buried in a dress of blue cloth that she herself had woven two winters ago, for her hand at weaving was among the finest in the land. 'Twas a glorious shade, like the sky at dawn. With her hair brushed smooth, she looked almost as I wanted to remember her. Mrs. Pinkett, Thomas, and even Thomas's mother said words for her. But I said nothing. I could not say what was in my heart. I could not ask her if she was at last joining my father, or if he had abandoned her even in death.

Thomas was the one who found the map. He helped me go through my parents' things. There was not much in the chest. Mostly tools and odd bits of cloth my mother had woven. There was a lovely mirror, small and silver, that we found by the back door of our cottage one winter's night. And my mother had saved the small velvet bags filled with coins that showed up mysteriously on the porch from time to time. I'd keep the mirror, for my mother had loved it well. Perhaps it was a gift from an admirer. I had wanted to believe it was from my father, but my mother was certain it was not. *Why would he leave a gift and disappear? Nay, he's probably still composing lullabies for dragons,* she'd say. Regardless, I would keep it. The velvet bags, though now empty, were of good quality and could be traded possibly. And there, underneath a fine cloak my mother had woven for special occasions, rolled up in a cracked leather canister, was the map.

"Trinket, mayhap the map shows where your father traveled about," Thomas said.

"Then why did he not take it with him the last time he

went?" I asked, although I knew the map had been my father's. But it helped me to argue with Thomas. I could only know what I was truly thinking when I had to defend one thought against another.

The map was soft and faded, drawn by my father's own hand in the black ink he always kept a small jar of on the shelf. But the ink in the jar had long since dried up, and the lines on the map had paled to a dirty brown. I traced an imaginary path from our town, through trees, to a far-off castle. Then I drew another, this time down the coast and to the villages by the sea.

"What are you going to do with it?" Thomas asked.

"What do you think?" My fingers trailed yet another direction, over the mountains to the forest.

He looked at me with eyes that widened as he understood my purpose.

"You are not going to follow it!" He spit when he yelled, which made it a good thing that Thomas the Pig Boy yelled very little.

"I am."

"You are only eleven."

"Almost twelve. A year older than you."

"What will you do out there?" Thomas asked, flicking the map with his hand.

"Why, find my father, of course."

And I will leave this place, and all the pain, behind.

But I did not say this aloud.

Thomas thought for a moment.

"If you go, can I come?"

I could have tortured him by not answering, or by saying no, but I had secretly hoped that he might want to journey with me. I could not imagine that he'd want to go back to spending all his time with his battle-ax of a mother, getting scolded if he breathed too loudly. As for myself, it would be easier to travel with a companion. And Thomas was a fairly brave boy, not to mention my only true friend.

"Could be dangerous, you know. Life on the road will not be easy."

Thomas's large brown eyes were already dancing. "Will there be excitement, do you think, and adventure?"

"Aye, mayhap. But if I let you come, you cannot complain," I said, though I knew he would from time to time. He was Thomas, after all.

Thomas nodded, his eyes alive with thoughts of great escapades.

My own thoughts were more focused. There was a truth I sought.

And I hoped with all my soul I would find it.

"Yes, Thomas," I said, "you can come with me."

THE FIRST TALE

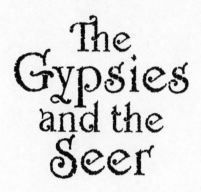

The
Gypsies
and the
Seer

THE DARK-EYED GIRL

We'd been traveling for many days and many nights, asking each person we met along the road about the story-teller known as James the Bard. My father.

But of him there was neither word nor memory.

And following the old map was not as easy as it looked. We could not tell how long it would take to get from one place to the next.

"Perhaps beyond this glade, and whatever that is," Thomas said, pointing to a cluster of what looked like trees on the map, "and over toward the east, we will find that village."

It sounded like a good plan, and I had none better, so we

continued. But it was not a village we stumbled upon as we followed the road and the faded smudges on my father's map. 'Twas a Gypsy camp. Nestled between two lush groves of trees were exotic caravans and wagons, speckling all the way up the hillside.

Thomas could barely contain his excitement. *Gypsies!* How fortunate we were to meet with such adventure so early on our journey.

My hand tapped nervously against my britches. Thomas's mum had given me the old trousers when I agreed to take Thomas along, so grateful she was at having one less mouth to feed. My only dress was rolled up tight in the bottom of my sack. I thought it best to keep it nice for when we met my father.

If we ever found him.

There was but a breath of wind as we approached the strange-looking camp. We walked a few steps. Then a few more.

Thomas's stomach growled monstrously loud.

When you are first traveling, you learn that few things are as important as food, especially if you are carting around a pig boy with a bottomless stomach. We had run out of the provisions we'd packed, and if we did not get bread soon, I feared Thomas would roast and eat his own foot.

We brushed against the low branches of trees, scuffling and dragging our feet noisily upon the gravel, clearing our throats in order to make our approach known, hoping to be heard, pitied, and fed.

In the space between two heartbeats, the Gypsies surrounded us. Shiny knives poked at us, daring us to move. My back was against Thomas's, and I could feel his spine shaking in unison with my own.

"Please, we mean you no harm," I said, my voice close to a sob. Then I took a breath and willed my tears not to fall. Were my father here, I would not want him to see me cower.

"We're just hungry," cried Thomas. And he truly cried tears of hunger. 'Twould take a cold, hard heart to ignore the sniffles of a starving boy. And, as bad luck would have it, that was exactly the kind of heart the enormous Gypsy standing in front of us possessed. He also possessed the largest, hairiest eyebrows I had ever seen in my life. I guessed him to be the Gypsy King, for none of the other folk looked near so imposing.

"Bind them!" he bellowed, and the Gypsies grabbed our wrists.

"Wait." And there, stepping out from behind the Gypsy King, was a dark-eyed girl, her black hair blowing against her cheek in the twilit breeze. She did not yell or shout at the men with knives. There was no command in her tone, yet our arms were instantly released.

She walked over and stood before Thomas and me, her eyes looking deep into ours. My own sniffling embarrassed me. Dragging Thomas along on this quest had been reckless. Surely he would have been better off at home. As for myself, well, though I did not want to lose my life, I had little left but that.

She touched my sweaty hand with her own cool one and closed her eyes, not moving even to breathe for one long moment.

Then the dark-eyed girl turned to the Gypsy King and said simply, "Do not harm these two, Father. I cannot yet see the reason that they have come, but no ill wishes travel with them. They are, after all, only children."

The Gypsy King raised a giant eyebrow at his daughter, then scowled at the pig boy and me. He took in my plain, moss-colored britches and messy plaits. His eyes moved slowly over the elegant cloak my mother had kept in the chest. Beautiful it was, of many shades and hues. I stood straighter, trying to look worthy of such a fine piece of clothing. He turned his gaze to Thomas but in less than a second he looked away. Truly, Thomas appeared to be no threat at all, with his gangly legs, stringy arms, and threadbare shirt. Thomas's feet were big and awkward. He was like a puppy or a colt that hadn't yet grown into himself.

The king said nothing. He turned to leave, gesturing with his hand, and all of the Gypsies stepped back together, as if in a dance. 'Twas strangely beautiful as they all faded into their caravans and tents, leaving Thomas, myself, and the Gypsy girl alone together.

She led us into the center of the camp to a small campfire. From a pot over the flames, she ladled out bowls of broth and handed them to Thomas and me, along with chunks of bread. I chanced a smile as Thomas slurped three bowls, one after the next. I did not eat so quickly, though, for I found my head full of cautious thoughts. *Why was the Gypsy King so quick to obey his daughter? What kind of girl was she?*

As if she read my mind, the dark-eyed girl spoke. "You wonder about me, as well you should."

I paused, my bread midway to my bowl of broth.

"I am a liar," she said.

TO TELL A LIE

———◆◈◆———

I thought I must have heard her wrong, for though most people have told small lies in their lives, 'tis few who will admit even to those. I did not speak, fearing to look the fool for misunderstanding.

"They call me Feather," she said, nodding at me to respond.

Feather. A name birds would carry on their travels with the wind.

"This is Thomas," I said, wishing his hair looked a bit tidier, not sticking out in all directions. He wiped his mouth with the back of his hand and grunted a greeting. Obviously

I had not chosen him for his manners. "He is the pig boy in our village. He agreed to accompany me on my quest . . ."

Her delicate black brows rose.

"I seek my father; he is a bard. I was hoping I might find word of him here."

She said nothing, so I continued. "A bard is a storyteller who travels from place to place, trading songs and stories for coin."

"I know what a bard is." There was a hint of annoyance in her voice. I had not yet given her the information she wanted. "What is your name?"

"I am called Trinket," I said.

"Well met, Trinket," Feather said. "We have not encountered a storyteller on our travels since I was younger than you are now, most likely. Mayhap the tales of my father's temper keep them away or perhaps it is his unwillingness to pay. Whatever the reason, none have stopped at our camp for a long, long while." Thomas and I were quiet except for the sounds of chewing and swallowing, so Feather continued. "But I remember the last one's voice, clear as a cloudless night."

"Do you remember his name?" I asked. She shrugged.

"My father was called James the Bard. They say I have his eyes." I opened my gray eyes wide, unblinking.

She returned my gaze for a moment, then shook her head. "I was far too short to look into the eyes of the last storyteller that came our way. Perhaps if you had his knees." She laughed. "Maybe *you* would be bard for us one night?" she asked.

"Nay," I answered. "I do not think so."

"What is the matter? It is only the repeating of a story. Are you afraid?" she asked.

It was my turn to shrug. 'Twas not that I feared telling a tale. The fear was that I would be horrible at it.

"Well, perhaps soon you will change your mind," Feather said. "Now, are you going to ask me about the lying or not?" She rose and stretched like a cat, the bracelets around her wrists tinkling.

It was obvious she wanted me to. And she had saved us from being tied up, so I politely inquired, "You are a liar?"

She nodded. "Yes, I lie all the time."

What do you do when someone tells you they lie all the time? Do you believe it? Or could they be lying when they tell you that they lie?

And why does any of this matter? 'Twas what I asked myself. Why should I care if a Gypsy princess tells lies or not? It's none of my affair at all.

Except that I felt a shiver down low on my spine. And I was most curious.

"Why do you lie?" I asked.

"Because if I don't, I surely will die."

Thomas choked a bit on his soup. I patted him on the back and offered him water. Feather smiled. Her dramatic words had had the desired shocking effect.

"You will *die?*" I whispered. "Truly die?"

"Well, I won't be struck with lightning and fall to the ground in agony. But my father will kill me and I would be just as dead."

"Surely your own father wouldn't kill you," I said.

"I am the seventh daughter of a seventh daughter, Trinket. I am a seer. With but a touch I can see the path a life will take. With but a dream I can see when death is coming. And I know without a doubt that if I stop lying, my life will be over."

And with those words, she rose and left Thomas and me

sitting with our soup, wondering which of the nearby trees would make the best shelter.

Or if the smartest thing to do would be to leave altogether.

—

"What's it like, to see what is to come?" I asked Feather as we went to the stream in the morning to fetch fresh water. Thomas was helping with the chickens. He preferred his pigs to chickens, naturally, but he preferred chickens to people. And since we had decided to stay a few days with the Gypsies, we hoped to work a bit for food and information. Maybe one of the Gypsies might remember my father. I had the secret intent of asking each and every one of them.

"Imagine the worst feeling in the world." Feather knelt to fill her bucket. "Then imagine a feeling even worse than that. That is what it feels like when a vision comes. 'Tis the curse of a seer."

"But can't you use your sight to help others? I would think having the sight would be a gift."

"You would think that, of course," she said, "but seeing

the future is no gift. For I cannot undo what is to come and it only frightens people to know the truth."

"You cannot warn people of danger?"

"Of course I can!" she reproved. She rose, her hands on her hips. "You do not understand at all."

She stomped off, leaving me four buckets to carry, instead of my two. It took me until the sun was high to return to the camp with the pails. Indeed, my arms were sore.

Feather was waiting for me, sitting on a crooked wooden bench near the silver-haired woman in charge of the water. The woman's soft purple skirt swayed as if underneath she tapped an impatient foot. She looked at all the pails I carried, then back at Feather's empty arms. But she said nothing and merely pointed to where she wanted the buckets placed. Apparently, one did not question the Gypsy King's daughter.

"I am sorry," Feather said. "I foresaw that you would be carrying the buckets alone, but I could not understand why I would leave you. Now I know why. I was angry with you."

I rubbed my elbow and my wrists, not responding.

"You see, that is what it is like for me. I see things, but I do not understand them. I do not know what to tell people..."

"So you lie?"

"Yes."

"Why do you not just tell them the truth?" I asked.

Feather led me to a small tree near a beautiful tent made of dark ruby and golden silks. We sat in the shade of its branches. Feather glanced from side to side, then whispered, "Because I don't understand what I see. How can I explain what I don't understand?"

I did not have an answer.

"I see flashes when I touch a hand or search into a palm. But then again, maybe they are just thoughts, the same as you have a thousand times a day. Sometimes, I see nothing at all. And people won't pay gold coins for nothing at all. There is an expectation, you see. Seventh daughters of seventh daughters have *the sight*. Everyone knows that." Feather cut her eyes to where a line was beginning to form outside of the tent and lowered her voice even further. "Perhaps I have no gift at all . . . but . . ."

"But?"

"But there are things that I *know* will come to pass, but I have no words to explain them and then . . ."

"You started lying."

"Well yes, to keep my father happy, though even he cannot tell whether my words are truthful or not. I like to think of it this way. I can either foretell the future—or I can *create* it." Her face turned smug and there was something in her eyes that made the hairs on my arms stand straight up. "Whatever I predict, well, it happens simply because *I* say it will."

"That makes you very powerful."

"Doesn't it, though?" Feather smiled. She had found a way to become an even more imposing figure than her father, the Gypsy King.

Was even *he* bound by her prophecies, true or false?

"Why are you telling me this?" I asked, not to be impolite, but out of curiosity. I had just met the girl the night before and now she was confiding her secrets.

"Why indeed," Feather said, as if to herself. "I do not know. But for some reason, it feels good to be truthful at least to one person."

I nodded. I understood about truth. Wasn't I searching for truth myself?

At that moment, the very figure of the Gypsy King loomed over Feather's head.

"Do not neglect your duties, daughter," he scolded. "Do you not see the line? There is gold to be made. Leave the chores to the girl." He dismissed me with a wave of his hand. "Go. And let the seer do her work."

He dragged Feather by the arm until she shook him off and walked of her own accord to the lovely tent with dark silks covering the entryway. Winding through the camp was a line of Gypsies and folks who must have traveled from nearby villages we'd not yet encountered. The procession trailed past the bushes and into the forest. Feather turned toward me before she entered the tent, her dark eyes sad. She glanced up at her father, who was not looking, and made a face.

THE STORYTELLER'S LULLABY

You should have heard the lies I told today," Feather whispered to me a few nights later as we huddled under a quilt by the small fire Thomas had built near our campsite by an old tree. It was just far enough away from the Gypsies' caravans that Thomas felt it safe to sleep. He'd not forgotten how quickly they could pull out their knives. He had already fallen asleep, his snores gentle and rhythmic. "I told a man he would marry a woman far better for him than the selfish one he pines for," she continued. "And I told an old woman her young grandson would get more work done if he were fed well rather than beaten with a stick."

"And what will happen now?"

"Well, I might have just changed the future. But I am not certain. I will know next week, when they come back, of course."

"What if they are angry because your fortune did not come to pass?"

"Oh, I shall place the failure of the fortune back upon them. *Oh, you must do more to earn such a future,* I will say. *The fates are fair. Sometimes gold payment isn't enough.*"

"So truly, you just stall for a while," I said.

"Of course. Sometimes up to three times. Or I think of tasks for them to do to keep them busy. Then they come back with more gold to hear their new fate. It is good business, really, to keep them wanting more." She rubbed her temples with her fingertips. "Oh, but I do grow tired of it all sometimes. Especially thinking of new lies. It makes my head ache."

We were quiet then. There was comfort in the hush of the night. Was this what it had been like for my father? Meeting strangers, sharing meals, becoming friends? Had he become so intertwined with life in a town or village that he stayed there and never came back?

Perhaps he had. However, I would not be so easily distracted from my quest. And I was finding out nothing from the Gypsies about a storyteller who might have visited them five years ago. Each time I asked about James the Bard, I was met with shrugs or shaking heads. Even if they did know anything about him, I had a feeling that they'd not tell. Though the Gypsies fed Thomas and me for our work, and tolerated our presence, none of them had offered us a sleeping place inside their caravans. Thomas thought that was fine enough, for he claimed he'd always have to sleep with one eye open.

Only Feather had offered friendship. However, I was not following my father's map in order to make friends.

"I think we shall leave soon," I confessed. "Thomas was eavesdropping on the people waiting in line for their fortunes. He heard that an old bard is telling stories but a day or two from here. Maybe he knew my father. I am thinking that bards likely know of other bards; perhaps they are even friends."

"Ah yes, you and your precious quest." There was no emotion in Feather's voice. I could not tell if she foresaw our leaving or if it surprised her. Either way, she was not pleased.

"He is called Fergal the Bald and he is quite famous," I

said. I wanted to say, *And I do not want to stay here much longer lest it become too hard to leave*, but I had better manners than that. "And there is another teller, the Old Burned Man, who is but a few days in the other direction."

"Ew. Bald and burned? They sound so unsightly. I myself would like a handsome bard." Feather sighed. "I wager that your father was a handsome bard. What was his name again?"

"James," I said. "James the Bard. And yes, he was handsome." When I closed my eyes, I could still see his dark wavy hair. I could feel the smoothness of his cheek against mine as he hugged me before I slept. And I could see his clear gray eyes. The same as my own.

Feather shrugged. The name meant nothing to her. "Why do you seek a father who doesn't even want you? After all, 'twas his choice to leave and not return."

Her words were harsh, though I did not think she meant to be so cruel. And it was a question I had asked myself again and again.

"Of course, mayhap he has not returned because he is dead," she added.

Yes. I had considered that as well.

"I am looking for the truth," I confided, at last trying to put into words the longings of my heart. "I must *know.*"

Feather took my hand in hers, placed her other hand over it, and closed her eyes.

"I have to find out," I said. "Why would a man who loved his wife and child leave and never come back?"

When she opened her eyes, she spoke in a whisper.

"Trinket, why do you seek only *that* story? There are many out there, you know. And you, with the blood of a bard! Were you to collect several tales, say seven, why you could trade for food and shelter for a whole week. Maybe even coin. It must be better than hauling buckets of water. You are a teller, Trinket, whether you believe it now or not."

Her words froze my blood. I'd never spoken the words to anyone, but it was my secret dream to become a storyteller myself someday, though I feared I'd never be good enough. True, I told stories to Thomas as we walked, but that was just to pass the time. *Wasn't it?*

The idea of becoming a bard galloped around in my head for a moment like a wild horse I was trying to coax back into its pen. If you have a dream and you hold it close to your heart, then you always get to have it. But if you let it out into the world then you discover, one way or another, if it will come true or not.

"Perhaps your father *was* the storyteller that came long ago. The women all said he was comely. I only remember that he sang the most beautiful lullaby," Feather said, interrupting my thoughts. She hummed a bit of a tune that stirred the hairs on my arms. "I loved that song, for I heard him practice it in the forest every morning as I woke. But he would not sing it for me. He said he would sing other lullabies if I had trouble sleeping, but he would sing this song for only one girl. *Only one girl.*" She let the words hang in the air between us. "My own father was angry, of course. Told him that if he would not sing the song for me, the Gypsy King's daughter, he would be banished from the camp. Or perhaps my father threatened to slit his throat. I do not remember. The bard packed up and left the next day."

"The lullaby. Do you remember it?" My voice shook slightly.

"I do not remember the words—only the tune. I so loved the tune."

Feather hummed again. Alongside her soft, low voice, I heard another. Deeper, but smooth like butter and honey on a slice of warm bread. A voice from long, long ago.

But Feather did not hear this voice, since it traveled from somewhere deep in my heart and sang in only my own head.

"'Twas something about baubles, pearls, and small night birds," she said.

Yes, I remembered the birds.

Feather tilted her head to the side, watching me.

"You look odd, Trinket. Have you heard this lullaby before?"

For the first time in longer than I could remember, no words would come.

"Perhaps it wasn't about pearls after all. 'Tis possible it was about domineering fathers with fat eyebrows. You are not laughing, Trinket."

I *knew* the lullaby. Not the words, precisely. But my heart knew the tune.

It was his lullaby.

He had been here.

I rose and began to walk. My stomach fluttered, and my

palms started to sweat just a little. I had found the first footprint my father had left behind. James the Bard really *had* been here.

And I was not sure how I felt about it.

Feather caught up to me, clasping my hand again within her own, and swung me as if to dance. "If only I could find a man to sing to me like that . . ."

"Feather, you are far too young to be thinking of men singing to you!" I scolded lightly, rubbing the goose bumps off my arms, hoping she would tell me more about the storyteller of long ago, yet fearful at the same time.

"Trinket, are you not aware that I will be sixteen soon? For some, that is marrying age." A breeze blew Feather's curls around her shoulders as she looked past the wagons and the trees, into the starlit night. "Do you not think of marriage, Trinket? You will be pretty someday, you know. If you wore your hair loose and brushed it until it shone instead of braiding it, it would be quite lovely. So many shades of gold and brown. Mayhap someday a young man will see you and fall in love."

"Ha!" I snorted. "We were not speaking of my marriage.

We were speaking of yours." I was glad Thomas was not awake to witness this conversation. The teasing would be endless.

"My father will make the match—sell me, more likely, to whoever offers the most. Of course, I have a plan for dealing with it . . ." Feather's voice trailed off.

"Did you foresee something?" I smiled.

"Not yet, but I will."

—

The next day and the day after that, Feather was again dragged away from chores once a line formed at the dark silk tent. "Your value grows steadily, daughter," her father mumbled to her as his pockets jingled with coins.

Thomas and I had decided to stay only for the rest of the week, to store up as much food as we could before we ventured off. So, for the third day in a row, I drew the water from the stream alone and hauled the buckets back to the silver-haired woman. It was not the worst chore, indeed, and everyone did a job or two to pitch in. But as I rubbed my aching arms and raced over to Thomas, I could see he was becoming restless working among the chickens. "It's too feathery here," he complained.

"I know exactly what you mean," I muttered as we split a boiled egg for lunch and stuffed the extra bread in our packs.

"Drawing the water doesn't involve birds," Thomas said, obviously confused. I reminded myself that I hadn't chosen Thomas the Pig Boy to accompany me for his talent at finding hidden meanings in cryptic phrases.

Thomas smacked himself on the head with his open palm. "Oh, I get it. You are talking about *her*."

I shushed him.

However, my feeling that our stay had become *too feathery* remained. Each night, Feather told me of the futures she had made up and the bits of true visions that she had seen and did not understand. Sometimes we tried to piece things together and puzzle out what the odd images foretold. Most of it just made my head spin. Did the vision of the bird flying over the old man's head mean a journey was to come? Or death was near? Or was it just a bird?

And there was the fact that when she was not in her silken tent, Feather watched me like a hawk watches a mouse. She was always nearby, and she had the uncanny ability to simply pop up whenever I turned around. When I asked her, nicely I hoped, why she was always so close to me, she replied, "Why,

Trinket, can you not see that there are few girls our age around the camp? It gets so tiresome to talk with old women or little boys all the time."

When I told her there were plenty of young girls to talk to, and that I was not her age at all, being only almost twelve myself, she replied, "But you, Trinket, are the only one who doesn't want something from me."

Was it true? Were Thomas and I the only ones in the Gypsy camp who did not want our fortunes told by Feather?

I had thought about it, of course. One does not enter into a friendship with a fortuneteller and *not* consider it.

And yet I could not bring myself to ask her.

Because perhaps, I did not want to know. What if she predicted horrible things for my future?

What if she told me I would never find my father?

RED MORNING

———————

'Twould have been better if Thomas and I had left earlier, for the day of our departure dawned deep red.

"Have a care about yourself today," Feather said, pointing to the crimson sky. "Not a good omen." She emptied her bucket into the barrel, then reached for mine. This would be the last time I performed this task for the Gypsies.

"You read signs as well?"

"It does not take a seer to read the signs of nature. Three birds crossing the skies above you mean good fortune. A halo around the moon means a change in the weather. Did your parents not teach you such things?"

I shook my head. "What does the red sky mean?"

"Within a week's time: Battle. Violence. Death. Take your pick."

—

"Can she really see the future, Trinket?" Thomas asked. We were at our little campsite nestled against the old tree near the outskirts of the Gypsies' clearing. As I rolled up my blanket, he packed his satchel with all his earthly possessions: a seashell from his uncle who sailed, a soft cloth for cleaning, a copper or two, several boiled eggs, and bread loaves for the trip. He handed me the old map, which I placed in my own bag.

"Aye. I think she can sometimes."

"We should go now, before all of those terrible things happen," he said. I glanced over toward the Gypsy camp, feeling torn.

"Feather hummed a lullaby I've heard before, long ago. One written just for me, I think," I confided. I'd been too afraid to speak the words until now. Too afraid I'd imagined the song, or if I told someone about it, it would fade into the mist.

The look on his face was blank, as if I'd spoken in a foreign tongue.

"Thomas, she remembers my da."

"*I* remember your da."

"Not the same thing and you know it well. He was here."

"Are you sure? Maybe she is just pretending so that you will stay. She seems to like having you around. And she herself said she was a liar." He sniffed and plucked a feather from his trousers, then another. Working with the chickens had made him look a bit like one.

"And there is a tale here. I can feel it. I think I might collect it. So that maybe . . ." But I could not finish. What if Thomas laughed at my idea of becoming a storyteller myself?

"A tale about what?" he said, instantly curious.

I narrowed my eyes. "'Tis a mysterious story, I think, of a girl with a gift of telling the future." Dramatically, I swept around Thomas, placing my fingers on my temples. "I see . . ." I cried, swooning from side to side. Thomas tried not to smile, but he could not help it. I grabbed his palm and began to read. "Let me see, you will marry a beautiful princess and have eleven children—"

"Only one princess?" He laughed.

"Well, not a real princess," I said, "a chicken-princess."

A noise from the bushes caused us both to freeze. I turned, and there, coming out from behind a tree, was the tallest man I'd ever seen. He was dressed in green and had a bushy black beard.

"I've found her," he called out. "Who knew it would be so easy to capture the seer? I would have thought the king would keep a guard with you." His eyes swept over Thomas and he smirked. "Obviously not."

Thomas and I edged our way closer to each other. I cleared my throat and prayed for boldness. "I am not the seer."

"And I am not interested in your lies. I heard you. I saw you take his palm." He pointed to Thomas's hand, which was shaking slightly.

A shorter, fatter man, also dressed in shades of green, came out of the bushes then. "Well done. Lothar will be pleased."

"Who is Lothar?" I asked.

"Our leader. We have traveled across the hills and through the forests to bring you back with us, seer." The fat man's voice was sharp and hard like a stone.

"Truly, she is not the one you seek!" Thomas piped up, his scrawny fists clenched at his sides.

Both men laughed at Thomas, whose face turned red as a berry.

"Protection from a pup?" the tall man taunted. "Let's have a go, mate. You and I." He circled Thomas, eyeing his gangly legs and skinny arms. "I'll keep one hand tied behind me, pup. And I'll give you the first blow."

"No! Leave him alone," I cried.

The fat man thrust his palm in front of my face. "Go ahead, seer. Tell me what you see. Quick-like, before we take you to Lothar."

"That won't be necessary," said a voice softer than a whisper on the wind. The tall man stopped teasing Thomas and the fat man's chubby palm instantly dropped to his side. A man swung down from a branch overhead and landed right in front of me. He put a finger to his lips and motioned to the other men, who promptly clamped their hands over our mouths before we could think to shout for help. We were flung over the shoulders of the men and carried off, away from the Gypsy camp.

THE MEN OF FORESTHILL

*H*ow long we were bounced up and down, upside down, I could not say. 'Twas not comfortable at all and my head ached most horribly. I wanted to cry, but I was too frightened to make a sound.

When they finally dumped us none too gently upon the ground, I leaned over to Thomas. "Do not say a word," I whispered. "Promise me?"

Thomas nodded.

"If they find out they carried off the wrong girl, they might not think twice before killing us. We must be very careful."

Thomas nodded again. His eyes were bright and glassy, but not a tear did he shed. He had hoped for adventure on the journey, but I rather think this was not what he'd had in mind.

The man with the soft voice came to us then.

"I apologize," he began, "for my methods. One never knows how the warriors of Foresthill might be greeted." He sat on a stump near where Thomas and I huddled together. I said nothing, my mind awhirl, thinking of what to do. His voice was kind and he seemed gentle. Surely he would not kill us.

"I am Lothar of Foresthill. These are my men." He motioned to five men, all dressed in green. Their sleeves and trousers blended into the leaves of the forest. Horses with manes as black as shadows were tethered to the trees. I could see why 'twas so easy for the men to sneak up on us.

I nodded, still silent.

"We travel from far over the green hills. My men say you are the seer."

I kept still. 'Twould do no good to reveal their failure at capturing Feather until I knew more.

"What say you tell us what you see?" he said, pulling a

brown glove from his hand and holding it gently in front of me.

"Why do you require a seer?" I asked.

"There have been rumors of disputes between the lands to the east of us and the lands to the south. We wonder which will be victorious so we can throw our lots in with the victor. And then my wife, she is with child—"

"Halt. Tell me no more," I said, knowing not from where the words came. "'Tis not so easy to see the future. Surely you know fortunes are not read quickly."

Lothar raised an eyebrow in question.

"There are things that must be done to call forth visions of what is to come."

Thomas raised his eyebrow as well, but I saw him relax for the first time since our capture. He knew the tone of my voice well enough to understand that I had some kind of idea. Whether it was a good or poor one remained yet unknown.

"In order to foresee what fate might bring, you must . . ." I tried to conjure a picture of Feather. What would she do in my position? She would either lie or stall. I chose stalling. "You must earn your future. The fates cannot be forced."

"I have never heard of such a thing."

"Do you want to know your future or not?" I asked, feeling slightly bold.

That gave Lothar pause. We stared at one another, sizing each other up.

Finally, he inclined his head toward me. "Very well, how do I earn the right to see the future?"

"Well, it is very simple, really. First, you and your men must circle the camp three times."

A look of disbelief crossed his face.

"That doesn't sound like much," he said. True. I would have to do better.

"There is more." My voice was more commanding than I'd ever heard it. "If you choose to listen."

Lothar rolled his eyes slightly, then nodded for me to continue.

"You must give us three loaves of bread."

He nodded again.

"And you and your men must stay awake for three days and three nights. Then your fortunes shall come to me."

"Three nights? Truly, three nights?"

"Yes," I said, "all of your men must stay awake for three nights."

"But why? It makes no sense."

" 'Tis the way of the fates. It does not have to make sense." I sat up straight, and I noticed Thomas did as well.

—

'Twas a long three days, to be sure. But the men of Foresthill were not unkind to us. I almost felt bad for deceiving them. But one must keep one's wits about her when traveling the countryside, and this was one case in which my storyteller's blood was quite useful. Perhaps I *could* create tales worth listening to.

Thomas and I barely spoke for fear of being overheard. The men of Foresthill were everywhere, it seemed, watching when we ate, even when we slept.

However, none of them could stay awake for three days. 'Twas near the end of the third day when even Lothar's eyes failed him and closed. Thomas and I gathered our things, and faster than an owl can blink, we left the men of Foresthill, and headed back to the Gypsy camp.

"I think it's a stupid plan, Trinket," Thomas said, out of breath from running. "Well, not all of it. The part where you got them to stay awake so they would be too tired to give chase, that was brilliant." I smiled. "And the bread part was good, too." He patted his sack, still filled with the loaves.

"But the part where we go back to the Gypsy camp is dumb. We should go off in the other direction. They will just find us again."

"The other direction leads to Foresthill!" I snapped, pointing to the place on the east side of my father's map where in faded letters it said *Lands of Foresthill*. That was the last place I wanted to go. I could not tell from the map how large the lands were, since it only showed the edge of them. But if my father ventured there often, he would have drawn it better, I thought. If we traveled west we would eventually hit the villages on the coast, even if we didn't find the Gypsy camp again.

"Besides, I've got to try to warn Feather," I said. "She showed us kindness. Kindness should always be repaid. How could I live with myself if I didn't try to tell her that the men of Foresthill are just waiting to carry her off?"

Thomas humphed. But he followed.

We walked through the night till dawn, only going in circles twice. Once the sun began to rise, finding west was much easier. When we reached the outskirts of the Gypsy camp, we met Feather, carrying the water buckets.

"Feather!" I cried, running to hug her.

"I thought you left. Off on your journey to see a bald, burned-up old teller," she said, though she hugged me just as tightly.

"No, I've come to warn you. Feather, you are in danger."

"I know," she said. "I know."

And we raced back to the camp as if demons were on our heels.

I could feel them before I heard them. And I heard them before I saw them. Six horses as dark as a moonless night. Atop them, six riders, all men. The men of Foresthill.

"We come for the seer," the tall man said to the forming crowd. Many Gypsies had gathered at the sound of the hooves, their knives drawn.

This must be the violence and battle Feather saw in the red sunrise.

The Gypsy King came out of his tent, his sword glinting in the morning light. "Who asks for my daughter?"

One of the riders guided his horse forward. "I am Lothar of Foresthill."

"Lothar is it?" asked the king. "And what do you, Lothar, want from my daughter?"

The Gypsies formed a barrier in front of Feather, Thomas, and me. I chanced a glance at Feather, but I could not read her face.

"She is a seer. We require a seer." He pointed to where Thomas and I stood next to Feather. Apparently, our escape hadn't gone unnoticed. Unfortunately, we had led them right to Feather.

Lothar was prepared for the possibility that the king would not part with his seer, let alone his daughter. The men of Foresthill began to advance.

"You need but to ask . . . and pay," the king responded slyly, motioning for his men to lower their knives. He grabbed Feather's arm and propelled her toward Lothar. The Gypsies parted and the king's daughter stood before the tall man on the horse.

"You?" he said, looking at Feather with puzzled eyes. He glanced over at Thomas and me. Did he understand yet that he had been tricked?

Feather said nothing. Perhaps she was afraid, but her shoulders were straight and strong.

She remained silent. She put out her palm and waited. Lothar got down and pulled his brown leather glove from his hand. He placed his hand, palm up, into Feather's own.

"Wait!" the king cried. "We have not talked of price."

The king took Lothar aside and their dark heads bent in negotiation. I could not make out anything they said, so I turned my attention to Feather. She was staring off toward Foresthill. Thinking of a lie.

Or perhaps genuinely seeing.

When the price was agreed upon, Lothar returned to Feather and gave her his hand.

"I have already earned the right to see my future," he said. "I have obeyed the ways of the fates."

Feather shot me a quizzical look, a smile tugging at her lips, then turned her head back to the large hand before her.

She pondered Lothar's palm for an incredibly long time. For a while, the silence did not seem to bother anyone. Then small coughs came from the crowd. I could hear the restlessness grow. Finally, her father approached.

"Feather, if you see so much, I will have to charge Lothar more." It was a joke and the Gypsies laughed, but there was a hard edge to the king's voice.

Feather looked up and blinked a few times. An unshed tear sat upon her eyelashes, waiting to drop.

Then she spoke. She did not use her low, seer voice, but instead the voice I was accustomed to hearing when we spoke to each other as friends.

"Sir, you must go now. Back to your home. Neither side will be the victor, for there is another threat . . ."

"And my wife? What news of my wife? Has the babe been born?"

There was silence.

"I see terrible sorrow."

Lothar's head snapped up and his eyes filled with pain. He mounted his horse and sped off, throwing a small bag of gold behind him. His men followed.

The Gypsy King could not grab the bag fast enough. "Well

done, my girl. I shall perhaps have to increase your bride price." He smiled at his daughter with no warmth, patting her shoulder absently as if she were a horse who had won a race, or a dog who had fetched a bone.

Feather did not even nod in acknowledgment. As they touched, I saw Feather shiver as something invisible passed from his skin through her own. She stood for a moment, as if in a trance, and then shook her head and walked away from the Gypsy King.

"Let us go, Trinket," said Thomas. "None of this bodes well for us. We should have left by now."

"Aye, you are right, Thomas. But Feather has become my friend. I do not know if it is the right thing to do, to leave her like this. Perhaps we should—"

I could not finish my sentence. Perhaps we should what? Wait and talk to Feather? Become further entwined in the daily lives of these Gypsies? Become so attached that I would never be able to go, never be able to find my father? *Never be able to find the one story I most needed?* With effort, I stopped my spinning mind. These were thoughts I did not want to think.

WARNINGS

——◆✦◆——

I entered Feather's exquisite tent, my fingers caressing
the silken flap. 'Twas the softest thing I'd ever felt and I could
have touched it forever, but then I looked back at Thomas. He
bounced lightly from one foot to the other, as if he needed to
use the bushes, but I knew better.

"Do not take too long," he said. "Please."

And I would not. Thomas had been patient, and I had no
wish to torment him, especially since I agreed with him. We
needed to leave this place.

"Oh, you are still here. I thought you would have gone."
Feather did not look up at me. She sat, staring at a lovely piece

of cloth. "For my bridal dress, someday," she said softly as she folded the fabric. She did not even glance in my direction, but continued folding various pieces of beautiful clothing and placing them in a bag.

"You are going to run away."

"And they say I see the future," Feather said.

"But they will follow you. They will bring you back."

"Again you are probably right."

"But why?"

Finally she looked at me, smiling as if I were a very simple child. "Trinket, when you are born, it is your destiny to die. It is everyone's future. Does that mean you should curl up in a ball and just let death take you?"

Puzzled, I shook my head. I did not like talking about dying.

"Of course not, you go out and live anyway, even if the end is inevitable," she said.

"But—"

"So maybe they catch me, maybe not, but should I just curl up and let my father sell me to a husband for gold, or bargain away my sight as he sees fit ... or should I create my own future?"

"What did you see, when your father touched your shoulder?" I asked.

"You do not have to be a seer to know what my father plans for me. He has made the arrangements already. He will not admit it, but I saw it—a foul tyrant across the water waits for me. Whether my father has promised me as a wife or a slave to such a beast, I do not know. But I shall be neither."

It was silent in the tent as Feather placed items in her bag. Bracelets, colorful hair ties, and necklaces jingled as she untangled them, wrapped them in cloth and put them on the top.

"I might need to trade these," she explained. "For meals and such."

"Won't you use your gift?"

"Of course, I am not a fool. I will use the gifts I have been given. But I must be quiet for a while, lest my father hear rumors of a fortune-telling girl."

I paused, wondering how Feather could leave her family. Did she not know how lucky she was to still have a family? Then I thought of her father, with the hairy caterpillar eyebrows, who always scowled. Perhaps a hideous father was worse than no father at all.

"What did you see when you took Lothar's hand? I know you saw something."

Why did I want to know? I could not answer, but I needed to understand. Thomas, on the other hand, felt the need to go. I could see him pacing outside, for he did not feel it was right to enter a lady's tent without permission.

"His wife has died in childbirth. He will be angry. He will rage at those he left behind to watch over her. Violence. But then . . ."

"Then?"

"He will feel great remorse. His heart breaks and he vows to do kind deeds. Perhaps, after time passes, I will seek him out."

"That seems like a lot. Have you ever seen so much before?"

"Never. Perhaps our lives are intertwined and that is why I could see. Mayhap his future lies beside my own."

I felt my eyes widen. Feather was choosing Lothar as her future husband.

"Don't look so surprised," she chided. "Remember, I believe in making my own fortune." Feather came to me then and hugged me. She also gave me a few coins from a small purse she wore around her neck. "'Tis best if we don't leave together. They will assume you and Thomas stole me away against my will and think nothing of slitting your throats to get me back." Feather hid her bag beneath her cot. "I will leave in three days' time. My father will be so busy with the preparations for the tyrant's arrival, he will not even notice."

"Goodbye, Feather. You are the first friend I have met on my travels." I felt the heat of tears behind my eyes.

"I am sure I shall not be the last." She smiled, then looked at me thoughtfully for a moment. She took my palm. "Would you like to know?"

Did I want to know? Did I want to know what the future held for me?

Or did I want to make my own future?

"Don't tell me," I whispered, curling my hand in a fist before I could change my mind.

"I foresaw you would say that." She laughed.

I turned toward the tent flap, hoping I had decided correctly.

But Feather could not help herself. "You will find your answers, you know," she said.

"The truth? I will find the truth?"

"That is not exactly what I said, Trinket. I said you would find answers. Every question has more than one answer. Every story more than one ending."

She held up seven fingers. "Were I you, Trinket, I would make my own future. Find your own tales for the telling. Seven. Being a teller is in you. I saw it there."

I hugged her as she hummed the lullaby for me, my father's lullaby, one last time, strong and true so I could carry it with me in my heart. "'Twas his song for you, was it not?"

———

"Finally," Thomas grumbled as I came out of the tent, but he was not really angry.

I did not answer him. Instead, I turned back to Feather, still unsure.

"We will meet again," the Gypsy King's daughter said, following me out. "And do not worry that the guards will come after you. I will tell them I foresee a plague from the plants in the forest. Those having to drop their breeks when nature calls will suffer from boils erupting on their cursed backsides!" She laughed. "That will stop them."

We regarded each other one last time, neither of us willing to say the word *goodbye*. Strangely enough, Feather grabbed Thomas into an awkward embrace. He blushed, and she whispered something to him, but I did not hear.

She returned to her tent, the tent flap closed, and Thomas and I walked out of the Gypsy camp.

—

I found myself glancing backward every few minutes, and Thomas doing the same. The Gypsy camp had been the first real stop on our adventure, and now it disappeared into the trees as if it had never existed. We did not leave empty-handed, though, for I carried with me a song from long ago. And perhaps a tale as well.

Thomas was unusually quiet. I caught him peeking at me from under his unruly locks, then looking away quickly.

"What is it, Thomas?" I asked.

"Nothing," he tried to lie.

"Feather said something to you. I know she did."

Thomas did not respond.

"Just tell me."

Thomas fidgeted, kicking hard at any stone unfortunate

enough to be in his path. "You said you did not like fortunes. You said you didn't want to know."

Ah, 'twas a prophecy then.

"'Tis not fair if you know something that I do not know, especially if it is about me." Whether I wanted to know or not no longer mattered. I could not let Thomas bear the burden alone.

"It's not about you. It was about me. She said . . . she said to watch over you."

I tried not to roll my eyes. So far, Thomas needed much more watching over than I did.

"And she said you would need my ear for listening," he said with a bit of confusion. "I dunno what she meant by that. I already have to listen to you all the time."

I punched him in the arm, but not too hard.

"And she said that I would do great things." His cheeks flushed as he told me.

"You will, Thomas. I am sure you will."

"And she said to follow the song. The lullaby. Follow the lullaby."

THE FIRST SONG

To a Gypsy on a Moonless Night

'Twas my first song, and there was nothing fancy about it.
Just a heart's own voice. For that is what a song is,
even if there is only a tune and no words at all.

Tell me true,
If thou could see
What could happen,
What might be.

Would thou take
The reckless chance?
Would thou peek,
Take but a glance?

And if thou saw
Thy future sold,
Could thou change
What fate beholds?

I have not
Answer nor opine,
But I'll not look—
The risk is thine.

The Harp of Bone and Hair

THE MISTRESS OF THE SEA

◆━━◆✕◆━━◆

*M*y father's map was dotted with small coastal villages. Rugged they are, as are the people who inhabit them. You must be strong of spirit to live with the ocean as your neighbor. Sometimes, she is as gentle as a new lamb, soft and placid. You might not even know she is there, but for her salty scent and the gifts of fish she bountifully brings. But other times, she is angry. She takes things that do not belong to her, and she does not return them.

The people who live on the land are not the only ones who are at the whim of the Mistress of the Sea. There are others.

Thomas and I came over a hill and upon a village called

Conelmara that looked as if it had just lost an argument with the Mistress of the Sea. The thatch was blown off the houses, trees were uprooted from the ground, bits and pieces of everything lay about.

"Perhaps this is not the best place to take shelter. These poor folk probably have not much left to eat themselves, let alone anything to share with two roamers," I said. Checking the map, I could see there were other villages a bit farther along. I wondered if my father had told tales at every village he passed on his travels, or if he had let his stomach determine his stops.

Thomas just grunted his response.

"You know, you've really got to learn to converse. Ask a question or two. I get tired of hearing my own voice all the time."

Thomas groused, "Fine. I've a grumble in my belly so loud and fierce it could be heard all the way to heaven and back." He paused. "Here's a question: What would be worse, Trinket, to be starving, but have no food, or to be dying of thirst and have no water?"

"I don't know, Thomas."

"Well, I can't tell myself, because I've both. I've a thirst big enough to drink a lake and a hunger loud enough to frighten a ghost."

"'Twould be a good story, Thomas. Mayhap if we keep going, we will find the Old Burned Man, and you can share it with him." I laughed and tried to make light.

"Me? I've no wish to tell tales."

"Mayhap . . . I do," I said tentatively.

"Mayhap you what?"

"I want to tell stories. Do you think I could, Thomas?" I spoke quickly, afraid I would lose my nerve and keep my dream forever trapped inside. But since we'd left the Gypsies, I'd thought of little else.

"Well, of course you'll be a teller, Trinket. What else could you possibly be?"

I smiled. I'd feared Thomas would tease me. His belief in me made my heart feel not quite so hollow.

"Would you sing songs, too? A good bard always has songs, you know."

"Yes. I suppose I could write a song or two." Already words and rhymes danced in my head, joined by fleeting melodies.

As I thought more about becoming a bard, I remembered

that my mother had always encouraged my tales. She'd laugh and tell me I was like him. Like my father.

Those were, however, babes' stories. Not what I sought at all. Now I quested for words that would sing in the hearts of those who heard them. Tales that were made of dreams. And I would need seven. Then I could stay in one place for a whole week and tell a new tale each night.

"What would you like to do then, Thomas? What do you think your path is?" The longer we talked about things other than his hunger, the better.

"I dunno. I've given some thought to it, though. Sometimes I feel it in my bones to be a healer."

I gave him a look. *Thomas the Pig Boy a healer?* Now *that* would be a story.

"Oh, not for people. For animals, mayhap. Do they have those, do you think, animal healers?"

"I suppose they might."

Looking up from where he'd been kicking a pebble down the road, Thomas groaned. "This is really a wreck of a town. But maybe we can find a meal here. Or a bed. Or both." I had not the heart to force him on. So we stopped at a rather dilapidated house, the closest one to the road.

The owner, Mister Fergus, surprised us with his kindness, offering us chowder and warm pallets for our rest.

"You are a wiry lad, but perhaps you have strength in your bones?" said Mister Fergus. He was strong and weathered, with a roundish nose that sat atop a gray moustache. Thomas looked from side to side, then, realizing Mister Fergus was talking to him, puffed himself up a bit. "We can use a lad like ye to help us rethatch the cottages." Thomas nodded over his fish stew. He was not a lazy lad, most days anyway, and if the work meant food in our bellies, he was more than willing.

"I am not as strong as Thomas, but I can help, too," I offered, glad I was wearing my britches.

Mister Fergus looked me over. "Have ye an ear for a tale, lass?"

I nodded. *An ear for a tale? 'Tis what my ears were meant for!*

"There is a lady who lost her husband to a storm a month ago, and just the other night lost her babe, too. Nigh on crazy she is, insisting the babe is still alive. We searched and searched, but the Mistress of the Sea must have claimed him."

I could feel tears welling in the back of my eyes. I, too, had lost loved ones. Mayhap I did not want to do this task, whatever it might be.

"She's in need of a lass who will listen to her, dry her tears, and pat her shoulders, so the rest of us can get the work done. She's done naught but stagger from one to the next of us, begging us to listen to her story. Begging us to keep looking for the babe." His voice trailed off and he sighed. "In the morn, I'll take you to her. Best you rest well now." He motioned to the pallets he'd arranged by the hearth. "You'll be warm enough there, I think." Mister Fergus did not wait for me to say yes. And Thomas was asleep before I could even talk with him about it. So I laid my head on the straw and closed my eyes, but no slumber came. Thoughts of mothers without their children and children without their mothers drifted through my wakeful brain.

THE MOTHER'S TALE

—◆◆★★◆◆—

*T*he sun had just peeked over the hill when Mister
Fergus took me to the cottage closest to the sea.

'Twas obviously the first house to be repaired, for on its
roof was fresh, new thatch. The people of Conelmara must
care for this woman a great deal.

"Catriona, there's someone here to see you," Mister Fergus
called, and with that, he shoved me inside the house, closing
the door behind me.

I expected her home to be a mess, for what care would a
grieving woman have for neatness and order? But it was not.
Everything was tidy. Linens were folded, chairs pushed into

a small table, floor swept. "Hello," I called. "Mistress Catriona?"

She appeared in the doorway of what must have been the bedchamber. Her long hair was brushed and the green dress she wore was clean and unwrinkled. She might have been beautiful, but for the swollenness of her eyes and the purple circles underneath. She looked as if she'd shed every tear she was capable of shedding. Before she could ask, I blurted out, "I am Trinket. I am the daughter of James the Bard. I am searching for him but I've not found him. I've come to gather stories as well." Well, that did not sound very compassionate at all. "Mister Fergus told me about your baby, and your husband, too. I am very sorry." My voice faltered on the word *baby*. It was horrible to lose a parent, as well I knew, but it was dreadful to think of a baby dying. "My own mother departed this life not long ago . . ."

"Thank you," she said, her voice deep and soft. "I was sorry to lose my husband. The Mistress of the Sea was greedy. 'Twas not only *my* man that she took. Many lost their lives that day."

I had no other words, so I said again, "I am sorry."

"However, she did not take my child." Her voice was fierce.

"Well, perhaps I misspoke. She may indeed have taken the babe . . . but he is still alive."

I waited. This was the story I'd come to hear.

"We were out on the boat, the babe and I, catching fish for our supper. The Sea Mistress had drowned my husband not a month before, so we had to provide for ourselves. Certainly, the good people of Conelmara offered to feed us, but I am strong enough. I'll not survive on charity. We were returning to shore when the greedy Mistress reached in with her great wave-fingers and carried my wee babe away. I saw her bounce him up on top of the foam, not drag him down to her depths as she did my man. I cried out, cursing her, begging her to return my child. That's when she sent the storm that demolished the village."

I did not speak. What could I say? Everyone knows that the sea does not return what she takes. 'Tis not possible.

"And you, Trinket *the Bard's Daughter*, you have come here to help me find him." Her face changed instantly from anguished to hopeful. She grasped me by my shoulders and shook me with crazed joy. "I know that is why God sent you!"

"Mister Fergus sent me."

Mistress Catriona just smiled at me. "He is not dead, my babe. I would feel it if it were so."

She rose and placed small cups of tea in front of us, hot and steaming, and a plate of oatcakes. But I was not hungry.

"Sometimes, the Mistress of the Sea will give a young human babe to a grief-stricken selkie mum whose own babe has died," she said. "That is an ancient agreement between the Mistress and the seal people."

"Seal people?" I asked.

"I thought you were the daughter of a storyteller. Did your father teach you nothing?"

I wanted to tell her how my father had left before he could teach me much of anything, but she merely shook her head and continued. "Selkies are creatures who can appear as men or women, but are most comfortable in their seal forms. They wear their sealskins in the ocean, but store them in secret places when they wish to walk on land. 'Tis a lucky fisherman who finds a selkie woman, hides her skin, and takes her for a wife. They are the most devoted of mothers."

"And you believe one of these seal mothers has your baby?"

Mistress Catriona nodded. "And I will get him back." Her voice was cold, like a winter's morning.

"I know what you are feeling, I think," I began. "I, too, have been separated from my father—"

"We shall need music. The selkies can be tamed with music," she interrupted. "Have you a voice for singing? And a mind for conjuring tunes?"

"I-I-I do not know, actually—" I began, but before I could get any more words out, Mistress Catriona had clasped her hand around my own and pulled me out of her cottage and down the narrow path toward the rocky coast.

THE MAKING OF MUSICAL INSTRUMENTS

As we approached, the ocean splashed playfully against the shore. The Mistress of the Sea and her angry storms were long gone from this stretch of the world, though the wind was brisk enough to tug at my braided hair and chill the tops of my ears. I was glad for the warmth of my mother's cloak. I turned back to see Thomas, who trailed behind determinedly. Was he not supposed to be repairing roofs with Mister Fergus? It seemed wrong to be heading for the waves when so much work in the ruined town still needed doing. "Perhaps we should go and check on the thatching," I began, releasing my hand from hers. "Mister Fergus may need some help . . ."

"Nay," said Mistress Catriona, a determined look on her face. "Mister Fergus bid you keep company with me, so as to keep me out of everyone's way. I know full well that none of them believe me. You will do your duty to Mister Fergus and come with me. 'Tis what an honorable soul would do."

I wanted to be an honorable soul. So I followed Mistress Catriona as she led me down the dirt path.

Thomas raced to catch up.

"You did not have to come, Thomas," I told him. "Doesn't Mister Fergus need you?"

"Mister Fergus would not want you to go and let the lady do something stupid, that's what I am thinking. And I am supposed to watch after you. Besides, I've been helping the whole time you've been sipping tea."

"How did you know I was sipping tea?"

"Peeked in the window. How did you think?"

"And how could you peek in the window if you've been working the whole time? Hmm?" I attempted a big, disgusted sigh, but Thomas interrupted.

"She's crazed, Trinket. Can you not see it in her eyes?" His voice was a whisper. I hoped the wind would not carry it down to where Mistress Catriona navigated between the large rocks of the shore.

I shook my head and turned to join her.

There were bones on the shore. Bones of large sea beasts called whales. Whiter than the clouds, they rose from the rocks like the ghosts of old tree branches. I could hear Thomas gasp at the sight of them.

Jagged and sharp, the rocks of the beach created a wall of sorts between us and the bones. Carefully, so the rough edges would not pierce our shoes, we made our way past the barrier to where the bones rested. But why would we require such things? Did she not say that the selkies liked *music*?

Mistress Catriona pointed to a large curved bone. "That is what we need. You will see, Trinket."

Around the bone that Mistress Catriona desired nested a family of swans. Their beaks were pointed and they squawked most miserably about our approach. The mothers must need to protect their babies, I thought. Thomas once told me that the most dangerous animals were mothers protecting their young. Perhaps Mistress Catriona did not realize the peril she was in. "Have a care, Mistress Catriona, they have beaks that would slice your finger from your hand before you could blink twice."

"Nay, they will not harm us," she said, stealthily moving forward.

But Thomas ran ahead of Mistress Catriona, scattering the lovely birds. Not one pecked poor Thomas as he flailed about, dispersing them to the four winds. 'Twas a brave gesture, to be sure, for he could well have returned with cuts, bites, and bits of flesh missing.

Thomas smiled proudly at his victory.

"Mayhap 'tis a good thing I came after all," he said smugly.

Mistress Catriona walked among the downy feathers of the swans' nests. She motioned for me to join her, so I did.

"Now, Trinket the Bard's Daughter, you will need this, to accompany your singing, of course." Her fingers delicately stroked the elegant white arch of the bone she'd pointed to but a few moments ago.

The truth was, I didn't know if I could sing well or not. I'd sung for my mum, but what mother doesn't think her own child's voice sounds like that of an angel? However, a story-teller must sing, for there are tales that lend themselves only to song. So I nodded, hoping my voice would not be too hideous to other ears.

"Here, take this. It will make a fine harp, and you'll be our singer."

We went back up the narrow path to her cottage. I carried the bone under my left arm. It fit there most remarkably well. As we walked, she drew from her pocket a straight, long bone, with small holes carved in it. "I have been working on fashioning a flute from this. We shall create such music that the selkies will have no choice but to give me what I want." And the sound she made when she blew gently and moved her fingers over the holes was like a song from heaven.

"I've never heard anything like it," I said softly, not wanting to disturb the magic in the air.

"Yes, 'tis a fine flute. But alas, I do not play as well as a true bard." She sighed. "But I believe it will be good enough—"

"Have there been tellers here of late, mistress?" I asked, taking a seat upon the stump in front of her cottage. Thomas sat on the ground next to me. Mistress Catriona paced whilst polishing the flute with her sleeve.

"One performed for us not a fortnight ago," she said. I

held my breath. Could it be? "This flute is more beautiful than his. But the tunes he played . . . none can compare."

I felt my shoulders slump. My father played a harp, not a flute.

But still, hearing another teller, *any* teller of tales, would help me learn the trade.

"He was aged and rough-sounding," Mistress Catriona offered.

"Probably the Old Burned Man," Thomas whispered, giving me a look. "Bald Fergal plays upon the drum."

I nodded. Perhaps the Old Burned Man was still nearby and we would catch up to him soon. For if I were to become a teller, I had much to learn. And there was no James the Bard around to teach me.

"Now for the harp," Mistress Catriona said, changing the subject. She quickly untied one of my braids and unwove the locks with her fingers. Then, she pulled from my head three long hairs.

"Ouch! Why do you need those?"

Mistress Catriona began wrapping the strands, up and down, creating strings between the unusual curved ends of the bone.

And when she plucked the strings, 'twas the sound of a majestic lyre.

We were silent, Thomas and I, until the hum of the notes completely faded.

"Most likely, you could have done all of this by yourself. Why do you need me along?" I asked. I wasn't trying to be impertinent. She had long enough hair. She could have used her own. And she could have completed her tasks without the help of Thomas or me. I had gotten the impression from Mister Fergus that I would be sitting with a woman half crazed with grief, much like I would sit and watch over a baby. Mistress Catriona certainly needed no one to watch over her. Nor was she getting in anyone's way. She was resourceful enough to make a plan. I wasn't convinced that Mistress Catriona wouldn't be successful.

"I need you, Trinket, for two reasons. First, because it is always easier to do something difficult if one has help. And second, because you are the daughter of a bard. Your hair in the harp will give it life, like blood does for a body. And," she continued, "you will compose a song for us."

I swallowed, feeling strange in my belly. What if I could

not do this? What if I could not write this song? What if I wrote a horrible one?

"Mistress Catriona," I said. "I must tell you. My father left these five years past and never returned. I was but a small thing. I never learned most of his songs." I did not know how to finish. *Mistress Catriona, I fear that I will fail.*

Mistress Catriona placed a long finger beneath my chin. She tilted my face up until I looked at her. "Trinket, we have been brought together to help each other. Do you not see that? And, if we are successful and get my baby back, I will give you the harp to keep. What bard wouldn't want a harp as fine as this?"

'Twas true. I had not, in my young life, seen many fine things. And this harp was the most magnificent thing my eyes had ever beheld. I would be foolish not to want to have it for my own. Imagine how my fame might spread as the lass who played heaven's harp.

I nodded and Mistress Catriona smiled. "Now, Trinket, we shall require a small boat."

THE ISLE OF THE SELKIES

Thomas found Mistress Catriona's boat washed up on the shore with only a small hole in the hull. With some patching, it would be watertight enough to get us to our destination.

"Trinket, yer a fool to sail with a loony woman," he said as he sealed the bottom of the little boat with tar pitch.

Thomas made me think sometimes, which was a good thing and a bad thing. True, 'twould not be the smartest course to follow a woman the village regarded as deranged. Follow her into the ocean, no less! And yet, I felt in my blood that there was a story to be found among the selkies. My mother once said that the secret to a good story was to listen to the hum in your veins. My father would have done so, I thought.

"Perhaps it is not the wisest of ideas, Thomas, but it is the most adventurous. And when you agreed to accompany me on my quest, you knew then that there would be the chance of adventure."

"But I thought that it might involve pirates or monstrous beings, or battles even." He finished painting the tar and stuck the brush in the wooden bucket. "And I thought I would be there, not stuck fixing roofs."

It was true. It wasn't fair, really. But the boat was quite small and I doubted there was room for him. Thus, I would get the adventure and Thomas would do the work.

"I won't be long, Thomas." I picked up the bucket to return it for him. "And if I don't come back soon, you can lead the expedition to find me. That would be exciting, do you not think so?"

Thomas grimaced. "Nay. I do not think so."

"Well ..." I began. Did I really want Thomas along as Mistress Catriona and I searched for her babe? Could we all manage in such a tiny craft? "I suppose ..."

"Trinket, you don't have to beg. Of course I'll come."

When the tar was dry, Mistress Catriona and I climbed in. She sat in the bow, carrying the harp and the flute. Thomas pushed us out into the waves and then climbed over the edge, sitting next to me and smashing me a bit. However, I was glad to have help managing the oars. As we left the shore, I looked back at the village by the sea. Mister Fergus carried a bundle of thatch over to a cottage with no roof. He paused and turned his head toward our small boat. I thought I could see his bearded face shaking back and forth in disappointment. Most likely, he thought I was as crazy as Mistress Catriona.

My arms ached, for it had been a long time since I rowed. Though my mother and I had lived near the sea, we were not fisher folk. There was enough to do with wool-gathering and weaving to keep us busy. Only occasionally did the opportunity arise for a journey on someone's boat. But Mistress Catriona had ventured out with her husband many a time before the sea took him. She knew how to find the proper currents to push our little boat along. All the way there, Mistress Catriona asked me to sing. The fact that she could scarcely hear me over the waves made me brave. I sang little songs and rhymes I had learned from the children of our village when I was a wee thing. Thomas remembered the tunes, too, for we'd often sung them around the house and out in the yard. He whistled along, helping when I'd forgotten a melody.

The isle of the selkies was small and rocky. The waves splashed against it ruthlessly, as if the ocean wanted to swallow the jagged bits, but thought them too sharp to digest properly. I could not see any place where we might be able to land. I was about to voice my concern to Mistress Catriona when she bid us row again, hard. We did as we were told and in but a moment we saw a small, crystal lagoon where the waters were calm. We all smiled as we put our shoulders into the oars and forced the small boat over the rough surf and finally into the lagoon. When at last we pulled up to the shore, I was unaware that I was still humming.

"What song is that? It is lovely," Mistress Catriona asked, breathing heavily as we dragged the boat across the pebbles.

"Something so old I do not even remember it much." I said these words too quickly, and without confidence.

"Trinket, isn't that your father's—" Thomas offered, then he caught the look in my eye and gave his full attention to moving the boat. I did not want to tell her it was the lullaby from my own father, or that I practiced the tune every night before I slept. 'Twas something I was not yet ready to share.

Luckily, Mistress Catriona was less concerned with my lie than with the tune. She retrieved the musical instruments from the boat and carefully placed the harp in my hands.

"I'd like you to play that tune upon the harp. I think that is just the melody I am searching for. It haunts, but it is not sad."

She looked at me, expecting that I would be able to pluck out the tune with ease. She obviously overestimated my ability. I feared failure. Again. "I shall need practice, mistress . . . perhaps a different tune—" I began, but she interrupted.

"Do not pluck a string yet, Trinket," she scolded. "We must first find out where they keep my babe. You must not play the tune until I am ready. You will just have to practice it in your mind."

I gave her a look of disbelief, but she was staring off into the distance. Perhaps Thomas was right and Mistress Catriona was a loon. Who could possibly play a tune with no practice?

—

Though the beach appeared deserted, Thomas and I hid the boat behind a large rock, just in case. Mistress Catriona set out down a path to find where the selkies might have taken her baby as I began practicing the lullaby in my mind. It helped if I hummed quietly to myself and plucked the strings of a pretend harp.

Thomas got bored and began throwing pieces of shells he found on the beach back into the sea.

The sun was beginning to sink in the sky. Mistress Catriona had not returned. We had been on the selkies' isle all afternoon, but I had not seen even the shadow of a seal. Mayhap we had pulled up on the wrong shore?

I kept imagining what it would feel like to actually play upon the strings of the bone harp. My mother always told me I had been born with my father's imagination. *You could create an amusement from a stone and a stick*, she'd say. But I was having a difficult time imagining the notes. I was going to have to experiment. If I did not, there was a good chance that when Mistress Catriona needed me to play the lullaby, I would not succeed.

There seemed no reason to be silent, for I was certain no one could hear me. Thomas was kicking at the waves now at the far end of the beach, his silhouette tiny in the dying light of day. So, I began plucking away at the harp. I gasped at the sound. Whereas my father's harp had been low and deep, this one was light and magical. The harp had been made with a mother's love and for good purpose, and perhaps that is why it sang so sweetly. Truth be told, every random note rang out so pure that it would not have mattered if I could play the lullaby or not. But, either by miracle, magic, or sheer luck, I saw in my mind the fingers of my father, long, long ago, dancing upon the harp strings. I tried to pluck the same ones, in the same way.

My father's lullaby, the song the Gypsy seer hummed for me, sprang from my fingers and onto the strings. Rugged and rough though my playing was, the tune was strong and true.

WATCHFUL EYES

At first, I did not notice the rustling in the nearby bushes, so absorbed I was in my playing. And, tickling somewhere inside of my brain were words that went with the music. I could feel that they were there, but I could not speak or sing them yet.

You can feel on the back of your neck when there are eyes upon you. Slowly I turned around.

"What are you doing, Thomas?" I asked. I knew it was him. The pig boy did not even have the decency to look embarrassed as he stepped from the bushes.

"I just wanted to sneak up and surprise you. This is kind of boring for an adventure, don't you think?"

"Be quiet. I am practicing."

"I'm not deaf. I could hear your harp all the way down the beach. I didn't know you could play that well." His hand bent to pluck a string, but I swatted it away.

"It is the harp. It makes even foul notes sing sweetly. But I shall never be able to play a whole song unless you go away and let me practice!" I did not mean for my voice to sound so harsh, but it had the desired effect. Thomas skulked off, muttering to himself.

I started strumming, but was struck by that feeling again. The feeling of being watched. And I was, but not by a person this time.

The seal was misty gray and not very large. I looked into its eyes. Dark and glossy they were, like deep pools of tar. The seal cocked its head to one side, then the other, then came closer. When it finally stopped right in front of me it nudged me with its black nose.

"You want me to play again?" I asked. I searched around wildly for Thomas, but he was nowhere to be seen.

The seal nudged my leg once more.

Well, what do you do when a magical creature nudges your

leg? And I was quite certain this was no ordinary seal. It gazed at me with eyes far too intelligent to belong to an ignorant beastie, as if it was trying to communicate with me. I looked up, hoping to find Mistress Catriona walking out through the trees to join me, or Thomas strolling down the beach, but I was not so fortunate.

The seal nudged a third time.

"Very well. I shall play for you," I said, trying to treat it as I would a person. I did not want to offend it. Slowly, shyly at first, I began again to pluck out the tune of my father's lullaby. Like all lullabies, this one was meant to lead a babe down the mystical road to dreams. The seal's beautiful black eyes blinked once, then again and again, staying closed longer each time.

The seal drifted off to sleep at my feet. I hummed along with the melody and felt encouraged that my voice was clear and pleasant. I could use my newfound skill when I became a bard.

However, I would not be able to keep the harp if I did not help Mistress Catriona rescue her child.

As if summoned by my thoughts of her, Mistress Catriona appeared through the opening in the trees, walking briskly.

When she was close enough that I could see her face, it became apparent that she was angry. Very.

She started to speak, but I put my hand up and pointed to the sleeping seal. She had not noticed its slight form, as the sun was setting and its body was hidden in my shadow.

Her eyes widened and she slowed her step, walking very quietly on the tips of her toes, until she was right beside the sleeping seal. She bent down.

"What are you doing?" I whispered. The seal moved slightly in its sleep.

I looked around again for Thomas. *Where was he?* Why was he not here when I needed him?

"Keep playing," Mistress Catriona whispered, as she rolled the little seal over on its back.

"What's that?" I asked. The sleeping seal had a dark line down the center of its belly.

Mistress Catriona did not answer. She gently prodded the stripe with her fingers, as if she was looking for something. I gasped as she pulled on the skin and it came away from the seal.

"Do not stop playing!" she whispered sharply under her breath.

I closed my eyes, not able to look at what she was doing. *What if she hurt the little thing?* I could not continue the song.

"Mistress Catriona!" I whispered fiercely. "I cannot let you—" But I was too late. She held in her hand the gray skin of the seal. Sleeping at my feet was a small boy about half my age with silver hair and pale skin.

"Is he . . . ?"

"No, he only sleeps. And he is not my son," she said coldly, answering the two questions I had been afraid to ask. "But I will not return his skin until they agree to return my child." She walked briskly down to where we'd hidden our boat and dug a shallow hole. She dropped the boy's sealskin inside and covered it with sand.

The boy began to shiver in his sleep. I felt sorry for him and placed the cloak my mother had woven over him. Her decision seemed cruel to me. And yet, what lengths would a mother not go to in order to retrieve her baby? What would I not give to have my mother back?

"Here is what we shall do," she whispered, brushing the sand from her hands. "We shall agree to trade this boy's sealskin for my child. If the selkies do not agree, then I shall take this child for my own. I shall burn his sealskin. Without it, he can never return to his life as a selkie." She looked down at the sleeping boy with the silver hair and chubby cheeks, then glanced up at me, her eyes wild.

"I think that is an awful idea," I said, my tone no longer hushed. I did not care if the child awoke. "You grieve the loss of your own child, yet you would do that to another mother? Mistress Catriona, what happened when you traveled down the path? Did you meet with the selkies?"

She nodded. "Aye. I found them basking on their rocks. I began to play my flute, to tame their wild hearts. But the music did not bewitch them. When I grew tired of playing, I advanced. They made way for me until I found myself before the Selkie Queen." Mistress Catriona was speaking quickly, and I had a glimpse for the first time of the crazed woman Mister Fergus had such concern for.

"Go on," I said gently, as if I were the adult and she the child.

"I begged the Selkie Queen for my son, but she claimed she could not give back a gift given to her by the Mistress of the Sea. 'Twould be bad form and seem ungrateful." Mistress Catriona began to cry. Sobs racked her body and I could do naught but gather her in my arms and hold her.

"Did you see him? Your babe?" I asked softly against her hair.

She shook her head fiercely. "Nay, nay, they would not let me near enough. And there were many baby seals. They will have given him a sealskin." She sniffled loudly, causing the silver-haired boy to turn in his sleep. "But if I had gotten close, I would have known him."

"How?"

She looked up at me for the first time since her tears came. "Did I not tell you? His eyes. One is green and the other brown."

GRAY

———◆◆◆———

*T*he boy slept for a long time. **Mistress Catriona** decided that someone should guard him but she was close to collapsing from exhaustion. I volunteered to watch over him so she could sleep before we tried again in the morning to bargain with the selkies. I wondered again about Thomas the Pig Boy. *Where was he?* Chasing this story was perhaps not the cleverest thing I had ever done. I was beginning to wish I'd disappeared with Thomas.

The seal-child roused and looked up at me with gray eyes. He saw the harp lying next to me and motioned for me to play. He seemed not to notice that he no longer wore his sealskin. I pretended I didn't understand. I wanted to see what it was like to talk to this boy. Maybe there was another solution to Mistress Catriona's situation other than holding him ransom and trading him for her babe.

He crawled over to my leg and nudged me with his head. "Do you wish me to play again?" I asked quietly, so as not to wake Mistress Catriona.

"Yes, I should like that very much," he said, then stopped in shock at the sound of his own voice. He looked down at his hands and his feet. He felt his face, his hair.

His frightened eyes captured mine and I felt instant pity. I could not participate in the kidnapping of this boy. But I *would* find a way to get my lady's child back.

Children should be with their mothers.

"Do not be afraid," I said gently. "I'll not harm you." His small body was shaking. "Are you cold?"

The boy nodded.

"Well, wrap my cloak about yourself. There, now, what is your name?" I asked gently.

"Gray," he whispered.

"Very well, then, Gray, I think it would be a good idea to

go and find the rest of your family. Will you take me there?"
I picked up my harp, waiting for him to agree.

He rose, then looked at me pleadingly. He did not like my cloak. He wanted his skin. "Listen to me, Gray. I shall get your skin back, but I need your help. Will you help me?"

Gray nodded.

"Good. Now first, what were you doing out here all by yourself?"

"The island is ours. We can go anywhere we choose."

He didn't seem to mind answering my questions, so I continued.

"There is a babe newly arrived. Have you seen him?"

Gray nodded. "Him belongs to the queen. The Sea Mistress brought him to her. The queen's own child died in a fisherman's net." Gray swallowed and I could tell we were both thinking it was a horrible way to die.

"Gray, the babe does not belong to the queen. He belongs to my lady asleep over there." Gray glanced at Mistress Catriona. "She misses him so much. Her heart grieves for him, for the Sea Mistress took her husband as well. My mistress suffers doubly, but we can help her. We must hurry, or my plan will fail."

With a slight nod, Gray agreed to lead me to the court of the selkies.

Though he spoke not a word, I could hear Thomas behind us, following. I would know the sound of those footsteps anywhere. I wanted to turn and poke him for being gone so long, but I did not want to scare the seal-child.

"There," Gray said at last, pointing to a rugged formation that resembled a ruined tower. I pulled Gray behind some rocks, hiding us both. I peeked around the edge and there were the selkies, all in their seal forms.

"Listen to me, Gray, for I might not have the chance to speak to you again. Your skin is buried under the small mound of sand on the beach near where we left my lady sleeping. Soon, I will begin to play the lullaby I played for you on my harp. I believe it is bewitching to your kind. If I am right, all of the selkies, yourself included, will fall asleep." Gray's puzzled eyes showed he had no memory of the magical music I had played. "When you awaken, Mistress Catriona and myself and her babe will be gone."

"I understands, miss." Gray curled his small body into a ball, awaiting the sleep I had promised. I patted him on the head and thanked him, then rose and walked toward the selkies.

"Thomas, if you can hear me, we need to find the seal with one green eye," I whispered. I thought I heard a cough, but it could have been the wind.

THE SECRET OF THE SEALSKIN

The selkies did not notice me at first. I sat on a rock that poked me none too gently in the behind. However, no one had ever promised me that the search for stories would be comfortable. Then the selkies started coming toward me. I could not afford to seek a more pleasant-feeling seat.

I began plucking the strings of the harp, as I had done for Gray when he first nudged me with his cold black nose. The advancing selkies slowed. I took a deep breath and began to sing words, not my father's words, for I could not pull those from my memory. Instead, I called for the words that had been resting in the back of my head since I first saw the island. A selkie song.

The same song Feather had heard, the same tune that had lulled me to sleep as a babe, was sprinkled with magic. With the harp, the melody, and the words I had created on my own, I cast a spell of drowsiness upon the selkies.

How long I played, I do not know, for once the song ended, I began it again and again. The strange creatures drifted to sleep, some curled against others, some stretched out alone. Eventually, I silently placed the harp in the sand and made my way to the slumbering selkies. I decided to examine the smallest ones first. Most likely the young cub I was searching for would be nestled up against a larger seal.

The moon had risen full, huge, and bright enough to guide me. I hoped the moonlight would be sufficient for me to tell whether the seals' eyes were both the same color or not.

Thomas emerged from the darkness then, yawning widely. He stepped silently between the slumbering seals, motioning that he would start on one side while I checked the other.

As gently as I could, I lifted the eyelids of the sleeping cubs, searching for the one with eyes of different colors. By the time I was on the fifth seal, I had gotten pretty good at stepping between the sleeping bodies as if I were the dream faerie herself, and nary a sound did I make. My own breath was so soft and shallow, I would have doubted I was breathing at all, except that I did not fall over and faint. Finally, I peered into one brilliant green eye and one muddy brown one. I had found the babe.

I cradled him in my arms, and he did not rouse. Instead, he cuddled against my chest. I motioned for Thomas to follow and on the tips of my toes, I made my way out of the sleeping mass of selkies. Noiselessly, I reached down and swooped up my harp as we sneaked back to where Gray lay asleep.

I wanted to wake him up, to say goodbye and to thank him, but thought better of it. Perhaps they would blame him if he appeared to know my plan, and they would punish him, and that was something I did not want. The less he knew, the better.

Thomas gathered Gray in his arms, understanding the need to keep the child out of trouble. For a boy who had a tendency to get both of us *into* trouble, he was certainly showing his responsible side.

I met Mistress Catriona halfway between the selkies' court and the shore. She had a wild look on her face, which immediately softened when she saw who I bore in my arms. She did not even notice as Thomas placed Gray on the sand, quickly dug up his skin and draped it over his trembling body like a blanket. I hated to just leave him there, but I had little choice.

"Are you sure?" Mistress Catriona whispered as she took the sleeping bundle from my arms.

"I checked the eyes. One green, one brown."

She turned the seal-child over in her arms and began feeling for the seam in his belly, to release him from the seal-skin.

"Nay, my lady, I would not do that just yet."

"Why ever not?" she demanded.

"It may cause him to wake and cry. 'Twould be better to wait until we were far gone from this place."

She nodded and we ran to the boat.

I did not tell Mistress Catriona, but I also feared the Mistress of the Sea. If she knew we had reclaimed the baby, she might upset the boat and take us down to her murky depths as punishment. If such a thing happened, I wanted the child to find a way back to his other family.

We rowed as silently as we could, away from the isle of the selkies. 'Twas more difficult than you can imagine, attempting to cross the sea without much of a disturbance upon the surface. Luckily for us, the Sea Mistress was otherwise occupied and caused neither whirlpool nor storm to interrupt our escape.

Whispering, for we were still too frightened to speak in our normal voices, Mistress Catriona asked, "How did you do it, Trinket? How did you sneak my babe away from them?"

Should I tell her about the enchanted lullaby that causes seals and seal people to fall asleep? Would she keep such knowledge safe?

"They were sleeping," I said simply, which was partly true. "And Thomas helped." The fact that it was a spellbound sleep would be my secret. I was beginning to realize that part of being a bard was knowing when to tell your story and when to keep your lips closed tight.

DECISION

We arrived at Conelmara just as the sun was rising. Mistress Catriona removed the skin from the seal, revealing her small, pink son, still sleeping. The look of love on her face made me glad I had risked so much to help her. A mother should be with her child. A tear scalded my windburned cheek. Was my mother with me now? Was her spirit beside me holding my hand, although I could not feel it? I glanced at Thomas, his eyes full and glassy. Mayhap he missed his brute of a mother as well.

"Get rid of this," Mistress Catriona said absently, handing me the sealskin, not taking her eyes from her son.

"Yes, my lady," I replied, thinking to return it to the waves. But as I walked to where the tide washed over my feet, I could see them out there, several black heads bobbing on the horizon. The selkies. One swam forward, ahead of the rest.

My head whipped around, but Mistress Catriona was already on her way to her cottage. So, I slowly walked toward the seal, then stopped just before reaching the water. She did not approach me, but stayed in the surf, regarding me with her deep, soulful black eyes. She loves him, too, I thought. I dipped the edge of the sealskin into the sea, preparing to release it, when the selkie started acting strangely. She prodded the sea foam with her nose over and over again, as if shooing me back up the path. When I pulled the skin out, her nudging ceased. I clutched the sealskin close to me, making a quick decision.

"What are you doing, Trinket?" Thomas called as I ran off. I could hear his breath behind me as he raced to catch up.

"Why should I tell you? I am not the one who completely disappeared on the selkies' isle last night." I had not realized how angry I was at him until now.

"Aw, Trinket, you can't blame me for trying to find adventure. I was bored sitting around on the beach."

"So, did you find it? Your adventure?"

"No. I got lost. Would have stayed lost, too, I suppose, if I hadn't heard your harp."

I humphed and went faster, but it was hard to stay mad at Thomas.

I ran with the sealskin as fast as I could, all the way to Mister Fergus's home. I reached the door first, but only by a hair.

"Got the babe back, I see," Mister Fergus grunted. 'Twas obvious he'd been watching out the window.

"Aye, we did."

"Well, 'twould seem we were wrong. The babe is alive."

"Aye, he is."

"What are ye hiding behind yer back?"

I pulled the sealskin out. "I was supposed to get rid of this, but then I thought, maybe someday, the child might want ... a choice." He looked at the sealskin and nodded once, then took it and hid it beneath a large stone on his hearth.

The air in the cottage smelled of fresh bread and butter. I thought Thomas would either faint from the scent or jump over the table like a hungry bear. Luckily, Mister Fergus cut us each a chunk of the bread and slathered it with butter. We ate greedily.

"I'll keep the secret, till the time be right."

We ate more bread and butter than had ever been eaten in the history of time and slept without dreams on the floor of the cottage.

———

"'Tis time to go," I said to Thomas the next morning, packing the beautiful harp of bone and hair in my sack. Mistress Catriona had offered me the flute as well, but I told her to save it for the babe. "Mayhap he'll be a bard someday."

"Nay, he'll be a fisherman, just like his da," she had said. Then she hugged me and whispered, "But you, Trinket, you strum with the touch of an angel. And what an angel you were to find my son for me! May the ground be soft and the wind gentle on your journey."

For the first time, my dream of becoming a teller seemed within my grasp. I had a harp. And if I was closer to becoming a bard, maybe I was also closer to finding the truth I sought.

After we bid farewell to the folks of Conelmara, Thomas asked, "Trinket, what really happened to the selkies when you played that song? Was it magic, do you suppose?"

"Well, that is a story best told as we walk."

Every storyteller needs to practice.

THE SECOND SONG

The Selkie's Lullaby

*These are the words that came to me when I sat on the rock on
the isle of the selkies with my harp. If you feel your eyes
tiring and your mind drifting away during the course of this song, 'tis
possible that at least a drop of selkie blood runs through your veins.*

Come lay your heid,
Come lay thee down
Upon my knee
Of woolen brown.

A song I shall sing
Of salt and sea,
Of waves and foam,
Lad, come with me.

Thy flippers are tired,
Thy skin is cold.
Slumber awaits,
Thy dreams to hold.

A song I shall sing
Of salt and sea,
Of waves and foam,
Lad, dream with me.

The spray is soft,
The moon so bright,
Come lay your heid,
And rest tonight.

The Wee Banshee of Crossmaglin

A LOVELY LITTLE TOWN

We'd heard rumors of tellers on our travels. Bald Fergal. The Old Burned Man. Stephen of the Swift Tongue. But no word of James the Bard.

Sometimes, I feared that we would not find him, but I did not say so to Thomas. However, if I could not learn how to be a teller from my own father, then 'twould be good to hear stories told by a true bard, not just by the local folk. Mayhap one would even allow me to apprentice. So we followed the road, hoping to meet a teller.

Crossmaglin was a lovely little village, surrounded by green and rolling hills. On the top of one of these hills sat the ruins of a castle older than time itself. Only the white tower remained intact, and that was quite surprising for the stones were placed together with no mortar, looking as if even the most delicate of breezes could knock them down. But the tower did not fall. It remained tall and strong, a watchtower, perhaps, over the small village.

When Thomas saw the tower looming over the village as we approached, he was ill at ease instantly.

"No good can come of this," he said. He reached for the map I'd been holding and pointed with his grubby finger. "Look at the map, Trinket. Says right here 'tis called the *Banshee's* Tower."

"So what?"

"*So what?* I'll tell you what. I do not want to go to a town inhabited by banshees. *Banshees!* Cross, ghostly old women who moan and wail when death is near?"

"I know what a banshee is," I said. And I did. They were the messengers of death. There were lots of legends about banshees. I'd heard bits and pieces of tales about them, how they'd once lived in clans and ruled the night.

But those were tales from long ago. No one believed such things anymore.

"I heard the banshees, you know, on the night your mum died," Thomas said quietly.

I was silent for a moment. We did not yet talk about *her*. There was an unspoken agreement between us that we did not speak about our mothers. Thomas most likely missed his mum more than he wanted to say. As for me, the loss was still too fresh, too painful to think about. So, I tried to make light.

"Nay, 'twas only the wind that blew the night she passed. And a peaceful, gentle wind it was." But I remembered the way it whispered through the cracks in the shutters as if it knew my secrets, then burst into the room in her last moments.

However, I did *not* believe in banshees, though I thought a good tale about one would be a nice thing for a bard to have. And a town with a Banshee's Tower simply had to have a banshee tale.

"Are you not hungry? I'm famished," I said, changing the subject.

"Aye, Trinket, you know I am. Never was a lad born with as fierce a beast in his belly as myself." It had been many days since we left the village by the coast, and we had eaten all of our supplies. The few folks we met along the road could spare a crust or two, but no tales. And since Thomas hungered for food, and I hungered for stories, did it not make sense to venture to Crossmaglin? It would have both, I was certain.

"Looks like a place that should be at the bottom of a lake where kelpies lie in wait to steal your soul . . . until a priest throws holy water on the lot of them and they get burned to a crisp."

I had not expected Thomas to be so superstitious.

"Thomas, I don't think—"

"Would you rather be carried away by a kelpie or burned to a crisp, do you think?" he interrupted.

"Neither. Come on, Thomas, I think I smell chickens roasting over a fire." I sniffed the air dramatically.

'Tis the truth when they say that the way to a man's heart is through his stomach. Thomas begrudgingly agreed to come with me. "But do not say that I didn't warn you."

We raced to the village, my lovely harp jostling gently against my side as I ran. I was glad it fit inside my bag, for I did not want anyone with thieving intentions to see it. We followed our noses to the most heavenly scent we could imagine: roasted fowl, rich stewed vegetables, and fresh bread and butter.

We peeked through the window of the public house to see a white-haired woman serving plates of deliciousness to the folks sitting at the tables. Thomas and I exchanged a look, messed up our hair even more than it already was, and tried to look as pathetic as possible. We entered as two pitiful waifs in search of a meal. The pub mistress rolled her eyes and sighed, then directed us to two stools over by the fire.

"Just because I feed you today doesn't mean I'll feed you every day," she said as she placed small plates of meat and bread before us. "Folks earn their keep here in Crossmaglin. That goes for food as well." Had I nothing else but bread and butter for the rest of my days, I would be happy, so long as the bread was as crusty and tender as the bread of Crossmaglin. I gave Thomas my share of chicken, so I could fill my belly with more bread. The only thing that could have made the meal better was a story.

"Is there a teller here?" I asked the pub mistress between bites. "We heard that perhaps there might be one—"

"Nay," said a man at a nearby table between slurps of soup. "But one might come next month." I tried to hide my disappointment.

The man who spoke to us was named Mister Quinn. His voice was gruff and his manner as well, but he was not unkind. He offered a place for Thomas and me to stay, in his barn with the animals, so long as we helped to care for them. Thomas was thrilled, of course. I was not. Goats chew on too many things, including fingers, not to mention they smell. However, the only way to get myself inside a nice warm house for a night's rest, like a *real* bard, was to trade a story for the comforts of a bed. And I was not ready to do so. Yet.

So, in the barn at night, after the animals had dozed off and Thomas had doused the lantern, I practiced my harp and my singing. Softly, of course. It would not be bragging, though, to say that I was truly getting better.

I was singing the second song I had created, a song of loss and death, for bards must be known for their tragedies as well as their tales of good fortune, when it happened.

By *it*, I mean the fierce storm that whipped up from nowhere.

The air felt heavy, like before a rain, yet there was no lightning, no thunder. Only wind. Rough wind, the kind that howls and moans and causes the hairs on the back of your neck to stand on end. The kind of wind that does not go around you, but through you.

STORM

━━━◆◆◆━━━

"What *is* that?" cried Thomas as the door to the barn was ripped open, waking all the goats and the various other animals.

"I don't know!" I yelled, trying to be heard over the howling. "Storm?"

I shrugged. It most certainly seemed like a storm. And the animals were certainly agitated enough.

"Oof," Thomas groaned, as a goat kicked him.

It was difficult to see in the barn with the lantern out, and too dangerous to remain there amidst wild beasts, so Thomas and I decided to brave the wind. We battled the door, attempting to get through the opening without getting thrashed. The door scraped against the side of my face and whacked Thomas on the knee, but we managed to escape the dangerous building.

The gusts became harder and harder, nearly blowing us over. We held hands and proceeded, heads ducked down, across the road and to a nearby house. With the whitewashed wall acting as a windbreak, we paused to catch our breath.

"Thomas!" I called out tentatively over the sound of the wind.

"I know, Trinket, I am scared, too," he yelled, still clutching my hand. I could feel my nails digging into his flesh, but I could not make myself loosen my grasp. The howling became screaming, then shrieking. Goose bumps spread across my body and probably through my hand to Thomas's grubby palm and up his spine as well.

Then, as suddenly as it began, the storm ceased. One moment the noise was so loud there was no room in our brains for even the smallest of thoughts. The next moment, 'twas silent.

The air was still. I brushed the hair from my eyes and looked at Thomas.

We were too afraid to speak and still breathing hard from fright. We expected to hear stirrings throughout the village, the noises of people trying to get themselves back to sleep, perhaps the sounds of babes crying or dogs barking. But the silence continued. We walked, hand in hand, down the streets of the village, searching for, well, we were not quite certain what. I wanted to call out, *Hark, is anyone awake?* but Thomas put his finger against his lips and looked hard at me.

We were followed only by the sound of our own feet crunching against the gravel as we made our way back to the barn. Thomas tried to pull the heavy door open, but it was stuck standing slightly ajar. Something was wrong with the top hinge, as if it had been stretched and bent. Thomas pulled again, but it would not budge, so we squeezed between the door and the wall.

I could hold my tongue no longer. "'Tis strange, Thomas. Very, very strange."

Thomas only nodded and walked over to the pile of straw he'd fashioned into a bed.

"How can you sleep?" I whispered fiercely.

Thomas simply shrugged and closed his eyes. "I am tired, Trinket. We walked quite far. And 'tis only wind after all."

But I heard him moving restlessly in the straw. He could pretend to be brave all he wanted, but I knew he was scared, too.

THE BROKEN DOOR

Early in the morning, Thomas and I examined the barn door, but it was still stuck. Deciding to leave well enough alone, we squeezed out of the barn and went up to the house of Mister Quinn. We found him coming down the gravel path, and he divided up the tasks for the day. I was given the chore of milking the goats and Thomas had to muck out the sheep pens outside the barn. I was not certain which of us had the more unpleasant job. I'd only watched milking in the past and had been in no hurry to learn how, but the sooner I started my chore, the sooner I could talk to someone about the events of the night before.

"Quite a storm last night," I said.

Mister Quinn grunted. He handed me a pail and a stool. We approached the stuck barn door; then he paused, taking in its awkward angle.

"I had never heard wind so fierce. It nearly blew the barn door off," I explained.

"Are ye telling me ye broke the door?" he grumbled as he pulled on the handle with no luck. The door did not move.

"Nay. I'm telling you that the wind near blew the door off."

"Ye'll have to pay for the repair if the hinges are shot." He touched the rusty metal of the pin of the hinge and shook his head.

"But we didn't break the door. The wind did. 'Twas most fierce!"

He didn't look at me but managed to shimmy his spare form in between the door and the wall and gave a huge shove. The hinge fell with a clink to the ground, warped and twisted, as the now-lopsided door swung open wildly.

"Coin for the hinge," he muttered.

I stood with my hands on my hips and gaped at him. He

did not notice, or chose not to look. How could he expect us to pay when we'd done nothing wrong? Nothing at all! However, he was a grown man, and we were but children. It would not do for us to be thought of as vandals. Who would invite a bard who destroyed things to their town?

So, the hinge would have to be paid for. I supposed I could sell the small silver mirror in my sack, but 'twould be better if we found another way.

And I would not sell the harp.

—

Being only thrice kicked by the goats, I was assured by Thomas, was a good thing. Truly it could have been worse. But perhaps Thomas was right and it was a bad idea to come here. Leaving the ill-tempered goats behind would be a relief.

"Excuse me," I said, handing the pail of fresh goat milk to Mister Quinn, who was squatting by an old wagon, repairing a wheel. "Here it is." He looked at the pail disapprovingly. He must have expected more milk; however, not a sound escaped his lips.

Thomas was still mucking out pens, so I went to the village

square to offer myself as a chore girl. I listened carefully as I walked through the town for the sounds of conversation. Surely people would be talking about the horrible storm. And if I could gather a tale while I worked and paid for the hinge, well, that would be grand. Asking a question or two about a bard named James was also in my plans. What a busy day I had before me! The public house loomed ahead, bustling with business. I entered slowly and quietly. All speaking stopped.

"Good morrow." I bobbed a curtsy to the pub mistress, whose head popped up as I entered. In the light of day, I could see that her white hair was kissed with a touch of old fire. Some curls escaped from her bun and tickled her cheeks, which were plump and wrinkled. "I am Trinket, do you remember me from the meal last evening? This morning I milked the goats for Mister Quinn."

She nodded briskly, but said nothing.

"I thought perhaps you might need help? I could wipe tables."

She looked me up and down, then handed me a broom. I began to sweep as she said, "I can give ye a meal, but not coin, if that's what yer after." Though I was disappointed, I continued sweeping. Perhaps if I swept well enough, I could earn a meal for both Thomas and me.

"I am surprised to see all the roofs still on the buildings, what with that horrible windstorm last night."

The woman glanced at me as if hoping I would just be quiet. Most likely she had bread to bake or vegetables to stew. Then she sighed and asked, "What storm?"

"The one last night, the one that near blew the door off the barn. The storm that shrieked so loud it sent chills through my very soul." The woman cocked her head to the side, looking at me as if I had claimed I'd seen a fox flying through the air wearing a king's crown.

"Last night, you say?"

"Yes, Thomas the Pig Boy and I barely got out of the barn alive."

Both eyebrows rose.

"Well, perhaps I exaggerated. But the goats began kicking and the barn door knocked into Thomas's knee and scratched my face." I pointed to my scrape. "When we left the barn for the safety of the open path, the wind bowled us over. And the sound . . ." I felt like I was explaining something to a child who had never even heard of wind, or perhaps to a person who did not speak my language.

"What did it sound like?" she asked, trying not to appear too interested. But I could tell she was, for her cheeks were flushed. And her eyes no longer showed boredom. 'Tis something a storyteller learns to look for.

"Like screaming. Or maybe shrieking. I could not tell really." I laughed nervously. "But it was horrible."

She turned brusquely away. "Quite a story, lass. But I heard not a thing."

I did not know why she would lie, but I did not believe her.

"It was not a story, but the truth," I said. But if she did not want to talk about the storm, there were other questions I could ask. "But I do like stories, you see," I said, sweeping the floor in front of her to keep her attention. "I am collecting them to tell. My father was a teller. James the Bard was his name. Perhaps he came here once?"

"Might have," she replied. "Might have come years ago. But I'd remember if he were one of the good ones. Bald Fergal, now he tells a good tale. Plays the bodhran well, too. Does your da tap the wee drum like Bald Fergal?"

"I don't think so. I think he played the harp," I said.

I worked for a while, making certain to get every crumb and bit of dust. "A most amazing tower that is, at the top of yon hill," I said as I finished sweeping under the last table.

"I would not be so curious, if I were you, to find out about the Banshee's Tower. There have been those who have ventured there and never returned," the woman whispered.

"If it is so fearsome, then why do you not move your village to a place more pleasing than the shadow of the Banshee's Tower?" I asked.

The pub mistress threw her head back and laughed. The white curls that dangled in front of each of her ears swung merrily. "Move a village? Indeed! You are not as smart as you look, child. Folks just cannot up and move a town, you know. And besides, the land here is good for grazing and the crops grow bountifully." Then, suddenly serious, she leaned down and whispered to me, "We have learned how to live in the shadow of the tower. We ask no questions, we tell no tales."

Moving her mouth even closer to my ear, she urged, "Do not go there, child. You might not find your way back. 'Tis foolish to go to the Banshee's Tower."

———

When I returned to the barn with bread and cheese to share with Thomas, I mentioned my strange conversation with the pub mistress.

"Same thing happened when I asked the neighbor boy about the storm last night. Claimed I must've imagined it. But he didn't say anything about the old tower," Thomas said with his mouth full of bread.

"We didn't imagine it, though, did we?"

Thomas shook his head. "I'll never forget how that sound rattled through my bones, like it could have pulled them apart if it wanted to."

"Thomas, you talk about the wind like it was a person or a monster or something," I teased.

He did not laugh, nor would he return my gaze. I knew he thought it was a banshee, but if he wasn't going to say so, then neither was I.

We slept little that night due to the howling winds and the agitation of the barn animals. Thomas's face held a cranky scowl, so I left quickly in the morning to do my chores. After milking the goats, I returned to the public house. I would sweep, scrub, wipe, wash, or do whatever was required to learn the story of the tower.

The pub mistress sighed when I asked for the third time. "Fine, I'll tell you the tale, if you've the stomach for it."

We sat at a table in the kitchen, our heads close together. The pub mistress began, "Once, the tower was the stronghold of a clan of banshees that watched over Crossmaglin. Perhaps *watched over* is not the right way to say it, but in the tower above the town, the banshees dwelt, shrieking and crying when death was coming to one of the folks in the village, for banshees call a wailing wind when death is near."

I nodded, encouraging her to go on.

"There was once a young banshee who was so full of trouble and mischief that she was cast out of the banshee clan," she continued. "They say she grew bored with hair combing and clothes washing, which is what the banshees do when death is far away. Whatever the reason, the wee banshee started wailing in the wind for no purpose at all, except to annoy the folks of the town and the other banshees. Every night, the wee banshee wailed and moaned until the other banshees got so tired of it, they disappeared into the mist, not telling the wee thing where they were going."

My heart went out to the little banshee, just a bit. I knew what it felt like to be abandoned.

"But did that stop the banshee? No. She kept on hollering, shrieking, and creating terrible winds. At first, the villagers tried to stop her. A few brave men went up to the tower at night, but they were cocky, thinking how easy it would be to dispatch a wee banshee. They did not bring the proper protection." The pub mistress tapped the small dish of salt on the table. "The wee banshee must have led them to their doom, for they never returned."

I gasped.

"One of those men was my grandfather. I was but a girl at the time. I remember traipsing up the hill the very next day searching for him." The pub mistress was silent for a moment, then dabbed at her eye with the end of her apron and continued. "Oh, the hill that day was so lovely, the grass so green, and the tower itself so white against the blue sky. But not a trace of my grandfather or the other men did we find. Since then, no one in the town pays attention to the wails of the wee banshee. No one is brave enough, nor foolish enough, to try to banish her away. We mind our business and she minds her own."

TRIP TO THE TOWER

———◆✦◆———

'Tis a bad place, Trinket. We should leave. I care not for that stupid door. We did not even break it. The wind did," Thomas said the next morning as he moved an old wagon back to the other side of the barn. He had placed it between the goats and us each evening since the first. Though there were not many goats in the barn, they kicked at us, bleated, and tried to chew our fingers whenever the wind blew wildly, which was turning out to be every night. And then there was the smell. Even though the wagon did nothing to block the odor, it did keep the goats away. And the farther away the goats were, the less it stank.

The morning air held its chill as Thomas and I picked bits of straw from our clothes. Purplish circles resided under his eyes and probably mine as well. Neither of us had slept much, but for moments between gusts, wails, and the bleating of the goats. Thomas must be truly terrified to want to leave a place where the food was so plentiful and tasty. I, too, was frightened. But we had a door to repair, and there was the fact that I had hoped to find a story in this strange little town underneath an ancient tower. The pub mistress had told me some of it, but I knew there had to be more. How far was I willing to go to capture my tale?

Mister Quinn was waiting as we left the barn. He examined the door hinges again, though we all knew they were still broken. "'Tis your fault," he said, pointing at us. "The wind's been a-wailing more than ever since the two of you came to Crossmaglin."

"I thought you did not notice the wind," I said.

Mister Quinn's right eye twitched. "Either go up to the tower and have her done with you, or hurry and earn the price of the hinges before she blows the whole barn down."

"She? Who is she?" I asked, but he stormed away and disappeared into his house, slamming the door behind him.

I had a fair idea who *she* was: the wee banshee.

"Told you so," Thomas muttered.

I milked the goats whilst Thomas tended the other animals. When I was kicked for the second time, I gave up and felt in my pocket for the few copper coins I'd been given by Feather. It would have to be enough.

"You win, Thomas. We'll leave. But before we go, would you come and explore the ruins with me? I should like to go up this afternoon and have a look around. Nobody will answer my questions about it except for the pub mistress."

"And what did she say?"

"Just small specks of a story. You probably wouldn't believe it," I said, hoping that would be enough to make him curious.

"Try me."

"She said that once there was a young banshee who was so full of trouble and mischief that she was cast out from the banshee clan."

"Banshees! Did I not tell you?" he interrupted.

I threw a handful of straw at him.

Thomas pulled a pretend key from his pocket and proceeded to lock his lips.

I told him all that I knew. Thomas's eyes got wide, the way

a person's eyes get when they want to hear more. His mouth was no longer shut tight, but gaped.

"The pub mistress didn't say much more," I said. Thomas's face dropped in disappointment. A breeze came by at that exact moment and ruffled the hairs on our heads.

"The wee banshee is there still, or so the pub mistress says."

Outlandish was the word my mother would use about a tale such as this. And she would have laughed and said that scary things like banshees didn't exist. But Thomas was more fanciful.

"Do you suppose *she* makes the wind every night?" he asked.

I shrugged, for I did not even *think* I believed in banshees. But had I not met a seer? Had I not met seals who could change into people?

"Will you come with me?" I asked.

Thomas paused. I could see his indecision flopping around in his mind, like a fish on land. I let him take his time, for I would not force him if he was too frightened.

I did not have to wait long before he nodded.

He would come.

We climbed the hill in the early afternoon. When we began, it appeared we would reach the tower quickly. However, the hill and the old ruin were both massive. We walked up the trail for an eternity until we finally came to the peak of the hill and the tower itself.

Like a giant from a lad's tale, the tower loomed over us. Thomas's excitement grew. Thoughts of banshees must have flown out of his mind.

"Look, Trinket, its tip touches the very clouds! How did folks build such a tower? How many years do you suppose it took? More than a hundred, I think."

But I was not looking up at the clouds. I was watching the sun, which was beginning its descent. We would have only a little while here before it became dark. I dreaded the walk back down the hill in the blackness of the night. We had not thought to bring a torch.

"Thomas?" I called, for I could no longer see him. "Thomas!" I shouted, my voice echoing against the silence of the hill.

No birds sang. The air was still. I could hear my own breathing and my pounding heart, but that was all.

"Thomaaaaaasssss!" I yelled, from the very bottoms of my feet.

"Trinket! Up here!" There was Thomas, hanging halfway out a window and waving wildly.

"There are stairs!" he called, as if I would not be able to determine how he got up there.

I entered the tower and easily found the stairs, which looked horribly unstable but felt strong and sturdy as I stepped. Up and up again. The stairs wound around the edges of the tower, creating a spiral that made my head spin. I had never before feared heights, but I had no desire to climb all the way up.

"Thomas! 'Twill be dark soon!"

"I've almost made it to the top!"

"If we don't leave now, we will miss our dinner!" Again, Thomas's stomach would probably be my greatest ally.

"Trinket, I am almost there!"

"Fine! Go on, then! I'll meet you below." I was put out, and angry with myself for feeling so. Had Thomas not come with me whilst I dealt with the selkies? I walked back down the steps and out of the tower to an ancient stone bench. I pulled my harp from my bag, glad that I'd brought it along.

'Twould be good to practice. I plucked the strings, trying some new tunes, then played once more the old lullaby. How I wished I could remember my father's words.

The ruins that surrounded the old tower created fascinating shadows on the ground as the sun set. A broken wall to the north. A crumbling gateway to the west. Only the tower stood untouched by time. I imagined the people that might have built it. Were they fierce warriors? Were they gentle scholars whose castle had been destroyed by invaders? That would have been before the banshees came, of course. *If* the banshees had even come at all. Inspired by these imaginings, I plucked new melodies that bounced from wall to wall, then drifted off into the sky above.

I did not notice when the breeze began, only that one moment I was contemplating old rocks, and the next I was wishing my mother's cloak was thicker.

"Thomas!" I shouted. "You are taking too long!" I placed the harp gently back in my bag and rose.

I doubted that he heard me, as my voice was carried away by the wind. I looked for shelter from the strengthening gusts and found it behind the stones of the gateway. I peered around the edge frequently, hoping to see when Thomas came out from the tower. The shadows cast by the ruins grew longer and longer until there was more shadow than light.

"Thomas!" I called, more in frustration than in hope that he heard me. I cursed the idea that had led us up the hill in the first place. My own idea, of course.

The sound was small at first, so small that I almost didn't notice it.

"*Trinnnnkkkkettttt,*" the wind called. And then a second time, louder.

"*Triiinnnnkkkkkkeeeettttt.*"

"Thomas, is that you?" I yelled, knowing that it was not Thomas, could not be Thomas.

THE WEE BANSHEE

Fear finally caught up with me.

'Twas the wail of a banshee, I was certain.

I peered around the stone once more, but I caught no glimpse of the pig boy. Naturally.

Perhaps knowing that death is close makes you strong. For, indeed, if death is coming for you, what do you really have to lose by being brave? Things could hardly get worse.

So, I stepped from behind the stone, faced the wind, and cried, "Who calls me?"

A girl appeared before me, but she was not really a girl. She was a wee banshee, crying most mournfully as her white hair whipped around her head. I had never believed in the stories of banshees, but what do you do when one is looking you in the face? And this child was *not* human. She was combing her hair with a silver comb, although the instant she smoothed a lock, it was tangled by the wind once again. Her gown was also white, paler even than her face. Glistening in the early evening light like diamonds on her cheeks were perfectly formed tears. She was beautiful and terrifying at the same time.

"Did you call me?" I asked bravely.

"Aaaaaaayyyyye," she wailed.

I swallowed and looked at my hands for a moment. *Did I want to know why?* I remembered my time with the Gypsy King's daughter. Back then, I had not wanted to know my future. Now, with a small banshee calling my name, was I strong enough to know if I was meant to die now?

"Am I going to die?"

She said nothing for a moment, then the wind became softer, as did her voice.

"I have a message for you, Trinket the Bard's Daughter."

I had thought it impossible to be more scared, yet her words sent a fresh wave of goose bumps down my arms.

"Who is the message from?"

"Your mother."

An eternity passed before I could form any words of my own. *"My mother?"*

My mother was dead.

"And the price of this message is a small, small thing. So small," she said.

At that moment, Thomas came up behind me. I could hear the gravel crunching under his feet, the same rhythm he made when we walked together mile after mile after mile.

"Trinket . . . do you see what I see . . . or think I see?"

"Aye, Thomas, I see a banshee girl."

The wee banshee glared at Thomas, then returned her gaze to me. "Come back on the morrow, as the sun sets." Her voice floated on the wind.

"Wait!" I called to the mist that now swirled about in the space where she had been.

Thomas grabbed my shoulders and shook me hard. "You are not stupid enough to think of doing what she says, are you?"

"Thomas." I pulled away from him. "She has a message from *my mother.*"

"It's a lie, Trinket. She is tricking you. She will carry you off."

I scoffed. "She is too small to carry anyone off."

"She's a banshee! God above only knows what she can do!" he cried.

"I am not afraid of a tiny little banshee," I lied. Of course I was afraid. But the chance to hear words from my mother made me courageous.

"You should be. I will not let you come back," he said simply, and turned to walk down the hill to the village.

You cannot stop me.

We did not speak all of the way back to Crossmaglin.

ALONE

The wind blew more fiercely than ever that night. And I could not be sure, but I thought I heard my name whistling through splintered planks of the old barn walls.

In the morning, I awoke to the sound of Thomas stuffing his meager possessions in his sack. "Trinket, we are leaving."

My head was still foggy with dreams of a pale ghostly girl calling my name, floating over clouds and stars.

"You are not my master, Thomas."

Thomas swallowed. He knew he could not force me to do anything. "Please, please, please do not do this, Trinket."

Until that moment, I had not known what I was going to

do. I did not in truth want to face the frightsome child again; yet, she bore a message from my mother. *My mother.*

How could I not try to find out what she might tell me?

"I have to, Thomas," I said, laying a hand on his arm. He brushed it off and threw his sack over his shoulder.

" 'Twill be your funeral, then. I'll not stay to watch it."

"I thought you were brave. But you are not. You are nothing but a scared little boy!" I cried.

"I'll be heading west and . . . well, I won't walk too fast."

And he left.

I was alone in the town of Crossmaglin. Well, not completely alone. There was cranky Mister Quinn and the strange pub mistress. And there were the goats.

It was better the pig boy was gone. He would only distract me from finding my tales. And if he was not brave enough to stay with me, then perhaps he was not the friend I thought he was.

At least this was what I kept telling myself.

I worked that morning, milking the goats one last time. I left my copper coins on the milking stool, but I no longer cared if it was enough to pay for the hinges. I swept the pub in the afternoon and tried to eat a small plate of bread and cheese.

Though the food curdled in my stomach, I willed myself to finish it, hoping it would give me strength. 'Twas a short distance back to Mister Quinn's barn, yet I found my feet dragging, and when I slung my bag over my shoulder, it felt heavier than usual with my harp and my map inside. But I had decided. I would go and receive the message from the small banshee. The message from my mother.

I readjusted my bag, thinking how much lighter it would soon be without my precious harp. Didn't the banshee say my mother's message would have a price? The harp was the most valuable thing I owned. There was nothing I would give it up for, except this.

The pub mistress blocked my way as I left the barn, startling me. "Thought I'd find you here." She took in my bag as I edged my way around her. "Leaving are you? I'd not go that way, girlie. Your friend went the other way."

"I know," I said, and continued toward the hill.

"You've a mind to see the banshee, then?"

I nodded.

She grabbed my hand and placed a small pouch in it. I peeked inside.

"Salt?"

"Protection," she said. "And turn yer cloak over, inside out. 'Tis also a shield against magical creatures, not as strong as salt, but you'll need all you can get if you've a mind to attempt this."

"Attempt what?"

"To banish the banshee, of course. That is why you are going, isn't it?" She cocked her head to one side, trying to read my mind. "You've been there once already, haven't you? Even though I warned ye not to go?" she asked knowingly.

I nodded.

She shook her head slowly back and forth. "Tsk-tsk-tsk. You're lucky to still be alive. Most never return at all. Are ye sure ye want to do this?"

I said nothing.

"If she promised you something, it will have a price. A price you won't want to pay. Do not fall for her tricks." Her brow furrowed and she tapped her chin in thought. "It would help if you had a mirror. A banshee cannot abide its own reflection."

I thought about the mirror still hidden in the bottom of my sack.

It gave me a little feeling of strength, but not much.

As I walked on the path to the ruins, I made up my mind and dropped the pouch of salt on the hard ground. I did not turn my cloak inside out for I did not want to keep the wee banshee away. I wanted the message from my mother. I remembered her hair, soft brown and gently curling. Her face was shaped like a heart, except that her chin was round, rather than pointed. Her eyes were deep blue, and in summer months the slightest sprinkling of freckles danced across her nose and cheeks. I, too, sprouted a new crop of freckles each spring. *Kisses from the angels*, my mother called them. Her arms, before they became so thin, had held me softly as I drifted off to sleep. And she told me stories.

Not stories like my father would have told, not *bard* stories, but stories about when she was a girl like me and the things she discovered as she ventured out into the world.

I missed her so much.

And I missed Thomas, though I wished I didn't. He had been there with me, caring for my mother, helping me cook vegetable broths and oatcakes in hopes of making her strong.

Before the illness, she mothered him as well as me. 'Twould be strange to hear her words and not have Thomas there.

But he had made his choice. And so had I.

The late afternoon sun glinted off the Banshee's Tower. Soon, the sun would disappear, the sky would darken, and I would receive her message.

As I neared the top of the hill, the wind kicked up, as I had known that it would. The low moaning began, rising to a shrill shriek as gloom descended upon the ruins. I found the stone bench and sat on it. I would not be waiting long.

"Trrrriiiiinnkkeetttt," the wind called.

I did not reply. If the wee banshee was looking for me, she would find me easily out in the open. I tried to sit with my back straight, looking fearless. But there was a bone-deep chill in the wind and I clutched my mother's cloak tightly, though it was nearly useless against the icy gusts.

I hoped 'twould be the spirit of my mother that found me cowering in the wind. She would wrap me in a soft blanket, the one full of colors she had woven for me long ago. I would cry and she would tell me not to weep, that it rarely did anyone much good. And then she would impart her message.

It was, however, the wee banshee who came to me, her pale eyes alive with devilish joy. "Yooooouuuu caaaaaaaame baaaaack." Her voice sailed on the wind.

"What is the message from my mother?" I asked. I had hoped to leave this place before the sun finished sinking in the sky. Perhaps I could catch up with Thomas in a day or two—if I decided to forgive him for deserting me.

"You have payment?" she whispered.

"Aye." I placed the bag with the harp on the ground in front of me.

She beckoned with fingers that looked far too long for a child's. I followed her carefully.

"Where is she? Where is my mother?"

The banshee did not answer, but continued on her path. I could do naught but follow, though the evening light vanished more with each step.

Gravel slipped beneath my shoes as she led me down a steep path on the other side of the hill.

"Wait! I cannot keep up!"

She floated faster and faster along the path and I started to run. Were I brave enough to look down to my left, I would have seen the pebbles skid out from under my shoes and fall hundreds of feet below, for on one edge of the path lay a cliff, on the other a wall of stone.

"Please, slow down!" I called, gasping for breath.

The wee banshee slowed and pointed over the cliff.

Did she want me to jump?

I shook my head, as no words would come. Thomas had been right. This fiendish child only sought my death, the chance to carry my soul off and cry most mournfully about it. Why hadn't I listened to him?

She pointed again as I clutched the rocky wall. I closed my eyes and bent my head. I would not look where she pointed, nor would I jump. But the wind was so strong, I could move neither forward nor back along the path.

I began to cry.

MESSAGE FROM BEYOND

*T*rinket," a voice called. It was not the whiny cry of the wee banshee. It was a gentle voice, the most beautiful voice I had ever heard in my life.

It was *her.*

It was my mother.

I was afraid to open my eyes. What if she was not here with me? What if, in my moment of death, I was imagining that she was here? Would not everyone want their mother with them when facing something so frightening?

"Trinket."

Bravely, though I was sniffling, I opened my eyes and looked into the empty air above the cliff.

'Twas no longer empty.

She was more lovely than I remembered, her skin not as drawn as when I last saw her, although it was paler than the face of the moon. Her hair did not swirl in the wild wind, but hung silkily past her shoulders. She wore the dress they buried her in, the most gorgeous blue I had ever seen. The color of dawn.

I reached out my arms to pull her to me, but she put up her hand.

"Trinket, do not move."

I looked down. If I had taken but one more step, I would have joined my mother in death.

And when I stopped to think about it, perhaps it would not be so bad.

I could fly through the air in a dress of sky, by the side of my mother. I had no one else now. All it would take was one little step . . .

"Trinket, stop."

Her tone was sharp. I knew that tone. When I tried to take more than my share of oatcakes, she used that tone. When I would not go to my bed at night, she used that tone.

I learned early not to ignore it.

"Why?" I asked.

She smiled so sweetly, I thought my heart would break. "This is not your time, Trinket. But you already know that, don't you?"

I said nothing. The urge to run into my mother's arms was strong. It was all I could do to keep my feet planted on the ground.

"Trinket, you must listen to me."

I nodded. I had come to listen to her message. *But I wanted so much more.*

"There will be a time when you will need these words. I have risked much to see you, Trinket, as have you."

Her face was fading in the dusk.

"I'll not be allowed to come again, Trinket, so listen well."

My eyes filled with tears.

"Your heart, Trinket, keep it safe and strong. It will guide you on the right course."

I nodded.

"And, Trinket, do not judge by appearances. Evil may lurk in a harmless package. And something pure and good may reside under old, crabbed wrapping."

Her lips curved delicately and I sniffled. She faded even more, her body but the steam above a boiling kettle.

I wanted to smile in return, but I was confused. If you had one moment with the dead, what questions would you ask? What would you tell them?

"Mother, I love you."

"I know that, Trinket. Please forgive me for leaving you. *Forgive.*"

"Mother, what about my father? Is he d-d-dead, too?" I choked out. "Is he with you?"

She was vanishing, and the small banshee drifted in between us, an endearingly innocent look on her face.

"Forgive."

"Stay . . . please . . ." I begged.

"Oh, my little Trinket," I could hear my mother's voice echo as she was lost to the mist. "I am with you more than you know."

I wiped my tears with my sleeve only to find the wee banshee there again in the space my mother had just vanished from. The wee banshee's long fingers opened and she held out her hand to me. So easy it would be to grasp it, to fall into the abyss and not feel this pain anymore.

I wanted my mother.

The banshee's outstretched hand slowly came closer.

"The harp," I said between sobs, pointing back to the tower where I had left the bag on the ground by the bench. "I offer it in exchange . . ." Paying the price was hard, but I had come prepared.

"I do not require the harp, Trinket," she said. Her voice was cheerful, almost kind. "I want *you*. Think of it. We could play all night, in the tower. We could comb our hair. We could fly on the wind."

Her bony finger beckoned and I watched as my own hand moved stealthily forward.

"You'll never hurt again," the banshee said. "You'll cry for the loss of others, but the pain will not be your own."

Sweet words. Never to feel my own pain again. The pain from a father who deserted me and a mother who died and abandoned me. Everyone left me. Even Thomas left.

Perhaps I drove them away.

"Yes, Trinket, you drove them away. They never cared for you," she crooned, her small face filled with compassion. "But I would not leave your side. We would stay young and ride the moon. We'd shriek at the world and watch as foolish mortals are carried off by Death."

Was I such a terrible person that no one ever wanted to stay with me?

"Your message has been delivered. Now 'tis time to pay," the wee banshee said. "The price is your life."

My hand was almost touching hers, but I could not reach her unless I took a step. I looked down. That one step would send me so far below that I could not see exactly where my bones would crash and break. Would they join others, there at the bottom of the cliff? Would my body lie next to the pub mistress's grandfather, and no one would ever know what happened to me?

Would I feel this searing hurt no longer?

"Trinket!" called a voice from the path above.

"Just one more step," the wee banshee whispered. "One more tiny step . . . no more pain . . . come, Trinket . . ." Her hand stretched out to me, just beyond my grasp.

"TRINKET!" Thomas shouted. "STEP BACK!"

The banshee grabbed at my wrist. Her nails scratched against my skin and I lost my balance.

THE BLUEBIRD

—◆◆◆—

*F*alling was not as peaceful as I thought it would be. It felt hard and rough and was over much too fast.

That is because I did not fall from the cliff.

Thomas had thrown himself at me and knocked me out of the banshee's grasp. She roared and wailed in despair. He landed on me and squashed me uncomfortably, but I would thank him later for it. Thomas had kept me alive.

He pulled on my arm, dragging my body upward, and forced me along the path. "Do not look back, whatever you do, do not look back." But I could not help it. Her eyes were fiery, like a demon's, and her face grimaced like a gargoyle. Thomas opened a small pouch of salt and flung it over his shoulder. Luckily, the wind did not blow the grains back at us, but carried them through the night, blasting the tiny specks against the thrashing, wailing form of the wee banshee. I could hear a *hiss* as the salt touched her skin.

Thomas pulled from his pocket my small silver mirror and flashed it at the wee banshee. Her moans and screams pierced the night.

My cloak whipped around and between us. Thomas batted it out of the way and clutched my hand, not letting go until we were far away from the top of the hill and the Banshee's Tower. All the way down the path, the wind did not let up, nor did the howling cease. We ran and ran as if Death itself was at our heels.

And it may have been.

When we got to the road that led back to Crossmaglin, Thomas took us in the other direction.

"Thomas, my things . . ." I sobbed, but my words were covered by the sound of feet on gravel. 'Twere the first words I had spoken in all time it took us to reach the fork in the road. Nay, I had not spoken, but I was not silent. I cried all of the way, until there were no tears, only dry coughing sounds, and still I did not stop. Thomas said nothing but held my hand as we traveled, helping me along when the going became difficult.

There is a time to talk and a time to hold your tongue. Thankfully, Thomas knew the difference between the two.

At last we were so far away it seemed safe to stop and catch our breaths. I sat on a log and buried my face in my hands. "My harp," I said softly, thinking only I could hear. 'Twas selfish to be thinking of a mere instrument when my very life had just been saved. I knew it, but I could not help it.

"It's here. It's all here," Thomas said simply, patting the bag on his shoulder that I'd been too shaken to notice. "I found this inside, see?" He pulled the mirror from his pocket and placed it gently in the sack. "When I went back, the pub mistress told me you'd gone. She gave me some salt and asked if I had a mirror. I didn't, but I knew you did. And when I got to the ruin, I saw your bag on the ground by the bench."

I noticed then that all of Thomas's garments, every last one, were on backward and inside out.

"Do you suppose we banished her away from the tower?" he asked.

I shrugged. The wind around us was gentle now, like the breeze in the room after my mother had died.

As long as the wee banshee was nowhere near us, I did not care where she was.

"Thank you for coming back," I whispered, my voice hoarse from the tears.

"Ah, Trinket. You'd have done the same for me." He smiled a bit, grateful, perhaps, that I wasn't crying for the first time in a few hours.

———

Later, when we were miles from Crossmaglin and could no longer see the Banshee's Tower, I asked the question that had been rattling around in my brain.

"Thomas, how did you arrive at just the perfect moment? Had you been an instant later . . ."

"You know, Trinket, 'twas the strangest thing. I was already on my way along the path leading away from Crossmaglin, when a bird appeared. A beautiful bluebird. Well, I'd never seen such a bird before, and I've seen lots and lots of birds, and so I went to get a better look. Was flying all strange, it was, darting all around as if it were trying to get my attention. And I was afeared the poor thing was injured. So I ran to keep up, thinking maybe I could help it. 'Twas approaching twilight already, yet this bird fairly glowed. Never seen anything like it. I *had* to chase it. It stayed always just ahead of me. So there I was, running to catch a better look at the bluebird, and the next thing I knew, I nearly stumbled over the pub mistress. She handed me a bag of salt and . . . well . . ."

He did not go on with the story.

I did not blame him. But a warmth and a tingle went through me.

"Thomas, what color of blue was the bird?"

"The color of the sky at dawn."

THE THIRD SONG

The Bluebird Song

To fly in the sky
With thee, dear bird,
Betwixt the clouds
Of white.

A-floating, a-darting
Up high, dear bird,
From morn
Until twilight.

What wouldn't I give?
A treasure? A tune?
To fly with feathers
'Neath the cold, pale moon.

Like a mother who watches
Over her nest
And teaches the young
To fly.

Against the blanket
Of sparkling stars
'Neath the Mistress
Of the Night.

What wouldn't I give?
A treasure? A tune?
To fly with feathers
'Neath the cold, pale moon.

The Faerie Queen and the Gold Coin

ORLA

———◆✦◆———

*E*ach village has its own way about it. Some have a
tragic sense to them and some can only be described as sleepy.
Thomas and I like the happy villages the best, the ones where
music can be found in the very sounds of bees buzzing or the
mooing of cattle. The ones where laughter trickles from under
the cottage doors like water over smooth rocks. Such a village
was Ringford, where we met a girl who was born to dance.
Perhaps the moon and stars twinkled in harmony the night
she was born, or the ocean waves beat against the shore in the
same rhythm as her little beating heart. Whatever the reason,
the lass was born with dancing in her soul and she could do

naught but move about, this way and that, every single minute of every single day.

Now, everyone knows how the faerie folk like their dancing. It's one of their favorite things, next to cake and revelry. And possibly romancing. But this tale is not about faerie romance. Or cake. 'Tis about dancing. And a bargain. And the girl who was born with the rhythm of the twinkling stars in her feet.

—

Thomas and I came upon the dancing girl's town after many days of walking. We were at the end of our rations and here was the fine-looking village of Ringford. We watched the townsfolk from behind a hedge, making sure the folks were friendly before revealing ourselves. Thomas and I had found that some people were kind and some were not, and the easiest way to tell was to watch how they treated their children. Villages where children were beaten were not places we stayed long, for where there was little tolerance for children, there was less for a young storyteller and her pig boy.

Instead of yelling at the dancing girl to be more helpful,

her family encouraged her, making the cutting of the turf a celebration.

"Dance, Orla, dance!"

Joyful voices frolicked through the breeze and to our ears, married with the sound of clapping. And then we saw Orla, dancing deftly in the peat bogs alongside her family as they worked. Tall and graceful, swift and strong, she was the best dancer Thomas and I had ever seen.

—

"If I were a true bard, I'd stay a whole week in a village just like this," I whispered to Thomas. It was impossible to say the word *bard* and not think of my father, but finding James the Bard became more of a foggy dream each day.

"I bet the Old Burned Man's been here. Maybe he's even here now." Thomas nudged me with his elbow. The more we searched for my father, the more we realized how difficult our task was. By this time, we were happy when we found *any* bard.

"Perhaps," I said, though I secretly doubted it. It seemed luck was never with us as we sought the Old Burned Man.

We had been fortunate enough to hear Bald Fergal tell tales the week before. His stories were mostly jolly and we'd giggled about them for days on the road. But when I had asked him about my father, he had supplied no information.

Thomas was about to laugh out loud at the scene the family created as they whooped and jigged on the turf when I poked him into silence. (Poking has its benefits.) Could he not see how amazing Orla was? Never before had I seen anyone dance so elegantly, yet with such power. Orla was a fine name for her, too. Her hair shone like gold and she carried herself like royalty. A golden princess, indeed.

We watched, spellbound, for a while. Then the bushes became too itchy and the family seemed kind enough, so Thomas and I came out and introduced ourselves. Orla's family, the McGills, offered us shelter and food, if we helped with the turf cutting. Naturally, we agreed. Thomas, of course, would rather have worked with the animals than alongside people, but he was learning to carry on a conversation quite well, as I made him practice when we traveled between towns. He'd developed a fine love of questions.

"Do you suppose 'twould be better to be a goat or a toad?" he might ask.

Or, "Why do we have five fingers and not seven? Then you could count the days of the week on one hand."

Or, "What if people got younger instead of older? Then I'd be bigger than you . . . somehow . . ."

That was what it was like to converse with Thomas. Though I hated to remind him, he already *was* growing bigger than me. His britches were no longer as saggy and his sleeves scarcely covered his wrists. If he kept up at this rate, we'd have to get him new clothing soon.

Perhaps if I worked more on my stories and songs, they'd be worthy of trade before long.

———

I practiced my harp that night by the fire as the McGill family sat around the old wooden table in their kitchen. Though I still got nervous when playing for folks, I found my fingers growing more sure of themselves each day.

"Do you play songs other than lullabies, though that is a lovely one," Orla asked as I strummed my father's lullaby, for

I played it every day. I had indeed picked up a few other tunes along the road. I nodded and Orla leaped from her chair with joy. "Will you play for me? I've never danced to harp music before."

"'Twould be an honor, Miss Orla," I replied.

"Been a long time since we've seen a harper in these parts," said Orla's father. He was a tall man with a reddish beard and an easy smile.

"Long time, indeed," said Orla's mother. "Oh, but he could play. Long fingers he had," she said as she took one of my hands in her own. "Like yours."

"Was he called James the Bard?" I asked, hoping with all my heart to hear *yes* for once instead of *sorry, no* or *I don't remember.*

"Oh yes, lass. That was him. Not heard a harp like that for years. But your hands, child. Yes, I've seen hands like that strum a harp before."

I could not help but feel warmth travel from my heart to my fingertips. He might have once sat where I was now sitting. *His* blood made my fingers play more beautifully.

Orla's father nodded to me that it would be acceptable to

play a dancing song, so I played a lilting jig I had practiced in the evenings when Thomas and I camped. And though Orla was but a child, she danced more fair than any woman I had ever seen.

THE FAERIE QUEEN

———◆∙◆∙◆———

'Twas my own fault that word of Orla's dancing skill made its way down to the faerie kingdom, for there was a faerie mound nearby. If you've not seen a faerie mound, I should tell you that 'tis not a sight you'll soon forget. Imagine a perfectly round hill, covered in grass that is both brighter and deeper green than any of the other grass around. And not a bush nor tree grows on this mound. Once a year, in the spring, a ring of flowers may sprout. Or it may not. Depending on the Faerie Queen's whim.

"If you see such a ring on the mound, do not attempt to pass through. Few have ever made it to the other side," Orla's mother told me as we sat around her table on our second morning there, eating fresh berries, cream, and bread. Her green eyes twinkled and her voice fairly sang. I liked how she spoke with her face as well as her voice and I told her so.

Her cheeks turned the color of strawberries and she said, "Well, I'm not so good as a proper teller."

"Have there been many tellers in these parts?" I asked, trying to summon enough bravery to bring the conversation around to my father once more.

She patted my hand as if she sensed the importance of my question. "If you are asking about that James the Bard, I've not heard of him being about for years. But the Old Burned Man comes from time to time. Ye'll have heard of him, no doubt."

Aye. I had.

Thomas's eyes lit up. "Did I not tell you, Trinket? I told you he came here." He smiled smugly.

He was becoming good at collecting gossip; his eavesdropping skills improved with each town we came upon.

"And Bald Fergal will be coming soon," Orla's mum said.

Aye. Bald Fergal. We had already heard *his* tales.

Thomas and I ate our midday meal by the faerie mound. He thought it would be exciting. I hoped there might be a story nearby. Instead, we both found it rather dull. No faerie ring to be seen.

We laid my cloak upon the ground and ate in silence, listening for faeries inside of the mound. I chewed my cheese slowly and frowned at Thomas as he made noise whilst peeling his egg. He dropped a bit of shell on the fine fabric my mother had woven and I glared at him until he picked it up and flicked it away. Finally, deciding there was nothing to hear, not even the buzzing of bees, we began to talk, though we should have known better.

"The girl, she can dance, no?" Thomas asked with his mouth full. Regardless of how many times I reminded him to chew and swallow before he spoke, he uttered whatever thought crossed his mind, the moment it crossed.

"Thomas, village folk would not want to see your food once it is inside of your mouth." *Especially boiled egg.*

"The way her feet move. Never have I seen a person move

their feet so fast." He stuffed the rest of the egg in his mouth, followed by a chunk of brown bread. "And she leaps so high, it's as if the sky holds its breath until she lands."

'Twas true. And the girl had rhythm in everything she did. The way she walked. The way she drew water from the well.

There was the crisp sound of a branch snapping, unusual because there were neither bushes nor trees nearby. Unfortunately, we kept up our conversation, going on and on about Orla, never suspecting that we had been overheard by curious faeries from the mound.

—

At first, we only noticed a few things going amiss. Like Orla's shoes being misplaced, or the fact that it took much too long to run a comb through her hair, so matted and knotted it was each morning. Or how the milk in Orla's cup would spoil before midday.

None of these minor catastrophes, however, had any effect on Orla's dancing.

'Twas Orla's duty to gather small, dry branches for kindling the fire. I accompanied her one day, for turf cutting was hard work and I preferred a good walk to a sore back. And with Thomas off investigating the sheep, I felt a bit lonely. Orla didn't talk much, but she twirled and leaped with her empty kindling basket, her feet barely touching the ground. I had to run to keep up.

"Which one of ye is Orla the Dancing Girl?" said a mysterious voice.

As if it wasn't obvious.

Orla turned around and found herself not a hand's length away from a most unusual creature. At first small of stature, the creature rose until she was tall enough to look the girl in the eye. Her hair was almost as fair as her skin but her eyes were of the black of a moonless night. Her clothing was sewn with a fine hand; I could tell as much, what with my mother being such a skilled weaver. The dress, of deepest rose, swirled delicately to the ground. Her cape was a rich emerald green. Afraid we were, but smart enough not to show it. Fear makes itself large if you let it out.

"I am," said Orla.

"I am the Faerie Queen, and I've come to make a wager with ye." She ignored me as if I weren't there at all.

"Nay, I'll not wager. Wagering brings nothing but shame to a family." Orla was bold to speak in such a way to a queen. "My great-grandfather warned me against making gambles from the day I could first take a step." And wise, too, for a girl so young. "Wealthy he once was, till he gambled it all away."

"Would this change your mind?" The Faerie Queen pointed to the ground at Orla's feet. Each pebble changed into a coin of gold. We gasped in unison as the path sparkled before us.

"Ahhhh," said Orla, bending to pick up one of the golden discs.

"Not so fast," laughed the queen, her voice echoing through the trees, the clouds, and the sky. "'Tis simple, you see, we will have a little competition between the two of us. A dancing competition."

Orla could not help but smile, for she knew no one could dance as fine as she.

I, on the other hand, felt frozen in place. I could not speak the words that formed on my tongue: *Orla, do not trust the Faerie Queen!* I had learned from my experiences with the wee banshee and the selkies that humans and magical beings often see things differently.

"Whoever wins gets the gold," the Faerie Queen continued. "Whoever loses never dances again."

Orla stopped smiling. "Never?"

"Never."

Orla, no! 'Twill break your own heart in two if you can never dance again. But I was frozen in my tracks. I could not even catch her eye. It was as if I wasn't even there at all.

Obviously, I had been bewitched.

The thought of being able to help her family and restore their wealth was too much for Orla. She balanced her weight from one leg to the other, back and forth, more and more quickly until . . .

"'Tis a bargain!" cried the girl, and she held out her hand to clasp that of the Faerie Queen. As they shook, the sky clouded over and a crack of thunder filled the air. Then the Faerie Queen and the gold coins on the ground vanished in a blink.

"Orla, what have you done?" I whispered to the morning breeze when my voice finally returned to me. But Orla was no longer there. She was skipping and dancing merrily down the path, dreaming of the gold she would win for her family.

THE DANGERS OF GAMBLING

News of the contest spread quickly, through both the village and the faerie kingdom, like green over the hillside in the spring. The challenge would be danced at midnight under the full moon in five days' time. Orla practiced from sunup to sundown. Her family did not know what to think, but what was done was done. The best they could do was help Orla prepare for her challenge.

"We'll stay, then, to see it through?" Thomas asked me as I paused to adjust the tightness of the strings on my harp, then started plucking again.

I nodded. I hoped he did not mind too much, for we could not leave the family in their time of need. My harp playing was necessary for Orla's practicing. Since daybreak I'd been working hard to keep up with her feet as she created more and more intricate steps. My fingers flew over the strings until small blisters appeared under the skin. But if the blisters on her feet did not stop Orla from dancing (and I was certain her feet must be sore and swollen), then the small eruptions on my hand would not slow my strumming.

Thomas placed his hand next to mine, then turned it over, front to back. "Look here, Trinket, not a blister nor a cut." He took in the red bumps on my fingers. "Mayhap I've got the easier job this time!" He whistled as he trotted off to join the men for an *easy* day of work.

The day before the competition, Orla's great-grandfather called her to his bedside.

"Trinket, please come with me. Great-grandfather often frightens me. He never leaves his room nor gets out of bed," she said.

I had been most curious about the closed door at the back of the house. But this was not something you asked about in polite company. I was learning that hunting for stories required patience.

Usually, when a story lurked, it revealed itself in time.

His hair was white and sparse and even his wrinkles had wrinkles.

"It's been fifty years, fifty years, I tell ye," he croaked, "since I, myself, struck an ill-made bet with the faerie folk."

Orla gasped. "Is that how you lost all of your—"

"Aye. That was the gamble that ruined me."

"What was *your* wager?" asked Orla.

"Same as yours." Great-grandfather's voice was like slow steps on a gravel path. "Oh, aye. These feet that can no longer walk"—he lifted a threadbare blanket to reveal a pale, shriveled foot—"once danced the sharpest steps. The Faerie Queen challenged me. She cannot abide there being a better dancer than herself. Oh, it should have been easy for me to win. I was the most fleet of foot there was, but she was tricky. Faeries always are. She changed the rules at the last minute."

He sat up higher in his bed, leaning toward us, beckoning us closer with his finger. He looked to the left and to the right before he continued.

"You there, harp girl, make sure there's no eavesdropping faeries under the window. Orla, look ye well under the bed."

When we assured him that no one was listening in, he went on.

"She changed the rules. I was made to dance upon a gold coin and not fall off."

Orla's eyes were as large as goose eggs. *"What?"*

"Foolish and full of myself, I was. I took the wager, and increased it, betting all of my wealth, *my family's wealth*, against hers."

We held our breaths, though we knew how it turned out. We knew that he had not triumphed, for Orla's family was the poorest in Ringford. But still, it was painful to hear him say it.

"I lost. We became poor because of it. In shame, I left my village a pauper. I came to Ringford to better my lot, but . . ."

He reached his gnarled hand under his pillow and drew out a beautiful golden coin. "This is the coin from the bargain, the last gold this family has known. I was saving it for my burial so it wouldn't be a burden to the family." He grabbed Orla's hand and pressed the coin into her palm.

"I want ye to take it."

"I cannot." Orla shook her head as she tried to pull away from the old man.

"Ye must!" he commanded. "Worse than losing the family money was losing my dancing." His voice caught and I looked out the window awkwardly. I would have left altogether, but Orla was between me and the door. "Money is just for buying things." He sniffed. "Dancing is life itself. I'll not have ye meet the same fate."

I could hear Orla swallow. Her eyes glassed over, but she did not cry. The full weight of her bargain landed upon us both as we stood in her great-grandfather's bedroom. I felt the cold finger of fear tracing circles on my spine. I wondered if she felt it, too.

"Do not be afraid, child," the old man said gently. "You, harp girl, take her out to practice." He waved us off.

"That is what ye must do," he called after us. "Practice, practice, practice!"

A COIN AND A HOLE

Outside, Orla tried without luck to balance her steps on the small circle of gold. Good as she was, she was not good enough to land each leap on the coin. Not only that, she practiced so hard that she wore holes in the soles of both of her shoes.

"These will need mending," she sighed as she unlaced the ghillies from her feet. "Have you a hand for sewing, Trinket?"

As if I could sew with my fingers so bruised and blistered from playing the harp hour after hour!

I shook my head. "I've no skill. And stitching through leather is no easy task. Have you a needle strong enough?"

"Nay," sighed Orla. "If I were to break one of mother's bone needles on my shoe, she'd be more angry with me than if I lost this match."

"Perhaps the cobbler?"

"'Tis worth a try," said Orla. "Mayhap he can help me."

The cobbler was not at his shop. As a matter of fact, the shops were all closed. The streets were deserted and our voices echoed in the emptiness. The excitement of the competition that night must have caused everyone to go home and rest up for the big event.

"I bet the Faerie Queen herself wears enchanted shoes made by leprechauns," Orla complained as we walked through the empty streets of the village. "And here I am, the afternoon of the match with nothing but ruined ghillies and a gold coin."

Orla was beginning to lose hope. I could not let that happen. There had to be a way to repair the shoes.

And there had to be a way to thwart the Faerie Queen.

If she was planning on changing the rules, we must plan as well.

Our steps echoed through the streets of the small village. The only torch still burning was at the blacksmith's shop. We had nothing to lose, so in we went.

The blacksmith's apprentice was a friendly young man with hair as dark as a crow's wing and eyes to match.

"Can you help me?" Orla asked as she slowly pulled the gold coin from her pocket. "I've holes in both of my shoes and this is all I have. I've been practicing my dancing on this coin, for that is what the Faerie Queen will ask of me. If I cannot do it, I must never dance again."

"Orla, ye wee fool," said the apprentice. "Why did ye go and do a crazy thing like that?" He looked at me accusingly, as if it had been my idea.

"The fault is my own," said Orla. "I was too proud of my dancing. And now I'll never get to dance—" A small sob escaped her.

"Now, don't despair." He took the gold coin from her and flipped it into the air. "'Tis about time someone beat the faerie folk at their own game." He winked at us both. "Give me the shoes."

Orla untied the laces and handed the ghillies over. The

smith began to measure the tips of the soles. *Was he planning on patching her shoes with iron?*

"Will it cost all of the gold?" Orla whispered. "My great-grandfather wanted me to practice dancing on the coin . . ."

"Nay, I'll not charge ye at all, Orla. 'Twould be accursed money if I did."

He flipped the coin back to Orla, who caught it with one hand. The sight of the coin twirling through the air gave me an idea.

"Orla, may I see the coin?" I asked.

It was not very large, but it was thick. If the fire was still hot enough, it just might work.

THE CHALLENGE

———◆►✕◄◆———

At supper, Orla hummed a reel quietly to herself as she sipped her soup and chewed her bread.

"Are ye not nervous, dearie?" asked her mother.

Orla simply smiled, tapping her feet under the table. Her mother moved her gaze in my direction.

"Trinket, has she been practicing too hard? She looks soft in the head this evening."

"Nay, she's been practicing a great deal, but not over much. She'll be ready."

I winked at Orla and she winked at me. We looked down at our bowls so as not to giggle. *Was this what it was like to have a sister?*

I heard a snort from Thomas. He gave me a *what have you gotten yourself into this time, Trinket?* look.

Orla's mother sighed and glanced up to the heavens, muttering something under her breath.

—

When the sun went down, people began to gather on the hillside. And by moonrise, the crowd covered all of the green. The faeries were in attendance as well. Oh yes, they can be invisible when they choose, but when they gather in such a great number, well, they sparkle and shimmer most visibly. The queen wanted them there, of course, to witness her victory over the mortal girl who was fool enough to bargain with the fey.

Thomas and Mr. McGill carried Great-grandfather, bed and all, out to witness the contest. He smiled, but his old eyes held the worry we all felt.

Just as the moon found its place in the center of the sky, the Faerie Queen arrived in a carriage drawn by six tiny white ponies. The wagon stopped in front of Orla and the queen stepped out. She pulled herself up to her full height and asked, "Are ye ready for the challenge?"

"Aye," Orla said, bending down to adjust a lace on her ghillie.

"And ye agree that the loser of the battle shall never dance again?"

Orla's father made a move as if to protest the terms, but though his lips formed words, no sound came out. Bewitched most likely, as I had been when we last met the Faerie Queen.

"Aye," said Orla, "and the winner shall have your gold?"

"Aye," laughed the Faerie Queen, and she clapped three times. Musicians appeared on either side of her, one with a flute and one with a fiddle. "You have your own musician, do ye not?" She pointed disdainfully at me, though I saw her look at my harp with envy. 'Twas, after all, a most unique harp.

"Trinket is the finest harper in the land," Orla bragged. I stood tall as those around, human and fey alike, whispered and mumbled.

"Indeed?" said the Faerie Queen. "Then 'tis only fair that she play for me as well as for you. I would not want anyone to say that the contest is not a fair one."

I swallowed hard.

"Of course, the harper must have some stake in this as

well." She turned her beautiful face. "The harp, of course, should you make a mistake in playing, will be forfeit," she said.

A boy's voice piped up from the crowd. "What does she get, then, if she plays without error?"

Thomas.

The queen glared at him, but quickly replaced her nasty look with a sweet smile. "She can have her choice of reward, of course."

I only nodded. I had no idea what I might ask for because I did not expect to be able to play without a slip. My hands shook, causing my harp to quiver, as the queen motioned for me to sit on the chair the McGills had brought for me from their house.

"So, we begin." The queen stood on one side of the wooden plank floor Orla's father had laid for the competition. Orla took her place opposite the queen. My fingers were poised over the harp strings.

"Oh wait, I forgot one small detail." *Ah, here it was.* She pulled from the pocket in her cape a gold coin. "All dancing must take place upon a gold coin. Each step, each leap, each twirl must land upon the gold!"

Orla's mother gasped and I thought she might faint, but Orla's father and Thomas fanned her with large leaves and held her upright. Murmurs, mumbles, and grumbles wove through the crowd, laced with the occasional cries of "Unfair!" and "Cheat!"

The queen might have expected to see Orla crumple in disappointment. If so, then she herself was the disappointed one.

"You first." There was the slightest bit of cheek in Orla's request. But perhaps I was the only one to notice.

The queen rose as Orla stepped back from the floor. The coin flipped into the air and landed smack in the middle of the planks. She snapped her fingers and I played.

The Faerie Queen began her dance. The village folk could not help but *ooh* and *aah* as she leaped gracefully about, the tip of her toe never touching anything but gold. My fingers raced along the strings, desperately trying to keep up with the queen's wickedly fast feet. My hands started to sweat, but never once did the queen look tired. Never once did she look anything but fresh and strong. And amazing. The villagers clapped as she finished her dance, pointed her toes one final time, and bowed.

She nodded her head the slightest bit in my direction. I had made no mistakes.

"Your turn." She looked Orla up and down, her mouth smiling, her eyes not. "I hope you enjoy your last dance ever." As Orla took her place on the dance floor, her eyes twinkled mischievously. She motioned for me to begin. The queen caught the glimmer. "Remember, you must dance upon a gold coin! Every step!"

ORLA'S GAMBLE

———◆◈◆———

*M*y fingers sprang to life again and I played. 'Twas harder this time, for I could feel fatigue rolling in like the fog on a fall evening. I'd no doubt the queen would count a fault against me even if I botched Orla's tunes instead of her own.

Not too fast, at first. *Give Orla time to ease in.*

Orla danced in a way that no one had ever seen before. Instead of leaping and prancing, as a lady should when she dances a reel, Orla's feet rallied and trebled, creating an intricate, pulsating beat. If you listened, you could hear her shoes click slightly each time she touched the wood. But the queen was too busy savoring her soon-to-be victory to listen. "Look how her feet do not even touch the gold!" she jeered. "She has lost the bargain already."

Orla's mother began to weep. She hid her head in her husband's red beard. *"Never even had a chance,"* she sobbed. Orla heard nothing but the music and continued to create the most amazing dance ever danced. My fingers, inspired by her feet, leaped over the strings, never missing a note. The villagers clapped in time with the tune.

"You're not following the rules!" the Faerie Queen shrieked.

Orla's feet hammered out a crisp rhythm, more musical, more graceful, and more entrancing than the Faerie Queen's performance. When she clicked her heels together for the last time, both faerie folk and townsfolk stood, clapping and yelling wildly. Orla pointed her toes and bowed regally.

"You lost! You lost!" cried the queen. "Now you'll never dance again! You stupid, foolish girl! You did not even try! It doesn't matter that your dancing was the finest, for even the fey cannot deny it." She gestured to the faeries on the hill, who were all leaping about and clicking their heels, imitating

Orla's spectacular performance. "But your foot never touched the gold!" she roared.

All were silent then.

Orla was out of breath and still smiling. She nodded at me to rise, which I did. "If you'll permit me, your highness." I bowed to the queen, then bent down and unlaced Orla's ghillie. I flipped the shoe over, revealing its sole. "You never said she had to dance on *that* particular coin." Nailed to the bottom of Orla's shoe with horseshoe nails was half of her great-grandfather's coin, pounded flat and covering the hole that had been there. The other half was nailed neatly to the shoe's mate.

"As you can see"—I held the shoes high, visible to all—"Orla completed all of her steps upon a coin of gold."

The queen was furious. Some even said they saw lightning behind her eyes, and many of the villagers, fearing her wrath, escaped down the hillside. Angry words in a language I did not understand spewed from her lips.

But she did not combust there, under the moon that night. Nay. She simply took in a deep breath and disregarded Orla altogether.

Instead, she turned to face me.

She tried to hide her ire, but faeries are of a passionate nature. I knew I would have to watch my step, and my words, very carefully.

"Come forward," she said, pointing to me. "Bring your harp."

I picked up my harp and held it close to me, lest she try to grab it away. I walked two paces forward, then stood my ground. If that was not close enough, then she could come to me.

"'Tis exquisite," she said. "Perhaps you would let me try?"

I knew I was foolish to refuse, but I could not bring myself to allow it. I wrapped my arms tighter around my harp and shook my head slightly.

"Very well," she said. "I did not expect that you would. We have other matters to discuss, do we not? Your payment. Have you thought about what you might ask of me? I could come back another day, when you have had time to consider your options."

I could see Orla's great-grandfather out in the crowd,

shaking his head. Yes, indeed she might come back...in a hundred years or so!

"I would prefer my reward now."

"Would you really?" Her voice, the quietest of whispers, was still so fierce that gooseflesh rose on my arm.

"Aye."

REWARD

———◆━◆◆◆━◆———

*B*efore you think too hard about what you might have wished for yourself, consider my situation. I was but a young storytelling lass accompanied by a pig boy, traveling through the land, attempting to find my father and learn enough stories so I could make a living for myself one day.

'Twas a hard enough path I had chosen for myself.

I did not need an enemy.

"I would like . . ." My voice was small, even to my own ears. I cleared my throat and started again. "I *demand* as my reward . . ."

The heat from the queen's glare was burning my own eyes. I felt them water and blinked twice. Oh, she was angry, but smart as well. I was certain that, at this moment, she was in her mind thinking of the things I might ask for and finding a way to turn my request into a curse.

'Tis the way of the fey. They'll not be bested.

I turned from the queen and looked into the remaining audience. The faces lit by torchlight under the midnight sky were scary to behold. Too much shadow around the eyes, and the grins all appeared evil, villager and faerie alike.

"I demand that the Faerie Queen be released from her punishment of never dancing again."

There were a few gasps and shocked murmurs. I was not facing the queen now, for I was too frightened, but I could hear her sharp intake of breath, followed by a slow exhale.

"Turn around, harp girl."

Slowly I turned.

"Why?" Her black eyes narrowed as if trying to search inside my mind. Perhaps she gained entry, for in the next instant, she smiled softly. Her face was so luminous in that moment, outshining even the stars and the moon.

"I'll not be outdone, girl. Faeries do not like being in the debt of humans." She spoke so softly I was not certain if anyone heard but me. "For your troubles," she said as she raised her hand and flipped a gold coin in the air toward me. I was too shocked to catch it, and it clattered on the wooden dance floor at my feet. I reached down to retrieve it. 'Twas larger than a regular coin, with strange shapes on it, perhaps serpents, all interwoven with each other, with no beginning and no end. Faerie gold.

By the time I looked up again, the Faerie Queen, her carriage, the ponies, and all of the faeries in the audience had vanished in the night, leaving behind Orla's newly won gold in several sacks of fine, heavy brown velvet.

The people whooped and hollered, raising Orla over their heads and lugging her fortune back to the McGills' cottage.

As I watched the villagers disperse, a hand clamped around my hand that held the coin. 'Twas sweaty.

Thomas.

"My palms were wetter than a crying babe's cheek." He laughed, and I hugged him. Neither mother nor father had I, but I had Thomas. And I was glad for it.

———

A traveling bard cannot remain in one place forever. Though I liked Ringford well, 'twas time to journey on and find new yarns to spin and eager new ears to hear them. And I could not forget what had led me here in the first place—the search for my father.

The farewells the next morning were both sweet and sad. Orla hugged me like a sister and the McGills thanked me over and over again. And Orla's great-grandfather clutched my hand tightly as a tear rolled down his withered face. "She would have lost it all without you," he said. I decided not to mention that 'twas probably my own conversation with Thomas by the faerie mound that caused the challenge to be issued in the first place. Some tales are best left untold.

"Why did you not ask for riches?" Thomas asked as we left the town of Ringford. "Or food. This sack will not last forever."

The sack in question bulged at the seams. Orla's mum had loaded us up with more food than four fat men could eat in a month. A heavy bag, indeed. But Thomas did not mind carrying the extra weight. It was worth it.

"You could have asked for a magic sack that would have filled with food whenever it was empty."

"And take the chance that the food would be cursed? Take the chance that if you ate it, you'd be under an enchantment?"

I knew Thomas would have chanced such a thing, were he hungry enough. But now, on a full belly, he nodded. "Didn't think of that."

"But what about riches?" he continued. "Come on, Trink, did ye not think of wealth?"

"Probably cursed as well. And if not a curse from the Faerie Queen, than the curse of greed. Yes, Orla's family has wealth, but they must now be on guard for someone who might want to take it from them."

"You sound like a know-it-all, you *do* know that, do ye not?"

We walked in silence then, but for the sound of our steps as we traveled farther and farther from the village. Sure steps, strong steps. Steps that said with each crunch of gravel that there were more important things than wealth and food.

"You're not going to tell me why, are you?" Thomas was getting annoyed, which would make for a cranky next few hours.

I sighed. "Thomas, with my reward, I bought us freedom. Freedom from the faerie folk chasing us down to reclaim whatever it was I'd asked for. And the freedom to continue on our quest for stories."

He said nothing for a long time.

"*Your* quest, you know."

"Hmmm?"

"It's *your* quest for stories. I am only along for the food."

THE FOURTH SONG

The Faerie's Reel

*These are the words I sang in my head when Orla and the
Faerie Queen danced their reels. I found if
I concentrated on the words, I worried less about
my fingers slipping.*

Oh, she is fair and fleet of foot
When she spins,
When she spins.
Oh, she leaps o'er the dust and soot
And makes the laddies happy.

And nae mistakes does Lady make
When she twirls,

When she twirls.
She dances on a golden stake
And makes the laddies happy.

A Pig Boy, a Ghost, and a Pooka

IN THE BUSHES

'*T*was late in the afternoon and the wind crackled between the trees, coaxing dead leaves to swirl devilishly through the air, into our eyes and our hair. It seemed like only days since we had danced under the late summer moon. But in truth, it had been weeks.

We wanted to reach the next village before nightfall. 'Twas rumored that the Old Burned Man had visited villages to the south. We still held out hopes of meeting up with him and hearing him weave tales, though he was proving to be more elusive than a butterfly on a winter's day.

We unrolled the map in the light of the dying sun. I wished, not for the first time, that we had been more orderly in our travels. I wished we had followed a more sensible trail. Instead, we had visited a hodgepodge collection of places. Up to the hills. Down to the coast. Back up the coast. Over to yon valley. Wherever we thought we might have a lead on a bard or a story of any kind, that is where we went. Or rather, that is where we attempted to go. Our latest stop had been the village of Moreglin, a tiny town with neither a teller nor tales. However, there were cows that needed tending, so Thomas and I lent a hand in exchange for food and shelter, as usual. How I wished I was brave enough to do my own telling and charge a fair price, instead of forever just practicing bits of songs and tales on folks. Oh, to sleep far away from the smell of cattle! Perhaps in the next village . . . except the next village was not there.

"Maybe they were wrong. Maybe the next village was more than three days away," I said.

"Then why did they not just say that? *The village is four days away.* How hard is that? If they'd told us right, we'd have the proper amount of food still." Thomas's complaint was punctuated with a loud growl from his stomach.

'Twas always food with Thomas.

"Perhaps we walked too slowly. They could have marked the days it would take a grown man, not a girl and a pig boy."

"Nay and nay again," Thomas argued. "If so, then why not just say, *It takes a grown man three days, but it will take you lot four?*

"And," he continued, "we've not been walking too slow. We've kept a steady pace." He kicked a rock, which traveled halfway up the hill we were approaching, then rolled back down to him. "If we cannot see the village of Agadhoe when we get to the top of this rise . . ." he said.

And yet, when we reached the top of the hill and looked down into the valley, no village lights greeted us in the twilight. Not a single torch.

I glanced at the map again, but it was no help at all.

We had not taken the wrong road. At least, I was fairly positive we had not.

Thomas muttered a word under his breath that I was certain his mother would have punished him for. I should have scolded him, 'twas my duty, being a year older and all, but I, too, was bothered by the lack of a town.

"I suppose we should make camp. I've still some bread left."

"Stale bread," Thomas said.

"And a few berries . . ."

"Mashed berries, probably rotting," Thomas said.

I gave him a look and began searching for a place to camp.

'Twas always a bit tricky, finding a camping spot. Not too close to the road, for there were stories of highwaymen that robbed and terrorized travelers at night. But close enough so that we could hear anyone approaching on the road and determine if they were friendly or not. Of course, there were times we traveled when there was no road at all . . . but those stories are not in this tale.

There we were at the top of the hill, out in the open. The nearest patch of trees and bushes was back behind us, still visible in the dusk, but it would take us several minutes to get to it.

"Those bushes are too far from the road."

"Thomas, just exactly what do you propose? It is near dark. It is getting colder by the minute. Unless you want to sleep right here in the middle of the hill, I suggest we start walking to yon bushes."

He gave a *humph* and followed me there.

Thomas whacked at the bushes with a big stick to make certain no small creatures already sheltered there.

"'Tis safe," he proclaimed. So there we slept.

IN WHICH OUR POSSESSIONS
ARE STOLEN

I heard hooves clopping down the path. I was dreaming of a man whose face I could not see, riding a horse against the moonlit sky. The sound grew louder and I could feel the ground vibrating against my back.

Thomas felt it, too, for he was shaking me awake. It was not a dream.

We scrambled to pull loose branches over us.

The clip-clopping slowed.

We held our breaths. I could see a horse-shaped shadow with a rider atop whose cape billowed in the wind.

"Stand and deliver," commanded a deep voice that echoed against the leaves and made them rustle.

We remained frozen.

He saw us, or heard us, or perhaps felt our presence. He called out again, "Stand and deliver!"

Thomas squeezed my arm and slowly released it, willing me to stay under the branches. He rose awkwardly, his hands in the air. "Sir, I have nothing but a stale piece of bread and some mashed berries," he said, sounding like a pitiful runaway boy.

Quite convincing. I was proud.

"Have it and welcome," Thomas continued, bending to reach for the crust of bread in his bag.

"Do not move, lad, not an inch nor a muscle." The outlaw's voice was harsh. I could see now that he had a large sword pointed right at Thomas, close enough to run him through. "And do not lie."

I could hear Thomas gulp as the blade moved closer to his throat.

"I'll have the bag. The one next to the lassie."

How he could have seen me, I know not, for I was completely hidden in the shadows of the bushes. At least, I thought I was.

"The bag, missy. Ye'll hand it to me, now."

Slowly I rose and stepped out from behind a branch, brushing leaves from my hair. The horse stood massive and mountainlike, and the rider's head reached the moon. A black mask covered most of his face, but peering out through two holes were a pair of eyes so dark and so cold they sent a new wave of shivers down my spine.

"I want the bag with the silver mirror, the harp, and the faerie coin."

The coin I did not care about, despite its obvious value. I had thought we might need it, or the mirror for that matter, to bargain with at some point. I had not expected the price to be our lives. But my harp. I did not want to lose my harp. With it, I was beginning to feel like a true bard. How could I be a bard without it? Perhaps if I fought. Or ran.

Thomas made the decision for me, choosing our lives over our possessions. He grabbed the bag from my hands and threw it up to the man.

"Sorry, Trinket," he said.

I said nothing.

I swallowed my anger and bit back my tears.

"Much obliged," the outlaw said, tipping his hat with a

flourish. Then he looked at me, cocking his head to one side, then the other. "Well, well, well." He chuckled. "How lucky I am to have stumbled upon you." I thought he would look the harp over, or make certain the coin was inside the bag, but he did neither. He continued to stare at me. Then, he reared his stallion and galloped off into the night.

He was gone faster than seemed possible.

THE GRAVEDIGGER

——◆▸✦◂◆——

*H*ow did he know what was in the bag?" I asked between sniffles as we waited for the sun to rise. I had tried not to cry too much, but being robbed was very frightening. And I knew it made Thomas feel better that he was not the only one to shed a tear. We'd found neither dreams nor sleep for the rest of the night.

"Followed us?"

"How could we not have seen? The countryside for the past few days has been open. There was nowhere to hide."

"Mayhap someone in the last town spoke of your harp. Ye did play it, after all."

"Mayhap . . . but I do not think . . ." My thoughts stopped as the sun finally burst over the horizon, so bright it made the insides of my eyelids turn red when I blinked.

"We'd best start looking for the village. Who knows how many days away it is," he said. I nodded, remembering that since my father's map was in my bag, the robber had that as well. I hoped we'd find a town soon.

Thomas led us to the top of the hill where, in the distance, we saw a most unusual sight.

The village of Agadhoe.

'Twas not there the night before, but now stood plain as day. Small thatched cottages sat clustered and golden in the morning light.

So confused we were, I did not even have time to cry about my harp or the map, not that there were many tears left.

We saw no people as we walked down the hill and into the town, which was unusual. In most places, many of the folks rise with the sun or before. There is always more work to do than there is daylight to do it in. But the streets were more silent than the inside of an egg before it hatches.

We went from house to house, knocking on doors, but

nobody ever answered. How utterly bizarre for a village to be completely deserted. Slowly and carefully, lest the highwayman be lurking, we continued on through the town. We saw not a soul.

At the far end there was a graveyard. Most villages that have a church also have a graveyard somewhere close by so that those who die can rest in holy ground. Near the gate to the graveyard was a small cottage with a sign on the door that read: Gravedigger.

I'd never met a gravedigger before.

I moved my hand to knock on the weathered door.

"What are ye doing?" Thomas grabbed my wrist.

"Knocking on the door, perchance it looks like something else?" We'd tried every other cottage in town without any luck. And this was the last in the village. Why not give it a knock?

Before Thomas could tell me why we should not knock on this door, it creaked open and an old man stood there, no taller than myself.

His head resembled a round, mossy stone, and he had a twitch in one eye. He looked us up and down. "Aye, ye'll do," he said. "Come on." And he grabbed the shovel that was leaning next to the door and motioned for Thomas and me to follow.

Thomas shook his head most emphatically. I grabbed his arm and yanked him along. I wanted to see what would happen. Would we be digging graves? I wondered.

"Excuse me, sir," I asked, struggling to keep up. For an old man, he was quite spry. "But if I may ask, where is everyone in the town?"

He stopped short and looked at us with his twitchy eye. Then he croaked, "Who wants to know?"

"I am Trinket," I said. "This is Thomas. We have traveled many days to find your village. We were set upon by a robber last night and have neither food nor money."

At the word *robber*, the eyebrow above the twitchy eye raised. The gravedigger looked around to the right, then the left, and asked me to describe the thief.

"Tall, on a horse bigger than a house. He wore a cape and . . ." Thomas had finally decided to enter the conversation. Unfortunately, we both realized that it had been too dark for any further description.

"But his eyes," I remembered. "When I looked him in the eye, it nearly froze my blood and bones."

"Humph," said the gravedigger. Then he turned and continued down the path through the headstones.

"Sir," I persisted, following. "We will gladly work in exchange for food."

"Will ye, then?" he asked, stopping in an open spot and handing the shovel to Thomas. "Dig then, boy. You, girl, you can clear the large rocks out of the way. It makes the digging go faster if the large rocks are gone."

He turned to leave us there to dig what could only be a grave. I tried once more. "Sir, where is everyone in the town of Agadhoe?"

"Do ye not know the day, girl? 'Tis Samhain. They'll be a-hiding in their houses, too afraid to walk the streets, too afraid to light a lamp, until the dead rest again. Tomorrow, most likely, or the next day."

Samhain. I'd heard of it, of course. The night when the dead visit the living. That was why there were no lights in the town below so it appeared as if there was no town at all. The townsfolk wanted to hide. They feared the return of their dead.

I wondered for a moment if *all* those who have passed return on Samhain, though I held little hope for seeing my mother again. Lucky I'd been able to receive her message in Crossmaglin. Had she more to tell me, she would have done so then.

She would not call upon me tonight.

Nay, if the entire town were concealing themselves, the spirits who walked tonight would not likely be gentle mothers paying loving visits to their children.

DIGGING

—◆✦◆—

After the man went back to the cottage, Thomas threw the shovel on the ground. "I am not digging a stinking grave."

"What are we going to do then? I cannot believe you are not hungry." I did not want to dig a grave either, but we simply had to eat.

"I think the old man knows something about the robber," I continued. "Mayhap he will tell us what he knows if we ask him during the meal."

Thomas glared at me. "You're just trying to find another story, are ye not?"

"Aye, I suppose I shall need even more now that my harp is gone."

Perhaps it was cruel to use the loss of my harp to get my way. But it worked. Thomas began to dig.

And truly, what choice did we have?

—

Digging a grave is hard work. Morbid, too. It made me think about death. I didn't like to think about . . . about people I loved being buried in the ground. Better to think of my mother flying like a beautiful bluebird, across the sun, looking down at me from time to time. The grave made me think about my father, too. *Was he dead? Or was he still out there, somewhere?*

My search had still turned up no clues as to why he disappeared. And I knew he must have existed, because I existed. But there were few along the way who remembered him. I wondered if I would ever find an answer. However, I did not regret this quest. It had led me on many an adventure and given me my own set of stories.

Sometimes, when you search for one thing, you find something else.

I said a silent prayer for James the Bard, wherever he was.

We were starved when we finished digging what we thought was a respectable grave. It was past midday and the sun was getting lower, so we ran to the little cottage by the gate. A mess met us inside, with brown leaves and broken branches strewn about. Obviously, the gravedigger was not the tidiest housekeeper. Had I not known better, I would have thought the only inhabitants of the cottage of late had been mice and squirrels.

Nonetheless, the old man's stew smelled wonderful. A rich, brown broth with bits of turnip, parsnip, mutton, and the tiniest onions ever glistened in our bowls. And there were slices of apples and pears, warmed by the fire. I could not stop eating the sweet, tart wedges. I wanted to ask the gravedigger about the robber, but my mouth was too full, so the only sound during the meal was the slurping of stew and the clinking of spoons against the pottery.

"Thank you, sir," I said at last, mopping the remains of the stew with a crust of bread. "'Twas the best meal we have had in many days."

He nodded, and then looked at Thomas with a wink. "I

expect you'll be needing all your strength tonight," he said as he ladled another helping in each of our bowls.

Thomas stopped chewing and looked at the man. His mouth was too full of apple to blurt out his question, so I helped him.

"What do you mean, exactly?"

The man sat back in his chair and lit his pipe from the fire. He did not even have to reach far, for the small table was next to the hearth.

"If ye are wanting to catch the Highwayman, it has to be tonight, else you'll never get your things back from him."

THE POOKA

———◆◆×◆◆———

*T*homas choked on his apple. I patted him on the back and handed him some cider. Neither of us had considered chasing after the outlaw.

"Here's what ye do," continued the old man, leaning toward us. "Ye've already dug the grave to trick the pooka. Once you've caught the pooka, he'll owe ye a favor. And pookas keep their word, they do. Ye'll ride the pooka out past the wall between the living and the other side and steal your wealth back from the Highwayman. Simple as pie." He chuckled to himself.

Thomas was the first to respond. He laughed out loud. "I

must tell you, old man, I didn't understand a word of what you just said. Not one word!"

However, I did understand. I had heard of the pooka, the enormous spirit horse that can speak to humans. There are tales of pookas carrying unsuspecting riders away, never to be seen again. My mother once tried to tell me one such tale (that she learned from my father), but I was too scared and I begged her not to finish. But I remembered that pookas, in addition to being large and terrifying, were surprisingly civil. They were also most easily bent to the will of humans on Samhain. There was, however, something in the gravedigger's instructions that did not make much sense . . . unless . . .

"Sir, the fact that we must cross the wall between the living and the other, does that mean that the outlaw is *dead*?"

"Nay. It means the Highwayman who robbed you was a ghostie."

Finally, Thomas stopped laughing.

Food remained in our bowls, but neither Thomas nor I had the stomach to eat it. The meal was finished.

—

"'Tis too dangerous," I said to Thomas that night as we walked back to the grave, remembering how close I'd come to following the banshee to the other side. The other side, I was convinced, did not play fair. "Perhaps if we wait . . ."

"Nay, it has to be tonight, or the wall will be too thick to pass through for another year." Thomas paused, then pressed on. "Do you not want your harp back?"

Of course I wanted my harp back. But if I had to choose between a harp and a pig boy . . . well, I would choose Thomas.

"You were the one who promised adventure would befall us if I agreed to accompany you on your quest for stories."

He had a point. But still, this was far too dangerous.

"Look, Trinket, you know the stories about Samhain. You've heard them since you were a babe, same as me. And if we get the help of a pooka—"

"*If* we find one," I interrupted.

"As I was saying, if we get the help of a pooka, I should be able to ride in and ride back out." He threw a crust of bread down in the grave, as the old gravedigger had instructed. I'd never seen Thomas so excited about anything.

"You've grown braver, I think, Thomas."

He paused, then looked me in the eye and said simply, "I had a good teacher."

The wind began to rise. We threw more and more crusts of bread down into the hole. 'Twas tradition to leave a feast for the pooka in the graveyard on Samhain, else ill luck was to follow for the year. At least that was what the old gravedigger told us. But when we searched again for the gravedigger, hoping he'd help us put together a feast, we could not find him. Perhaps he, too, feared the night of Samhain, like the other residents of Agadhoe, and was hidden inside one of the lifeless little cottages. Thus, our pitiful feast was leftover bread and apple slices.

We hoped it would be enough.

We heard a sound carried on the wind. Perhaps it was a large horse blowing gusts of air from his nostrils. We could not tell, however, if it was the pooka we were expecting, or the Highwayman atop his stallion, so we hid behind the nearest gravestone.

"Weeeeeeellll, what have we here?" said a surprisingly pleasant voice. "Crusts of bread? What kind of a feast for a pooka is that?" The voice changed from kind to perturbed.

'Twas not the outlaw, of course. 'Twas the pooka.

I chanced a peek. Deep gray, he was, with a mane the color of midnight and a tail to match. Quite handsome, but comical in the way his mouth moved when he spoke.

"And, putting the crusts down a hole? What way is that for folks to tell ye how much they appreciate ye? No way at all, I tell ye," he muttered, shaking his head back and forth.

"Mebbe something else is under the bread. Can't really tell from up here . . ." He leaned over the grave.

Before I could blink, Thomas jumped up and pushed the pooka from behind.

The horse wriggled and waggled and tried to keep his balance, but fell, as we had planned, into the grave.

"Och, now, why'd ye have to go and do a thing like that?" he whined.

Thomas and I peered down over the edge. The pooka sat with his legs crossed, nibbling on a crust.

"It's stale, ye know," he complained.

"Sorry," I said.

"Now that I've captured you, you have to honor me with a favor," said Thomas in his most commanding tone. Quite impressive for a pig boy, really.

"Perhaps I do not want to," said the pooka.

"Pardon me, sir pooka, but the custom says that you are to be most civil and agreeable when honored with a feast on Samhain." My voice sounded like I knew what I was talking about.

"Ye call this a feast?" he moaned. "It's more like table scraps a dog wouldn't eat, that's what it is. Now help me out of here."

"Very well, you have given us no choice but to leave you here." We turned our backs and took a few steps away.

"No! Wait!" cried the pooka. We glanced back over our shoulders. "I apologize. If you would assist me in my effort to get out of this . . . this . . . this whatever it is, I shall help you." His voice was most civil, now.

Not wanting to insult him by asking for his word of honor (as the custom says that pookas are most honorable creatures), we helped him out of the grave. 'Twas not easy, hefting a horse twice the size of a regular nag out of a hole in the ground. Thomas climbed down and leaned against the horse's huge rump with all his might.

"I beg your pardon!" the pooka cried.

"Forgive me . . . er, um, sir. It's just that if I don't push

253

against your bum while Trinket pulls on your mane, we might never get you out." Thomas grunted between pushes.

I was already pulling on his mane, the coarse hairs cutting into my hand fiercely.

"Of all the indignities," the pooka muttered.

"You could help, sir," Thomas groaned. "Just place your forelegs on the edge and—there you go—now when I count to three—one, two, THREE!" Thomas cried, and with a final shove, the pooka stumbled up out of the grave. A sweaty Thomas emerged after him, breathing heavily. "I hope I never have to do that again."

"You are not the only one. I've probably got bruises all over me rump," said the pooka.

I quickly explained to him our situation.

"So," he began, taking a deep breath, still munching on bread crusts. "Ye want me to take ye through the wall between the living and the other so ye can find the Highwayman and steal back your harp, your mirror, and your gold coin? You're serious about this?"

We nodded.

"The Highwayman, nasty piece of work, he is. If he catches ye . . ." His voice trailed off.

Thomas said bravely, "Well, we just won't let him catch us. Are you fast?"

"Fast enough for you, laddie. Fast enough for you."

"Fast enough to carry the both of us?" I asked.

The pooka considered the situation before replying, "Aye."

TO THE OTHER SIDE

Nay, Trinket, you're not coming—" Thomas began.

"Aye, Thomas, you'll not stop me, and we both know it. So we can stand around and argue, however I myself think that it is rude to quarrel in front of company." I nodded to the pooka, who winked back at me. "Or we can get this over with."

I handed a jug of water to Thomas. "Remember to drink up before we ride. There might not be time after."

Thomas glared but took several swigs from the jug. This was the part I was glad Thomas was willing to do. "Don't drink too much, though. It could be a bumpy ride." He did not laugh at my joke, but the pooka snorted. Bending down, the pooka allowed Thomas and me to climb on his broad back.

"You will not fall, for I will not let you. But hold tightly. I shall gallop faster than you have ever traveled. 'Twill feel like flying." The pooka seemed to be enjoying this. "And remember not to get down from my back while we are on the other side."

"Why not?" I asked.

"How can you not know this?" the pooka scolded. "If your feet touch the ground, you'll stay on the other side until next Samhain, plus one day more."

A year and a day with the dead? Perhaps it would not be so bad if I found my mother. She would not come to me, but if *I* found her . . .

"Do not think about it, Trinket," Thomas said. He knew me far too well. "There is a reason there's a wall between the living and the other, don't ye think?"

"Aye," said the pooka, "there's a reason indeed." And he left it at that.

True to his word, the pooka galloped faster than either Thomas or I could have imagined. The trees blurred into one long and eerie shadow that trailed after us. We traveled so fast that even the light of the moon could not catch up. Breathing was difficult, for the air was sucked out of our lungs as we rode faster and faster still. My mother's fine cloak flew behind me as if it had wings of its own. The pooka did not speak. With his head down, he raced against the night, speeding us toward the wall between the living and the other side.

I thought I would be able to tell when we passed through the wall. Perhaps there would be a sense of utmost despair. Perhaps it would be even darker. Perhaps there would be a tiredness in my bones that would compel me to seek eternal rest. Alas, I noticed no difference. The pooka whispered, "We are here. Do not get off my back."

He stopped. We listened to the silence, waiting for a clue as to which direction to pursue. I thought there would be the sound of wailing on the other side, like the wee banshee from

Crossmaglin. However, there was nothing but the faintest melody.

"Do you hear that?" I whispered in Thomas's ear. He shook his head. "'Tis my harp a-playing. I'm sure of it."

He whispered back, "Which way?"

I pointed to the left. Slowly and silently, we trod along. The pooka's hooves made no sound on the ground, if there was indeed ground under us. I could only see mist.

The tune became louder, proving we were going the right way. But no spirits did I see. Weren't there countless dead folk? I would have thought the other side quite crowded.

As if reading my mind, the pooka whispered, "The other side is vast. More so than you can imagine. And, of course, 'tis Samhain. Many souls have gone frolicking amongst the human folk."

"But not the Highwayman," Thomas said with a gulp.

"Nay, the Highwayman is a ghostie. He does not have to wait until Samhain, when the wall is at its thinnest, to travel betwixt the lands of the living and the dead. He can pass back and forth as he pleases." The pooka was most knowledgeable. I was glad we had him for our guide.

"Why, then, are not all of the dead folk ghosties? Wouldn't they like traveling back and forth of their own choice? I know I would." Thomas's voice was so quiet, only the pooka and I could hear.

"Would ye now? Ghosties are tortured souls who cannot rest. They long to feel blood rush through their veins again, to be alive. But they cannot return to life, nor can they feel comfort in death. 'Tis not a fate anyone would choose, lad. Like being more tired than ye can comprehend and not being able to sleep."

I felt a bit of pity for the Highwayman. Certainly, he had stolen from us, but an eternity of no rest sounded dreadful indeed.

The music was loud enough for me to discern the melody. And I recognized it.

Gooseflesh spread across my shoulders and down my arms. Thomas felt me shake off the chill.

"What is it?" he whispered.

"'Tis a song I know . . . a lullaby . . ." *My father's lullaby.*

And then, through the mist, I saw him.

THE HIGHWAYMAN

The Highwayman sat on a rock, playing my harp. His long fingers moved over the strings deftly. He finished the lullaby and began a sorrowful piece that broke my heart. I longed to get off the pooka and speak to him, but Thomas held my arm tightly.

Now what to do? Should we demand the harp back, or try to get close enough to grab it?

"You've come a long way to retrieve such a small treasure," the Highwayman said, turning slowly and facing us. "And on a pooka! 'Twould seem I underestimated you."

He rose, placing the harp on the rock, and took a step closer to us. Thomas clutched the pooka's mane even tighter.

The Highwayman smiled cruelly. "Your harp?" He addressed his question to me. "Come and get it." He stepped out of our way and bowed gallantly.

Ever so slowly, we moved toward the harp.

"Your eyes are familiar, girl." His voice was between a sneer and a whisper.

"Don't listen to him," warned the pooka. "I told you, he is evil."

"And the point of your chin," the Highwayman continued. "Aye, girl, I've seen it before. I knew when I first looked at you, I'd seen it. Somewhere . . ." His voice trailed off.

We were almost close enough. If I leaned far over and Thomas held me, I might be able to grasp the harp. If only we did not have to pass the Highwayman first.

"Who is it that you look like, dearie? Your mother? Or your father?"

I froze as the Highwayman chuckled. "Mayhap you do not know."

We inched forward, just past him, almost even with the harp.

Thomas pinched me hard. I'd have to grab it now, fast, or miss my chance altogether.

I reached out, the tips of my fingers touching the smooth white bone. The pooka moved us closer.

As I clasped the cold side of the harp and pulled it to me, the Highwayman's hand snaked out and jerked at the creature's mane. The pooka stumbled, nearly throwing me off. Had Thomas not been holding me so tightly, I would have fallen and I'd have been cursed to live a year and a day on the other side. Thomas dug his heels into the pooka's flanks and the creature reared back.

"A challenge it is, then!" The Highwayman laughed. He climbed upon his stallion, which had appeared from nowhere.

The pooka galloped hard and fast. I clutched the harp tightly with one hand and Thomas with the other, hoping we were going the right way, but at this point, any direction away from the Highwayman was a good one.

He was but a breath behind us. I could feel the stallion panting on the back of my neck.

"A gentleman of the road, I am," the Highwayman snickered. "Always willing to offer kindness to a fellow traveler." He reached out and caught a few strands of my hair and yanked. "Hmm, the father's hair or the mother's?"

I screamed, tempted to throw the harp back in his face. But that would not have stopped the Highwayman. He cared not for the harp.

He sought trophies of another kind.

We sped through the other side, the wind so harsh on our faces we were near blinded. I thought once or twice I felt a tug on my hair, but whether it was a strand caught in the branched fingers of a decrepit tree, or the Highwayman closing on us, I could not be sure.

I was far too afraid to look back, for if he were to catch us, I would not have his cold eyes be the last things I ever saw.

We crossed through the wall between the living and the other, but that did not stop the Highwayman. He was not as close to us now, but he didn't need to be. He could follow at his own pace and never tire. He was dead already.

But we were gasping for breath. Even the pooka was wheezing as we arrived at the gravedigger's cottage. "Hurry, Thomas, HURRY! You've got to do it now!" I cried, hoping he hadn't sweated off all of the water he'd drunk earlier.

A VISIT FROM THE QUEEN

We got off the pooka and Thomas proceeded to relieve himself on the gatepost of the small house.

"The only way to keep a ghostie out of your house," the gravedigger had told us, "is to piss on the gatepost. They won't pass through. They cannot."

Thank goodness Thomas had no problem. Seemed like, in fact, he'd not relieved himself for days. I wanted to say, *That's quite enough, Thomas,* but preferred instead to look off into the distance. I caught the eye of the pooka, who was doing the same.

I did not see the Highwayman approach. But I could hear him circling.

"Ye'll be safe, if ye stay inside," the gravedigger had told us. But where was the old man now?

The door to the cottage was just large enough for the pooka to fit through, though Thomas had to push on the horse's large rump once again.

"Sorry," Thomas mumbled.

"Well, ye should be. Twice in one night. Now, close the door, will ye?" the pooka ordered. Thomas closed and bolted the door.

———

Through the window, we could see movement among the gravestones. Those from the other side, perhaps, paying a visit on Samhain. But nothing came near the house. We sat inside the cluttered, filthy cottage, a girl, a boy, and a pooka, trying to pass the time until daylight came, hoping the sun would keep the Highwayman away.

"They cannot go far, you know, ghosts and such," said the pooka. "A ghost cannot pass over water. Cross the stream half a day's walk east of the village and you'll be safe."

We heard clip-clopping again, louder, sending new waves of chills down my arms.

"Do you suppose..." Thomas began. "Ah, never mind."

"Go ahead. Ask me."

"Well, the Highwayman talked a lot about your folks... do you suppose..."

"Are you asking me if he knew my parents?"

"Or, maybe, could he *be* one of them... like your father, I mean? Think about it, Trinket. No one seems to know much about James the Bard. Mayhap your da became a robber—"

A loud growl interrupted us and we flew back to the window. The Highwayman stood at the gate, anger fairly spewing from him. But he was not alone.

I gasped as the familiar, terrifyingly beautiful form of the Faerie Queen emerged from the fog, cracking her whip overhead and driving her miniature ponies across the dry ground of the old graveyard.

"I'll have the coin," she said, her voice just as I remembered. She drew herself out of her carriage and up to the Highwayman's full height. Her pale hand gestured impatiently. "You should know better than to steal what the faerie folk have given, you foolish shade."

The Highwayman appeared as if he would refuse. But

then, all around the graveyard, spirits materialized from behind the headstones. Some young, some old, all as pale as the
clouds at night. "Give it back," they whispered. "Give it back
to the girl."

Whether 'twas a trick of the Faerie Queen, or the dead
speaking for us, I did not know.

Slowly, Thomas and I walked onto the cottage porch. If
the Highwayman had been able to venture past the gatepost,
I was certain he would have done it by now.

Shaking with fury, the Highwayman gave the coin to
the Faerie Queen. "It does not belong to me." She flipped it
through the air and it clattered on the porch at my feet, just
as it had after the contest in Ringford. "It belongs to the girl.
Return all that is hers." She then turned to me. "You would
do well not to lose a bargaining coin given by the folk. Prove
yourself worthy, girl, for 'tis more valuable than you can
imagine. I'll not help you retrieve it should you part ways
with it again."

My sack flew through the air as the Highwayman glared
at us one final time. Thomas raced through the doorway and
caught the bag before it could fall to the ground and shatter

the mirror. The Highwayman's eyes were no longer cold, but hot with rage, his mouth twisted in a sneer. *Was that the face of my father, hidden behind a thief's mask?* Then he turned and galloped off into the new light of dawn. The air was rent with the queen's laughter.

Naturally, the pooka was gone when we went inside, for 'twas daybreak and he was, after all, a creature of the night. And a magical one at that.

We wanted to say goodbye and thank you to the gravedigger, but he was still nowhere to be found and we were too anxious to get past the stream, half a day's walk from the village. And we'd no desire to bide with the folk in this town, who had cowered in their homes for the past two days and nights. Strangely, though, as we passed the farthest edge of the graveyard, we saw a weathered headstone with a small shovel leaned up against it.

HERE LIE THE BONES
OF OLD MACGREGOR
OF ALL HE WAS
THE BEST GRAVEDIGGER

That night, miles away, I felt for the bargaining coin deep inside the pocket of my britches. 'Twas warm from being so near my skin and I rubbed it twice for courage. Was I finally brave enough to speak aloud the thoughts that had crowded my head all day?

"Thomas," I said carefully, "what if that outlaw, what if he really *was* my father?" I swallowed, trying to sound like I didn't care as much as I did.

"What if he was?" asked Thomas. "Doesn't make you any different, does it? You're still Trinket no matter what."

I wanted to bury the bard's map in the dirt, for I'd follow its trail no longer. What if it had been drawn by the evil hand of the Highwayman? But Thomas would not let me.

"A map's a map, Trinket. We can still use it even if you don't like who made it."

Wise, wise Thomas.

"Still Trinket no matter what." I said those words over and over to myself for the rest of that night.

And many nights to follow.

If James the Bard was really James the Ghostly

Highwayman, then I wanted no part of him. And if he was not, sadly I was no closer to finding him. Though some folks remembered my father, no one had seen him for years. He was as good as dead.

Perhaps some truths are never meant to be uncovered.

THE FIFTH SONG

The Dangers of the Road

*To tell the truth, this is not my favorite song, and
I cannot play it without getting a chill upon the back of
my neck. However, it is the duty of the teller to
warn the unsuspecting traveler, I think.*

*Go not, thou unsuspecting lad,
Oft through the blackened night,
For in the mists
And tree-claw limbs
There lurks a fearsome sight.*

*Hooves of fire,
Flanks of coal,*

Only a moment
To forfeit thy soul.

And there, behind the callous swirls
Of danger and despair,
The clipping, clopping follows thee
Through empty evening air.

Hooves of fire,
Flanks of coal,
Look not upon him
Or forfeit thy soul.

The Old Burned Man and the Hound

CASTLE CHORES

Thomas and I were still determined to find and hear the Old Burned Man. Most villages considered it an honor when he paid a visit. No feast was too extravagant, no bed was too soft. He ofttimes visited castles or fine manor houses, and though it would take him a hundred days to tell all of his tales and sing all of his songs, he was not known for remaining long in one place. I could not even imagine what it would take to remember a hundred stories! I was still working on gathering and polishing seven.

I had become more courageous with my harp. Perhaps it was that I was tired of milking, drawing water, thatching roofs, and digging graves. Or perhaps, after being chased by creatures and beasties worse than Death itself, it seemed foolish to fear a quiet fire, shining eyes, and ears ready for the listening. In the last village we'd been to, a woman took one look at my harp and said to me, "Have ye songs to go with your harp? Or mayhap a story, lass?"

Aye. I liked how that sounded. The Story Lass.

—

But now we had finally arrived at a true castle, called Castlelow. It had received its name from being situated on a low, grassy meadow. The legend was that another castle, called Castlehigh, once sat at the top of the nearby hills, but now only ruins remained. 'Twas a good thing we chanced upon Castlelow, for each night as we camped, the sound of howling wolves grew louder. Never before had we heard such howling. Perhaps it was normal for this time of year, with winter approaching. Neither Thomas nor I were certain, though, for there were never wolves howling near our village on the coast. We were grateful to find the shelter of thick stone walls.

There are all manner of beings that live in a castle. Not

just kings and queens and lords and ladies. Not just servants down below or knights in the field. There are animals as well. Pigs, goats, and chickens running free through the castle yard and hounds, lying under the tables, waiting for crumbs to drop.

I'd met hounds before, of course. But a castle hound is a different breed from a village hound or a road hound. You can tell by the way he holds his head and the way he stands close to his master.

The way he'd give his life to protect him.

———

I was somewhat nervous, of course. Would Castlelow want to hear the tales of a traveling lass? Mayhap it would be better to do odd chores and such, taking the time to listen to the stories of the castle bard, if they had one.

I decided not to ask about my father here. He was the past. I had to focus on the future.

The Lord and Lady of Castlelow were kindly. They had a new babe, their first, a boy with sandy hair that stuck out from his head like the down of a newly hatched duck. I was assigned to help look after the child, which would allow me to practice my lullabies and perhaps a story or two. Thomas was assigned to the pigs, his first pigs in a long, long time. He was jubilant.

"Aw, Trinket, mayhap we can stay here a while. The food is plentiful and the straw is clean." He had a small piglet, pink and quite adorable, tucked under his arm. "And the work is not hard."

"Not like digging a grave." I laughed.

"Nay, not like digging a grave at all," he said.

True, we'd done much hard labor on our journey, slept on the ground, and gone hungry more oft than not. Life at the castle looked to be easy. My task was not difficult, either. I did the things the laddie's nurse would rather not do, which mostly consisted of dirty jobs like changing soggy clothes, feeding him gruel, and following him wherever he wanted to crawl. Unfortunately, the babe had a hard time getting to sleep and the nurse bade me stay with him in his nursery in the tower until he slumbered. I missed the storytelling for the first four nights we were there. 'Twas torturing me to be so close to a true bard and not be able to hear him, even if it wasn't the Old Burned Man, who was due to arrive any day, or so everyone said. Thomas had been luckier than I, for there was no need for a pig boy to lure the piglets into dreamland.

"They said if we were good and quiet and all, that we could come and listen," he told me the fifth morning of our stay. I could feel jealousy rising, and Thomas saw it in my face. "He wasn't near so good as you," he sputtered.

I only humphed.

"Trinket, they've seen your harp. They know you're a teller. Why do ye not just—"

"I am not ready for a castle, Thomas."

He walked off, but I was sure I heard him mumble, "Of all the things, never thought she was a chicken."

Thomas was right. I was being ridiculous.

One must be brave to tell stories.

I had met with creatures of unusual magic and lived to tell the tale. I had even escaped a deadly rider atop a phantom stallion and outwitted the powers of darkness.

Was I not brave?

FINN

———◆※◆———

I practiced, singing soft songs to the young babe
each night with the lord's gigantic hound at my feet. He loved
the songs, too. A larger dog I'd never seen in my life. Were he
to stand on his hind legs, his head would have risen far above
my own. His coat was the color of wheat in autumn. But the
most amazing thing about him was that, for all of his enormous stature, he was gentler than the evening breeze. They
called him Finn the Great. I thought of him as Finn the Oversized Kitten.

He watched over the babe each night while he slept. As I
drifted off to sleep in my small closet of a room next to the

nursery, I could see the hound lying still and protective on the floor at the foot of the boy's crib.

Perhaps I would have a dog of my own one day, I thought as I strummed and sang softly in the early morning before the babe awoke. A dog could watch over Thomas and me while we slept. What an odd family we would be. No parents, just a boy who tends pigs and a girl who tells tales.

There were worse families, I was certain. And yet—

The voice that interrupted my song was gravelly and rough. "I heard music on the stairs and followed it here. 'Tis a nice song. Is it yours?" 'Twas a damaged voice, but there was beauty in the ragged way he spoke.

I wish I could say that I answered, *Aye, sir, my own tune as well as my own words.* But when I turned to face him, I could not speak. His face was fiercely scarred and he wore a gray hood that covered his head. The scars were white and twisted his smile (I thought it was a smile) into a frightening skull-like grimace. I gasped and nodded stiffly. I could feel heat rush to my face. What horrible manners I possessed.

After all, exactly *what* had I expected him to look like? The Old Burned Man, for he could be no other, the bard I'd searched for, was standing *not halfway across the room.* The famed teller had finally arrived at the same place at the same time as Thomas and I. I should have been jumping with excitement. *He was here!* But all I felt was horror.

The Old Burned Man looked down.

I stammered, "Er, 'twas a song I wrote for my mother. She reminds me of a bluebird."

"She is blessed to have such a song written for her."

"She's dead."

There was silence, but it was not uncomfortable this time. 'Twas like he was offering a bit of silence in respect for my mother. That was nice.

"Well." He cleared his throat, which sounded painful. "The ones we love often leave us, don't they?"

"Aye."

"But my guess is they'd prefer not to, if given the choice."

His ruined eye winked at me, and I found myself smiling slightly at this gruesome-looking man.

"If given the choice," I repeated.

—

'Twas not simple to sneak down the stairs of the castle to hear the storytelling that night, but how could I miss my first chance to hear the Old Burned Man? As if the babe knew I needed him to sleep, and quickly at that, he refused to lie down for a long time. Even when he finally slumbered lightly, the quiet sound of my footsteps roused him and I had to start singing all over again. I found myself making up unpleasant words.

> *Go to sleep, little piglet,*
> *Lest I roll ye in the mud*
> *And make thee eat on worms and scraps*
> *'Twill be for thy own good.*

"Ye'll have to teach me that one. I might use it sometime," said Thomas with a snicker.

I carefully placed my harp on the cushion, tiptoed across the room, and whacked him hard in the gut.

"Oof."

"Shhhhhh." Most likely I should not have thumped him, but I was in a mood due to missing the very reason we had come this far.

Luck was with me, for the babe did not stir. "I got tired of waiting on the steps for you to come down," Thomas whispered. "He must be halfway through with the stories."

"Aw, Thomas, you didn't go and hear him without me? You waited?" I asked.

"Now, Trinket, how could I leave you with the wakeful babe and go listen to the Old Burned Man *and* live to tell the tale?" Thomas grabbed my hand and pulled me toward the stairs. Finn the dog opened one eye and watched us leave. Feeling the babe was in good hands, or paws, we continued on our way. I stumbled once on the hem of my dress, which I'd pulled from the bottom of my sack and worn for the evening. Finally hearing the Old Burned Man was worthy of my nice clothes.

'Twas not the Old Burned Man, though, but a string bean of a lad named Berthold.

Thomas rolled his eyes. "Not him again," he muttered.

"Where is the Old Burned Man?" Thomas whispered to a lady as we squeezed in beside her on the bench.

"Cough or fever," said the lady. Thomas groaned and was promptly shushed by the woman. "Now quiet down and give proper respect. Berthold is the nephew of—"

"Aye, I know. I heard him the other night," Thomas said, then mouthed the words *he's horrible* so that only I could see.

Berthold's voice quivered like a leaf on a branch. He kept clearing his throat and he forgot important parts of the story, so the ending made no sense. The crowd was beginning to get restless and the lord and lady looked annoyed.

"Is there not someone else who has a tale this night?" asked the lord. "Where is the girl who arrived but a week ago with a harp?"

I was determined to have courage this time. I raised my hand. "I am the Story Lass," I said.

"Well, go on, lass," said the lord, "give us a story."

I took my place on the three-legged bard's stool as Thomas raced up the stairs to get my harp. I felt in my pocket for the faerie gold, which I now carried with me always, and pulled it out. The coin felt heavy in my hand.

"A-hem." The lord cleared his throat. "Any time now, lass."

Whether I rubbed the coin for courage or for luck, I do not know. But I rubbed it thrice and placed it back in my pocket.

Then I began my tale.

My voice was timid at first, and I swallowed a couple of

times until I felt the shaking stop. *No better than Berthold.* I took a deep breath and calmed myself. Though 'twas my first castle, I hoped it would not be my last. This is what I had worked so hard for.

"The Story of the Gypsies and the Seer," I began again, "a tale of a princess with a rare gift and her father, who would stop at nothing to sell it."

With my words, I painted pictures of the places I had been. The exotic caravans of the Gypsy camp came alive in the great hall, so real, in fact, that I could smell the chicken coop and feel the silk of the tent under my fingers. The words were flowing from my lips now, into the ears and hearts of my audience. Their eyes shone with unshed tears at Feather's plight and they gasped when Lothar's men drew their swords. Best was the cheer at Feather's escape, and then the call from the crowd for another tale.

'Tis one thing to learn a story, word by word, to tell it the right way; 'tis another altogether to bring a tale to life, where moments before there was nothing but emptiness.

Thomas had placed my harp at my feet sometime during my tale, so quietly that I hadn't noticed. A hush filled the hall as I plucked the first note and sang the first song I had ever written myself.

The great hall of a castle is an amazing place to play a tune, for the notes echo and bounce between the old stone walls and out to the folks sitting on their carved benches, hoping to be whisked away to another place and time.

I have had many adventures. But this . . . this was the most magical.

For five nights they asked me for my stories. I sat on the bard's stool, rubbed my coin for luck, and told my tales: Gypsies, selkies, banshees, faeries, and pookas danced across my harp. Each yarn I spun was better than the last, each song sweeter.

Then, the Old Burned Man recovered.

IN WHICH I FINALLY HEAR
THE OLD BURNED MAN

The great hall was full, for Lord John had planned a hunt and a banquet for the next day and had invited many to the event. The room was overwarm and the air sticky, but I did not care. We wedged ourselves through the crowd until a lady in a dress of fine blue velvet tweaked my braid hard and glared.

The Old Burned Man cleared his throat and spoke.

Perhaps it was because his voice was spoiled and the effort to use it sounded painful, but I felt honored to be the recipient of his words. They sang in my mind, though the back of my throat ached in sympathy. The spell he cast with his story was more wondrous and mystical than I could have imagined, and that says a great deal coming from a lass who spends most of her time imagining.

The bench we sat on was hard and we were quite squished, but I did not care. The legend of a lady who tended swords for only the bravest knights and lived underwater in a lake that never froze over was both lovely and tragic.

I listened.

I dreamed.

Though his voice was ragged, his telling was far smoother and silkier than even Bald Fergal's. My heart soared at one moment with the magic of the story, then sank the next moment. I felt quite the fraud. My tales could not compare. I was no bard. What had made me think that I was?

And then the Old Burned Man pulled out his flute.

"I'll only do the one song tonight," he said, "for my throat's still a-paining me. 'Tis a lullaby I composed myself many years ago."

'Twas lilting and sadly sweet. But beautiful.

And all too familiar.

My blood stilled.

I knew the song.

And in my heart, I knew the player.

—

Thomas gulped, then he looked at me and his eyes grew wide. Did he, too, recognize the tune? His hand touched my sleeve, but I jerked my arm away and ran down the corridor and up the stairs. The tears on my cheeks were hot. I could not sniff them back no matter how hard I tried.

Finn raised his head when I stumbled into the room, saw it was me, and lay back down, his eyes still open. The dog watched me as I sobbed and grabbed my harp, clutching it so hard the strings bit into the flesh of my arms. But I did not care about the pain.

When you cry, your mind is a jumbled mess. Part of your brain is trying to make you stop crying and stop thinking about the things that are making you cry. *Hush, hush now, do not cause a scene.* The other part of your brain is lashing back, thinking thoughts so numerous and difficult that reason runs and hides for a while, until things die down.

Thomas was a reasonable fellow, and he did the same. I

heard his footsteps come up the stairs, pause, then go back down.

The only creature brave enough to offer comfort was Finn. He nuzzled his enormous head under my arm. My throat was too thick to even utter, "Not now, dog, go away." So I let him stay at my side as I sobbed, watching the tears splash on his golden coat. There was something terribly reassuring about the dog's presence.

I was glad to have such company.

I cried myself to sleep and the night was filled with dreams.

I dreamed that I saw my father and that he told me stories and kissed me goodbye and never came back.

I dreamed my father rode on a dark stallion, with a cape that flew behind him.

I dreamed my father smiled at me with a scarred and ruined face.

—

When I awoke, I was no longer overwhelmed with sadness.

I was confused.

How could a man that old, scarred, and hideous-looking possibly be my handsome father? How could he have been so heartless to have not returned if he was actually still alive? WHY?

And I was angry.

THE HUNT

*E*ven before the sun rose the nurse poked her head into my small closet room. "You're all red and blotchful. Been ye crying, girl?"

I sniffled and nodded, but quickly looked away. I did not want to speak of my suspicions.

"Never mind about it, girl, whatever it is, ye must get the babe dry and fresh. He needs to say goodbye to the lord. Off to the hunt, he is." The nurse tugged on my arms and pulled me up. "You're a weed of a girl, you know. I swear you've grown in the days since you have come here."

I only sniffed.

"'Tis a good thing you arrived when you did, what with the wolves in the forest and all. The pack's been a-howling each night. Had you met them on your journey, ye might not have made it here whole."

I swallowed, remembering the forlorn howls we had heard as we traveled. Sadly, it was more pleasant to think about being attacked by wolves than about having a father who stole for pleasure and laughed a dark laugh like the Highwayman. Or a hideous father who left you five years past and could have come back but chose not to.

"Seems foolish to go on a hunt for boars with wolves about, do ye not think?" the nurse continued, unaware that I was a poor contributor to the conversation. "I would think the wolves would have eaten the boars or scared them away. Alas."

"Aye. Alas," I offered.

"But if the lord says there shall be a hunt, then a hunt there shall be, I s'pose." She handed me a little gown of white lace with gold trim for the babe. "Dress him. Clean his wee face, too."

Finn the Great was at my side as I changed the babe from

his soggy clothes. The hound looked at the boy with deep, soulful eyes, perhaps thinking him a pup instead of a baby.

The wolves howled in the distance as I took the child down the stairs to see his father, who promptly kissed the boy's head and led his band of hunters out of the castle. Thomas was with them. 'Twas a boar hunt, after all, and a pig boy might be useful, for what were boars but meaner, more dangerous swine?

I was both glad and mad Thomas was gone. Glad, for I didn't want to speak with him about last night, and mad, for I did not want to spend the day alone with my thoughts.

After feeding the infant down in the kitchens and taking him to visit his lady mother until he became cranky, I sat him in his bed and began to play my harp for him. My fingers started to pluck a familiar tune and then stopped. I would not play my father's lullaby ever again.

Instead, I played the new tune I had composed for the selkie boy's song, and his eyes were closed before the last verse.

"You've a strong voice," a voice said, "for one so young."

The Old Burned Man stood in the doorway. I chanced a look at his scarred face. *Were those the eyes of my father behind his gargoyle's features?* I supposed they could be. They were similar to mine in color, but the shape wasn't right.

Nay. He could *not* be my father, James the Bard.

But then there was the lullaby.

My thoughts were muddled.

I had sought the Old Burned Man for such a long time, just to hear his stories, not thinking for a moment that he might be my father. He looked far too old, but perhaps he was younger and just horribly disfigured. What happened to him? I wondered, then shook my head. No, I would not pity him. It was his choice not to return.

Would I prefer that my father had died? Would I prefer him to be the Highwayman?

"I thank you, sir," I said, my voice hard like stone.

"You're a teller, too, then. I heard you the other night. Held them in your grasp, you did, lass. Where did you learn such skill? You are quite young, as I said."

Perhaps it is in my blood, I wanted to say, but I did not. I merely shrugged.

The silence was awkward.

I wanted him to leave, but then ... perhaps ... *Was I completely certain?*

I cleared my throat. "The song you played on your flute last night. 'Twas lovely. It was yours?"

He smiled, but it did not reach his eyes. "Just an old lullaby, written long ago, for a very special child." He sighed and looked off, his voice quiet. "Some say it has magic."

He had his secrets, too, then.

He asked to see my harp, so I showed him. "Unusual and fantastical," he told me.

The conversation continued in such a manner, stilted and uncomfortable. *Are you my father? If so, why did you leave us and never return?* The words screamed in my head.

But I could not make them come.

TRAGEDY

After the Old Burned Man left me, the nurse
reappeared and began tidying the room as the babe continued
to doze. She took one look at my face and shooed me off.
"We'll be fine here, lass. The hound can help amuse the boy
when he wakes. Go try and shed whatever heavy weight you're
carrying around. You'll do no one any good brooding about
like that."

I grabbed my mother's cloak and set off, leaving through
an old door at the bottom of the tower held ajar by a heavy
rock. "'Tis cleaning day," I was told by a woman with a
broom when I asked about the open door. "Got to sweep out

the hall to make things nice for the banquet tonight." Ah yes. The banquet. In my dark mood, the thought of fine food made my stomach turn. I wandered under trees and down the green paths of the castle grounds, hoping that the farther away I was from the Old Burned Man, the clearer my thoughts would become.

Was I not happy, then, to have found the man I thought was my father? Truly, it was more likely that James the Bard was the Old Burned Man than the Highwayman. After all, the Old Burned Man was a teller. That was a clue right there.

But nay, I was not happy. All I felt was anger. When I set off on my quest for my father, I did not know what I would find. I hoped to hear of my father, of course. Had I expected to hear only of his death? Perhaps tragic, yet heroic. But that at least was an acceptable reason for him never to return.

If he was alive, he *would* have come back.

Should I tell him that my mother had died with a broken heart? Mayhap yes, if that would hurt him. Although the fact that he'd never returned showed his lack of care. It would not matter to him at all. And if *he* was not my father . . . well, those were thoughts I did not want, either. *How did the High-wayman know the lullaby?* I blocked this question from my mind.

I sat under the trees until the sun was low in the sky.

That was when screaming started.

"Wolves! A pack of wolves!" I heard someone cry. I dashed through the castle gardens toward the keep, bumping into a large figure wrapped in gray.

"Nay, lass," said the Old Burned Man, "'twill do you no good to run. Best to stay here and safe, until the guards round them up." He held me by my shoulders, the fine fabric of my mother's cloak in his scarred hands. I glanced to where his fingers softly touched the threads. *Did he remember when she made it?* I looked away.

"The wee lad might be afraid. I am going to him and you will not stop me," I said. "'Twould be sad, would it not, for the child to feel abandoned?"

His hands dropped in an instant, as if I had burned him myself, and I ran, red-faced, to Castlelow.

Had he noticed the cruelty of my words? The angry, beastly part of myself hoped so.

Up the stairs I climbed, taking two at a time when I could. I could tell he was panting and huffing behind me, but his legs must have been damaged as well, for he was not fast for a grown man.

I arrived in the babe's room to find the nurse wailing.

"He's dead! He's dead! I left him for but a moment alone with the hound. Just a moment! The beast!" she cried. Her arms were flailing and she clutched the hem of her dress against her face. Then she pushed past me and ran down the stairs. Finn was there, by the babe's bed, blood on his coat, blood on the floor. He looked at me and bared his teeth.

"The hound killed him! The hound killed my master's son!" The nurse's voice echoed eerily through the tower.

And truly, that is exactly how it appeared. Why Finn should attack the babe, I could not say. Had the howls of the wolves thrown him into a canine frenzy?

"There," said the Old Burned Man, "behind his left flank, the babe's arm . . . 'tis *moving*."

I gasped as my eyes followed where the Old Burned Man

pointed. The babe's chubby arm stuck out from behind the dog, and the fingers twitched. Most likely, the arm was still attached to the boy.

"We need to get the dog away from the baby! I think he's still alive!" I took a hasty step toward the hound and then stopped when he growled.

"Stay back, Trinket!" cried the Old Burned Man, pulling my shoulder.

Trinket? How did he know my name? Everyone except Thomas simply called me *girl*, or *Story Lass*.

I jerked away and cried, "The babe needs me!" I took another step forward. "Finn, be calm." I placed my hand palm up and moved closer.

Finn growled again, showing blood in his teeth. He lay on his side and his breathing was labored, but he glared at me in warning. The hand behind him moved again, followed by a soft cry.

I turned to the Old Burned Man. "See, the babe's alive. We just have to get to him!" I saw my harp on the bench by the door, the whiteness of the bone fairly glowing in the afternoon light. I slowly tiptoed over to it.

"Stop! Do not do this!" the Old Burned Man warned me. But I would not be stopped. I reached the creaky wooden bench and sat down to play. If my tunes could make selkies sleep and faeries dance, perhaps they would be able to calm a crazed hound.

LULLABY

I don't know why, but I began to strum the song I had sworn but hours before to never play again. My traitorous fingers were plucking my father's lullaby, the most soothing, gentle song I knew. After a moment or two, my playing was joined by the sound of a flute, sweet, clear, and strong.

We played together as moment after moment drifted by. Finn stopped baring his teeth. Whether it was the tune that tamed him, or the fact that neither of us was approaching him, I do not know, but he relaxed. The Old Burned Man continued the melody as I put the harp down and rose.

When I got close enough, I could tell that Finn had been

hurt, very badly. The blood on his coat was his own. 'Twould have been impossible for a small child to inflict such damage upon a dog.

Finn's eyes softened and his head slumped down. "The hound is bleeding," I whispered. I knelt by the dog as the lullaby's final note faded into silence and the Old Burned Man crept around to the other side of Finn. There he found the babe, who was sobbing quietly, like a mewling kitten.

"He's unharmed." The Old Burned Man cuddled the child close to his chest. The babe's eyes were wide and his breathing strong. Placing the boy on the mattress, the bard continued to soothe him. "He's just scared. But look," he said, pointing to another furry mass on the far side of the child's bed.

"Where is the foul hound?" Lord John bellowed as he charged into the room, sword drawn. He pointed his weapon at Finn and cried in anguish, "You will die now, you filthy cur!" And he raised the sword over his head, ready to swipe at the back of Finn's bloodied neck.

"No!" I screamed with all my might. I stepped between the man and the beast, which was foolish, for Lord John was crazed. He only had eyes for the hound. Too late, I realized he would kill me in order to destroy the dog, if that's what he had to do. "No!" I cried again, cowering now, in a useless attempt to save myself from the blow.

"My Lord!" The Old Burned Man's ragged voice ripped through the air, louder than I'd ever heard him. He tried to grab Lord John's arms from behind.

"I'll have your head, man!" yelled Lord John. "The horrible beast attacked my son!"

"Nay! He did not attack! Finn did not attack the babe!" Breathlessly, I pointed behind the bed. "Can you not see?" I ran to the bed and held the child up.

The Old Burned Man did not let go of the lord. The two men struggled until finally, Lord John shifted his gaze from Finn to me and the babe.

"Look!" the Old Burned Man said, forcing Lord John's vision to the floor near the bed.

There, bleeding on the cold stones, was a large black wolf.

"What in . . ." the lord began, but did not finish as he realized what had happened. The hound had not attacked the child. The wolf had. He'd probably crept in through the open

tower door, though he must have been sly indeed to get inside the castle walls in the first place. And Finn had protected the babe from the wolf. The fury faded from the lord's eyes as his sword clattered to the ground.

He ran to me, gathered the lad in his arms, and sank to the floor, weeping.

Gradually at first, so stealthily that none of us noticed, the black wolf rose slowly, teeth bared, and emitted a low, demonic growl.

We all froze. I glanced at the Old Burned Man, whose intense gaze willed me not to move, not even to breathe.

Thomas skidded into the room. He ran past the lord and the bard, straight toward me, and unknowingly placed himself between Finn and the wolf.

"Trinket! What in the world ... ?" Thomas gasped, bending down to the wounded dog. A snarl made him turn around.

He stepped back, but it was too late.

The wolf lunged at Thomas.

I screamed.

The wolf sank his claws into Thomas's shoulder and pulled him roughly to the ground. Thomas cried out as he went down, but when his head slammed against the floor, he fell silent.

Whether 'twas the shrieks of the quick battle or the unnatural quiet that followed that roused him, Finn, injured and bleeding though he was, sprang at the wolf. The wolf released his hold on Thomas and growled again, his dark eyes fairly screaming, *I have nothing to lose now, hound. My life is forfeit. But I'll not cross into death without taking a human child with me.*

But Finn, brave, strong Finn, could not be taken down. Their fight waged on, hound versus demon-wolf, creating a barrier between poor Thomas and myself.

"Thomas!" I cried.

But he did not answer. I could see naught but his still form on the ground, a puddle of red surrounding him.

I tried to go to him, but the firm hands of the Old Burned Man held me back.

"You can't help him if the wolf takes you as well."

The wolf latched onto Finn's throat, but in that instant, Lord John was there, still holding his babe in one arm and thrusting his sword into the wolf with the other.

"Look away, my son," Lord John cried. He held the whimpering boy close, shielding his eyes from the grisly scene.

"Thomas!" I yelled, tears making it hard to see in front of me. I stumbled away from where Finn lay breathless beside the dead wolf.

Thomas was still. So still. I put my head down to feel his breath on my cheek.

So very faint. But there nonetheless. He lived.

The useless nurse returned with her lady, both gasping from running up the stairs.

"The babe!" cried the nurse, pointing to where Lord John stood with the child in his arms. Lord John's lips moved, as if he were praying silently. The lady let out a strangled cry and then dashed across the room to her husband and their babe.

"I'm so sorry, lass. I know he was your friend," the nurse panted as she approached Thomas and me, wiping her nose on her sleeve. "A pity to lose one so young and strong. Died like a hero, he did, trying to save the lord's son."

She reached for my arm.

"Go away!" I screamed, using every bit of my voice. *"He's not dead."*

But she was not to be stopped. "Mayhap not yet, but soon most likely. Wolf gashes are nasty and foul. Do ye not see all the blood on the floor?"

I held firm to Thomas, lest she try to wrestle me away. I would not leave him, and I would not let him leave me.

We had been through too much together.

"If you be so certain he is going to pass, then you best get the priest," said the Old Burned Man. The nurse nodded, then turned and ran back down the stairs, her footsteps and wheezing fading into nothing.

I cradled Thomas's body in my arms. He did not move.

"Trinket."

The voice was even rougher than usual, and right against my ear.

I did not answer.

"The bargaining coin. I know you have one. I saw you rubbing it before you told your tales." The Old Burned Man's hand was gentle on my shoulder and he patted my hair as if he were soothing a horse.

"Do ye have it still, the bargaining coin? The faerie gold?" he persisted.

I sniffled against Thomas and nodded.

"Place it on the floor, next to Thomas," he whispered. "Quickly, there is little time."

I released Thomas and reached in my pocket for the warm coin. I looked over to where Lord John and his lady were still sobbing over their son, planting kisses on all his fingers and toes. They noticed nothing in the room but the babe. Finn was panting and bleeding. The sword stuck out of the wolf and glinted in the last bits of afternoon sun that streamed through the castle window.

"Quickly, now," the Old Burned Man said. "Place it next to Thomas."

And so I looked into the gray eyes of my father, which shone silver with unshed tears, and set the gold coin next to Thomas's own head.

In a blink, the coin glimmered and was gone.

The blood vanished.

And Thomas's eyelids fluttered, just like they did in the mornings when he first awoke.

"What happened?" Thomas asked, his voice raspy and tired sounding.

Then he sat up. "The wolf! Finn!" he cried, and rushed over to where the hound lay suffering.

Thomas was just as skilled with dogs as with swine. Finn

let him examine his injuries and stroke his bloodied coat. "'Twill be all right, Sir Hound," Thomas murmured. "Ye've done well today. Your sire would be proud."

He knew not the danger he'd just been in. He did not even know that I had bargained his life back with the use of the coin the Faerie Queen had given me. I watched him tend the hound, as tears of gratefulness trailed down my cheeks.

When I turned around, I found the Old Burned Man staring at me.

He blinked twice, then cleared his throat and said, "You are brave, Story Lass."

"The coin," I said, "how did you know?"

"I thought all bards knew the tale of the bargaining coin," he said quietly.

I should have thanked him. I should have thrown myself at his feet and thanked him a thousand times for saving Thomas.

But I had no words.

In a bluster of robes and legs, the priest and nurse bolted into the room.

"Him!" the nurse cried, pointing to Thomas. Puzzlement filled her eyes as she took in the dead wolf, the injured dog,

and the quite lively boy. "He—there was blood—and he—"
she sputtered.

The priest, still breathing heavily from the run up the
stairway, walked over to Lord John and delivered a blessing
to the babe, just as if that was the reason he'd come.

Not to bless and comfort the dying at all.

—

I sighed. I did not want to talk with the Old Burned Man
about the things between us. I wanted only to leave this room.

Obviously, the Old Burned Man felt the same. He was no
longer there.

REMORSE

That night, there was a large banquet in the great hall celebrating the hunt, the safety of Lord John's son, and the bravery of Finn the Great.

Finn, his body striped by bandages, gnawed happily on an enormous joint of meat. I was presented with a beautiful case for my harp, crafted from the softest leather. Thomas received a pup that Finn had sired, and although it would be one more mouth to feed on the road, the protection he would offer would be quite worth it, we thought. Thomas promptly named him Pig.

The Old Burned Man was absent from the fine banquet table.

"Ah, yes, our storyteller, our Old Burned Man. Where is he? We've a token for him as well." Lord John raised an elegant pillow upon which was a golden cup. Next to him, the puffy-eyed lady held the boy upon her lap. "The life of my son is beyond price," she began, "however, we ask for the Old Burned Man to come forward and accept—"

"He's gone," interrupted the nurse. "He's a-packed and left from the castle."

I should not have been surprised. But I was. I thought perhaps he would seek me out.

But he did not.

However, 'twas not a helpless child who he left this time.

———

Thomas, Pig, and I took our leave from Castlelow the next morning. It still amazed me that Thomas bore neither scratch nor bruise nor memory of his encounter with the wolf. But I would spin it into a fine tale for him on the road. He'd be proud.

It would not be hard to catch up to the Old Burned Man, for his pace was never quick. Though I felt like I did not want to see him again, I *would* know the truth I had sought for so long.

And James the Bard alone could tell me the story.

THE SIXTH SONG

Hound Victorious

*This song sounds best if there is a drummer in the audience
who agrees to strike the beat, strong and true. If no drum
can be found, spoons from the kitchen tapped against the
wooden benches work almost as well.*

*Oh, thee, my hound,
From heaven thou come'st,
Where birds and angels
Sing.*

*Soft and sweet,
They bring thee down
In honey'ed arms to
Dream.*

Valiant and brave,
A babe's life to save,
Valiant and brave,
Ta-roo.

We honor thee, Finn,
Of the wheaten coat.
Of the lion heart
So true.

A nobler beast
Ne'er did roam,
To fight
The wolven doom.

Valiant and brave,
A babe's life to save,
Valiant and brave,
Ta-rooo.

The Storyteller and the Truth

THE OLD BURNED MAN SPEAKS

*I*t took us only a day to follow his path and find him. He was sitting by his campfire, silhouetted against the last of the daylight.

"You've come for the tale, then, Trinket?" he asked without looking up.

"I've come for the truth."

The Old Burned Man cleared his throat. His voice scattered against the clear evening air like a jar of pebbles that had been dropped.

Stories are like stars. They shine brightly for us in times of darkness. Some of them draw our attention and hold

it. Some we forget, but these are no less beautiful simply because our careless minds cannot hold on to them all.

But then there are stories that burn inside of us, waiting for the right moment to be told. My dear Trinket, this story has burned inside of me for a long, long time. Finally, it can be told.

The Old Burned Man cleared his throat once again and continued.

I loved your mother. Of all the things I will tell you, this is the most important. I loved her like the sun loves the moon or a moth loves a flame. She was the best person I ever knew. Lovely Mairi-Blue-Eyes.

And I loved you, too, Trinket, with your sparkling raindrop eyes.

You must believe that I wanted to come back to you. Sometimes I think about how different all of our lives might have been had I not taken to the road to begin with. But that was my calling. 'Tis the way of a bard. This is something I think you understand, now.

I left, that early spring day, prepared to travel and tell my stories until the appearance of winter's first frost. I would have come home, bearing a small bag bursting with gold and perhaps some thread in exquisite colors for your mother to weave into fine things. But, as you know, life does not often go as planned, and the road is fraught with adventure.

The ruined eye winked.

I spent my days away from you doing what I do best, telling tales and playing songs on my harp. Yes, I had a harp once, but my fingers are now too scarred and clumsy to pluck the notes. And my voice too withered to sing the songs. A flute works best for me now.

I met Gypsies along the way and stayed with a caravan many weeks. They offered me beautiful silk, in a lovely shade of blue I thought your mother would like, if I stayed and told my stories. I sang a song to the Gypsy King's daughter every night to lull her to sleep. She was a smallish girl plagued by bad dreams. The king wanted me to stay forever, until I refused to play for his daughter a special lullaby she'd heard me practice. I'd created that song for only one child. You.

I met all manner of creatures on my journey. I played sleeping songs for the seal people, told ancient tales to a wandering clan of banshees, and strummed jigs and reels for dancing faeries. And though I knew hundreds of tales already, I gathered a hundred more as I traveled. Some from folk in rare and unusual places, some from my own experiences. Yes, there were many of those.

But none of those tales are the one you want to hear, are they? You want the story, the reason I never went back to the small cottage by the sea. Very well. But I warn you, 'tis a frightening tale, where all is not as it seems. And in truth, dear Trinket, I did go back to the cottage, not once but several times.

SO PERFECT A DAY

◆—◆◆◆—◆

*M*ost accounts of a terrifying nature begin at night. This one does not. This one begins on the most gorgeous day you could imagine. The trees were turning and the air was filled with the scent of dry leaves. The sun was not too hot nor the breeze too cool. 'Twas a perfect day.

I was walking between villages, making my way to a castle whose name I cannot remember. 'Twas taking longer to get to the next village than I had been told it would. But I had an apple in my pocket and a bit of cheese and a crust of brown bread. And, as I said, the day was beautiful and golden.

Through the forest came the sound of hooves pounding against the soft ground. I could feel the vibrations under my feet, traveling up through my legs. Around the bend galloped the largest horse I'd ever seen. Atop him was a gent in fine clothes and a flowing black cape.

"Good day, good sir," I said. 'Twas not unusual to meet others along the road. I'd found that being friendly to fellow travelers was the best course. However, I was no fool. I kept in my bag a large, heavy rock. Already, the rock was in my hand, hidden behind my own gray cloak.

The stranger swept down from his horse and brandished his sword. "'Twill be a good day, indeed, sir, when you give over your purse." He smiled with his mouth, but his eyes held menace.

I hurled my rock, but the stone hit the ground behind the man. The rock had gone right through him.

I gasped as he laughed and said, "I should run you through!"

Being a bard, naturally I'd heard tales of those who, though death had visited them, chose not to pass on. I'd even told stories of those who remained in the world of the living as shadows of their former selves. Ghosts. But I'd never met one on the road.

Until now.

Perhaps his sword is but an illusion as well, I thought, though the sound of it slicing through the air above my head was real enough, as was the feel of cold steel when he held it against my throat.

"Your purse, good sir," he said through closed teeth.

"I have no money."

"You'd prefer to forfeit your life, then?"

"Nay. I do not wish to die."

"Then convince me, good sir. What reason have I to let you live?"

What reason, indeed? I swallowed and thought of you and your mother. I would use whatever method I could to stay alive, to see you again. And I had but one weapon. My words.

"Do ye not become bored, sir, from time to time?" I asked.

His dark eyebrows rose in question. "What are you about?"

"I, sir, have a gift worth more than sacks full of gold." Strangely, my fear made me brave. Perhaps you have felt this along the road as well. "A gift so fine that even the wealthiest lords pay handsomely for it."

He rolled his eyes in disbelief, but allowed me to continue, which I took as a good sign.

"The chance to experience great adventure."

"I am a gentleman of the road. I've plenty of adventure, sir."

His voice was mocking, but I was glad for each second I managed to distract him from killing me.

I looked from side to side, as if I was imparting a sacred secret, which indeed I was. "I offer the chance to feel alive again."

This gave the Highwayman pause.

"'Tis not possible to cross back into the living and remain," he said at last. "I have tried."

"Nay, I am not offering life, I am but a poor bard. I could not possess a secret so amazing and majestic."

"Then what do you offer, sir?" The sword lowered slightly, then poised over my heart.

"Feeling. I offer feeling. Would you not like to feel as if your heart were racing, as if your blood were once again thrumming through you?"

"You talk circles, sir, and I grow tired. State your intentions or meet my sword." The tip of his sword pressed against my chest.

What had I to bargain with but my craft? And truly, I could weave a story like no other in those days. My voice was smoother than the velvet on a king's robe. With but a whisper, I could send chills up any spine.

Were my stories fascinating enough, and could I tell them well enough, to win my life back from a ghost?

I would find out.

A YEAR AND A DAY

I should have known better. I should have known not to expect one who steals from others to honor his word. And these were his words: "I shall keep you with me, sir, until I feel what you say I will feel." He flicked at the edge of my cloak with the tip of his sword. "Or until I grow tired of you and kill you." He laughed without humor.

He pulled me up onto the back of his horse and we rode faster than I could imagine riding to a place I had never seen before. The trees were cold and dead, although winter's chill had not yet touched the land. There were mists and the sky was neither dark nor light. I got down off of the horse—

The Old Burned Man noted my gasp, but continued.

—and sat upon the large rock. The Highwayman smirked and commanded me to begin.

So I did.

I began with a rollicking tale of betrayal, heroic triumph, and a magical coin. 'Twas one of the old tales, from when the land was young. The kind of tale that sings in the veins, for even though parts of it are impossible to believe, every word rings true.

He feigned boredom, at first. But he could not maintain his pretense for long. When a story decides to claim you, it takes both your heart and soul during the listening.

"Too bad *you* did not possess such a bargaining coin," he jested. "Mayhap you could have bargained yourself a better deal."

I remained silent, letting the story have its final

moment. Like a song, a story needs that one last note, as it flies off on the wings of the world.

"Or perhaps *I* could have used a coin such as that... to barter my way back..."

He was thoughtful then.

A good tale always makes one thoughtful afterward.

Next he asked me to play my harp, which I did most willingly. I played lullabies guaranteed to calm and relax the fiercest of beasts. Perchance, he would doze...but even I should have known that 'tis impossible to lull a ghost to sleep. For those who do not join the dead, those who stay in the shadows in between, never rest.

After that, one story per day was all that I would grant him, thinking each day he would release me.

But he did not.

He could not. I should have remembered from the old tales what happens to those who travel through magical boundaries. When I'd stepped off the horse and touched my foot to the ground, I had committed to spending—

"A year and a day."

—

Yes, a year and a day on the other side.

Truly I had hundreds of stories. And I told one each day, to save myself from being run through . . . but sometimes . . .

The withered voice cracked.

Sometimes, when I felt I could go on no more, when the loneliness and longing for you got to be too much, I would tell tales that made you and your mother come alive in my heart.

I told stories of you, Trinket, and of my memories of your sweet face and clear gray eyes. I told tales of your mother's beauty and the way her laugh made the flowers in my heart bloom.

And in desperation, I played for him the lullaby I had composed for you. Yes, the one I played for you, and only you, when you were a babe. It became his favorite and he demanded it after each tale. And so, to stay alive, I played.

You may ask what else I did on the other side. The

truth? I cannot remember. Perhaps time moved differently, for the year passed more quickly than a leaf falls to the ground. I am certain that I met other souls, there on the other side, but I can recall neither their names nor their faces.

I was true to my word. The Highwayman *felt* for the first time since his foul life had been cut short by the hangman's noose, years and years before. He laughed at the escapades of a luckless prince. His eyes glistened with unshed tears when the last of the great warriors was betrayed by a friend and killed. The thief, however, was not true to his word.

"The souls here are restless," I said to him before one telling, for it was not unusual for us to converse before or after the story.

"'Tis the eve of Samhain, sir. Only natural they should be excited."

"Samhain? Already?"

"Aye." He sat polishing his sword, though it never grew dull, so there was not much point.

"Then—" I began.

"Nay, I have not yet tired of your tales, sir." He kept

polishing. He liked the way the sword flashed with the light of the moon. "You shall stay."

But I was determined not to.

There were few who were willing to help a mortal soul lost on the other side. Fewer still willing to cross a shade as cunning and ruthless as the Highwayman. However, luck was with me when I met the ghost of a gravedigger the next day.

"Ye don't belong here," said he. His hair, what was left of it, was long and white, and he walked stooped over, leaning on an ancient shovel.

"Nay, I don't. I'd very much like to go back. 'Tis Samhain, after all. Isn't the wall between the living and the dead at its thinnest?" I asked, even though I knew this to be true from the tales I'd told.

He handed me the shovel and said, "Ye'll do."

The Old Burned Man nodded as if to say, Aye, 'tis true.

And so, a year and a day after the Highwayman captured me, I dug a grave, captured a pooka, and rode him back across to the other side, to the land of the living.

THE WRATH OF THE HIGHWAYMAN

The Highwayman was angry, though, for he had been deprived of his prized entertainment. If I had crossed a stream or lake before he caught up with me, things might have been different.

But I did not.

Soon after the pooka let me off, I was walking through a village, down deserted streets where not a sign of life could be seen or heard. But there was light. On the outside of each house a torch burned fair and bright, perhaps to keep the ghosties away. On a night like Samhain, the torchlight was not enough.

I could hear the clip-clopping of his horse's hooves, not behind me but as if he was next to me, or on a nearby street.

I tried to hide in a doorway, but I could not flatten myself enough. The clip-clopping echoed between the buildings, louder and louder still. The Highwayman was advancing. I started banging on the door.

"Let me in! Please! I beg you!" I shrieked. I am not proud of the fear I felt nor of the way I screamed. I could hear stirring in the house, and the door opened but a crack. Staring up at me, through the narrowest of slivers, was a clear gray eye.

He paused and stared off, then gazed into a different set of clear gray eyes.

"Mum," said a tiny voice, "there's a man here at the door. Sore a-feared he looks. Should we let him in then?"

"Please," I begged. "He comes for me. The Highway-man comes!"

"That's exactly the reason we shan't let you in!" cried

a stern voice on the other side of the door, which was being pushed against me hard. "Ye think I'm a fool?"

I gave a shove and tumbled into the house and closed the door behind me. The wood was rough and my hand was filled with splinters from all my banging.

"How dare ye bring the wrath of the other side down upon my wee home!" yelled a woman with her hair stretched back so tight as to pull her eyes apart. "What are ye thinking? Me here with only me daughter." She probably would have sobbed had she not been so angry with me.

And I didn't blame her. What *had* I been thinking, bringing the horrible Highwayman to the doorstep of a mother and her lass? I thought of another mother and lass left home alone.

Another lass with cool gray eyes.

The Highwayman laughed, the sound harsh and cruel. The mother and her child huddled close together, and I crouched behind the door, cursing myself for involving this innocent family in my struggle with the dark side.

We heard a crash, as if something had been thrown

upon the roof of the cottage. Then smoke, light at first, but quickly growing thicker and darker, engulfed the room. The thatch on the roof must have been dry, for it erupted in flames like a bonfire. I heard the girl cry and the mother yelling at the girl to stay close, but I couldn't see anything in the dense black smoke.

There were screams, naturally. And I am certain some of them were mine. I only knew that I had to get the woman and child out of the house before it was too late. I grabbed them to me, though my own cloak was ablaze, and somehow found a way out of the fiery cottage.

He was silent for a long time, and his eyes filled with unshed tears.

The next thing I knew, I was wrapped in bandages, feeling like I was still aflame. I could barely see and my skin was red, blistered, and painful, indeed.

The woman and the girl with gray eyes had been saved from the fire. I had rescued them, though 'twas my own fault their cottage was burned by the vengeful

Highwayman. Lesser folk would have turned me out, injured or not. But the woman was a healer. And so she practiced her remedies and potions upon my hideous burns.

They looked after me, filling my dry mouth with cool water and restorative broth, keeping my bandages fresh and applying ointment as I would let them. 'Twas sore painful, to be true.

My harp was destroyed in the blaze, as were my hopes of seeing you again.

But time heals. If it does nothing else, time does that.

Slowly, the anger I felt at being horribly disfigured, and their anger at me for causing the roof of their cottage to be torched, melted away as a cautious friendship grew. I told them about you, you know. They did not understand why I could not someday go back to you.

But I could not.

I left your mother and you a whole man. A handsome man. How was I to return, a shell of my former self?

Thus, I stayed in the strange village, hidden from view, as the healing ointments and remedies gradually did their work. Until one day the girl woke afrightened in the night and asked me to tell her a nice tale to help her sleep.

And so the stories came to me, again.

I had no harp, but the woman carved me a flute and I told stories and played. Although my body would forever be scarred, my heart was healing.

I no longer possessed the handsome looks of a young man, but instead a destroyed face and ruined white hair. So, I called myself the Old Burned Man and took to the road once more. My fame as a teller grew. Far more fame than I had ever known as my former self. Perhaps folks were intrigued by my scarred face and body. I know not, but with that fame, I gained courage.

Mayhap enough courage to go back.

RETURN

The woman and child begged me not to return to you and your mother. True, once they had encouraged such a reunion, but we had grown fond of each other and they feared losing my company, and quite possibly my purse, for many a lord paid amply for my tales. My guilt would not allow me to keep much for myself, so the woman and child were well cared for. But I had to go back. I had to.

And so I returned to that little cottage by the sea and watched from afar, too self-conscious to show my hideous face. I kept hidden behind my gray cloak and watched.

Oh, your mother was so beautiful!

Mairi-Blue-Eyes tended the sheep and sheared their wool. She carded the wool in the evening whilst sitting on a stool outside the cottage. The sunlight caught the gold in her hair as she smiled. And you, Trinket, you played at her feet, or danced. Or sang. Even then, you had a voice that carried on the wind, true and sure.

As I watched, I felt a tear on my cheek. *She* no longer *needed* me. *You* no longer *needed* me.

The Old Burned Man put up his hand. He did not wish to be interrupted.

It had been more than three years since I'd seen either of you. Much of a year spent tale-telling, one year spent on the other side, and over a year spent healing from my wounds, for I even had to learn to walk again! And I realized that your lives had gone on during that time. Mayhap you would not even remember—

Again the hand went up.

⸺

Whether it was the wrong decision or not, it was the one I made. I would not be a burden to your mother nor an embarrassment to my child. I had left the village a strapping, handsome man. James the Bard. Now I was so scarred and twisted, folks thought I was aged. And pitiful.

I journeyed from then on. Village to castle. Castle to Gypsy camp. Gypsy camp to manor house, and all sorts of dwellings in between. The stories were my life now, even though I could not help myself from looking in on you, and you'd blush if you knew how I swelled with pride at how you grew. Tall, strong, and filled with such promise.

I left things from time to time, on the back step, small bags of gold and such. Once I left a small silver mirror given to me by a princess who liked my tales. Mayhap you remember it?

An ever-so-slight nod.

Now the story becomes even more tragic, for a chance encounter with the Faerie Queen convinced me of my selfishness.

"Do you really believe," she said after listening to a story. (For the faerie folk are always around when there is a tale to be told. Watch for the way the light moves in the corners of the room, or the way the trees sway just so. That is them.) "Do you really believe that your wife and child only loved your looks? Are you foolish enough to think they would not care for you? The true you that lurks beneath the damage?"

At least, I think she said these words to me. I'd fallen asleep after telling the tale, near a perfectly round mound, dotted with the most lovely flowers. I awoke after dreaming of you and your mother and hearing the Faerie Queen's words. I knew then that I would return. However, I was struck ill, which happens often. My throat never healed well and I spend many weeks each year nursing myself through fever. By the time I went to visit you again, your mother had died and you were gone.

If I live to be one hundred, I will never forgive myself for not taking the risk sooner that she would reject me, just to see her alive once more.

There was silence for a long time. What words could be left? At length, he cleared his throat and continued.

> Then I heard of a girl with a white harp, a Story Lass, traveling with a grubby boy, and I thought, Could it be her? Could it be Trinket?

The words were but whispers.

> So I began to follow your trail, though illness and my scarred legs made me too slow to catch up to you, until you came to Castlelow.
>
> And now you know, daughter, what became of your father.
>
> Now you know.
>
> Most stories have only one ending, but at this moment, this particular story has two. Two possible endings.

James the Bard stood, bowed slightly, and excused himself.

THE FIRST ENDING

I looked over to where the Old Burned Man was resting. He'd spilled his heart out, that much was true. Admitting to low feelings such as cowardice and vanity was most likely difficult. Cowardice, as he was not brave enough to return to my mother and me in time. Vanity, in assuming that we would reject him based upon his appearance.

It had taken courage, yes, to confess these things.

But perhaps it was a case of far too little, far too late.

Did he not remember my mother had died? Could he have saved her from the illness had he been there?

We would never know.

Therein lay the poison. We would *never* know.

It no longer bothered me to look at his scars, for they were as much a part of him as his eyes or his nose. No, it was not his physical appearance that bothered me. I could not look at him because he angered me still. Still.

I would not look at him because that would mean forgiving him. Forgiving him for abandoning me.

I motioned to Thomas to gather our things.

"Why, Trinket, we just got—"

I silenced him with a glare.

I felt the Old Burned Man's gaze and eventually returned it. I glanced at him with as little emotion as possible, then looked away, as if he were something insignificant, like an earthworm or a small beetle crawling among the dried grass.

From the corner of my eye, I saw him nod in understanding.

The Old Burned Man bent down and petted Thomas's pup. Thomas clasped hands with the Old Burned Man, as grown men do, then walked over to stand beside me.

I turned in the direction of the road.

I did not wave.

I did not look back.

THE SECOND ENDING

———◆►◄◆———

The second ending, were I to choose it, would be more difficult.

I let the silence settle around me, comforting like the cloak my mother had made for me. Thomas knew better than to disturb my thoughts, and the Old Burned Man, well, he was intelligent in the ways of people.

The question was, could I forgive him?

Could I?

I knew in my heart it was the right thing to do. I knew I *should*.

But could I?

Would I always, when I looked upon his scars, feel my

blood seethe beneath the surface? Would I blame him for the death of my mother? Not that he could have prevented her illness, but perhaps he could have been there. He could have been there for me.

And I would not have been so alone.

Is there anything worse than being alone?

There was a time when I thought not. But now I was uncertain. I had managed fine with just myself and Thomas. Now we even had Pig. We had made our own family. And a person didn't need much if they had someone as loyal as Thomas by their side.

I did not need a father.

But did I, perhaps, still *want* a father? Not an imaginary one who lived on pirate ships or lulled dragons to sleep. But a real father. A damaged, disfigured, and remorseful man who somehow still managed to touch my soul with his words and touch my heart with his own.

I could not imagine what it cost him to tell me his tale.

Perhaps, one day, I could tell him mine.

—

I readied my sack, but I did not leave.

We had food aplenty that night. The Old Burned Man taught Thomas how to set a snare and he'd captured a fine rabbit, which they roasted on a stick over the fire. 'Twas tasty, and it is always easier to think when your belly isn't growling. I watched the Old Burned Man eat carefully, out of the corner of my eye. He handed little bits of food to Pig and laughed as the pup stood on his hind legs, trying to get the morsels.

"Look, he's a dancer," he said.

And then he smiled.

The Old Burned Man's smile reached all the way to his eyes. Eyes that were silver gray, just like mine. And when he smiled, he didn't look like a gruesome, scarred man.

He looked like my father.

James the Bard.

In that instant, the tiniest sliver of memory came to me and I saw him kissing my mother goodbye. I felt him pat me on the head.

He could feel that I was staring at him and he turned toward me.

"Where is it you'll be traveling to, then, Trinket?" he asked quietly.

"I do not know, I'll have to look at the old map—"

His eyes grew wide and he interrupted me.

"The map? You have my map?"

"Aye," I said. "You left it." I took the leather canister from my bag and placed it in his hands.

"I always wondered where it was. Thought I'd lost it along the road somewhere. And here *you* had it." He unrolled the map with care and pointed to a place east of Castlelow. "We are here." He paused for a moment, then added, "The question is: Where next?"

There was something in his voice that just might have been hope.

"I am not yet certain," I said, making up my mind at last. "I have many more stories to learn . . . Father."

THE SEVENTH SONG

Of Baubles and Trinkets

My father's lullaby

A chest of gold,
For thee, my sweet,
A chest of jewels
To lay at thy feet.

For no other lass
In all the land
Can tame the world
With but her hand.

Thy eyes like drops
Of crystal rain,

I know thy heart
But not thy name.

So take my gifts,
But darling dear,
And come with me,
There's naught to fear.

And I shall give thee,
My one true love,
The blessings of
The morning dove.

And in return,
For days long gone,
The nightingale
Will sing her song.

There is no trinket,
Bauble, nor pearl
Can match the grace
Of thee, sweet girl.

AND SO . . .

—◆━━◆◆◆◆◆━━◆—

$\int$easons change.

So must we.

That which we hold on to so tightly eventually withers in our hands, and it is time to let go.

Time to let the winds carry the pieces away. For mayhap the small pieces are seeds. Seeds that will find a new, fertile ground somewhere to take root and sprout.

I took the small handful of seeds I had been clutching and cast them to the winds. Some took to the air; some fell in the nearby grass.

And one fell by my foot.

Only to be spirited away by a small bluebird.

"Do not judge by appearances," my mother had told me on the mountain overlooking Crossmaglin, "for something pure and good may reside under old, crabbed wrapping."

And so I was learning to see past the scars and sadness of my father and into his mending heart.

"Forgive." Her words drifted around me as she became a part of the evening sky.

And so I would learn to.

⸺

"Come now, Trinket," said Thomas.

"Aye," said my father. "Your harp is itching to be played again, and I know of a village not too far, just o'er the hills. They are soon to celebrate the marriage of their lord to a mysterious lass. Some say she's a Gypsy."

"Aye," I said, repeating it in just the way my father had said it. " 'Tis time."

⸺

It took us three days to travel to the wedding of Feather and Lothar. Three days of getting used to a different rhythm on our journeys, for there were three of us now, instead of two, although Thomas would claim there were four. He counted Pig as a person.

Banners of crimson and gold were displayed up and down the narrow streets of Foresthill. This marriage was more a festival than a solemn ceremony.

And when I finally got to see Feather, she looked truly happy.

"Little Trinket, you have grown much," she said, taking me by the hands and twirling me around.

I stepped back. She was right. I had grown. No longer was I timid Trinket, the girl who searched for a father. Now I was Trinket the Story Lass. I had learned from a Gypsy girl to follow the calling in my blood and make my own future. I had been to the isle of the seal people and earned my harp. I had followed a young banshee to hear words from my dead mother. I had played music for the Faerie Queen and won a reward. I had traveled through the wall between the living and the dead with the help of a pooka. I had saved the lives of a loyal hound and my best friend.

And I had found my father.

"Trinket, will you play your harp for the wedding and tell us a tale?" Feather asked me. I looked at my father, and he nodded.

So I sat and strummed my harp. The notes rose up from my heart, out through the air, and into the coolness of the evening as a smile played upon Feather's lips.

I smiled back and cleared my throat, for now I did indeed have a tale or two for her.

For that is what I do.

That is who I am:

Trinket the Story Lass.

AUTHOR'S NOTE

I drew heavily from Celtic folklore (Irish, Scottish, and Welsh) when creating Trinket's stories, attempting to weave in bits of magic from the tales I heard as a child, researched as a grownup, and told to audiences myself as a professional storyteller. A good *seanachai* (Gaelic for storyteller) always flavors a story upon the retelling with a bit of her own soul.

The Gypsies and the Seer. Often I have wondered about seeing into the future. If I could, would I want to know what my future held? Those born with "the sight" appear often in folklore, and in ancient times, many a king had his own personal fortune-teller. The seventh daughter of a seventh daughter (or the seventh son of a seventh son) is said to be gifted with "the sight" in many cultures.

The Harp of Bone and Hair. Harps made from bones and hair have appeared in folktales all over the world. More often than not, the bones used are human. However, there is an old tale of a babe stolen by faeries and a mother who bargains with a harp made from a sea creature's bones, which is the basis for this story. Famed storyteller Sorche Nic Leodhas collected a version of this tale, called "The Stolen Bairn and the Sidhe." Of course, because of my fascination with seals, selkies found their way into the mix in my version. Selkies, the seal people, are common in Irish and Scottish folklore, and are often called roans or silkies.

The Wee Banshee of Crossmaglin. When I first researched banshees (back when I was about Trinket's age), I remember wondering if they were always ladies, or if there were ever child banshees. I could find no evidence of banshee children, but then, maybe those who know did not survive to tell the tale. I named my village Crossmaglin, which is similar to the real village of Crossmaglen in Ireland, because I love how that name sounds. However, my imaginary village with its Banshee's Tower bears no resemblance to the real town of Cross-maglen.

The Faerie Queen and the Gold Coin. I knew a former Irish priest who, when my daughters were first learning Irish dance, claimed that the best Irish dancers could complete their steps on the face of a penny, or so his old aunt had told him. I later learned that in truth, dancers would often pound large horse nails into the bottoms of their shoes to create sound when they danced, or even the occasional coin. Perhaps Orla was the first. As for the faerie folk, they have always been known as fine dancers and dangerous competitors. Irish poet and playwright W. B. Yeats collected many stories about the faeries.

A Pig Boy, a Ghost, and a Pooka. Oftentimes stories get jumbled up in the telling, where elements from one tale meld into the next. The term "highwayman" wasn't really in favor until the eighteenth century, although robbery along the road has been a danger since the creation of roads. There is a famous poem, "The Highwayman" by Alfred Noyes, which is hauntingly lovely, though the highwayman in my story is far less noble. As for the pooka, he is perhaps the most misunderstood creature of Celtic folklore. A shape-shifter who can be a wolf or an eagle, he is most often known as a horse who can talk with humans. Whether his intention be good or foul depends upon the story (and the pooka). In some places, the *pooka's share* is still left out for him on Samhain (the ancient name for the holiday we call Halloween). I visited a graveyard in the west of Ireland called Aghadoe, and though no ghosts came out to haunt me, the image of the graveyard with its crumbling headstones still does. So I rearranged the letters a bit and made Agadhoe the name of my town.

The Old Burned Man and the Hound. There is an ancient Welsh tale called "BeddGelert," about a brave hound that protects a royal babe but is killed by the king, who unfortunately misunderstands the situation. There is even a monument to this dog in Snowdon, Wales. I always hoped they got the story wrong, and that the brave dog lived. The great thing about being a storyteller is you can create a better ending.

The Storyteller and the Truth. *A year and a day* is a magical unit of time. Some legends hold that marriages can be dissolved after a year and a day or that perhaps the dead can return in special circumstances, but only for this length of time.

As with all tales, the true meaning of each story is for the listener to determine. And though I enjoy researching folktales, I do not claim to be a folklorist. Just a simple storyteller with a desire to pass along the magic of stories, hoping they'll reside in your hearts and minds for more than just a year and a day.

ACKNOWLEDGMENTS

Above all else, two very extraordinary people are responsible for Trinket getting the opportunity to tell her tales. Joanna Stamfel-Volpe, my amazing agent, who e-mailed me before she was even done reading the story to let me know how much she was enjoying it and how beautiful she found it. That e-mail changed everything for me. And Beth Potter, my brilliant editor, who loved the story as much as I did and helped me weave the words even more tightly so that they would hold together, true and strong.

Thank you to teachers/writers Nancy Villalobos and Chris Kopp, who read each of Trinket's tales, one by one, as I slowly finished them, and always seemed eager to read another. And faraway thanks to friends Holly Pence and Kathy Duddy, whose long-distance support is worth more to me than a thousand gold coins.

I could not be more pleased with the work done by the copy editors, the art directors, the amazing Dan Craig, and everyone at FSG Macmillan. I appreciate you so much.

Special thanks to my parents, John and Nancy Moore, and the rest of my wonderful family in New Mexico: John Moore III, Tammi Moore, Hope Moore, Jacob Moore, Jim Daniels, Elora Daniels, and Mia Daniels. My sister, Susan Moore Daniels, plays the harp so beautifully that I am certain her strumming echoed in my brain as I wrote this book. My nephew John Moore IV composed a hauntingly beautiful version of "Trinket's Lullaby" that makes me tear up whenever I listen to it. I am not sure what I did to be part of such a wonderful crew, but I am thankful for them.

To the dancers of the Comerford Irish Dance School and their director, Tony Comerford: thank you for several years of amazing rhythms and the inspiration I've gained from watching your feet fly.

To the students and staff of Jefferson Elementary: every day you give me hope for the future of our world. And, kids, I never get tired of you asking for more stories. Never.

And finally, to my husband, Sean: you put up with a lot while I was working on this book and it is only because of your support that I was able to finish it at all. And to my beautiful daughters, Noel, Isabelle, and Caledonia: you are my muses. My stories are always for you, first and foremost. So is my advice: never be afraid to live your dreams and tell your tales. I love you.

NO SUCH THING AS A BAD DAY

A MEMOIR BY

HAMILTON JORDAN

FOREWORD BY JIMMY CARTER

LONGSTREET PRESS
Atlanta, Georgia

Published by
LONGSTREET PRESS
2140 Newmarket Parkway
Suite 122
Marietta, GA 30067

Printed in the United States of America

2nd printing 2000

Library of Congress Catalog Card Number: 99-068571

ISBN: 1-56352-578-X

Jacket design by Burtch Hunter
Book design by Megan Wilson

Cover Photograph by David Hathcox © 1996

Visit Longstreet Press on the World Wide Web
www.longstreetpress.net

The best is yet to come.

FOREWORD

The fascinating journey detailed in these pages will arouse the interest of every reader.

Imagine an author who has survived attacks from three different kinds of cancer, and is able to describe these experiences with courage and good humor.

Imagine that this same young man — a quarter of a century ago at the age of twenty-seven — analyzed one of the most complicated and daunting political challenges in American history, and planned the basic strategy for a campaign that brought an unknown Georgia governor into the White House.

As a young Southerner, Hamilton Jordan's personal tribulations while serving as White House chief-of-staff are the stuff of which fiction is ordinarily made. These challenges took on a bizarre and damaging life of their own when Hamilton was faced with a barrage of false accusations from men who lied in order to reduce their own prison sentences.

As a boy, Hamilton saw his Uncle Clarence Jordan become the founder of a racially integrated farm in deep South Georgia in the 1940s. He witnessed the intense hatred that this aroused among the Ku Klux Klansmen, whose bombs, fires, and bullets did not deter Clarence Jordan from demonstrating his Christian faith in action.

Fifteen years later, Hamilton was on the scene when Martin Luther King Jr. began his early civil rights marches in Albany, Georgia.

During the Vietnam conflict, the author volunteered to serve, but, when he was physically disqualified for combat, went there on a humanitarian mission. Instead of the Viet Cong, his unsuspected adversary turned out to be Agent Orange, an almost fatal encounter he later described to Admiral Elmo Zumwalt, whose order to use the chemical herbicide resulted in the death of his own son.

In summary, this is an astonishing collection of adventures and observations, woven into a dramatic account that helps to clarify some of the mysteries of our nation's recent history. But above all, Hamilton Jordan's book provides reassurance for cancer patients and members of every family who face the challenge of this disease.

Hamilton's story offers a rare combination of insight, wry humor, and real inspiration.

JIMMY CARTER
Plains, Georgia

DEDICATION

This book is dedicated with love and admiration

to Kathleen Jordan

— my eleven-year-old daughter — whose courage, joy, and spirit in dealing with a chronic disease inspires me and all who are fortunate to know her.

Her mother, her two brothers — Hamilton Jr. and Alexander — and I are very proud of her and grateful to her for her example.

TABLE OF CONTENTS

PART ONE

PART TWO

NO SUCH THING AS A BAD DAY

PART ONE

FIRST TIME AROUND

I remember it like it was yesterday.

I was lying in my hospital bed. My doctor had just left to review the tissue report with the pathologist . . . he promised to come back within the hour. I had been in the hospital now for five days and had had every test in the book. And it all came down to a person sitting in a laboratory somewhere peering into a microscope at my cells and deciding what kind of cancer I had . . . and whether I would live or die. Would it be curable, or even treatable? Would I have a fighting chance, or be left to hope for a miracle, racing around the world to off-beat clinics searching for a cure?

My dear mother and sister made small talk to pass time. A nurse's aide brought in a form for me to fill out evaluating the hospital services.

"Have you enjoyed your stay, Mr. Jordan?" she asked.

"I'll tell you in an hour," I joked. She didn't understand.

I found myself knotting up the bed sheet in my hand. The emotional mask that I had been wearing for my family's sake was close to being shattered. Just to escape, I turned on the television and surfed from channel to channel, hoping to be distracted, and was startled to see a picture of myself on the local CBS affiliate. I turned the volume up in time to hear, "CBS has learned that former Carter aide Hamilton Jordan is in an Atlanta hospital and has been diagnosed with inoperable lung cancer."

Panic gripped my body as I looked at an old photo of myself on the television screen and these strange words sunk in.

My mother's face dropped and my sister watched me closely for a reaction. Then logic returned. If my doctor, who just left my room, didn't know what I had, how in the hell did CBS News know? Like so many other times, the media had only half the story right.

The panic caused by the news report subsided as we continued to wait. Suddenly, my room was flooded with doctors: the oncologists, my pulmonary specialist, the radiologist. I tried to read them like a jury . . . one was smiling slightly, the others were not. What did it all mean?

The radiologist broke the ice. "Hamilton, when more than one doctor comes into your room, it is usually pretty good news."

"All I ever wanted was a fighting chance."

"Well, Mr. Jordan," my lead doctor said, "you certainly have that." He paused, glanced down at a written report and looked up. "You have diffuse histiocytic lymphoma. Ten years ago, this would have been a death sentence, but this is an area where we have made progress . . . there are a number of treatments that are reasonably effective in dealing with this disease."

I stuck on one word. "Reasonably, doctor? What does that mean?"

"This is one of those 'good news, bad news' situations. The bad news is that you have a very aggressive cancer. The good news is that aggressive cancers divide rapidly, which means that they are particularly vulnerable to chemotherapy and radiation at the time of cell division. We've got to find a treatment your cancer will respond to."

He went on to tell me that I would need to undergo further tests, but that the evidence at this point was that the cancer was confined to my chest area. "We plan to radiate your chest. The bottom line is that we have a good shot at curing this."

That was too vague, and I learned for the first of many times that cancer patients should only ask questions if they are prepared to hear the answer. "What is a 'good shot,' doctor?"

"Well, every patient is different. . . ."

"Just quantify it for me!" I interrupted.

"I don't like to use numbers, Mr. Jordan, but if you insist. . . ."

"I do," I said firmly.

"About half of the patients who have non-Hodgkins lymphoma would achieve a remission with the therapy we will give you. Half of those will be free of disease five years out."

I was doing the math in my head. "So overall, I have about a 25 percent chance of being in the group that obtains a remission AND is cancer-free five years later?"

"That's about right, Mr. Jordan."

I was devastated to hear my chances of being alive reduced to statistics, but I had asked for it. And from that point on, I insisted that doctors avoid vague terms and quantify my situation. When the stats were favorable, I believed them and clung to them. When they were discouraging, I either tossed them aside or made up my mind to be one of those who beat the odds.

But when the doctors left my room that afternoon, I was faced with the cold, harsh fact that the odds greatly favored the cancer winning this battle, not me.

I didn't sleep much that night.

The story had actually begun on August 24, 1985, a day frozen forever in my memory.

I knew something was wrong when my family doctor sent me to the hospital for my annual chest X ray, which he had routinely taken in his office for fifteen years. A couple of hours later as we sat in his office, he talked quietly on the phone to the radiologist. I strained to hear, but all I could make out was, "I understand, yes . . . I understand."

He hung up the phone, turned away as if to avoid contact, slid the X rays out of the large brown envelope, turned them upright one by one and lined them up on the illuminated viewer. What had taken him seconds seemed like hours. He took a deep breath, pointed with his finger to a smoky area on one film and said slowly, "Hamilton, I hate to tell you this, but you have an abnormal chest film."

He paused to watch me as his words sank in. "This spot here is some kind of mass . . . some kind of growth."

"Could it be a cancerous growth?" I asked quietly.

"Yes," he said slowly, picking his words carefully, "and most likely it is a cancerous growth, but we will not know for sure until we take a biopsy."

I was stunned and just sat there, staring at the film. I felt like someone had suddenly pulled a plug and all the energy and feeling were flowing from my body. I had a surreal sense of standing apart from this bizarre scene and watching myself sitting in the examination room, talking with my doctor friend, asking the predictable questions:

"Do we know for sure it is cancer?"

"What kind of cancers would grow in that area?"

"What can I do?"

"Will I live?"

After he had repeated six or eight times, "We won't know any more until we do the biopsy," I stopped asking questions and was ready to go home.

My doctor kindly offered to drive me home so that he could tell Dorothy, my wife. I thanked him but said that I wanted to be alone.

I was barely out of the parking lot when Dorothy called on the car phone to report something cute our eighteen-month-old son, Hamilton Jr., had said. Later, she would tell me that she had sensed something different in my voice. "What's wrong?" she asked.

This was not the way to tell her, I thought. I needed to be able to hold her in my arms, comfort her and be comforted, but I couldn't hold back. I needed her to know and simply blurted it out: "Richard found a mass in my chest and thinks it's cancer!"

Dorothy was shattered. She tried to be strong and brave for me, but I could feel the fear oozing out of her every pore. For the first of many times, I realized that it is often more difficult to be the loved one than the cancer patient.

I will never forget taking Hamilton Jr. for a walk in his stroller that same afternoon. I welcomed getting away from the house and from Dorothy and having time to think . . . but I could only think about him. I stopped, picked him up, and hugged him as I cried softly so as to not scare him. Would I live to see his second birthday? Or his third? I fought back tears every time I looked at him and was thankful he did not understand that something bad was going on with his "da-da."

Dorothy and I spent the evening on the phone alerting family and friends . . . these were terrible calls to make.

Everyone tried to be optimistic and struggled to say the right thing.

"Maybe it is just a virus you caught in Vietnam," offered my mother, who was battling lung cancer herself.

"It could be benign," my sister suggested.

"You hear about mistaken X rays all the time," a close friend said.

While my family was filled with wishful thinking, I chose to look at it differently. This was definitely serious, probably cancerous, and the big question was whether or not it was curable. I started off thinking that my chances were not very good while my family was hoping and praying for tropical diseases and mistaken readings of my film.

I checked into the hospital the next morning for a complete battery of tests. It would take a couple of days. I resolved to be brave for my family. If I fell apart, I would be no good for myself or for them. I hid my very real fears and spent the next several days cracking jokes and trying to make the best of a miserable situation.

While I was waiting for the report from the biopsy, a friend who happened to be a professional counselor stuck her head through the door. "In the mood for some company?"

"You bet . . . am I glad to see you," I replied.

She sat down on the side of the bed, grasped my hand, and — fighting back tears — said, "I have been thinking about you and praying for you."

My first thought was that she was going to have to pull herself together before she could help me. "I appreciate your prayers but right now I would gladly trade them for some advice on how to get my head straight. We've been on a roller coaster, and I have to settle down and live with this thing, whatever it is."

"Hamilton, the best thing you can do is to understand the various stages people go through when confronting a serious illness."

I nodded. That made sense.

She continued: "Most people deny their illness initially. They hope that they will wake up the next morning from a bad dream. They refuse to face reality by denying reality.

"The second stage is usually anger," she continued. "People get mad at the world, at their family members, themselves and at God. They ask, 'Why me? What have I done to deserve this?'

"Next, people usually bargain with God by making a promise that they will do something worthwhile with their lives if they are allowed to live."

"Finally, patients become depressed, but out of that feeling of despair, people ultimately face their reality. This is acceptance — when a person puts aside his anger and denial, looks squarely at his problem, accepts and deals with it."

"Look," I said, "I'm not trying to be different and maybe I am just hiding my real feelings, but what you describe is not the way I feel. Denial? Deny what? I've got a mass in my chest the size of an apple. I have seen it on the X ray, know it's there . . . so there's no use in denying it. Angry? At whom? I have lived a great life and have been blessed with much more than I deserve. I don't want to die, but if I died tomorrow, I wouldn't have much room to complain. I don't know 'Why me?' but 'Why not me?' Maybe God gave me this disease because he thinks that I am strong enough to handle it."

"Bargaining with God?" I continued. "The God that I believe in has all the cards. . . . I don't think that God has to sit down and negotiate with His creations. What am I supposed to do, say that I will be a television evangelist if I am cured?"

She smiled.

"I don't know if I want to be cured that badly," I added with a grin.

"Hamilton, you have totally blown my theory and obviously you have already accepted the reality of your disease."

"Is that okay?" I asked.

"It is terrific!" she said as she bent over and gave me a big hug. "It's terrific!"

LEARNING ABOUT CANCER . . . THE HARD WAY

Unfortunately, I know a hell of a lot about cancer.

Back in 1975, on a beach vacation with my parents, my father had complained of sharp pain in his hip, which he dismissed as "arthritis." Weeks later, my mother called to report that my father had been hospitalized with something she would only describe on the phone as "serious." I rushed home and went directly to the doctor's office. He held my father's bone scan against a light, revealing a perfect outline of his skeleton with what looked like twenty or thirty spots sprinkled across his frame. His body looked like a Christmas tree strung with white lights.

"Those are 'hot spots,'" the doctor explained. "Each of them is a cancerous growth in the bone. I'm sorry to have to tell you this, but your dad has metastatic prostate cancer."

I bombarded him with questions. . . . How did this happen? What was his prognosis? Was it curable? Would my father die?

"Sometimes we find a lump in a man's prostate gland during a physical. We do a biopsy. If it's cancer and there's no evidence of spread, we take the prostate out. If we are lucky, that's the end of it. The poor patient is impotent and incontinent as a result of the surgery, but he has a chance for a full life. Often, by the time we feel the lump in the prostate the horse is already out of the barn in many patients; the cancer has spread, and — like with your dad — it is already in the bones. Once the cancer escapes the prostate, it is incurable."

Soon afterwards, my father began his treatment, had his testicles removed and began taking female hormones, a course of treatment that usually puts prostate cancer into remission for a period of time. His was a textbook case as he enjoyed two years of quality living, learning even to joke about the enlarged breasts that resulted from the female hormones. Then, as they almost always do, the hormones lost their effect and the cancer came roaring back in his bones. He died within the year.

CAMP SUNSHINE

But it was at Camp Sunshine that I really learned about cancer and the enduring lessons of life.

Shortly after we married and several years before my first bout with cancer, Dorothy — a pediatric oncology nurse — organized Camp Sunshine, one of the first non-profit camps in the country for children with cancer. New to Atlanta, Dorothy was a dynamo: raising money; recruiting campers from reluctant parents not inclined to give up their sick children for even a week; recruiting volunteer counselors; organizing a sophisticated medical clinic fully staffed by pediatric oncologists and nurses from Emory; and organizing an outstanding camp program for these special children.

It was a major undertaking. Early on, I tried to help a little too much, second guessing some decisions she had made. Dorothy told me in no uncertain terms to back off, that this was not a political campaign but her project. I did, and ever since, Camp Sunshine has been Dorothy's volunteer project with my playing a minor, supportive role. (I am the perennial MC for Talent Night . . . one year I was M.C. Hammer-ton and another time, Judge Ito.)

We started with only thirty-eight campers and twenty-five volunteers. Today, Camp Sunshine has a year-round program for over four hundred children and their families: two weeks of summer camp, a family weekend that addresses the problems that affect the siblings and parents, a ski trip to Colorado for amputees and the physically challenged, a trip to Washington for our teenagers, an "Outward Bound" program and many other activities. Camp Sunshine has had a major impact on our lives, especially by giving us the opportunity to witness time and time again dramatic demonstrations of the power of the mind and attitude to alter the course of disease.

My favorite memory is of Corey Grier, a good-looking black teenager. A natural leader with a ready wit and generous spirit, Corey drew boys and girls of all ages to him like a magnet. He also had a tough cancer in his colon and battled it with great courage for several years. Finally, the tumor got the upper hand.

In July 1985, the doctors told Corey he had a short time to live. Corey calmly told his doctors that he

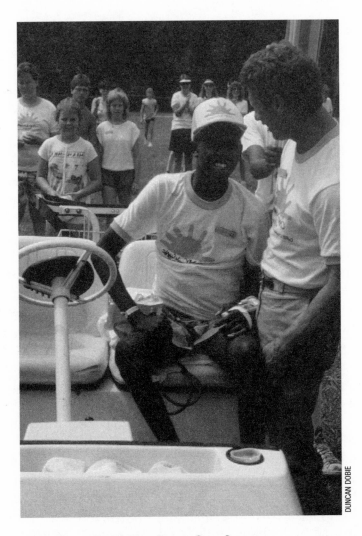

COREY GRIER DAY AT CAMP SUNSHINE

intended to live until June (1986) so he could return to Camp Sunshine to tell his friends goodbye and celebrate his seventeenth birthday that same week. The doctors humored Corey, but told his parents that he would be lucky to make it to Christmas and would never live to the next summer.

Eleven months later, a gaunt but smiling Corey was airlifted to Camp Sunshine on a helicopter to celebrate "Corey Grier Day." The campers held up hand-made signs, clapped and yelled excitedly as the helicopter touched down on the football field. Everyone crowded around Corey, reaching out to touch him or to slap a "high five." Several older campers lifted him carefully from the chopper and carried him gently to a specially decorated golf cart.

Surrounded on all sides by counselors and campers, Corey looked like the Pied Piper as he led the crowd to the lodge where we celebrated with ice cream, cake, and stories. Corey stayed for only a few hours but had a great time. As he rode back to the athletic field, he was talking a mile a minute, emotionally exhilarated from his visit. He even told one camper that he might live until the next Camp Sunshine. As Corey was hoisted into the helicopter, the harsh reality of the moment sunk in. The chopper paused about twenty feet from the ground and did a "360" so that we could all see Corey's smiling face one last time before he disappeared in the blue summer sky. We waved and waved, hoping that our forced smiles hid our tears. By the time the chopper was out of sight, several hundred people were wiping their eyes and hugging one another.

Corey returned to Egleston Hospital that night, celebrated his seventeenth birthday the next morning with his family and some favorite nurses, and died peacefully that afternoon.

Corey's story is just one of many of the brave children who have touched our lives in indescribable ways. They have taught us how to live and sometimes have shown us how to die.

DECISION TIME

With my biopsy behind me and my diagnosis complete, it was time to begin treatment. But what was the best treatment? My doctors told me that they could treat me locally. But was there a doctor out there somewhere who was having remarkable success curing people with my type of lymphoma?

In what I would later come to believe was one of many small miracles in my life, a doctor friend flew in from out of town just to be with me. I was counting on him to calm me down, to tell me everything was going to be okay.

Instead, he shook me up. He put his hand on my shoulder, and simply said, "Old friend, you have got to take charge of your own medical care."

"What?" I said. "Here I am worrying about dying. Don't I have enough to think about with my young wife and baby . . . and you wander in here and tell me I have got to be responsible for the medical decisions?"

"That is exactly right!" he shot back. "Tell me who has a greater stake in the decisions that have to be made than you do?"

The minute he said it, I knew he was right, and from that moment on, I did take charge. The stakes were too high. . . . I could not afford to be passive. I had to have the peace of mind of knowing that whatever treatment I received was the best available.

I shared my candid feelings with my own doctor that afternoon. He agreed to help me explore all my options. That night, I gave an orderly twenty-five dollars to sneak me out of the hospital and wheel me over to the library. In a few hours, I knew a hell of a lot about diffuse histiocytic lymphoma. While there was much I did not comprehend, I was able to understand the broad challenges that faced me.

This kind of lymphoma was usually aggressive, was considered incurable until recently and had almost always spread to different sites in the body when it was diagnosed — hence the name "diffuse." It was obvious from recent journal articles and clinical trials currently taking place that there were several centers in the United States that specialized in treating lymphomas.

In every article I read, "staging" the disease was

critically important. A test known as the "lymph-angiagram" was essential to assess the spread of lymphoma and could even detect internal changes in an individual node that might indicate lymphoma. This old-fashioned, painstaking test required that a skilled technician find tiny lymph veins in each toe and "push" dye into the veins which would then show up on a scan.

When I asked my doctor about the lymphangiagram, he called it "outdated" and declared that it had been replaced by the CAT scan. "We don't have anyone here who could even do a lymphangiagram anymore," he explained.

The moment that he said that, I made a resolute decision to go somewhere else for my treatment. Within twenty-four hours, I had talked with five cancer centers around the world that were developing experimental treatments for non-Hodgkin's lymphoma. The name of the National Cancer Institute in Bethesda, Maryland, popped up time and again for their pioneering work on lymphomas. In my research, I would ask the doctor or nurse whom I was talking to, "What would you do if you had my disease?" A majority said that they would to go NCI . . . others mentioned NCI as one of several options.

I made contact with a doctor at NCI who told me that they were getting 60 to 70 percent of their non-Hodgkin's lymphoma into complete remission and that 70 percent of those in remission were cancer-free after several years. I did some quick math in my head. "That means that you have a 50 percent cure rate?"

"That's right, and if your disease is localized and early, your odds could be slightly better."

I asked about having the NCI experimental treatment given to me in Atlanta so I would not have to move my family.

"Look, Mr. Jordan, you usually have one shot at curing lymphoma. I would want to have my treatment administered at the place where it had been developed, especially when that place has the broadest possible experience in treating lymphomas. Why go for a reproduction when you can have the original?"

It was difficult to leave our Atlanta doctors and the community where we have so many personal and emotional ties. And it was a logistical nightmare to contemplate uprooting our little boy and leaving the comforts of home. But this was my life, and I had to take my very best shot. There is a lot of difference between a 25 percent chance of cure (which I had been offered locally) and 50 percent when you are dealing with your life.

"I'll be there tomorrow," I said.

While packing, I got a call from NCI with an offer to have a limousine pick me up at the airport. I told the well-meaning staffer that I appreciated the gesture, but that I didn't want or expect VIP treatment. "Spread the word up there, please, that I want to be treated like Joe Smith."

There were selfish reasons for my attitude. During the Iranian hostage crisis, I had to negotiate with the Shah of

Iran and his medical team on the logistics of his treatment for cancer (ironically lymphoma) and had seen first-hand how doctors tend to overreact to public figures. In some instances, the doctors become too conservative and are not willing to take the normal risks required in dealing with a serious medical problem. On the other extreme, some tend to "overtreat" public figures, become too aggressive and take too many risks. I didn't want either extreme — I simply wanted the best care that NCI would give an ordinary patient.

I had also seen the egos of doctors and patients result in less than ideal medical care. The Shah of Iran needed to have his spleen removed and insisted that Dr. Michael DeBakey, the great heart surgeon, perform the operation. Dr. DeBakey, who had not personally removed a spleen in years, took the Shah's spleen out. Later, the Shah died in Egypt of cancer and complications from the surgery.

Conversely, when President Reagan was shot, the White House doctor opted not to have "the best" doctors brought in but insisted that the doctors on duty in the emergency room who dealt with gunshot wounds every day treat the president. Some doctors credit that decision with saving the president's life.

Once I got to NCI, I was indeed treated like Joe Smith and put on an accelerated batch of tests.

"We are going to work your ass off, Mr. Jordan," one friendly young doctor teased. And they did. In two days, I had a spinal tap, a repeat bone marrow, constant blood work, a liver scan, a brain and bone scan, and a liver biopsy monitored by a scope that was inserted into my abdomen by an incision through my belly button.

And finally the lymphangiogram, the test they were unable to do in Atlanta that had motivated me to look around in the first place.

This is a delightful four-hour procedure where you have to lie perfectly still while they cut tiny holes in your toes to find a lymph vein through which they inject dye, which illuminates your entire lymphatic system on X ray. The lymphangiogram revealed one or two suspicious nodes below my diaphragm that were not enlarged but that looked "funny" in the words of the radiologist. If there was cancer in those nodes, it would totally change my "staging" (the extent of disease) and the treatment they would give me.

"We want to know the truth," my doctor said. "If there is cancer in your abdomen, we need to know so we can adjust our treatment accordingly. I want to stick a needle through your belly and sample these two nodes." He went on to explain that this was a slightly risky procedure as the nodes which he would biopsy were adjacent to a major artery.

"If you want to know, I want to know," I said quickly. In the short time I had been there, I had developed absolute confidence in the NCI medical staff.

After giving me a mild sedative and a local painkiller, the radiologist pulled out what he described as "my favorite Japanese needle," which was about two feet long.

I asked if I could watch.

"Only if you promise not to faint," he said as he moved the table around so I could clearly see the X ray monitor. He quickly stuck the needle in my abdomen.

"I promise not to faint if you promise not to stick that damn thing into my heart or artery."

He laughed and with sure, steady hands, probed and pushed until the tip of the needle was about a half-inch from the target node. "The challenge here," he explained, "is that this node is not firmly attached to anything. I have to spear it free-floating to get a good sample."

I wished he had not told me that, turned my head away from the monitor, and gulped a deep breath. Maybe I shouldn't feel so cocky. The thought had barely crossed my mind when I felt the needle move.

"Gotcha!" said the doctor.

I turned quickly to the monitor and saw the needle stuck in the node like a spear in a fish.

I breathed a sign of relief.

He quickly drew the sample tissue out of the needle, placed it in a vial, and held it up to the light.

"Mr. Jordan, I got a good piece of the bottom of this node, but I would like to get a piece of that other node if you'll let me. It is important to know what's going on in there."

Sounding more confident than I felt, I said, "Go ahead."

In another minute, he had penetrated the top of the

second node and drawn the long needle out of my belly.

I shook his hand and thanked him. "With an aim like that, you must hunt birds!"

He shook his head. "I am a terrible shot."

"I wish you hadn't told me that."

It turned out that the lymphangiagram saved my life. The needle biopsy found cancer in one of the nodes in my stomach. This important new fact completely changed my staging and their treatment.

Without the lymphangiagram, I would have been staged a "1-A," which meant that the doctors believed the cancer was confined to my chest and could have been treated with radiation. I would have had my chest radiated, the mass would have probably melted away and for some period of time (my doctors guessed several months), we would have believed we had killed the cancer. But the cancer in my abdomen would have been unaffected by the radiation to my chest, would have spread throughout my body and greatly reduced the possibility of my achieving a remission or a cure.

I considered the fact that it had spread to my abdomen a tremendous setback. "How bad is that?" I asked my doctor.

"Not bad at all . . . at least we know now where we stand. We will zap you with this new cocktail. And it has been working pretty good. You have early disease, localized in your chest and abdomen, not in your blood or in your marrow. I believe that you can be cured."

The head of the medical team came in while I was eating dinner Friday. "We'll start your chemo Monday, Mr. Jordan."

"Do we have to wait?"

The doctor said that he was on duty Saturday and that we could do the first cycle then.

"Tomorrow is your birthday," Dorothy protested.

I gave her hand a squeeze and smiled. I thought about the cancer cells racing around my body while I ate birthday cake. I had no intention of giving my body the weekend off.

"Let's get started with it," I said, trying to sound brave about something that I didn't feel very brave about.

CHEMOTHERAPY

By random selection, it was determined that I would receive the PROMACE-CYTOBOM protocol, which was being tested in clinical trials against standard protocols in treating lymphomas. There were eight drugs in this protocol that would have some different and hopefully fatal impact on cancer cells. The good news was that by using them together in combination, there was a greater chance that they would kill all the cancer cells before any of the cells developed resistance to the drugs. The bad news was that in the course of killing the cancer cells, they also kill your body's healthy cells and are particularly rough on your blood components.

Because I had an aggressive lymphoma, my cells were dividing rapidly and were peculiarly vulnerable to chemotherapy. This meant that if the chemo worked at all, it could work dramatically.

The doctor told me that he would give me "almost lethal" doses of the drugs in order to kill the cancer and that he was willing to deal with any complications and side effects that might develop.

A doctor friend had given me a lecture on chemotherapy before I had left Atlanta. "If you expect to get sick from your chemo, you will get very sick. Do not assume the worst . . . prepare for the worst, but hope for the best."

In the abstract, it sounded good, but I was scared to death of these powerful drugs. I had seen too many cancer patients wandering the halls, stopping to use their plastic nausea trays. I had heard stories of people who developed "anticipatory nausea," who threw up when they drove by the clinic just at the thought of their chemo, and horror stories of people who vomited for days after each treatment.

My primary doctor brought me the consent forms to sign before I took my chemo. "Before you sign, I have to inform you of potential side effects and risks. You want generalities or details?"

"I had rather have the details so I can spot any side effects," I said.

"On day one through day fourteen, you will take prednisone. It is a steroid. It will cause some redistribution in your body fat, can cause mood swings, and will increase your appetite."

"What are mood swings?"

"You might feel depressed one hour and exhilarated the next. We had one patient on prednisone who thought he was Jesus Christ!"

He continued. "On day one, you will get the following drugs intravenously: adriamycin, cytoxan, and VP-16. Adriamycin causes vomiting, hair loss and is harmful to your bone marrow. It can cause heart and liver damage but you will be closely monitored.

"Cytoxin causes nausea, hair loss, mouth ulcers, frequent urination, bladder irritation, and sometimes skin discoloration.

"On day eight, you will receive your second cycle of four drugs: vincristine, ARA-C, Bleomycin and Methotrexate. Bleomycin causes nausea, hair loss, bone marrow damage and can cause lung damage, although this is not common.

"Vincristine usually results in constipation and hair loss. You may experience 'neuropathies,' which will include jaw pain and numbness or cramps in your fingers and toes."

"Great," I said sarcastically.

"ARA-C causes. . . ."

"Enough!" I said, holding up my hand. "I've heard enough. All this is doing is scaring me. Are these drugs going to kill me or kill my cancer . . . or both?" I added as an afterthought.

"Mr. Jordan, they are going to kill your cancer for sure. The challenge is for them to kill every bit of your cancer, every cell . . . to leave the cancer so weakened that it can be cleaned up by your immune system. Along the way, they are going to play hell with your body and push it to the very limits, but we will monitor you very, very closely and deal with any problems that arise."

"Let's get started," I said as I signed the consent form and handed it back.

In a few minutes, the nurses had given me the anti-nausea drugs and had begun to give me intravenously the first "cycle" of the experimental protocol.

My favorite doctor walked into my room, smiled, and said, "Happy Birthday!"

I forced a smile. "Thanks for the presents," I said, nodding toward the IV.

He put his hand on my shoulder and squeezed me. "Mr. Jordan, I believe you are going to have many, many more birthdays."

"Do you really think so, doctor?"

"I really think so . . . and it is important that you think so too."

Although I felt wiped out and was heavily sedated from the drugs, the nausea never came. I waited and waited to be sick but instead felt better and better. My nurses were surprised.

"Unbelievable," a large, jolly nurse said. "You've got an iron stomach, Mr. Jordan."

By six o'clock, I was eating yogurt, calling my mother and siblings and celebrating my first treatment without horrible side effects.

Dorothy finally left the hospital after ten. I was exhilarated to be feeling good and had trouble sleeping. When no one was looking, I walked outside the hospital to enjoy the crisp breeze and clear fall sky. It was invigorating. I had dodged a bullet that day and was grateful. I wondered how much of it was just dumb luck and how much of it had been my determination not be to sick.

LIVING WITH CANCER

With the first treatment behind us, Dorothy and I tried to develop a normal routine and focus on life in the present tense. It was not easy; there was always something to do medically that reminded me that I had cancer. I had to take several different medicines every morning and evening. I had to take my temperature four times a day to spot any signs of early infection. I had to rinse my mouth out with a special preparation six times a day to reduce the occurrence of mouth sores and fever blisters, and I had to apply a special fluoride treatment to my teeth each night to ward off the decay that was aggravated by the chemo. Sleep was precious as bladder irritation caused me to get up every hour or so during the night.

All of these little medical chores cumulatively did not take more than an hour a day, but they were a constant reminder of my illness. In addition, there were always two or three visits to the hospital each week for blood counts, X rays, and chemo treatments. I realized that having cancer could become your full-time job and preoccupation. But I was determined not to let this happen.

I started to focus on my work and found that I could still be productive. I could even — for periods of time — put the disease out of my mind. The chemotherapy had reduced my energy level to 30 to 40 percent, but on most days I felt pretty good. I started back jogging the day after my first treatment and got up to two or three miles a day. The fact that I could get out and do this, feel the wind against my face and sweat on my brow, gave me an enormous lift.

With my chemo treatments now scheduled on a regular basis, Dorothy and I worked hard to develop a routine and make a normal home life for Hamilton Jr. We took regular trips to the zoo and savored visits from our families. Dorothy resumed her jogging, went to great lengths to cook me nutritious and healthy meals at those odd hours of the day and the night when I did have an appetite. Most importantly, she was my cheerleader and best friend. After a few months, our cozy Bethesda rental started to feel like home, and things seemed pretty normal.

But things were not normal.

I knew that I was receiving the best medical treatment in the world at NCI. But after the first cycle of chemotherapy was completed, I realized that while the doctors were doing great things for my body, they were doing nothing for my mind. And I understood why.

At a major research center where doctors are treating very sick patients and testing new protocols, there is little time left to worry about a patient's emotional condition. In the abstract, they all understand the benefits of a positive attitude, but there are not enough hours in the day to play doctor and therapist. And even when acknowledging the importance of the right attitude, their advice is superficial.

"Have a positive attitude," one young doctor suggested during a check-up. When I asked him what he meant, he said, "Just hang on!"

I was not content to just "hang on." I believed that there was much I could do to assist in a return to good health. But I realized ultimately that I would have to look inside myself to find the emotional and spiritual resources necessary to develop and sustain a positive attitude.

An obvious starting point was to talk to other cancer patients. They — not my doctors and nurses — were the ones who really understood what I was going through.

Some patients were withdrawn, depressed, and didn't even want to talk. One man about my age simply cut me off when I asked about his cancer: "Look, I've got my problems and you've got yours . . . just leave me alone! I don't want to talk to anybody."

But there were others who were talkative, laughing, and extroverted. One little old lady of about seventy kept me in stitches for about fifteen minutes with jokes about doctors and death. When she ran out of cancer jokes, she started in with some dirty jokes chock-full of four-letter words that could have been told in a Las Vegas nightclub. She cleared the area where we were sitting and talking.

I found this second group of patients had come to grips with their disease and the realities of cancer despite — in many cases — poor prognoses. In more cases than not, these people were doing well medically and exceeding their doctors' expectations.

I got one doctor who was treating me to talk about the impact of attitude on disease. "Look," he said, "you have two cancer patients with the same disease and the same prognosis. One goes home, cuts himself off from family and friends, locks himself in a room watching television, expects to die and does die. The other surrounds herself with the love and support of family and friends, continues working, is determined to beat cancer, and either does beat it or greatly exceeds the medical prognosis. Doctors know this anecdotally and know it instinctively. The problem is that we have trouble dealing with anything that we can't prove or quantify. Most of us just don't have time to think about this stuff."

As I talked to more and more cancer patients who exhibited this joy of life, I was inspired by their attitude . . . an attitude that I did not yet have. I gained a deeper understanding that theirs was not merely "a will to live." Many were in the late stages of their illness, were not expected to live or were being treated for rare diseases with highly experimental therapies because nothing else had worked. Although expressed in different ways, I heard the same thing time and again. They described their cancer as a "strange blessing" that had "focused their life" or made them "appreciate life." They cherished each day, every friend, and each gesture of love or affection.

Some dwelled on the importance of a spouse or loved one. Most mentioned religious faith. Several recommended particular books.

I went to the store and bought so many books that I carried them out to my car in a grocery cart. Some were goofy, others relied totally on prayer, and still others recommended untested diets or vitamins. I read ten or fifteen pages before putting most of them aside.

But two authors — Norman Cousins and Dr. Carl Simonton — have written books about the mind-body relationship that opened my mind to thinking about my illness in a totally different light. Both authors are grounded in practical knowledge, but with a healthy respect for things that we know but cannot necessarily prove.

Norman Cousins, a layman, wrote in *Anatomy of an Illness* how he refused to accept his doctor's death sentence for a bizarre degenerative disease. He described how he fought back, designed his own "treatment," and over a period of time was returned to full and normal health.

Dr. Carl Simonton, a radiation oncologist, had worked for twenty-five years to understand the impact of attitude on cancer. His book, *Getting Well Again*, is an inspiration for anyone with cancer.

The theme of both books is that the natural state of the human body is good health and that the body contains enormously effective natural healing powers which can be employed to beat disease. Indeed, every day, the human body's natural system kills germs, viruses, and cancer cells run amok. Both Cousins and Simonton believe — based on personal experience and years of study — that a person can help to muster these powers, and that a person's belief in the natural healing power of the human body can have a significant impact on the course of cancer.

These books said, in essence, that just because we do not understand how something works does not mean that it does not work. The medical profession has a name for the impact of a person's belief on the course of an illness — they call it the "placebo effect." It seemed strange that many in the medical profession can accept the reality of the "placebo effect" while distrusting theories and studies based on that same phenomenon.

Both authors strongly recommended that cancer patients work in active partnership with their health team, emphasizing the importance of attitude, stress reduction, exercise, diet, and the happiness that comes naturally from family and friends. Above all, they recommended that a person must have a purpose in life beyond their own narrow and selfish desire to survive.

These books became very important to Dorothy and me. Not because they contained some easy "secret cure," but because they were compatible with our own values and beliefs. I believe in a kind and benevolent God, but I have always felt that God helps those who help themselves. I cannot expect God to fight this battle for me alone — I must do my part. Sure, God is capable of miracles, but it is unlikely that he will waste one on me.

These authors provided me an intellectual framework to think about my cancer differently. I began to regard my body as a battlefield for the war being waged between the cancer cells and the chemotherapy. It was my job to keep my body — and mind — healthy and positive. Some mornings I would literally roll out of bed onto the floor because I did not have the energy to stand up. Eventually, however, I would stand up, and no matter how weak I felt, I would walk or even jog a couple of miles every day. And without exception, that exercise, that attempt at being normal gave me energy and hope to keep going.

I began to see for the first time that this ordeal could be the basis for refocusing my own life. Cancer does not have to be a curse . . . it can be an opportunity to gain insight into your life.

Once I believed that emotionally, spiritually, and intellectually, I could undergo anything . . . and was prepared for any outcome.

My remaining treatments went well but were not easy. Over the long haul, the powerful chemicals had a cumulative, debilitating effect on my body. Because my white blood cell "count" (which is the essence of the immune system) stayed surprisingly high, I asked my doctors to increase my dosage on the accepted theory that the more your body can tolerate, the better. After much internal debate — and my signing an entire new set of forms — they gave me the increased dosage for the last two months.

CHEMO CARRIES ME BACK TO OLD SAIGON

"Just relax," the nurse said reassuringly, patting my arm as she guided me down into the brown leather recliner in the "chemo room," the playful yellow and blue walls punctuated by a number of what the staff called "stations." Each station was a serious-looking reclining chair surrounded by bottles — full of colorful poisons — sitting atop tall, shiny rods on rollers and tethered by long tubes to the arms of patients.

On my first visit, she had pulled out a card and said, "I am going to read you your rights . . . ha, ha!" — then read in a quiet voice the different drugs she was giving me and the risks involved:

"Adriamyecin can cause permanent damage to your heart and kidneys. . . ."

I glanced around the room . . . a couple of patients were dosing, others read and one fidgeted nervously as he watched the drip . . . drip . . . drip of the liquid into the clear tube taped to his pale, bony arm.

"Vincristine can cause permanent nerve damage, including neuropathies. . . ."

I signed the release and watched closely as she tied the rubber strap around my arm and poked around for a vein in which to insert the large needle.

She chatted nonstop, her commentary spiced with one-liners that were funny the first time. By the third visit, I had heard them all and had to force a smile or slight chuckle to acknowledge her effort.

I realized over time that — like most of the medical staff at the National Cancer Institute — her chatter was nothing more than a defense mechanism. While at one level, she was certainly "connecting" to her patients, her constant blabber protected her from real conversation and from getting emotionally involved with the endless stream of poor souls that came her way. I couldn't really blame her; so many of the cancer patients who showed up at NCI had failed first- and even second-line therapies elsewhere and had come there to take their last, best shot.

She started me with an antinausea drip, which made me drowsy, before she began to feed in the five drugs in my experimental protocol. I hated the feeling that followed as the grogginess spread over my body; I felt punchy and was no longer clearheaded or in control.

I had tried reading, which never worked, and sometimes closed my eyes and pretended to sleep just to avoid having to talk to the nurses.

I told myself over and over again that it was wasted energy to try to wonder how I had contracted this disease. I fought it and rarely thought about it — except when I was taking my chemo and would find my mind drifting to the hidden origins of my illness and remembering Vietnam. . . .

I thought about those long, hot, and humid, days in a small town in the Mekong Delta called Tan An, life with the Vietnamese family where I was in language training, the bowls full of rice and vegetables — occasionally augmented with a piece of tough, barely chewable "beef," which — having "gone native" — I struggled to master with the chopsticks. After I learned that dog meat was a Vietnamese delicacy, I made a point of avoiding all meats.

I could remember like it was yesterday watching Ba Chu, the old grandmother, teeth black from eating betel nut, sitting in the open yard scrubbing the vegetables that would later be sold to the stands along the road, complaining nonstop about the "American poison" that had ruined the field where her family rented land and grew their precious vegetables.

Everyone in the village had a different story, but it turned out that on two or three occasions low-flying American planes had dropped some kind of herbicide on the thick jungle which ran along the river in an effort to "defoliate" areas where the Viet Cong were thought to be hiding at night.

The spray didn't kill any VC but seemed to have destroyed broad swaths of crops in the nearby fields. The angry villagers complained to their local officials that the Americans were destroying their livelihood. The "official response" was that the wind had blown the spray intended for the nearby jungle over onto the crops.

The villagers didn't care about the intentions . . . all they knew was that a lot of their crops had been destroyed.

During the first few weeks there, we met a few young U.S. military officers who were intrigued with Americans not in the military. They listened skeptically to our "mission" and — like many of the Vietnamese — suspected that we worked for the CIA. We wrangled a chopper ride from them, which allowed us to see the Mekong Delta from the air and to witness part of the "pacification" effort. On that day the effort amounted to our flying at several thousand feet over what they called "hostile populations" and hand-throwing cartoon-style leaflets from the helicopter that said, in essence, that the Saigon government and their allies — the U.S. military — were the good guys and the Viet Cong were the bad guys.

From several thousand feet or so, one of the young officers pointed out brown spots where the "herbicide" had been sprayed in an otherwise lush, green countryside.

"The stuff the Air Force sprays is ba-a-a-d stuff . . . it'll kill anything!"

The Vietnamese family I was living with told us that the leaflets we had seen dropped were very useful — as toilet paper for the rural Vietnamese.

It was years later before I would understand that this herbicide, containing dioxin, had been widely sprayed all over South Vietnam and that it was called Agent Orange because of the orange-colored bands around the 55-gallon drums containing the chemical spray. In what the U.S. Air Force designated "Operation Ranch Hand," an estimated one-tenth of the total land mass of South Vietnam, or about sixty-six hundred square miles, were sprayed with Agent Orange, 1967–69 being the years of highest activity and volume.

Because the low altitudes at which they flew exposed them to small-arms fire, the "Operation Ranch Hand" crews were the most highly decorated air units in the war.

After a number of scientific protests, the United States ceased to use Agent Orange in 1970. Years later, veterans — who were showing up with inordinate numbers of neuropathies and certain types of cancer — began to demand investigation by the U.S. government.

STOPPING COMMUNISM IN ASIA

It was not the way I had planned to arrive in Vietnam. After the long stuffy flight from Manila, I hurried off the plane and ducked into the dingy, humid bathroom in the Saigon airport, barely lit by a single bulb hanging from a cord. When I started to urinate, I felt an intense burning — like someone had set my crotch on fire. I had never felt a pain like that before and understood what it meant to "climb the wall." I had a sinking feeling that the innocent-looking young Filipino girl at the International Voluntary Services "going away" party in Manila was not so innocent after all.

I went "cold turkey," didn't drink another thing to avoid urinating. After a long wait going through customs, I found my way to a military compound and a smart-ass Army doctor.

"Welcome to Vi-e-t Nam, Mr. Jordan," he said sarcastically after looking at my urine under a slide. "Congratulations. It takes most guys a few weeks or months . . . you set some kind of record by arriving here with a first-class case of the clap."

I was embarrassed to death. I had never had any kind of venereal disease before and felt filthy all over. My first reaction was to take a hot shower and burn my clothes. The crazy thought crossed my mind that this would be reported home, but I said to myself, "Hell, I'm an adult, twenty-two years old, and halfway around the world . . . they are not going to write my parents!"

All such thoughts vanished as he pulled out a needle big enough for a horse, made me bend over and stuck it in my buttocks. He seemed to enjoy my discomfort.

My noble mission to Vietnam had begun on a low and humiliating note.

"What are you? CIA or what?"

Trying to recover some of my dignity, I said in my most serious voice, "I am a civilian volunteer. I am going to work in refugee relocation."

"Whaddaya mean, volunteer?"

"Well, I volunteered to come here."

"What are you getting, thirty, forty thou a year?"

"I make $120 a month," I responded proudly.

"Bullshit! You are either lying or crazy! Or both. And if you are telling me the truth, you need to go down the hall and see a shrink . . . nobody volunteers for this place. Vietnam is the asshole of the world!"

While many other young Americans had powerful reasons to go or not to go to Vietnam, my motivation was pretty simple — a sense of adventure. I had flat feet and a bad knee, which earned me a medical deferment from the draft, but I had a feeling that something important was happening in that distant place, and I wanted to see it firsthand.

However, when people asked why in the hell I was going "over there," *adventure* was not a very good answer. So I hid behind the more noble cause of "supporting my country." It was years later before I could admit to myself what a foolish and dangerous decision I had made.

But going into my junior year at the University of Georgia, I had no idea what I would do after graduation. The expectation of my family — with attorneys on both sides — was that I would practice law. I worked as an orderly at a hospital my junior year and senior year and enjoyed my lowly job making life just a little better for my patients. But I ended up with neither the desire to be a lawyer nor the grades to go to medical school. That's when I started thinking about going to Vietnam.

The antiwar movement had not penetrated the "juke-box room" at my fraternity house at the University of Georgia, where the brothers started gathering in the early afternoon every day to drink beer, swap stories, and sing along to "Louie-Lou-ee, Ooo-ooo . . . shake-o your thang!"

I had two types of friends. Some were in ROTC, the guys who dressed up in their uniforms a couple of times a week, marched around the campus, and played sol-dier. The others were the guys who — through their families or political connections — got into the National Guard summer programs ("Army Lite"), which required six weeks of basic training and sentenced them to once-a-month weekend duty for a couple of years and pretty much guaranteed that they would not be sent overseas. "The Viet Cong would have to be invading Miami before any of us get called up to active duty," one frat brother explained. The Guard was "a royal pain in the ass, but better than being shot in the ass in Nam."

I suppose there was the third type — students who were against the war, but none were visible at UGA, or else they were too smart to reveal their true feelings.

Then I read a magazine article about an organization called IVS (International Voluntary Services), which had operated since 1954. For very little pay, young people were assigned to work in third-world countries doing "community development" and agriculture work.

Described by the writer as the "Peace Corps" of Vietnam, the IVS was showing the Vietnamese people the "human face" of U.S. concern and were making their own special contribution to the effort. I was intrigued by the article and privately found it exciting and romantic. I fancied myself as a kind of "junior diplomat" for my country, doing my patriotic duty in this faraway and dangerous place.

My parents saw nothing good in this new idea and argued strenuously against my going. Nevertheless, while my mother cried at the airport and my father dabbed at his eyes with the white handkerchief he always wore in his suit pocket, I also knew that they took a certain amount of pride in my volunteering to go when so many others were going to great lengths to avoid military service at all costs.

I had bought myself a dark suit with thin gray stripes, a red tie, and some new black shoes and showed up at a Harpers Ferry, West Virginia, hotel for the two-week

"Ambassador Jordan"

IVS "indoctrination" before going to the Philippines for language training.

I arrived a bit early at the hotel to find a scruffy-looking bunch of people with long hair milling around, and I wondered where my group was meeting. But when I began to notice that several of these folks had on IVS "Hello" nametags, I realized that this was indeed my IVS "class." So there I was . . . standing there in the middle of a bunch of hippies with my pin-striped suit on. A few were friendly, others were not.

I started to meet them and learned their stories . . . they went to schools like Berkeley, Harvard, and Goshen. After a long and boring welcome and lecture on the history of IVS, a small group gathered on the porch after dinner, talking quietly among themselves and passing around cigarettes.

As I walked up, one of the guys asked, "Want a drag?" and stuck a foul-smelling little cigarette in my face.

Taken aback, I held up my hand and said. "No, no, no . . . I don't smoke."

"'Ambassador Jordan' does not smoke," someone snickered sarcastically. The entire group laughed . . . but the name stuck for a while.

As I smelled the weird odor from the smoke and heard the wisecracks, I finally realized that I had been offered pot.

TAN AN, SOUTH VIETNAM

My initial IVS "training" assignment in South Vietnam was intense language study while living with a Vietnamese family in the Mekong Delta. A teacher would come in during the morning and we would work for hours on pronunciation and vocabulary. Vietnamese is a very difficult tonal language where the same word said five different ways has five totally different meanings. There were a few in our group who "got it," but most of my colleagues and I struggled with the language, constantly trying it on the Vietnamese family with whom we lived and at the little roadside stands that sold fresh pineapple and warm Cokes.

Our little house sat off the main road to Saigon, and during the day U.S. and ARVN troops moved freely up and down the road. But at night, the Viet Cong ruled. We lived right on the river, and every night we went to sleep to the sound of the choppers as they meandered up and down the waterway using infrared technology, hoping to catch small groups of VC moving through the darkness.

I began doing refugee work in the Mekong Delta, trying to relocate vegetable farmers from the highlands of Vietnam whose villages had been taken over by the Viet Cong. And I — a twenty-three-year-old American who spoke about fifty words of Vietnamese and had never grown anything other than a mild beard — was supposed to help these lifelong farmers learn to grow rice.

RICE FARMING IN VIETNAM

I began to spend a lot of time at night reading books on the history of Vietnam. Quickly I came to view the ongoing conflict from a slightly different perspective. For over six hundred years, the Vietnamese people had been fighting their Chinese neighbors and later the colonial French, whom they finally drove out of Vietnam in 1954. We seemed merely to be the next group of foreigners passing through, fighting for objectives that the people neither understood nor shared. And we were supporting a corrupt military government that lacked the popular support of the Vietnamese people.

I knew that our nation's goals were noble in Vietnam and certainly seemed so to those in the White House. It was pretty simple: We were trying to "halt" communism in Southeast Asia and bring democracy to Vietnam.

But it seemed a lot to expect that the Vietnamese people — who had been fighting "foreign devils" for generations — would understand or appreciate what our country was doing. Why were the Americans any different from the Chinese or the French who brought war and devastation to their villages, destroyed their rice fields, and killed their sons and daughters?

Certainly, through their eyes, we were no different.

In early December 1967, I developed a stiff neck followed by a violent fever. When I finally got a thermometer, I realized from my hospital work that my fever — sometimes 105 or 106 — was dangerously high. After lying in my bed for several days, sweating and sleeping and sometimes delirious, the family that I was living with sent for an IVS volunteer in a nearby town.

Stu Bloch, Harvard '67, a loud-mouthed, wise-cracking radical who had been unmerciful in ribbing me, turned out to be my true friend. He found a small wagon, laid me on it with a pillow and blanket, and pulled me several miles to a local U.S. military post, where I was put in a jeep and driven to Cam Ranh Bay, the largest U.S. military base in Vietnam and immediately admitted to the military hospital and moved to an isolation ward.

CHRISTMAS AT CAM RANH BAY, SOUTH VIETNAM, 1967

"Oh my God . . . he's coming here! Can you believe it? He's coming here . . . the president is coming to our unit!" shouted one of the male nurses, waking me from a deep afternoon sleep.

All of a sudden, the long, low quonset hut that had been turned into a hospital ward with about thirty beds was a beehive of activity as nurses and orderlies emptied trash baskets, picked up around the beds, and buttoned their uniforms.

It took me a couple of minutes to find out what was happening, but I soon figured out that President Lyndon Johnson — returning from a trip to the funeral of Australian Prime Minister Harold Holt — had decided to pay a Christmas visit to "see his boys" by visiting our hospital.

By this time I had been in the hospital for three weeks, my illness still undiagnosed. Now not just my neck but my entire upper body was bent over in stiffness. The air force doctors initially thought it was some strange form of meningitis, but they were not sure and chalked it up to just one more strange tropical disease. The first week or ten days I had been heavily sedated and could barely remember my time in the isolation ward.

But once it was determined that I was not contagious and had begun to respond to a battery of antibiotics, I was moved to a regular ward. I was still sick and heavily medicated, and like clockwork — every four to six hours — my fever would shoot up and this huge knot (the size of a large lemon) would well up on the back of my neck.

While in pain and sedated, I was not so sick that I didn't realize that the soldiers around me quickly figured out I was not one of them, but a civilian "volunteer" — something they could not even comprehend. Neither brave nor a fool, I didn't even try to explain IVS . . . maybe they would think that I was an intelligence agent.

Our ward was a mixture of guys . . . a few recovering from battle wounds and surgery, others like myself who had malaria or other strange tropical diseases that they simply called malaria. A handful of the guys had developed a strain of gonorrhea that did not responded to penicillin or any other drug. Their situation had stabilized and was under control, but they were still "sexually contagious." These poor saps were not going to be allowed to return to the States until they were "clean."

As these guys were "long-timers," who weren't acutely sick and knew all the ropes, they tended to have the run of our ward. Their leader was a loud-mouthed marine named Grimes, whom everyone called "Grimey" — not a term of affection but an accurate description of his coarse appearance and foul mouth. Short and built like a tank, Grimey acted like he was in charge of our ward, and at some level he probably was.

One morning early in my hospital stay when I was having a difficult time even moving my upper body, Grimey jumped on top of my chest, pinned my shoulders down with his knees, and yelled out, "Okay, Georgee-boy . . . tell us why you volunteered to come to this shit hole? You're not a really a volunteer, are you? Betcha you're a rich spy or CIA? Or maybe just a queer? I bet you are a queer . . . I've got something for you to eat that's better than that crap they serve here. Want it? Do you want it, Georgee-boy? I bet you do!"

Although on my back with the big marine sitting on my chest, I tried to hit him with my good left arm, but I telegraphed my feeble half-swing, and he easily deflected it.

"Oh . . . Georgee-boy wants to fight?" he mocked as he started to playfully slap my face with his open palms, then slapped me a few times really hard. He finally balled one fist and delivered a serious punch which glanced off my nose and hit my eye. I started to cuss him and struggled to get up when a large pair of black hands encircled the marine's neck from behind, literally lifted Grimes up in the air and threw him onto the floor.

I knew it was Willie Roberts, a black air force orderly from Bainbridge, Georgia, about sixty miles from my hometown of Albany, Georgia. A huge, soft-spoken man who carried himself with great dignity, Willie had changed my bed when I was unable to move and had brought me rags with ice to break my fever. We had long conversations about family back home or about his shopping trips to "Aw-benny" when he was a boy.

Grimey now found himself on the floor, with Willie sitting on his chest, his hands tightly gripping the marine's bulging red neck. Grimey was flailing his arms wildly when Willie got right in his face and said in a low voice, "You chicken-shit marine, next time I catch you messing with my sick Georgia buddy, I'm gonna whup yo ass, understand! I gonna wipe this floor with your ugly face, understand? Do you understand?"

Grimey's beet-red face shook up and down until Willie let him go. He lay on the floor for another minute or so, his chest heaving up and down, breathing heavily. He glared at me as he pulled himself to his feet, and the small crowd that had gathered drifted away.

I waited in fear for the next few days for Grimey to exact his revenge when Willie was off-duty. But Grimey never said another word to me, and his reign over our ward came to a crashing end. For the rest of my stay, he kept to himself and his few marine buddies and was ignored by the rest of the ward.

Life was easier for me as I began to recover.

Suddenly, the quonset hut door flew open and the president's entourage entered — Johnson towering above them, with large, almost floppy ears, and dressed in khakis and a tan shirt covered with a flak jacket. Johnson was bigger than I expected and moved easily and quickly and with purpose. When he stopped to talk or shake hands, he seemed to pull the person toward him at the same time or to bend over for those too sick to sit up. The effect was that the soldiers had the president of the United States right in their face.

He worked the quonset hut like he might have worked a crowd of voters, moving at lightning speed down the long row of beds — waving to one, shouting a greeting to another, flashing a smile, and stopping at each fifth or sixth bed. Occasionally — when directed by the docs — he would pin a purple heart on the wounded soldiers . . . and in one case a medal for bravery.

When the president was three or four beds away, he caught my eye and appeared to be moving in my direction.

"Where you from, soldier?" he shouted out.

"Georgia," I said proudly.

Johnson started to smile when suddenly Grimey yelled out, "He's not a soldier, Mr. President. He's a peacenik!"

Johnson's head jerked back like I was a leper; he turned to the air force doc in charge, who whispered something into the president's large ear. He must have confirmed I was not a soldier as Johnson's exaggerated smile turned to rows of unhappy wrinkles. He glared at me for an instant and quickly moved to the bed across the aisle.

I felt both humiliated and cheated . . . I had planned to tell him about my Georgia roots and about working in Washington as an intern for his old friend, Senator Richard Russell, but I was dumbstruck and just sat there as the parade moved on. My once-in-a-lifetime chance to actually meet a president had been ruined by some jerk with a big mouth. I was devastated and fought back tears.

I left the hospital at Cam Ranh Bay a few weeks later. The huge knot on the back of my neck had marched up and down for several weeks, and finally — after a sustained assault of new antibiotics — it gradually disappeared. The red-headed air force doctor told me, "I don't know what in the hell it was . . . whatever it was, we probably don't even have a name for it in American medicine. I'm going to put it down as 'dengue fever.'"

He sent me to Saigon with strict orders to take it easy for a few weeks before I returned to my assignment in the mountains near Nha Trang. I was too weak to do anything so I hung around the IVS house practicing my

RECOVERING FROM "DENGUE FEVER," CAM RAHN BAY HOSPITAL

Vietnamese with a young teacher who came to the house to coach anyone who needed language help. I certainly qualified.

On the eve of Tet, the Vietnamese New Year, we awoke in the middle of the night to the noise of shelling, which we assumed was directed at the air base not far away. But soon we heard small-arms fire in the street, and we began to "feel" the shells as they literally shook our house, the lights flickering off and on.

Although we had no sense of it then, the Tet Offensive — which would mark the turning point in the war — had begun.

The IVS veterans at our house — some of whom were ten-year Vietnam veterans — recognized that this was more than just random shelling and quickly agreed that a houseful of Americans in the middle of Saigon could be a prime target for the Viet Cong. Using flashlights, we were led quickly through the narrow streets that night to nearby houses, and I hid under the bed of a tiny house until the heavy shelling ended the next morning and the gunfire became sporadic.

Back at the IVS house, we heard over the Armed Forces Radio Network that the Viet Cong had launched a well-coordinated offensive all over the country, making a mockery of the U.S. claim that we were winning "the hearts and minds" of the Vietnamese people. Indeed, the Tet Offensive demonstrated that the Viet Cong could strike at will — whenever and wherever they wanted to — even in the capital city.

A few days later, we got reports that a couple of IVS volunteers were missing and believed to be captured and that one, a conscientious objector, had been killed. I was sure that the Viet Cong assumed that any Americans mingling with the people and attempting to speak the language were "CIA."

It was a cruel irony . . . conscientious objectors half way around the world trying to help war victims had been killed in the very conflict they had opposed. Just as there was no good way for the American GIs to tell the difference between a friendly boy running along-side their tank and a Viet Cong prepared to toss a grenade down the hatch, we could hardly expect the Viet Cong to know the difference between GIs, intelli-gence agents, and do-gooders.

In the aftermath of the Tet offensive, IVS offered to cancel the contracts of its volunteers. A few stayed, but many went home.

I was confused, scared, and ready to leave.

The hospital stay and the Tet Offensive had wrung all of the romance out of Vietnam for me. I realized that I had flirted with death and that no American in Vietnam was safe anywhere . . . from germs or from bullets.

I did not want to die in that distant land for a cause I did not understand and for a reason I could not even articulate. The war permeated every aspect of life in South Vietnam. I concluded it was impossible for a white American to have a significant impact helping these people. We could be in the villages each day, struggling to speak their language, eating their rice, and making tiny steps toward what the pacification experts called "community development." But at night the Viet Cong would return with a nationalistic message, rice, and weapons. It was no contest.

At best, we were a symbol of our country's good intentions. At worst, in the minds of many Vietnamese, we had become the enemy, the reason for the killings, the destruction of their crops, the suffering.

Not many had the chance to leave as I did. Not the young men drafted, trained, and dumped into the middle of this strange war. Not the Vietnamese people who had been fighting foreign invaders for the past six hundred years. Nor the tens of millions of Vietnamese people who had no particular political ideology and only wanted to be left alone to live in peace and to grow their rice and vegetables.

The reaction to my coming home was disappointing in every respect. I thought that people might thank me for my attempted service.

Those who were "hawks" only knew that I had gone over as a civilian, had come home early, and had not been in the military. Those few who were beginning to question U.S. involvement or were against the war only knew that I had been in Vietnam with some government agency. When I came home to Georgia and had time to clear my head, I was sure that my country — with the very best intentions — had made a huge mistake in undertaking what President Eisenhower had warned against — a land war in Asia. Most importantly, we had confused nationalism with Communism and had allowed our obsession with Communism to drag us into the wrong war in the wrong place for the wrong reasons.

As one general said, "The only way to win the war is to destroy Vietnam." Based on my short time there, that is exactly what we had tried to do . . . but we had neither destroyed Vietnam nor won the war.

I kept looking for black-and-white answers in Vietnam — a way to reconcile our good intentions with the mess that had been created — and all I could see were shades of gray.

——————

Lying there in the chemo room at NCI, I watched the slow drip . . . drip . . . drip of the clear liquid that I hoped would save my life. As I watched the liquid move in fits and starts down the tube enroute to my arm, I realized that neither Vietnam nor cancer made much sense.

Our country had lost one war where I was nothing more than a bystander. Now I was as totally involved as one could be in a battle for my own life.

I wondered if I would win.

NCI, ROY COHN, AND D.C. DAYS

Several months later, I was at NCI for a checkup, and, while feeling my stomach for possible enlarged lymph nodes, one of my favorite young clinicians teased me by saying, "You're not the only big shot around here."

"Former big shot," I said, trying to sound uninterested. I assumed he was talking about the famous Washington attorney Edward Bennett Williams, who was being treated at NCI while bravely battling colon cancer. I had bumped into him on several occasions in the chemo room.

"Yep, this guy was really big, but long before your time . . . Roy Cohn. You know who he was, don't you?"

I almost fell off the table. I knew him only too well. Unfortunately, he was not before my time. In fact, he had successfully smeared me just as he had many others in a long and controversial career that started as Joe McCarthy's henchman back in his red-baiting days in the early 1950s.

"What the hell is Roy Cohn doing here?"

"Officially, he is here for cancer," he said sarcastically, "But we are treating him for advanced AIDS, which he denies that he has."

It did not surprise me that this man, whose reputation and public image had been built on lies, might die living one.

———————

I had never met Roy Cohn, but I felt like I knew him. I remembered seeing old news clips of Cohn sitting at Senator Joseph McCarthy's side during the hearings which bore his name, whispering in his ear with tidbits and cues, which the Senator used to paint good and often innocent people as "Communist sympathizers" and "reds." I remembered the riveting response of Joseph Welsh, General Counsel for the U.S. Army, who was defending a young associate (Fred Fisher) whom McCarthy and Cohn were attempting to smear:

> Senator, I have ceased to be surprised by your reckless conduct and your willingness to stoop to any level to smear innocent people. Let us not

assassinate this lad further, Senator.
You have done enough. Have you no
decency, sir, at long last? Have you no
sense of decency?

That exchange in 1954 began to turn the tide of public opinion against McCarthy and Cohn and marked the
beginning of the end for McCarthy's reign of terror, as
more and more good people stood up to their bullying
tactics. McCarthy was quickly discredited and defeated,
and he died in 1957.

Roy Cohn never made a political comeback nation-
ally, but practiced law in New York City, cultivated
contacts with key members of the media, and would
pop up every now and then representing some
celebrity (like Donald Trump) in some highly public
divorce settlement or scandal.

It was an unbelievable irony that a quarter of a century later (1979) Roy Cohn could concoct a scandal
involving me and successfully sell it to the major news
organizations. Roy Cohn had shrewdly exploited my
vulnerability — my unattractive public image, which
had been largely created by the gossip columnists and
Washington pundits — for the benefit of his clients.

WUNDERKIND TO FOOL IN SIX SHORT MONTHS

When we arrived in Washington, I had been hailed as a political genius, but it did not take long for my reputation and image to be reduced to that of a cartoon character.

I thought about the long road to the White House, those hard years when I would drive the ex-governor of Georgia in my beat-up green VW to the Atlanta airport to catch a plane to New Hampshire or Iowa. In those days, our fledging campaign could not afford two tickets, and Jimmy Carter would fly coach to Iowa or New Hampshire and be met by volunteers who would drive him around and put him up in their homes.

People didn't laugh at us openly, but some of our friends and even some members of my own family snickered at us behind our backs — a peanut farmer from Georgia running for president of the United States? Preposterous!

The only thing that kept me going through those years was the dream of Jimmy Carter's presidency and the possibility of changing politics in this country — challenging the status quo and shaking up the Washington political establishment, so out of touch with the mood and needs of the American people.

Working in the White House was never a goal of mine, but when I was offered the chance to go with the president-elect to Washington, I was caught up in the excitement of the moment and said "Yes" to that once-in-a-lifetime opportunity. I never wanted to be a public figure, and I certainly never dreamed that I would become a controversial figure and ultimately a political liability for the man and the cause that I served.

Because Jimmy Carter was not a product of Congress or well-known to the political establishment, there was an inordinate curiosity about him. As a result of their long years in Congress and Washington, Presidents Ford, Nixon, Johnson, and Kennedy were well-known to the press and to the movers and shakers in the Washington political establishment.

But Jimmy Carter was an enigma, and his success was both celebrated and resented by the Democratic establishment. It was bad enough that they did not know him or have any stake in his candidacy, but to make matters worse, Carter had defeated their own favorites — Morris Udall, Birch Bayh, Scoop Jackson, et al. — in political battles all over the country.

By the time we arrived in Washington, there was a strong but subtle feeling: "You guys from Georgia won the White House by running against Washington, through politician gimmickry and just plain dumb luck . . . but we are going to show you who is Boss in this town!"

As a result of Carter's unexpected success in the Democratic primaries, Jody Powell and I had the highest public profile among the people around Jimmy Carter. Jody was always at Carter's side and became a familiar and popular figure to the members of the national press who traveled with Carter and covered the

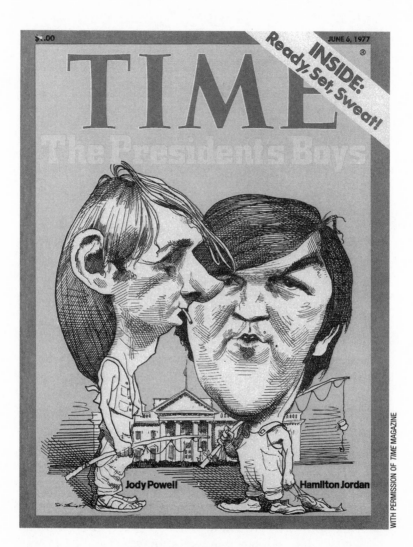

"FROM WUNDERKIND TO FOOL"

campaign. They appreciated Jody's quick mind, his access to the candidate, and his sharp wit. Initially, Jody was inaccurately perceived as playing the traditional and limited role of "mouthpiece." Over time, the press realized that Jody was a key influence on Carter as well.

Because I was the campaign manager and was given exaggerated credit for the campaign strategy that carried Carter to Washington, there was always great curiosity about me and my future role in the White House. I had never traveled with candidate Carter, and only rarely granted press interviews. . . . I figured it was my role to stay in the background and do my job. Consequently, I became a mystery to the national press corps.

After the general election, I worked closely with Carter and Fritz Mondale on the selection of the Cabinet, rarely granted interviews to the press, and ended up in the large corner office of recent chiefs-of-staff . . . even though we had vowed repeatedly throughout the campaign not to have a powerful chief-of-staff.

I realized that I was in trouble when I read an article in the *Washington Post* by Sally Quinn describing me as the "second-most powerful person in Washington."

"My God," I told Jody, "I've been set up for a great big fall!"

Even I could not imagine how big and how sudden my "fall" would be.

I had never been a public person and had trouble thinking of myself as one. I was wrong and naive in the extreme for failing to appreciate the fact that anyone who worked at the White House — and particularly someone like myself who had a long and close relationship with the president and worked in the office that had been occupied by Sherman Adams, Clarke Clifford, and H. R. Haldeman — was a highly public person, like it or not. And that public position carries with it certain responsibilities, including the need to be at least responsive if not proactive in dealing with the press. By shunning the national press in hopes of keeping a low profile, I instead helped to create an atmosphere that allowed a highly unattractive image of myself to be presented.

Despite the perception that developed of my being a playboy and a rube, I spent most of my first year physically at the White House, working fourteen and sixteen hours, seven days a week. I never went out socially and had no desire to be part of the Washington "scene." This was interpreted by many as a sign of my contempt, and one of the constant complaints about the "Georgia mafia" was that it was difficult to get them — "particularly Jordan" — to attend any of their gatherings.

Vice President Mondale — who had an office next to mine — had become a close friend and adviser. He was very much a part of the Washington establishment and strongly recommended that I "get out more" and let people get to know me.

I decided to attend a small dinner party given by Barbara Walters in honor of the Israeli and Egyptian ambassadors to celebrate progress made toward an

Israeli-Egyptian peace agreement. I was seated next to the Egyptian ambassador's wife at a table that included Henry Kissinger, humorist Art Buchwald, and ABC newsman Sam Donaldson. It was a typical dinner party with interesting people and congenial conversation. There were too many toasts, which made for a very long evening, but otherwise it was uneventful and enjoyable. I was glad to have gone and felt that I had at least begun to pay my dues to social Washington. Perhaps it would be another couple of months before I had to make an appearance at another one.

Several weeks after the dinner, a scathing article appeared in the "Style" section of the *Washington Post*, the theme of which was that the Carter people worked too hard, ignored the social mores of the Capital City, and were paying a big price politically for not being more a part of the cultural fabric of the city. And, of course, when the Carter people did socialize, they made fools of themselves.

The evidence cited was that when attending Barbara Walters's dinner for the Egyptian and Israeli ambassadors I had grabbed the bodice of the Egyptian ambassador's wife, peered down her dress, and declared loudly, "I have always wanted to see the pyramids!"

Because it appeared in the "Style" section of the *Post*, the reaction initially was not serious, and no one seemed too concerned about it. In fact, most people seemed to think that it was funny . . . except me, because I knew that nothing remotely like that had ever happened.

And it seemed to make absolutely no difference that I denied the story unequivocally, or that the Egyptian ambassador's wife, Mrs. Ghorbal — a lovely, matronly lady, old enough to be my grandmother — denied it emphatically or that every other person at our table denied seeing or hearing anything like the incident so vividly detailed in the *Post* article.

But the "pyramids" story just became part of my political biography and was accepted without question by others, adding to the litany of other funny and outrageous stories about me that started out in the gossip columns and soon gained momentum and credibility through their appearance in political columns or their mention on the television talk shows. Most of these stories were totally or largely untrue.

The muckraker Jack Anderson, for example, wrote that I and the president's close friend Charles Kirbo — himself a distinguished attorney — had taken a $10 million bribe from fugitive Robert Vesco to put the fix in for him with the Justice Department. Made up out of whole cloth, Anderson's story prompted a grand jury investigation that lasted almost a year just as another grand jury was organized to investigate alleged wrongdoings in the operation of the Carter Peanut Warehouse in Plains. (The special prosecutor concluded in his final report that "not one peanut" was missing.)

The last conversation that I had with my dear father — the night before he died — he was sobbing into the phone as he said, "Son, I just don't understand why those people up there don't just leave you alone?"

I put up a brave front, told people that it "came with the territory," but I was terribly embarrassed and hurt. Try as I could to laugh all of these stories off, I could not ignore the fact that I had quickly become defined — not by my actual work — but by these outrageous and largely inaccurate allegations.

As Jody was fond of saying, "The truth never, never catches up with the wild rumor or the interesting and funny gossip."

But when the FBI knocked on the door of my little apartment around 10:00 P.M. in August 1979, I was no longer able to dismiss it as gossip or as pundits taking potshots at me merely because I worked for the president.

While the FBI had interviewed me probably a half-dozen times regarding various charges made against members of our administration, this one seemed different — the call from the agent at night, the insistence that they interview me right away, and the refusal to discuss the reason.

The two agents who showed up at my apartment were polite but all business: "Anything that you say here can be used against you in a court of law . . . you have a right to an attorney. . . ."

I started squirming but tried to calm myself, thinking, "For God's sake, Hamilton, don't act like you have done anything wrong! How you react could determine whether these guys believe you or not."

Did I remember, they asked, being in New York with Jody Powell in the spring of 1978, and did I remember going to the fashionable New York City nightclub, Studio 54, with Jody?

I told them that I did remember going there briefly on one occasion, that I didn't remember the time or date, but that I did not remember Jody's being with me.

They asked me some more questions, and then showed me a series of pictures, and asked me to identify them. I told them that I did not know or remember any of the persons in the pictures.

Finally, the real purpose of their visit became crystal-clear: "Did you — while in Studio 54 on the occasion that you did visit — use the drug cocaine?"

I told them absolutely that I had not, that I had never, never used drugs and that people who knew me would confirm that. While I was still nervous at the idea of the FBI visit, I was actually relieved to learn how ridiculous the charge was and knew that no credible person anywhere could or would claim to having seen me use drugs. Ironically, I was considered hard-nosed and a "tiger" on drug use among people in the campaign and now in the White House. I was not naive as to what was going on socially in the late 1970s and the widespread recreational use of cocaine, but I had warned our young staff time and time again that drug use would simply not be tolerated. As I often said, "When you work in this building — the White House — you do not have the luxury to pick and choose which laws you will obey."

When I demanded the source of the story, they told me that two men, Steve Rubell and Ian Schrager, said that I used cocaine at Studio 54. They went on to tell me that Rubell and Schrager were the owners of Studio 54 and that they had recently been indicted for income tax fraud.

"Oh, I see . . . these guys are trying to plea bargain with the Justice Department. Trying to get off or have their sentence reduced by producing criminal information about me!" I would have taken the situation much more seriously if I had known then — as I would learn later — that Roy Cohn represented Rubell and Schrager, that he had taken the bogus charges to the Justice Department and had already leaked the story to the press.

But the agents told me nothing more, refused to comment on my observation and warned me not to try to talk with Jody until the FBI could interview him so that there would be no allegations of collusion between us.

It turned out that Jody was on a trip with the president down the Mississippi River. He called me the next morning after his interview.

"You weren't even with me the night I went to Studio 54," I told Jody indignantly. To me, the charges were utterly outrageous, lacked any credibility, and were obviously motivated by an attempted plea bargain. "Maybe this will be a three-day story and blow over," I suggested hopefully.

"Are you kidding?" Jody responded. "The president's

top aides, a president who is a born-again Christian, Studio 54, drugs . . . they will have to deal with it. Batten down the hatches because we are going to have a bumpy few days here."

But even Jody could not anticipate how seriously the charges would be treated. The next morning, the *New York Times* ran a headlined front-page story, which in turn stimulated calls to my office and the press office from the major networks and the top correspondents from other news organizations.

I sat in the office in the West Wing of the White House alone. Jody had been right . . . this charge against me was already a big story, and it was going to get bigger fast. I was totally vulnerable to these outrageous charges because they would be piled on top of all the other untrue but reported stories. I had very few real friends in the media who would stand up for me.

Still waiting for President Carter and Jody to return, I wrote the president a memo stating that I had not taken drugs and had never used drugs. I also said that I feared that my being under investigation while a member of his staff was unfair to him and I stated my intention to resign.

I was sitting in the Oval Office when the president and Jody returned. Jody was feisty, arguing that the charges were baseless and that most members of the press would believe us. I told him that I was not so sure after reading the *Times* story and seeing the flood of requests for interviews.

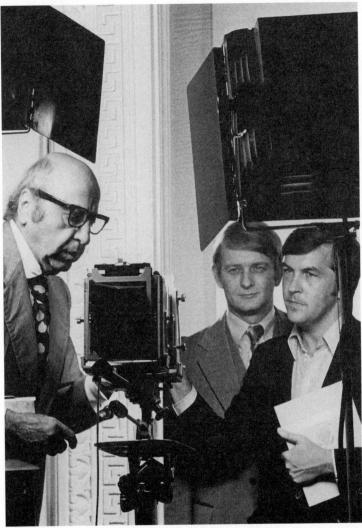

BEING PHOTOGRAPHED WITH JODY POWELL
BY RENOWNED PHOTOGRAPHER YOUSUF KARSH

Carter agreed with Jody but reminded us both that as the ultimate law enforcement officer of the United States, he would have to be careful and conservative in what he could say publicly.

After that conversation, I walked back into the president's small office, just off the Oval Office, handed him my resignation memo, and left.

In a few minutes, the president called me on the direct line and asked me to join him in the Oval Office. He came from around the desk, put his arm over my shoulder, and said, "Ham, your leaving will not help anything. . . . I will lose both ways. Some will see your resignation as confirmation of your guilt and I will be denied your services at a very critical time for the administration. It is in your interest and my interest to stay and fight this thing through."

The most damaging and outrageous treatment of the charges was a major story that led off the "CBS Evening News." It was introduced by Walter Cronkite, reported in detail by Mike Wallace, and finally concluded with an "analysis" by Bob Pierpoint, the White House correspondent. The three segments together lasted longer than eight minutes . . . almost half of the total "budget" (twenty minutes) of the entire news report.

The CBS News story focused on a trip I had made earlier in the year to a Democratic Party fundraiser in Southern California. Two well-known liberal fundraisers and political opponents of the Carter Administration (they were already actively raising funds for Ted Kennedy's primary challenge) told Mike Wallace that they had heard that I used drugs on that trip. Several other people who were interviewed also said that they had heard I had used cocaine, but they had not produced a single witness to my using cocaine.

I was devastated as I sat in my office and saw this outrageous report. . . . I felt like someone had punched me in the stomach. The Mike Wallace story took every single allegation and insinuation from the mouths of people I had never seen and did not know — however groundless or reckless — and treated them as absolute truth. Wallace accepted allegations made by third parties and discounted or rejected outright my unequivocal denial conveyed by Jody to the executive producer of CBS News, as well as the assertions by credible third parties that no one had ever known or even heard of my taking drugs.

Our denials were all for naught. Any reasonable person watching the "CBS Evening News" would have concluded that Carter's chief-of-staff was an out-of-control cocaine user and a jerk to boot.

After watching the CBS report, I began to think that my first instinct to resign was the right thing to do. Who knows, I thought, I might be asked to resign. I could not argue with anyone who went to the president (or came to me on his behalf) and simply said, "This thing is hurting the president . . . you need to step down."

It seemed that no one — not even the members of the press who knew me from covering the campaign — would risk coming to my defense or challenging the momentum of this story, which was running so strongly against me. It seemed to make no difference that my accusers were plea bargaining with the Justice Department and were represented by Roy Cohn. Had the press totally forgotten about the tactics he had honed in the McCarthy hearings?

The only person who spoke out on my behalf was Jimmy Breslin, a journalist whom I had never met but who had watched Roy Cohn and Company operate in New York City.

"Hamilton Jordan is the most maligned person in the nation today," Breslin wrote. "Whores shriek and deadbeats smirk that Jordan has sniffed cocaine in their presence. And the news industry rushes to make important their statements. The *New York Times*, using the claims of people from a place like Studio 54 . . . ran a story on the first page that left me with the impression that Jordan had killed several babies. CBS used six minutes of its evening news show to herald rumors spread by sleaze."

The investigation dragged on for ten months.

PRESUMED GUILTY

My grandfather used to say, "The road to hell is paved with good intentions."

I had become a victim of such good intentions — and had been practically to hell. With the abuses of the

Nixon White House and the "Saturday Night Massacre" (when Nixon had fired his own prosecutor, Archibald Cox) fresh in the national memory, we introduced a law that mandates the appointment of a special prosecutor when any serious charge is made against a "high government official." While the basic tenet of our legal system is that the accused is presumed innocent, under the special prosecutor's law — as a practical matter — we learned that the accused is considered guilty until he or she can prove their innocence.

The logic against me ran something like this: Jordan is guilty of outrageous social behavior . . . he made obscene gestures to the wife of the Egyptian ambassador, he has been a jerk around Washington, he was accused of taking a bribe from Robert Vesco, he probably has a drinking problem, so if he went to the "back room" at Studio 54, he probably used cocaine!

But truth ultimately prevailed, and I remember the "celebration" in my office in the White House on the afternoon that Independent Counsel Arthur Christy announced that the grand jury had voted 24–0 against bringing an indictment against me. Christy — who obviously had figured out the scam that Roy Cohn had almost pulled off — announced that there was no serious evidence against me and told a few key press people on background that I had been "set up" by Roy Cohn and friends.

Attorney General Ben Civiletti — who had replaced Griffin Bell when he resigned and had appointed the special prosecutor — visited the president in the Oval Office shortly before my public exoneration and told Carter that he had considered bringing indictments against Rubell, Schrager, and Cohn for their perjury and their obvious conspiracy to bring false charges against me. Attorney General Civiletti told the president that he had decided not to bring charges as it was "not in Hamilton's best interest to do so."

I wished the attorney general had asked me what I thought were in my best interests.

The spontaneous celebration that broke out in my West Wing office following the announcement that I had been cleared was awkward and embarrassing for me. Someone popped a bottle of champagne and friends from the White House dropped by or called to express their support. Some even "congratulated" me.

I was sure that I had not done anything to earn anyone's congratulations, and it was hard as hell to think that I had "won" anything.

I had embarrassed the president, and I had violated "Clifford's Law." Mr. Clark Clifford, a key aide to President Harry Truman and the dean of Washington "insiders," told me in my office soon after our inauguration, "Whenever the press is writing stories about the staff — good or bad — it is space that could have been devoted to the president and the administration's goals and policies."

To the extent that I cared about my "public reputation" — and at some level, I certainly did — I knew that it would be forever tainted by these silly allegations.

I should have taken some short-term satisfaction when Rubell and Schrager went to jail to serve time for tax fraud charges. However, after a brief stay in a minimum-security facility, they were out, celebrated in New York social and media circles.

Studio 54 finally closed as the disco era wound down, and Schrager and Rubell went on to other things. Rubell ultimately died of AIDS. Schrager opened the first of a series of trendy hotels in New York City and around the country and the world.

During the middle of the Studio 54 investigation of me, an anonymous person — maybe trying to be helpful or to even some old score with Roy Cohn — sent me some intimate photographs of Steve Rubell and Roy Cohn that insinuated a romantic relationship between the two. I did not know the real truth, but I did know that despite a highly publicized career of exposing people in government as "dangerous homosexuals" who were vulnerable to blackmail by the Russians, Cohn himself was widely believed to be gay.

I felt uncomfortable even looking at the pictures and never used them in any way. If the tables were turned, there is little doubt what Roy Cohn would have done.

And now, six years later, Roy Cohn was right here at the National Cancer Institute, fighting for his life just like the rest of us. And to think . . . he was right down the hall!

I remembered the scene from *The Godfather* where the assassin goes to the hospital to smother some ailing rat fink with a pillow. I relished the thought of walking into Roy Cohn's room, identifying myself, giving him a piece of my mind, and having him at least worry about my intentions.

Later that day, I used my friendship with a nurse to locate Roy Cohn's room. Ignoring the red "Warning" and "Posted" signs taped all over the door, I stuck my head in the door, ready to surprise Cohn and say my piece.

The room was dimly lit, and when my eyes finally focused, I could see that Cohn's famous bug-eyes were closed, his face and neck covered with dark splotches. The brash, in-your-face character from old news clips was taking loud and irregular breaths from an oxygen mask that covered his face.

I just stood there with my head poked inside the door for a few seconds, unable to enjoy his plight, seeing only another human being wasted by disease.

Suddenly I felt a tap on my shoulder. "Do you have a visitor's pass, sir?" the nurse asked.

Surprised, I mumbled an apology and hurried quickly down the hall.

Toward the end of his life, Roy Cohn's life began to catch up with him. A few months after I saw him at

NCI, the New York State Supreme Court, whom he denounced as "yo-yos" and a "bunch of blithering idiots," voted unanimously to disbar him from the practice of law, and said his behavior as a lawyer had been "unethical," "unprofessional," and, in one case, "particularly reprehensible."

Cohn did not take it laying down, showing people his personal "get well" notes from President and Nancy Reagan. He speculated in the *Washington Post* as to whether the president or first lady would attend his funeral and bragged about the fact that Attorney General William French Smith was a good friend and had attended both of his Reagan inauguration parties.

He died in August 1986. The *New York Times* repeated Cohn's claim that he had cancer. The White House issued a statement that "The Reagans are saddened at his passing and extend their sympathy to his family." Roy Cohn would have liked — and expected — that.

MAGIC WORDS

This part of my story ends where it began, with a doctor looking at X rays up against a viewing screen. The young NCI doctor held the films up to the light . . . one at a time.

"Nothing there, nothing there, nothing there . . ."

BALD AND BLOATED AFTER CHEMOTHERAPY

When he paused at one film, I held my breath.

"Nope, that's just scar tissue. Mr. Jordan, based on these X rays, I am happy to tell you that you are a CR for sure!"

"CR" stood for "complete remission" and meant that blood work, X rays, and palpation had revealed no sign of cancer. It didn't mean that there were not some hidden cells beyond the view of these modern tests and instruments.

"There is not a sign of cancer anywhere."

I gave the surprised doctor a bear hug that caused him to drop the X rays all over the floor. I babbled a quick apology, left him down on his knees picking up the film, and started running down the hall to the pay phone. I heard him yell down the hall after me, "Now, you will still have to have regular checkups and be followed closely. . . ."

"I understand, Doctor. I understand. Thanks so much!" I yelled.

By the time Dorothy answered the phone, I was sobbing like a baby.

We had probably beaten cancer. It had not been easy. I was completely bald, bloated from steroids, and vain enough that I stopped shaving in the bathroom so I wouldn't have to look at myself in the mirror. The industrial-strength chemo with the "kicker" tacked on at the end had taken its toll on my body, and, according to my doctors, had rendered me sterile.

The good news was that my cancer was gone. There were no guarantees. I would live under a cloud for a few years with monthly checkups, X rays, and blood tests. But I had earned at least the chance to live a normal life with Dorothy and watch my son grow up.

I considered myself a very lucky man.

ALBANY, GEORGIA

I followed my doctors' orders closely and continued to be checked regularly . . . once a month, then every three months, then six months, and finally once a year.

I didn't become a hypochondriac, but I listened to my body more closely than most and didn't hesitate to visit a doctor when I had a real pain or worry. I also began to see a lot of stories in the press about skin cancers and decided to see a dermatologist in 1991.

As I was shown to the exam room, several pale young doctors in their white coats dashed from room to room. No tans here, I thought.

Dermatologists must be the busiest, fastest-moving docs anywhere. Like so many in medicine, they are being squeezed financially, and their only way to stay even is to increase their volume of patients.

"These are the barnacles of age, Mr. Jordan," the young doctor said as he went over my body, covered only by boxer shorts. He would occasionally pause to peer through the magnifying gizmo strapped to his head at some suspicious mole or wart.

He moved quickly over my legs and arms, then came to an abrupt stop on my lower arm, asked for a can of spray that freeze-dried and numbed the spot, flicked it off with a small knife and then mumbled something into a hand-carried recorder clipped to his white jacket.

"This one is probably going to need to be biopsied. Did you get a lot of sun exposure when you were young . . . sit out in the sun a lot?"

"Only for about ten years, doc," I said. "I was a lifeguard every summer from junior high through college."

"Did you wear sunscreen?"

"In 1960 . . . are you kidding? We used Johnson's Baby Oil with iodine in it. Wasn't that as good as sunscreen?"

He laughed out loud, "Probably about the worst thing you could use. That iodine didn't block the ultra-violent rays, and that oil just baked your skin instead of protecting it."

"It sure made me tan."

"And probably produced these couple of spots which are probably some kind of skin cancer."

I quit joking when I heard the dreaded "c" word and turned into Dr. Jordan. "Skin cancer? If you looked at my chart, you know I've had my share of cancer. Do any of these moles look cancerous?"

"Won't know until the pathology comes back," he said matter-of-factly. "But I wouldn't worry. None of these is of any size or consequence."

Yeah, I thought. No consequence to you.

———————

Again, I had to think about cancer.

It was disturbing to me that something I had done thirty years before might be expressing itself today in some kind of abnormal cell growth.

I thought back to those hot summer days at the Elk's Club where I was a lifeguard, teaching the children of doctors and lawyers to swim as little tots, then baby-sitting them at the pool year after year while their dads played golf and their moms tanned themselves around the pool, sipping Cokes through the day and piña coladas — topped with little paper umbrellas — in the late afternoon.

By the end of the summer, I would be so brown that my father used to joke that folks were going to think I was integrating the Elks' Club pool. . . .

It was already hot enough that summer of 1961, but the temperature went up all over town when the civil rights struggle came to Albany.

A normally sleepy town tucked away in deep southwest Georgia, Albany was the retail hub for our agricultural corner of the state. The pace quickened on

Saturdays as pickup trucks and cars from all over South
Georgia swarmed into town, filled with farm families,
the men dressed in overalls or brown khaki work
clothes and the women in loose-fitting cotton dresses.
Some were plain looking . . . others had on their
"Sunday best." They had come to "Aw-benny" with
their paychecks and shopping lists.

This was the summer that Dr. William Anderson, an
idealistic black physician, organized "The Albany
Movement" to test the new Supreme Court ruling that
required the integration of all public facilities. The
organization's actions were aimed specifically at elimi-
nating the "White Only" signs at bathrooms and water
fountains, the most powerful symbol of legal segregation throughout the South, and to give black Georgians
access to the local bus system and trains.

But the good intentions of Dr. Anderson were not
enough. While Anderson had energized the black community, he had no plan for translating their activism into
leverage with the white authorities. After several months
of public marches followed by arrests, trials, and releases,
there would be more marches, arrests, and trials. The
word on the street was that the "movement" was floun-
dering, losing steam, and having trouble finding fresh
marchers as many "locals" could not afford more time in
jail or fines.

In addition, there was starting to be competition
between locals and outsiders for "leadership" of the
Albany Movement. The leadership of SNCC — the

Student Nonviolent Coordinating Committee — which had sent key national leaders into Albany, was increasingly concerned that other civil rights organizations might be invited in.

While the movement dominated the headlines and gripped the local community, nothing was really happening: there was no dialogue with the public officials and no strategy. The white community, in the meantime, smugly "stiffed" Anderson, refusing even to talk to him or his lieutenants. By strictly enforcing the law and never resorting to highly publicized violence (as Chief Bull Connor would later commit in Birmingham), the white establishment made its strategy obvious: they simply planned to wear the Albany Movement down.

Flustered and uncertain as to how to play his hand, Dr. Anderson finally turned to his old Morehouse classmate, Martin Luther King Jr., and asked him to come to Albany for a speech. King — who was still developing the nonviolent tactics that would later prove so successful — accepted the invitation for a single appearance simply as a favor for an old friend.

However, once King arrived in Albany and made a powerful and moving speech at Mt. Shiloh Baptist Church, he immediately realized that he had invested his personal reputation in the Albany Movement. What had been a local and state story became a major national story overnight.

At the age of seventeen, I saw Dr. King's first march

in Albany. Despite pleas in the *Albany Herald* for its white readers to refrain from glorifying these "trouble-makers and outside agitators," my father surprised me by inviting me to go downtown with him one Saturday morning for Dr. King's first march. In a few minutes, we found ourselves standing in the middle of the all-white crowd, two or three deep along both sides of Pine Avenue, the main street that was lined with huge palm trees.

By now it was December, and the day was cold and overcast. An eerie silence pervaded the downtown area as most stores and offices had closed and the major streets were roped off.

After several months of public demonstrations, a ritual had developed among the marchers and the police. The marchers would gather at one of the large black churches for coffee and donuts, speaking and singing and seeking inspiration from one of the gifted preachers from around the South who would recruit the worshipers to join in the march. They would then pour into the street in a flood of black faces, accentuated by the occasional priest or nun in official garb, and would march a scheduled route to the front of City Hall, where the police would stop them and ask them to disband. They would politely refuse and would be arrested, always without incident.

But with Dr. King in town, all bets were off. Rumors were everywhere that card-carrying communists, armed with weapons, were pouring into town. The

KKK responded by calling for a rally in Albany and declared an "alert," asking its chapters to send "white militia" to Albany prepared to fight.

We couldn't see the marchers yet, but we could see the advance guard of policemen on motorcycles that preceded them. Necks strained and people stood on tiptoes. We began to hear a quiet noise that became a chorus as it got closer and closer. Finally, we could make out the words.

> "We shall overco-o-o-m-me
> We shall overco-o-o-m-m-m-me
> We shall overcome some day."

The marchers rounded the corner and came into full view as they filled Pine Avenue. I was surprised — most of the marchers were high school and college age with a sprinkling of kids who were barely teenagers. It was easy to pick out the familiar face of Dr. King with his dark overcoat on in the front line, marching in locked arms with other men who looked like clergy.

Particularly noticeable was a toffee-colored, handsome young man marching next to King who looked like he was in high school. I would learn later that he was a preacher from Thomasville, Georgia . . . Reverend Andrew Young.

Someone else in the crowd had noticed the light-skinned marcher as well and shouted, "Go home, you high-yellow nigger!"

A farmer in overalls standing nearby voiced the ultimate fear, "That's what happens when you integrate . . .
niggers will marry our daughters!"

"Over my dead body!" another retorted.

"Go home, Commies!"

"Get a job, you lazy niggers!"

"Two, four, six, eight . . . we ain't gonna integrate!" a
group of teenagers repeated time and again.

The group kept marching down Pine Avenue. "My
God," my father muttered as he held up his hand and
pointed, "There's Hattie!"

Sure enough, bringing up the rear were several rows of
black women in their Sunday best, and right in the middle was our housekeeper of over fifteen years, Hattie
Jackson. In her sixties, Hattie was a proud, quiet women.

What did this mean . . . "our" Hattie in a protest march?

The crowd moved at a quick pace on down Pine
Avenue until they reached the area of City Hall where
they were met by a phalanx of big policemen in riot
gear, tall black boots, white helmets, and black leather
jackets. They chatted nervously among themselves,
standing across the street about five feet apart, twirling
their billy clubs.

Positioned in the middle to "receive" the leadership of
the Albany Movement was Chief Laurie Pritchett, a
large, round-faced man, who had won the grudging
respect of the black leaders by "shooting straight" with
them and never allowing for violence or mistreatment
of the prisoners.

THE ALBANY MOVEMENT: DR. MARTIN LUTHER KING JR.,
DR. WILLIAM ANDERSON, AND POLICE CHIEF LAURIE PRITCHETT

Looking down at the top of King's head, the chief blared over his bullhorn, "You are violating the laws of our city by marching without a permit. You have two minutes to disperse . . . you have two minutes to disperse or you will be arrested!"

There was no response from the crowd. Dr. King and another marcher knelt in prayer. After a minute, the light-skinned young man pulled out a bullhorn and stuck it in front of Dr. King. Avoiding the chief's glance, Dr. King said in a strong, clear voice, "We are exercising our constitutional rights to peacefully assemble. We are marching today to protest the failure of the City of Albany to allow its Negro citizens and taxpayers the use of its public facilities. We have broken no law and seek no trouble. We only request that you enforce the law of the land, Chief Pritchett, and allow us to exercise our rights."

There was no reply, and the chief looked around nervously as a television camera crew pressed through the crowd with a microphone extended to try to pick up the exchange. Chief Pritchett studied his watch . . . waiting for the two minutes to expire. It was going according to plan. The marchers knew they would be stopped, the Chief knew that they would not disperse, and the group expected to be herded into the area between City Hall and the jail where they would be led one-by-one up the stairs to be booked and put in jail.

The protest marchers waited quietly for what seemed like eternity. Most stared straight ahead at Chief Pritchett.

The Chief finally looked up, pulled out his bullhorn, and said calmly, "You have refused to obey my orders, and you will now be arrested. Do not resist arrest, and you will not be harmed."

The large crowd moved quietly into the area between the city jail and the courthouse, which were connected by a large, brick building, thus surrounding the group on three sides. The policemen took their billy clubs and gently prodded and poked until all the demonstrators had squeezed into the small space. They had started to sing again, but you could hear the voices of some starting to talk or complain out loud . . . one or two of the children began to cry.

I was never sure what happened next . . . whether the demonstrators had stumbled and tripped or had been pushed to the ground by a nervous or overzealous cop, but people began to pile up in the narrow alley and several ear-piercing screams penetrated the winter air.

A couple of the onlookers laughed, and one yelled out, "Looks like a bunch of niggers in a sardine can!"

Several marchers locked arms and circled King to protect him. Soon, the entire crowd had dropped to the ground, the singing had stopped completely, and screams and cries echoed out of the enclosed area.

The white onlookers began to shout their approval.

I looked anxiously for Hattie but could not find her in the sea of black faces. It turned out that a young lady had fainted and was being passed above the crowd to the outside where some medics were soon attending her.

My father, a normally gregarious man, had watched in silence, then tugged at my arm and said, "Let's go!"

I was gripped by the spectacle in front of me and just stood there until I felt another hard tug. "Listen to me, Hamilton, we are leaving," he said sternly, "Right now, do you hear me?"

He was silent for a while as we drove home. Then he started talking. "Those people ought to be ashamed of themselves . . . getting those children into that mess. I'll be glad when they all leave town."

"What about Hattie?" I asked.

"Hattie better be careful, or she's going to be looking for work somewhere else."

My father harbored no sympathy for the protesters and repeated the argument that the good, local "colored folks" had been brainwashed by these "outside agitators." But my father was a gentle man who would never harm another human being. I could tell that he was uncomfortable with what we had seen that day . . . the ugly mood of the crowd, the raw hate that we could almost feel.

In reading about the protesters in the local papers, I had felt threatened. These people were out to destroy our way of life. But seeing it up close was entirely different, and witnessing the march that afternoon changed my thinking forever. For the first time, I felt real shame in my life, watching quietly while decent people and children — including our own dear Hattie — were herded into the alley just like animals.

Later, I would mark that day as a moment of moral failure in my life. I had an opportunity to take a stand, to risk something . . . instead, I had just stood there. Like so many other "decent" white Southerners, I kept my outrage and my shame to myself.

We worried that Hattie might be in jail. When she did not answer her phone, I begged my father to call the jail and check on her.

"This is none of our business, Hamilton. Hattie got herself into this mess, and I am not going to interfere. If she calls and needs bail, I will help her, but I am not going to stick my nose in this civil rights business!"

We were surprised the next Monday morning when Hattie, who regularly rode the six o'clock bus across town to be at our house by seven, slipped quietly into the house, wearing her crisp white "maid's" uniform. She even gave me a good-morning hug, which was something she used to do every day, but less often now that I was a teenager. Later, I would wonder if that hug was a way of forgiving all of us and Hattie's way of bringing Dr. King's message into our home: I love you even though you have mistreated me and my people. That hug stuck with me the rest of the day.

Hattie followed her usual routine: took the garbage out, cleared off the breakfast dishes, and assumed her usual place at the sink to do the dishes before she went room to room, making up the beds and gathering clothes to be washed and ironed.

My father appeared in the kitchen dressed in a dark

suit, ready to go to work. He looked surprised to find Hattie there, and I wondered what he would say . . . or if he would take her aside and scold her for getting involved in the march.

"Good morning, Hattie," he said.

"Good morning, Mr. Jordan."

"Nice day, isn't it?"

"Sho is, Mr. Jordan, sho is."

I realized then that my father was confused by all that was happening and felt the same shame as I did.

No one in our family ever said anything to Hattie about her "marching," and she never mentioned it to us. She did seem to be spending more time at "church activities," which was a clear signal to us that she was heavily involved in the Albany Movement.

It was through Hattie's quiet commitment that I began to appreciate the depth of the civil rights struggle. I was sure that all over the South there were "good colored folks" playing the same game as Hattie . . . working in the homes, restaurants, garages, and businesses of white people for meager wages, but slowly and surely putting aside their fears and becoming the foot soldiers of the movement.

A few years later, Hattie surprised my mother when she announced that she was taking the day off so that she could drive people to the polls to vote in the 1964 presidential election. It was as close as she ever came to publicly acknowledging her political activism.

The courtroom was packed, but we knew some ladies in the clerk's office who slipped us into a row in the back just as the judge called the court to order. One section of people were scribbling furiously on pads, and we figured out they were the national press.

Judge Abner Israel presided. I knew him well—he was one of my father's golfing partners in his regular Sunday game. The judge peered over his glasses, glaring first at the press, then at the group of blacks huddled around a table in front of the courtroom. I half stood, hoping to see Martin Luther King, but could not find him.

Judge Israel tapped his gavel a couple of times softly, and the blacks standing around the table quickly took their seats. Several of the men in the press area were turned around in their seats, talking to one another until Judge Israel firmly banged his gavel.

"In the event some of you have not had the occasion to appear in this Court," he drawled, "I will expect order and respect." Unable to hide the sarcasm in his voice, the judge forced a slight smile and looked at the area where the press was sitting, "To our friends in the press who may not be accustomed to Southern courtesies, you are welcome here, but the very same rules apply. No talking, no noise. Clerk, read the charges."

A wiry little man, wearing a black suit, white shirt, and red bow tie, stood up and read the charges, "City of Albany versus M. L. King. Dr. Anderson and others . . . For organizing a march without permit, refusal to obey an officer's order, and disturbing the peace."

"Defendants," Judge Israel snapped. "Stand up."

As the famous head of Martin Luther King Jr. popped up, my brother leaned over and whispered, "He looks like Mighty Mouse."

I thought at first that he was trying to be funny, but when I looked at King, I knew what he meant. The small head perched on top of the compact body featured large ears and a slim mustache. King wore a tapered, dark suit that fit him snugly. He looked quite dapper.

"Mr. King, Dr. Anderson, you have heard the clerk read these charges against you . . . how do you plea?"

"Not guilty, your Honor," King said first in a rich, clear voice. The others joined in.

"Alright," the judge said. "Proceed."

The prosecutor slowly lifted his large, pear-shaped frame and waddled toward the Judge. "The City of Awbenny, Jawga, calls Chief of Police Pritchett."

The red-headed police chief took the stand and recounted how Dr. King had led a march that was not authorized, had disrupted traffic and commerce in the downtown area, and had refused his requests that the marchers disperse. After several minutes of questioning, the prosecutor turned to the judge and said, "Your Honor, the City rests."

The Judge turned in the direction of Dr. King and the others, "The defense will now be heard."

An elegantly dressed black attorney rose and started to speak, and I remember thinking that this was the first time that I had ever heard a black man talk like a white person. "My name is Donald L. Hollowell. I am an attorney for the NAACP, and am licensed to practice in New York State, Washington, D.C., and Georgia. Assisting me is the Honorable C. B. King of Albany and Miss Constance Baker Motely of New York State."

C. B. King and the other black attorneys rose briefly, acknowledged the judge, who just glared, and sat back down.

"I know C. B. King," the judge said sarcastically, seeming to enjoy the fact that he had withheld the simple courtesy of a "Mister." "I do not know these other lawyers and do not know if they are properly licensed and able to appear before this Court."

Hollowell jumped to his feet: "With respect, your Honor, these are distinguished attorneys," and started to rattle off the credentials of his fellow counsels.

"I don't care what you know about these others, Mr. Hollowell. You have not made the proper arrangements for these people to practice in my Court, and they will not be allowed to speak here today."

"But you Honor," Hollowell protested, "I would like to bring to your attention that this team has practiced before the Supreme Court, participated in the landmark *Brown vs. Board of Education* suit. . . ."

Abner Israel held up his hand, "Enough, Mr. Hollowell, enough . . . Please do not waste the Court's time. I do not need biographies here . . . proceed."

Hollowell went back to the table where King was sitting with the other black lawyers, picked up a handful of paper, turned around, and held up a document. "Your Honor, if it pleases the Court, I would like to read some selected portions of the United States' Constitution. Starting with the Fourteenth Amendment, which states . . . "

Bam, bam, bam . . . Israel was red in the face as he banged his gavel over and over and over again. I thought he might just explode.

"Mi-s-s-s-t-e-r-r Hol-l-o-w-e-l-l," he dragged the name out sarcastically. "I do not need instruction from you or anyone else on the U.S. Constitution. Do you understand?"

"In all due respect, Judge Israel," Hollowell quickly countered, "The Constitution of the United States is THE ultimate authority. The city's refusal to permit Dr. King, Dr. Anderson, and the members of the Albany Movement to peacefully assemble is a violation of the Constitutional rights under Article . . . "

Judge Israel was now standing, . . . "Stop, Mr. Hollowell, stop . . . you will not make speeches to me in my court about the law."

"Your Honor, my client has the right to a reasonable defense. Is this Court not aware of the following Supreme Court cases," and Hollowell started reading cases in a loud voice while the judge — his face beet red — was banging his gavel nonstop.

Hollowell continued to read in a normal voice.

"Mr. Hollowell, cease, Mr. Hollowell, stop right now!"

It looked like Judge Israel was not only losing his temper but losing control . . . the hearing was not going the way it was supposed to. The judge quickly ordered a recess, got up, and started toward his chambers.

Mr. Hollowell droned on.

The judge stopped at the door, turned, and glared at Hollowell and warned loudly, "One more word, Mr. Hollowell . . . one more word and you will find yourself in contempt of this court and spending the night in jail."

This time Hollowell stopped. Israel flashed a satisfied smile until he heard another voice.

"Judge Israel, please hear me out," a deep voice boomed.

A hush settled over the courtroom, and the judge turned to see Martin Luther King Jr. standing erect, his hands outstretched as if asking for quiet.

"Judge Israel, neither I nor my attorneys mean any disrespect to you personally or to this court. But this is a court of law. How can our very own Constitution and the rulings of our highest court be of no interest to you or no relevance to this court? Can you answer that question for me, Your Honor? Do you recognize and accept the rulings of the U.S. Supreme Court?"

The Judge froze at the door, his eyes no longer were filled with hate . . . he seemed confused as to how to deal with King's direct and respectful appeal.

King's deep voice rang out again, "Please answer me, Judge, do you recognize the U.S. Constitution and the rulings of the U.S. Supreme Court?"

The judge slammed the door and escaped to his chamber as the court crowd turned noisy with reporters trying to yell questions to King and Anderson, huddled at their table, surrounded by their legal team.

It was learned later that Judge Israel had met in his chambers with some of the city fathers who told him in no uncertain terms that he was losing control and that the routine hearing could turn into a "circus," giving Martin Luther King Jr. a platform for making derogatory speeches about Albany.

Using Police Chief Pritchett as an intermediary, the city fathers began a negotiation with King, Anderson, and their team with the main objective of getting King out of town in hopes of taking the wind out of the Albany Movement.

Judge Israel returned and — in a calm voice — refused to hear any more witnesses and postponed the trial of King and the others for sixty days.

The jail full of protesters were released, and King suddenly found himself on the courthouse steps, having to defend and rationalize the "deal" struck between the city fathers and his representatives. King claimed victory, and later told a cheering crowd at Mt. Shiloh Baptist Church that those in jail had been freed and that a biracial commission would be set up to address the overall issue of desegregation. King also mentioned that his presence in Albany was no longer needed.

Even as he spoke, Chief Pritchett was denying that the city had agreed to any "deal."

The press was hard on King, calling the "deal" between the city and King "a stunning defeat" for King's reputation.

King returned to Albany in July 1962 to be sentenced for his previous December marches. Faced with the choice of paying a $178 fine or serving forty-five days in jail, King took the jail sentence, fully expecting a long and publicized stay in jail to give the Albany Movement new life and momentum.

Two days after he began to serve his sentence, he was released and told that an anonymous, well-dressed black man had paid his fine. King was flustered and complained that, "For the first time, I was sorry to be out of jail."

It turned out that through local publisher and Democratic Party Chairman James Gray, the city fathers had been in direct negotiations with the Kennedy Administration, hoping to defuse the growing tensions. Federal Judge Robert Elliott, a Kennedy appointee, issued an injunction that ordered King not to violate the local ordinances. This meant that King would have to violate a federal order if he marched again. King felt uncomfortable disobeying a federal order (and possibly offending the Kennedy brothers) so he watched from the sidelines as the Albany Movement took to the streets. After Judge Elliott's injunction had been overturned by an appeals court, King returned to the streets and to jail.

After starting his third jail sentence, local Judge Durden suspended King's sentence and conceded that the Supreme Court had overruled the local segregation ordinances. Even Albany Mayor Asa Kelly admitted that Dr. King had " . . . accomplished his objectives."

King and the leadership of the Albany Movement celebrated their victory as "the end of segregation in Albany, Georgia." They found it quite hollow, however, when young Negroes — trying to integrate the public library, pool, and other facilities — simply found them all closed.

King returned to Albany, led marches, and received suspended sentences. The white leaders seemed to always find a way to give King a short-term victory and then take it away through the shrewd use of the media, the local laws, and the nonviolent tactics of Chief Pritchett.

King always regarded the Albany Movement as one of the early and most important lessons of the civil rights movement. The local black leadership thought that King's presence itself would assure success and alleviate growing strains between the local and national civil rights leaders. Instead, King's presence only sharpened these tensions over leadership and tactics.

The regular marches in Albany continued for a while, became smaller in size until they became only occasional gestures, covered only as a local story as King moved on to Selma, Montgomery, Chicago, Washington, and finally Memphis.

———————

Change came hard to the South . . . and to the Jordan family. My father could never bring himself to say "Negro" properly, but he stopped saying "nigger" around us and usually used the word "colored" or "nigra," which was the "polite" compromise between "nigger" and "Negro."

In the late 1960s, the reality of integration hit close to home.

A proud veteran of World War II, my father was serving as chairman of the local draft board, a thankless volunteer job that he treated very seriously. With the Vietnam War raging, the Johnson Administration was pushing hard for these local boards — which exercised considerable authority over the fate of young men of draft age — to add black members in symbolic recognition of the increasing number of black draftees and volunteers.

After much discussion, the board invited Dr. Thomas Jenkins, the tall, dynamic president of Albany State College (the local Negro teachers' college) to serve on the Board. Jenkins, a shrewd and gregarious leader, knew how far to push for what he wanted without permanently alienating the white elites. He made quick friends with the white members of the draft board and quickly became a force in their deliberations. It was not long before my father was telling us that Tom Jenkins was a "good man" and a "good example for the colored race."

However, my father was more shocked than touched when Dr. and Mrs. Jenkins, unannounced, dropped off a pecan pie at our home for the Christmas holidays.

Hattie seemed to take special delight when she walked into the family room where my father was reading the afternoon paper to announce, "Mr. Jordan, Dr. and Mrs. Thomas Jenkins are at the *front* door."

My father — flabbergasted to have a black couple at our front door paying a social visit — maintained enough composure to exchange pleasantries and to invite them in. He seemed surprised that they accepted his invitation and were soon sitting in our living room. He offered them a drink, and before long they were sipping on bourbon-and-water and making small talk.

Later, laughing at his predicament, my father said, "I suppose if I had invited them to spend the night, they would have slept over."

The Jenkins' visit was a landmark in my father's life. Although he told people about it in a joking way (I always thought to preempt or dispel any notion around town that he had actually invited them for a social visit), I could tell that he had taken a perverse pride that the proud black educator had chosen our home to visit.

Years later, when Dr. Jenkins was appointed by Governor Jimmy Carter to be the first black person to serve on the State Pardon and Paroles Board, Tom Jenkins invited my father to attend his swearing-in ceremony in Atlanta. My mother was sick and unable to go, but Hattie heard them talking about the trip and asked my father if she could ride up with him as Dr. Jenkins was one of her "personal heroes."

While my father didn't want to have to bother with

Hattie, neither did he have the heart to turn her down. So my father — with Hattie riding in the back seat, which was where blacks always rode when in a white person's car — drove all the way to Atlanta. My mother made sandwiches for them to eat in the car so my father would not have to deal with the complicated issue of the two of them eating at a public facility. My mother could not resist kidding my father later that, as they drove away, it looked like a black woman had a white chauffeur. He did not find her observation amusing.

My father reported that he learned more about Hattie in that drive than he had learned in fifteen previous years. Trapped in the car for six hours, they talked about things never mentioned before, and it changed their relationship forever.

I doubt if my father ever thought about the irony and contradictions of that trip to Atlanta: my father in the front seat and Hattie — part-time maid, part-time civil rights worker — in the back, driving to Atlanta to see his friend, the first black man appointed to an important state board (and the first black to ever come to our *front* door for a social visit) sworn in.

My father was very proud of Dr. Jenkins's success and loved to tell friends that Jenkins's service on the draft board had demonstrated his effectiveness in his dealings with whites and had been a major factor in his appointment to the important statewide position.

Years later, I made the trip home to Albany to attend Hattie's funeral at the church where she had sung in the choir for forty years. I was the only white person there.

My mother and father stayed home. They loved Hattie and appreciated her years of loyal service. But they simply could not bring themselves to attend a black church. What would people say if they heard that they had gone to black funeral?

THE CANCER GENE

Four years had passed since my bout with lymphoma when I got word that my mother was back in the hospital. Dorothy and I canceled our after-Christmas vacation with our young son and our three-month-old baby daughter. I drove all night to my mother's hometown in South Georgia to be with her.

Although she was finally coming to the end of her long battle with lung cancer, my mother had thrown — in the words of my sister — a "hissy fit" when she heard we had canceled our trip.

She struggled to sit straight up in the hospital bed and finally got vertical enough to shake her finger as she scolded me: "I will not stand for you canceling this vacation with Dorothy and those precious children. I'll jump out of that window over there if you try to stay here with me instead of taking your family on this trip. I am just fine in this wonderful hospital, and your sister is going to stay and keep me company."

I wasn't particularly worried about her jumping out the window since her room was on the ground floor, but I had no doubt that my dear mother would make my "visit" with her just miserable if I did not bend to her will.

It was this same indomitable spirit that had helped to keep her cancer at bay now for more than five years in spite of the dire medical predictions.

I remembered clearly the young doctor showing us the spot on the X ray indicating that the cancer had come back on her remaining lung only months after the removal of her other lobe. He was the same young doctor who, at her original diagnosis, asked my mother if she smoked.

When my mother responded that she did not smoke, my sister's jaw dropped.

"Have you ever smoked, Mrs. Jordan?"

"Yes, I did."

"For how long?"

"About fifty years."

"How much?"

"Four or five packs a day."

"When did you stop, Mrs. Jordan?"

"Yesterday, Doctor . . . right after you told me I had lung cancer!"

When my mother's cancer recurred, the young doctor had described her new challenge and prognosis: "As we feared, our initial strategy of removing the one cancerous lobe was not successful. The cancer has now spread to the remaining lung, and there is a significant amount of disease in that lobe. Radiation to that tumor will probably reduce the size of the tumor or stop its growth, but it will not get rid of it and will reduce her lung capacity even further. Since she has multiple sclerosis on top of her cancer, this only complicates her ability to breathe normally and comfortably. Bottom line is that I don't want to make her a respiratory cripple by overdoing the radiation."

The doctor told us that he would radiate her "tactically" to fight the cancer when it interfered with her quality of life, but that sooner or later, it was going to hit a spot or a vital organ where there was nothing else left to do.

"Doctor," I said, "someone has to ask, how long is she likely to live?"

"Your mother is one tough lady, but the cancer plus the MS . . . I hope that I can help her to have another pleasant six to nine months, maybe a year, but it will be downhill after that, very difficult for her, and she will not last long."

That was over five years ago, and here my mother was still bossing us all around, playing bridge every Wednesday with her "girl friends" and absolutely immersed in the lives of her seven grandchildren, with their pictures, little notes, and Christmas and birthday cards taped all over her refrigerator, her dresser, and the walls of the family room.

It seemed that my choices were pretty clear . . . go on our vacation or stay here with my mother and catch hell nonstop from her for not going. As I hugged her goodbye, she pulled back, looked me in the eye and said, "You understand, don't you, son, I am damned tired of being sick!"

"Mama," I said, smiling as I hugged her, "I know what you mean. . . . I know what you mean!"

It bothered me after I left the hospital and had time to reflect on it . . . my mother's "one cancer patient to another" tone of voice, saying she was "tired of being sick." It was as close as she had ever come to complaining about her cancer or even suggesting that cancer might prevail.

But her spirit was otherwise strong and my hunch was that it was just a low moment, being put in the hospital right after a wonderful Christmas with our family. We were all going to have to get used to her being in and out of hospitals for the next few months and then try to get used to life without this special woman who had loomed so large in all of our lives.

Twenty-four hours later, Dorothy, the kids, and I were out riding in a horse-drawn carriage in the beautiful foothills of West Virginia, covered by a sprinkling of light snow, when I suddenly turned to Dorothy and — for reasons I could not explain then or now — simply said, "My mother just died."

Dorothy was startled at my strange declaration and we rushed back to our hotel room to call her. The message light on our phone was blinking, and I was not surprised when I listened to my sister's voice asking that I call her immediately at the hospital. When she answered, I could tell that she was fighting tears as she told me that our mother had "passed away" peacefully that morning without any pain or discomfort. "I think she was just tired of fighting and not feeling good and finally just threw in the towel."

After the funeral, we invited all of her close friends, neighbors, and family members from out of town to come by our family home to visit. Not surprisingly, we easily fell into telling funny stories about my mother's rich and wonderful life. As the afternoon wore on, local family friends had come and gone, and we were left to take comfort in the company of my mother's and father's remaining brothers and sisters and their children.

As I looked around the room, I was struck by how many of my aunts and uncles shared a common experience with my mother and father and me.

My father's brother had prostate cancer. My mother's brother had prostate cancer and her sister was battling breast cancer.

I mentioned this to Uncle Frank, eighty-five years old, a wrinkled and gentle plain-spoken peach farmer from Talbotton, Georgia, who was actually my father's cousin.

"Hamilton," he said, "seems like we just got the cancer jinx in the Jordan family."

"On both sides," Uncle Hamilton, my mother's brother, added. "Our mother had two different cancers in her lifetime and Daddy had prostate cancer. What about Clarence? Did Clarence Jordan die of cancer?"

"No, no, no," Uncle Frank said, shaking his head vigorously, "My little brother Clarence didn't die of cancer. . . . Clarence died of a broken heart."

True, Clarence did not battle cancer, but he fought all of his life against something as deadly and pervasive as cancer — the prejudice and hatred that were so deeply ingrained in the world he grew up in.

UNCLE CLARENCE

My father's family lost everything in the stock market crash of 1929 and the Great Depression, and his father died shortly afterwards of a heart attack. Overnight my Daddy went from being the son of one of the wealthiest men in middle Georgia to selling Maxwell House coffee door-to-door to support his family. He spent more and more time with his first cousins who lived nearby in Talbotton, a small farm town in middle Georgia known as the "peach capital" of the world.

His seven Talbotton cousins became more like siblings. The middle son was named Clarence.

When I was growing up, Clarence Jordan was a

mysterious figure in the life of our extended family, rarely present at family reunions or the annual gatherings in Talbotton for Thanksgiving and Christmas when we would choose up sides and play football on the big lawn speckled with pecan trees before stuffing ourselves with turkey, country yams, and pecan pie.

I can remember family members whispering among themselves about "what Clarence was doing" and shaking their heads with disgust.

When I was eight or nine, I remember saying to Uncle Clarence on one of those rare occasions when we did see him, "We see Uncle Frank and Uncle George and Uncle Robert all the time. We never see you except at weddings and funerals."

The big man squatted down to look me right in the eye, smiled and hugged me, then pulled back: "Well, Hamilton," Clarence said, "You are half right . . . you only see me at family funerals because you have to be invited to weddings," he laughed with a twinkle in his eyes. "I love your daddy and mamma so much that we have got to get together more."

But we didn't, and Clarence continued to be the "black sheep" in the family. It was a long time before I would understand.

Later on, when I was in high school, Clarence, Florence, and their children visited us every couple of weeks throughout one summer. They always came at night unannounced, piled out of the same old beat-up car and usually brought pecans or peaches from their farm in a brown paper bag. They wore overalls or khaki pants, obviously farming clothes, but as we romped and played in the backyard, the kids seemed pretty normal to me. What didn't seem normal, though, was that as soon as Clarence and Florence left, my parents would shake their heads and agree that it was "just a shame what Clarence was putting his family through."

As I later came to understand, by this time (the late 1950s) Clarence Jordan was a marked man. Clarence himself eventually explained to me the reason for his frequent visits to my family that summer. Martin Luther King Jr. and "The Albany Movement" were trying to integrate the public facilities, and over a three- or four-month period, King and the leadership of the civil rights movement were in my hometown, either in jail or in hiding in the houses of supporters. Clarence told us that he saw Martin — as he called him — regularly during this period and that on the way out of town, he and Florence had enjoyed dropping by our house at night to catch up with the "Albany Jordans."

As I grew older, I learned to both understand and appreciate my unusual Uncle Clarence and began to visit him — without my parents' knowledge — once or twice a year, starting with my junior year in high school.

G. K. Chesterton once said, "The only problem with Christianity is that no one has ever tried it." Chesterton obviously never met my Uncle Clarence.

In 1942, while Martin Luther King Jr. was in the seventh grade, Clarence Jordan founded an interracial commune in rural South Georgia. It was eleven years before the Supreme Court declared the "separate but equal" doctrine unconstitutional and more than two decades before blacks could drink from a public water fountain or use a public bathroom. Strict segregation was not only prevalent in the South . . . it was legal.

Clarence Jordan committed himself to living his faith — ironically the same Baptist faith that rationalized segregation and racism, the same faith that first tried to silence him, then tried to run him off and finally attempted to destroy him.

Clarence lived his life in "scorn of the consequences," and risked everything . . . the love of his parents, siblings and friends, and the lives of his own wife and children. For twenty-five years, Clarence and his family stood alone against the rising tide of the white South's worst violence and bigotry.

Asked by a reporter after one bombing if he were ever scared, Clarence responded, "Was I ever scared? I am always scared, particularly for my wife and children. But being scared is not the question . . . the question we face every day is whether or not we will be obedient to a system and to a group of people who insist that we hate and mistreat our fellow man."

Martin Luther King Jr. called him "my friend, my mentor, and my inspiration." Recalling their first meeting, Dr. King said, "When I first invited him to speak at Dexter Street Baptist Church (in the early 1950s), Clarence told us about his interracial commune in rural South Georgia. It was shocking and inspiring . . . and sounded too good to be true. Here was a son of the old South, a white Baptist preacher doing what we were just talking about doing. I went to Koinonia later to see it for myself and couldn't wait to leave because I was sure the Klan would show up and kill us both."

Corranzo Morgan, a black farmer, recalled, "I almost fell off my chair when Mr. Jordan came over the first time, shook my hand, and invited me and my family for Sunday dinner. I hemmed and hawed and finally said we wuz busy. I'm athinking, this young white boy must not know that coloreds and whites eating together jest isn't done . . . he is going to get his-self kilt. My next thought was that we might get ourselves kilt too . . . living cross the road from him."

"When we first heard about Clarence Jordan and Koinonia," Andy Young recalled, "we considered it too radical, too dangerous. Martin and I were trying to get folks the right to ride on the bus and to shop where they wanted . . . huge challenges back then. But here Clarence was — smack dab in the middle of Ku Klux Klan country — going for the whole loaf. Clarence did not spend all his time telling others what to do or making a fuss about it . . . he just kept living his faith. And

Clarence put all the rest of us to shame until we did something about it."

Clarence himself was a bundle of contradictions. He was, in the words of his biographer, Dallas Lee, "a gentle man who thundered against injustice, a nonviolent man who stared down the Klan, a genuinely humble man who could walk into the home of a rich man and say, 'Nice piece of plunder you got here.' He was a dirt-farming aristocrat, a good ol' Georgia country boy with a doctor's degree, a teacher with manure on his boots, a scholar in working clothes."

Clarence's faith was not a remote, prissy, sanitized doctrine or ritual but a gritty, folksy, in-your-face way of life, based on respect and love for all of humanity and applied to every decision and every action. The hard moral choices that Clarence forced on a defiant white South were often sugar-coated in his rich sense of humor and sounded a bit less threatening when delivered in his melodious drawl.

The civil rights struggle dominated every aspect of Southern life in the 1950s and 1960s. Clarence saved his special scorn for his own Baptist Church. The white churches generally and the white Baptist churches specifically, caught in this moral cross-fire, were the major force for rationalizing segregation and maintaining the status quo.

"Here you are," he lectured a group of Baptist ministers, "sitting smugly on your hands while the greatest moral dilemma since the Civil War is ravaging your communities. What is your response, ye moral pillars of the South?" Clarence mocked: "I'm sorry, but I can't afford to get involved."

"Brother Clarence," one minister protested, "you are being too hard on us . . . every person here is praying for you."

"Save your prayers for each other," Clarence thundered. "You need them more than we do. Your silence in the face of this hate and violence makes you an active accomplice to the cowards who shoot up our homes, beat our children, and bomb our farms."

No one clapped as he sat down.

TALBOTTON, GEORGIA

Clarence Jordan was born in 1910 in the central Georgia town of Talbotton, where his family were prosperous farmers and merchants. The middle of seven children, there was little in his early years to suggest the remarkable life he would lead.

The fires that would erupt later in his life simmered quietly for years as young Clarence began to measure and weigh what people said against what they did. He attended Sunday School at the First Baptist Church and learned to sing the same songs of love and faith sung by Baptist children everywhere. One of his favorites went,

"Red and yellow, black and white,

. They are precious in His sight,
Jesus loves the little children of the world."

Years later, Clarence would write about the torment this little ditty caused him:

It bothered me greatly . . . even as a child. Were the little black children precious in God's sight just like the little white children? The song said they were. Then why were they always so ragged, so dirty and hungry? Did God have favorite children? I was puzzled and started to think that maybe it wasn't God's doings, but man's. God didn't turn these black children away from our churches — we did. God didn't pay them low wages — we did. God didn't make them live in another section of town in miserable huts and pick rotten oranges and fruit out of the garbage for food — we did. Maybe they were precious in God's sight, but were they in ours? My environment told me that they were not very precious in anybody's sight. A nigger was a nigger and must be kept in his place — the place of servitude and inferiority.

The sprawling Jordan home was just down the street from the courthouse. Clarence recalled that the jail was about one hundred yards from his home and a group of "chain gang" convicts was often camped in the jailhouse yard. Fascinated by these strange characters so different from his own experience, Clarence began passing through the camp in the afternoons after school. The acquaintances he developed gave him a glimpse of life that was totally alien to what he was being taught at home and in church:

> I saw men with short chains locked between their feet to keep them from running, men bolted into the agonizing shame of primitive pillories, men beaten with whips or their bodies torn under the stress of the "stretcher" — a small frame structure in which a man could be placed with his feet fastened at the floor and his hand tied to ropes above him that extended to a block and tackle on the outside. I saw that almost all these men were black. This made a tremendous, traumatic impression on me.

Another indelible boyhood memory was of a revival one summer night, when Clarence from his place in the church choir looked out into the congregation and saw the warden of the chain gang get carried away as he sang "Love Lifted Me." But the next night he was awakened by agonizing screams of one of his chain gang friends; the warden had the man on the stretcher. "I was torn to pieces," recalled Clarence. "I identified totally with that man in the stretcher. His agony was my agony. I really got mad with God. If the warden was an example of God's love, I didn't want anything to do with Him."

Clarence carried the contradictions of his early life with him to the University of Georgia where he studied agriculture but continued to read his Bible. The summer after graduation, he went to ROTC camp to complete the training that would allow him to be commissioned an officer in the U.S. Army. It was while playing soldier atop a galloping horse that what mattered most to Clarence became abundantly clear. Later, he wrote about it:

> The class that day was a mounted drill held on the edge of the woods. I was on horseback and galloping through the woods with my pistol and saber drawn. We were to shoot the cardboard dummies and stick the straw dummies with our sabers. Every time I would shoot one of those dummies, that verse, 'But I say unto you, love your enemies,' would flash through my mind. . . . At that

moment, I saw the conflict between the mind of Jesus and the mind of the commanding officer. It was crystal clear that Jesus was going one way and I was going another. Yet, I claimed to be his follower.

When Clarence had completed the obstacle course and cleared the woods, he found his commanding officer, dismounted, and resigned his Army commission on the spot. The officer tried to talk Clarence out of such a rash decision. When he got nowhere, he suggested that Clarence should become a chaplain.

"I told him," Clarence said, "that would be the worst thing I could do. I could not encourage someone else to do something that I myself would not do."

His course was set, and he surprised family and friends when he announced that he had decided to become a preacher.

THE SOUTHERN BAPTIST SEMINARY, LOUISVILLE

His fellow students at the Southern Baptist Seminary in Louisville were not sure what to make of the tall, high-hipped, slow-talking Georgia boy who quickly earned the nickname "Tall-Bottom." Clarence soon began preaching and working in the poor black neighborhoods of the city, and the idealism of theology school crashed headlong into the harsh reality of the urban poor. Clarence became a familiar face in the crowded shanties of "South Town," befriending people and inviting black families to dinner at his modest apartment on campus.

For these activities, needless to say, Clarence was rebuked by some of his professors. He offered a spirited defense, using the very Bible teachings of those now chastising him to devastate their objections. The flustered head of the seminary finally ended the discussion: "Brother Jordan, you are supposed to minister to these unfortunate people, not entertain them in your home. It just is not done."

Outraged to find the same hypocrisy in theology school that he had found as a little boy at the Baptist Church in Talbotton, Clarence set a course from which he would never depart: "I made up my mind then and there that I was going to try to live my faith . . . not act it."

Clarence was inspired to a new vision by Florence Kruger, the tall, blue-eyed daughter of German immigrants who worked as the assistant librarian at the school. Clarence started spending more and more time at the library with Florence, talking about their beliefs and faith, and soon they announced they were to be married. They conceived a plan to return to the rural South to establish a "demonstration" project where they could "live their faith" and combine their religious beliefs with their practical knowledge of agriculture to help the rural poor, black and white.

KOINONIA — THE EARLY YEARS

In July 1942, Clarence and Florence Jordan and Baptist missionaries Mabel and Martin England opened their "demonstration project" in rural South Georgia near Americus, down the road from Plains. They called it Koinonia, the Greek word for "community."

Clarence had a strategy for realizing his dream. He wrote one of his friends from theology school:

> At first, we'll set up simply as farmers, trying to win the confidence of the people as good citizens and good neighbors. Once we feel that we are part of the community, we will try to bring in some of the principles that we believe in. In this way it will be growth from within instead of a system imposed from without. We'll hold all things in common, distribute to people according to their need, and every worker will be given an equal voice in governing our community.

Fifty years later, it is difficult to comprehend the courage of white people in rural Georgia establishing an interracial commune flying under a Christian banner. Indeed, Clarence's vision was so radical for the times that it was not initially understood or taken seriously by

CLARENCE JORDAN AT KOINONIA

either the local whites or blacks. The white churches found the young man fresh out of the seminary a witty and entertaining preacher. Later, Clarence would say, "They must notta listened to what I was saying."

But the tolerant atmosphere changed when the good folks of Americus began to see blacks and whites eating, living, and working together at Koinonia. It was doubly threatening that Clarence was one of their own . . . a Georgia boy, a Baptist, and a farmer. Twenty years later when "outside agitators" were swarming into the South in support of Dr. King's activities, a familiar refrain of the white Southerner was, "You just don't understand the South." They could never say that about Clarence Jordan.

The churches led the attack when they realized that "race-mixing" was part of the Koinonia agenda. The local Baptist church voted Clarence and the Koinonians out for "violating the social customs of our community." Clarence feigned surprise: "I don't understand your action in throwing us out. If we are sinners as you suggest, we are in bad need of being at church and getting straightened out. If we are the saints, you are in bad need of our fellowship."

THE DIFFICULT YEARS, 1955-1965

When the Supreme Court ruled in 1953 that the "separate but equal" doctrine was unconstitutional as applied to public education, the South prepared to refight the

Civil War. Yet here, in the heart of Dixie, was Koinonia, which embodied the worst fears of the white South. The people of Sumter County resolved to either drive them out or snuff them out.

It started out as a series of mean-spirited "pranks" — threatening phone calls in the middle of the night, the signs torn down at the roadside stand on Highway 19 to Atlanta where Koinonia sold its eggs and farm products to passers-by, sugar poured into the gas tanks of cars and trucks parked at the farm. As the Koinonians tolerated these minor annoyances with little complaint, the harsh jokes turned into a stream of violence.

In July 1956, a bomb was thrown into the roadside stand in the middle of the night, causing significant damage.

Koinonia responded by running ads in the local paper, stating clearly that they were not there to harm anyone and asking the same of their "neighbors."

The plea not only fell on deaf ears but earned the official condemnation of the Sumter County district attorney: "Maybe what we need right now," he said, "is for the right kind of Klan to start up again and to use the buggy whip on some of these race mixers. . . . I had rather see my little boy dead than sit beside a nigra in the public schools."

With this official sanction, the violence escalated and became more focused on Clarence and his family. His son, Jim, subjected to constant abuse at the local high school, was shipped off to finish high school among friends in North Dakota.

Still, in the face of mounting violence, Clarence always argued against abandoning their project, saying that if they left, it would only give encouragement to the forces of hate and evil. As Florence expressed it at one meeting, "There was never any feeling in Clarence's mind or my own that we should leave. We would not be the first Christians to die for their beliefs and we certainly would not be the last."

One night while Florence and Clarence were driving from Americus to Koinonia, a pick-up truck of good old boys started to pass them, slowed down long enough to yell insults at them, then darted ahead. When Clarence rounded the curve, the same pick-up truck was blocking the road, and three men were standing in the middle with shotguns. Clarence screeched to a halt and later claimed to have set a "world record for a 180-degree turn on a dirt road. I recalled that the Scripture said, 'If a man strikes you on your right cheek, turn to him both heels.' They may have shot at us, but I didn't hear it if they did because I was traveling faster than the speed of sound."

Reports of violence against them was routinely reported to the police and routinely dismissed. In January, their roadside store was bombed again . . . this time completely destroyed, with a loss of more than seven thousand dollars' worth of goods.

The violence moved closer to home. In the middle of the night on January 27, 1957, the peace of Koinonia was interrupted by screams as a machine gun strafed several houses, miraculously missing the inhabitants. Several days later, two cars rode by the farm in the early evening and fired shotguns at the lighted playground where the children were playing volleyball. As the children ran for cover, Clarence erupted with anger and ran toward the cars shaking his fist and yelling, "Come back here and face me, you cowards! Come back!"

As the intensity of the violence directed at Koinonia increased, Clarence searched for ways to protect his followers. In 1957, he wrote to President Eisenhower:

> Dear Mr. President,
> A peaceful community of sixty men, women, and children is facing annihilation unless someone in authority does something about it before it is too late. Groups of ten to twelve cars are harassing us every night. We have been bombed, burned out, and shot at. Our children are beaten going to and from school. Until the Supreme Court decision and the rise of the White Citizens' Council, we were not molested. Since then, our life has become difficult and our existence precarious. We have been told that the end is near, but we shall not run, for this is America. Should freedom perish from our land,

we would prefer to be dead. Someone
in authority must do something before
it is too late.

Eisenhower did. He passed Clarence's letter on to J.
Edgar Hoover, who promptly initiated a federal investi-
gation of Koinonia as "known race mixers and probable
Communists." Hoover also passed the letter on to the
Georgia Attorney General and encouraged the Georgia
authorities to begin their own probe.

Emboldened by the federal and state actions —
ironically instigated by Clarence's plea for help to the
president — the Sumter County grand jury launched
its own investigation with the goal of ridding itself of
Clarence Jordan and Koinonia once and for all.
Clarence was called to testify and told a reporter when
leaving the courthouse, "I tried to explain to the good
folks on the grand jury the difference between Karl
Marx and Jesus Christ . . . ended up they didn't know
very much about either one of 'em."

The grand jury issued a public report which held the
white community blameless and accused Koinonia of
"bombing itself" and creating "incidents" for the purpose
of drawing attention and "stirring racial passions."

When Clarence read the report, he said that the
white community had sanctioned the past crimes committed against them and had given a "hunting license"
to anyone who wanted to do them harm.

BOYCOTT

Having tried and failed logic and violence, the white community turned to coercion and imposed a highly effective boycott on Koinonia. It was simple — any people caught selling anything to Koinonia would themselves be boycotted. It applied to everything — gas, fertilizer, food, and medicines — and soon the Koinonians were traveling seventy-five to one hundred miles to get outside of the area of the boycott and to make anonymous purchases in cash.

When the Birdsey Feed Store in Americus (owned by a Macon man who knew Clarence's parents) refused to honor the boycott and continued to sell to Koinonia, his store was completely destroyed by a bomb. The good people of Americus meant business.

During the boycott, a prominent Americus banker wrote Clarence's father, who was on his deathbed, to tell him that "Your integrationist son is tearing our Christian community apart." The sick old man sent for his son and chastised him for "bringing shame on our good Christian name." For once, Clarence bit his lip and did not argue. Instead, he marched into the banker's office unannounced, jerked the surprised man up by his necktie, and promised him, "The next time you bother my sick daddy, I am going to forget about Jesus Christ for about fifteen minutes and beat the hell out of you."

1965-1969 . . . HARD TIMES

By the late 1960s, Koinonia was running out of steam. The hard work of the civil rights struggle had moved to the ballot box and the courtroom. While people came and went, the actual number of devoted Koinonians dwindled sharply. Some left because of the violence, others left simply because it was a hard and demanding existence.

Clarence began to spend more and more of his time preaching and writing, translating the Bible into a modern version cast in contemporary times. He called it the "Cotton Patch Version" (which Harry Chapin turned into a successful off-Broadway musical in the early 1980s).

Unlike Clarence, I kept my own doubts about "the system" to myself but still managed to cultivate our friendship. The last time that I saw Clarence, I had just returned from Vietnam and was going to work for his neighbor, Jimmy Carter, who lived just a few miles down the road and was going to run for governor of Georgia. I wondered what Clarence thought of him.

"He is a nice fella, Hamilton, but he is just a politician."

He was in a reflective mood that day as we sat in his "writing shack," a cozy ten-by-twelve-foot structure where Clarence read, wrote, and studied. I had not seen him in two years, so there was some catching up to do. He talked with a touch of sadness about the past, the defection of so many of their people from Koinonia, and the hatred that persisted. I was surprised to find him low.

"Haven't you accomplished a lot here?" I asked.

"That is not for me to say. I hope that we have made a good try at living according to the Lord's teachings."

Then he continued: "We have made progress, but not much." And holding up his large, rough hands, he put his thumb and forefinger almost together. "Every inch, every centimeter has been so hard . . . and at such a great price. But we have survived and persevered. We have survived," he repeated. "A tiny light in a sea of hate."

He looked out the window of the little shack as if counting the years and remembering all the people who had come and gone, all the violence directed against them. His eyes glistened. He continued, softly, "We have accomplished so much less than we had hoped for when we bought this old run-down piece of land. I underestimated the raw hatred of these people for their fellow human beings . . . the lengths to which they would go to justify their own corrupt system . . . the good people who lacked the moral courage to speak out. My greatest disappointment was the hypocrisy of the church . . . these so-called preachers who should have been pillars of strength and examples, moving people toward understanding and reconciliation. Instead, they were moral cripples whose silence aided and abetted those who hate us and try to destroy us."

Clarence told me that he would never leave Koinonia, but that their struggle for economic justice must move to the cities, where the urban poor had no jobs, no houses, and no hope. He called his new vision "Dream for Humanity," which was focused on the reality that people without a home were not a family, could not live in dignity, and did not have self-respect. "I think the Lord is pushing me to be practical in my old age," he chuckled, "and become a house-builder in the city instead of a farmer."

Six months later, Clarence suffered a massive heart attack while working in his writing shack. His son Lenny gave him mouth-to-mouth resuscitation but was unable to revive him. Panicked calls went out to the emergency room and several doctors . . . but no doctor would risk coming to Koinonia, particularly not to save Clarence Jordan's life. Clarence was dead at age fifty-nine.

The "good people of Americus" tried to humiliate Clarence in death as they had been unable to do in life. The coroner refused to come to Koinonia to issue a death certificate and insisted that the body be brought to him. Millard Fuller, one of Clarence's most devoted disciples, loaded Clarence's limp body into the back of a broken-down station wagon and drove him to the hospital, where he had to wait before bringing Clarence in. The coroner insisted on doing an autopsy. Millard called Florence at the farm for approval; she assented, and in a few hours Fuller was ready to carry Clarence home.

"They may have cut out his heart," observed Clarence's older brother, Frank, when he heard about the autopsy. "But they couldn't get his soul."

Remembering Clarence's opinion of funerals ("a waste of money on an empty shell . . . you can send a kid to college for a year on what some people spend celebrating their dead selves"), Millard Fuller put a few coins, a pocketknife and a Timex watch — representing all of Clarence's worldly possessions — in a paper bag. On the way back to Koinonia, he found a used shipping crate and strapped it to the top of the car. The next morning, following a simple service attended by about a hundred friends, Clarence, with his few possessions, was buried in his work clothes in the pine box in an unmarked grave.

I was in Savannah organizing for Jimmy Carter's campaign for governor when my mother called me to tell me Clarence had died. I immediately asked about the funeral arrangements, but I was already too late.

I felt sad not to be able to say goodbye to this great man whom I had barely known but who had brushed against my own life. I smiled when I thought about Clarence's sudden exit . . . he left this earth just as he had lived — on his own terms as defined by his God.

No one would be more disappointed than Clarence that the hard lessons of his life and faith would still be so highly relevant twenty-five years later. It would bring tears to his eyes to realize that, forty years later, some of the grandchildren of the white Southerners who bombed Koinonia, shot up his home, and beat his children still today occasionally burn black churches in the South.

On the other hand, it would bring a smile to his face to know that one of his followers — Millard Fuller — took his new vision and transformed it into Habitat for Humanity. Clarence would also find it a great and pleasant irony that his farmer-politician neighbor down the road, Jimmy Carter, was one of its main supporters.

Maybe this good man who demanded so much of himself and others would take some small satisfaction from all of the good that had come from the example — he would call it "witness" — of his own life. But I doubt it.

PATHOLOGY REPORT

It took several days to get the pathology report on the "samples" that the dermatologist had nipped from different areas of my arms and face.

When I heard a message on my answering service from my doctor, I knew that it meant trouble. . . . My experience is that the nurse calls with the good news and the doctor calls with the bad.

"Mr. Jordan, it is a good thing that we took those samples because one showed an early skin cancer which we need to take care of."

Cancer number two was a hell of a lot easier than

cancer number one . . . a skilled dermatologist numbed the area around the cancerous lesions, quickly excised them — with a generous margin — and sewed me up with a few stitches.

And it was over . . . I hoped.

ON THE BEACH

August 1995. We were on our annual family vacation on the Outer Banks of North Carolina. It was a glorious morning, the warm sun bearing down from a cloudless sky while a steady breeze blew the sea oats back and forth on the dunes separating the wooden houses — built high on stilts — from the beach. I was standing on the back porch of our house watching my three children (conceived naturally, despite dire medical predictions) through binoculars as they romped in the surf with more than a dozen of their Pennsylvania cousins. In the old days, people might tease me that my kids look like the mailman . . . the 1990s version would be that these surprise children looked like the FedEx man. However remarkable their conception,

HAMILTON JR., KATHLEEN, AND ALEX ON THE BEACH

Dorothy and I considered ourselves especially blessed to have a wonderful daughter and a second son.

Hamilton Jr., eleven, was riding his "boogie board" in the morning surf while his little brother Alex, three, puttered around looking for shells. I could barely see Kathleen's laughing face who, at age six, was being "buried alive" by several cousins who were scurrying around and covering every inch of her little body with handfuls of wet, white sand.

Dorothy and her two older sisters had lined up their beach chairs in the usual spot on the edge of the surf so they could watch the kids while they baked in the sun, read their paperbacks and talked, pausing now and then to splash their feet in the water or to get up and call to a couple of the older boys who were out a bit too far on their surfboards.

I tried to enjoy the view but could not help myself as I paced back and forth on the wooden deck, anxiously awaiting a call from my doctor.

It had started earlier that week during my annual physical exam. Among other things, I had a digital rectal exam of my prostate, which was normal, and also had a simple and relatively new blood test called PSA (for prostate-specific antigen), useful in detecting prostate cancer.

A day after my exam, the nurse called to give me my report: "Everything looks good." I asked specifically about the PSA as it had edged up slightly the last couple of exams. "Your PSA is 3.9 . . . within the normal range."

While I understood it was technically "normal," I also knew that it had shot up a full point since my last check-up. I had read a Mayo Clinic study that indicated a rise of more than .75 in a year was considered abnormal. Mayo had also developed an "age-adjusted PSA" that meant my "normal" PSA was actually slightly elevated for a man my age. Armed with this new information and acutely aware of my own cancer history, I was not about to sit back and relax.

My regular doctor — Dr. Bill Waters III, who is one of the greatest doctors anywhere — was on summer vacation, so I called Dr. Paul Hatcher, a respected urologist in Knoxville who had been my urologist when we lived there. I described my situation and asked him if I should have an ultrasound, which would allow him to "look" at the prostate gland. He agreed and got my undivided attention when he told me that one out of three men with an elevated PSA have prostate cancer.

He did the ultrasound the next day but found no suspicious spots. "As long as we are in here with the ultrasound, we could do a random needle biopsy which will sample your prostate . . . it's the only way to know for sure if something is going on."

That was no decision. I knew first-hand the advantages of being aggressive in screening as well as in treating cancer and urged him to proceed.

"We are being aggressive," Hatcher admitted, "but you'll know where you stand." Using a "needle gun," he took six samples of my prostate, each of which would be examined under the microscope overnight. The procedure was only mildly uncomfortable.

I gave the doctor my vacation number and arrived back at our beach house just in time to join the Scrabble game, an after-dinner ritual that divides the family into fiercely competitive teams. I was glad to lose myself in letters and words and hoped that I seemed normal to Dorothy. We played into the night, and I was relieved when Dorothy called it quits and went to bed.

Our game ended after midnight, and I sat out on the porch with Dorothy's two older sisters, our feet propped up on the railing as we were swallowed up in a perfect summer evening: a full moon, teenagers huddled around small fires up and down the beach, and the sound of the surf crashing against the sand. It was the next-to-the-last night of our vacation.

"I am expecting some bad news tomorrow," I announced, "and I thought it would be better for you both to know while we are all still together so you can help Doffy (the family nickname for Dorothy, their baby sister)." I told them about my biopsy and shared my worst fears. They sat and listened quietly, reaching out to touch me and finally hugging me as they tried to reassure me.

Susan thought that I was unduly worried because of my first cancer. "Everything will be okay."

"Whoever heard of anyone your age having three different cancers?" Nancy asked.

Lying in bed that night, I tried to rationalize my situation, counting stats instead of sheep . . . going over and over again the same facts. Dr. Hatcher had found no "suspicious areas" with the ultrasound. Only one out of three men with elevated PSAs has prostate cancer. And Nancy was right. What are the odds of a person having three different cancers by the age of fifty? I calculated it must be one in one hundred thousand.

But these mental gymnastics provided little comfort. Despite the seemingly favorable odds, I had a strong premonition that I had another battle to fight with cancer.

I didn't sleep well, got up early, made a cup of coffee, and sat on the porch watching the sun come up while I waited for the call from my doctor on my prostate biopsy. By the time that sun goes down, I thought, I would either be facing cancer again or laughing about my overreaction to a silly blood test.

Dorothy called from the bedroom, and when I walked in, she was sitting straight up in the bed. "Hamilton, what's going on? Something's wrong!"

I had not fooled her after all. I hated to tell Dorothy that I might have cancer again. Although she would think me foolish for this thought, I felt like I had failed her.

"Dorothy, I am afraid that I have prostate cancer."

Later, she would tell me that she heard me say the words but simply could not absorb them. "You what?" she said in a disbelieving voice. "You have what?"

I told her my story of the rising PSA and my needle biopsy the day before. She was visibly relieved. "You don't have cancer, Hamilton, you are worried that you might, but you don't know for sure." Like her sisters, her hunch was that I had overreacted.

She was right, but, at another level, I knew that she respected my instincts and feared my premonition. She pulled me onto the bed, gave me a big hug, and said, "No matter what happens, we have a guardian angel looking over us."

The phone rang around ten.

"Mr. Jordan, this is Dr. Hatcher. . . . Sorry, but I do not have any good news for you. Your pathology is back and you do have prostate cancer."

I was really not surprised and heard myself asking, "What is my Gleason?" The Gleason score is a number assigned by the pathologist from the analysis of prostate cancer cells under a microscope. A low Gleason (3 or 4) is a slow-growing cancer that often requires no treatment in older men while a high Gleason (8 or 9) means the tumor is aggressive, fast-growing, and more likely to have escaped the prostate gland.

"Your Gleason is a six . . . in the middle. In a man your age a Gleason 6 prostate cancer has to be treated." He told me I needed a CAT scan and a bone scan to see if there was any evidence of cancer spread outside of my prostate. My own father had died of prostate cancer, and I remembered his doctor telling us, "The horse is out of the barn." Now, twenty years later, would I get the same death sentence?

I made plans to leave that night to return to Knoxville to have my tests. During that afternoon on the beach with Dorothy and my kids, I found plenty of excuses for extra hugs. As I watched my children, I wondered if they would grow up without a father. How many more beach vacations would we enjoy together?

While facing my first cancer, I did research on childhood memories and learned that children under the ages of three to four have only the vaguest memories of lost parents. By the age of six or seven, children have some specific memories, and children over ten have full and rich memories. I could not stand the thought that my younger children might not even remember me. I started thinking about making a series of video tapes that might capture who I was and would express to them my special feelings for each one of them. Could I pull that off?

As I often do, I put Kathleen and Alex to bed that night. I laid between them on the double bed, made up silly stories and ended with our usual "Five Finger Prayer," which little Alex proudly led, bowing his head, folding his chubby hands together, and raising his little fingers one at a time: "Thank you, God . . . I love you, God . . . I am sorry, God . . . help others, God . . . help me, God . . . Amen."

Totally relaxed and in a state of pure joy, I watched them drift off to sleep. It was tough to break the spell, get up, say goodbye to Dorothy and Hamilton, drive to the airport in a hard rain, and start to think once again about cancer.

My tests in Knoxville the next morning were routine . . . drinking a gigantic, twenty-ounce cup of dye — poorly disguised as "orange juice" — before the bone scan and the CAT scan. As always, the hardest part was the waiting, and wondering what the technicians in the other room were saying as they saw my film. Was it — "This poor fellow is in bad trouble!" or "This guy has dodged a bullet!"?

I pumped them for clues. You can sometimes squeeze good news out of nurses and technicians — a wink or an "I'm sure you'll be okay" — but they always, always let the doctor deliver the bad news. I struck out with this crowd; they told me absolutely nothing. It worried me. As I hand-carried the film over to Dr. Hatcher's office, I pulled out a couple of the X rays and held them up to the light. I couldn't see a damn thing but that didn't make me feel much better.

Waiting for doctors to read your X rays must be like waiting for the jury foreman in a capital punishment trial to read your verdict. Someone you hardly know is about to tell you whether you are going to live or die. All it takes is a little spot on an X ray that was not there before to indicate that you have cancer. With my follow-up checkups, I have been through this ordeal dozens of times — it never gets easier.

Dr. Hatcher was matter-of-fact as he examined the films one by one: "There is no evidence on the bone scan or CAT scan that your cancer has escaped the prostate. This means that we have probably, and I stress probably, caught it early."

I breathed — literally — an audible sigh of relief. Calmly, he outlined my options:

- radiating my prostate over a period of time in hopes of killing all of the cancer cells;
- implanting radioactive pellets in my prostate, which would have the same effect; or,
- removing my prostate through surgery.

Hatcher explained that many patients considered the radiation options the "easy" choices as they avoided the surgery and some of its possible complications. Yet, he pointed out, there was no long-term evidence — over ten years — that radiation or implants were as effective as surgery. In fact, most urologists currently believe that surgery provides the best long-term cure rates.

"Doctor, with three young kids, I need a home run . . . tell me more about the surgery."

"The operation to remove the prostate is major surgery. But the good news is that IF the cancer is confined to the prostate, once the prostate is removed, you are cured. Short-term, you'll have some incontinence problems as a result of the surgery . . . long term, you should have none. There is a significant risk of impotency, which is greatest in older men but much less in men your age."

He continued. "It is not only major surgery . . . it is also delicate surgery where a millimeter can mean the difference in success or failure." Dr. Hatcher encouraged me to take my time in making my decision and advised that if surgery was my choice, I should select a surgeon who had done at least a hundred of these operations and who currently performed at least fifty a year. "I will only operate on you after you have considered all your options as well as other surgeons." He gave me a short list of the best prostate surgeons in the country. In an age when many doctors fight to hang onto surgical patients, Dr. Hatcher was unconcerned and confident in his own skills and knowledge. I had great confidence in his integrity and in his ability.

I had missed my flight back to Atlanta but was anxious to get home as Dorothy and the kids were driving in from the beach. I was determined to be waiting for them in the driveway to share my good news.

I rented a red convertible with a tape player, bought a handful of "Golden Oldies," grabbed a Big Mac and fries, and hit I-75 South. I put the top down, turned up the volume, and sang at the top of my lungs all the way to Atlanta. I got some strange looks from others who saw a middle-aged geezer in a flashy convertible, driving a bit too fast and singing "Sugar pie, honey bunch . . . You know that I lo-o-o-o-ve you, I can't help myself . . ." They probably thought I'd just won the lottery . . . and I had. I woke up that morning thinking that I might die. While there were no guarantees, I knew now that I might live — that was something to celebrate!

DECIDING WHAT TO DO

The day after my return from Knoxville, I got a call from Jimmy Carter. I assumed it was about some activity at the Carter Center as those of us who know and care for him understand that President Carter is not given to idle chit-chat.

"Hamilton, I haven't seen you in a while, but you have been on my mind a lot the last two or three days. I have been worrying about you."

I was flabbergasted to hear that he had been "worrying" about me at the very same time I had been on my medical roller coaster. Outside of my immediate family, no one knew about my diagnosis.

"Mr. President, I have been worried about myself. . . . I have just found out that I have prostate cancer."

"Oh no, Hamilton," he said. "I'm so sorry to hear that."

I thought about his own family's sad cancer history, the fact that his father and three of his four siblings had died of pancreatic cancer at a young age. Jimmy Carter was the only one left.

"You really didn't know about my situation?" I asked the president.

He convinced me his phone call was spontaneous. He said that he would be praying for me and asked for a report after my surgery.

"Mr. President, based on this call, you'll know my outcome before I do!"

While touched by his kindness, I was stirred even more by the mystery of his call. I had not spoken with President Carter in several months . . . how had he sensed that something was wrong with me? Coincidence, divine intervention, whatever . . . I was happy to have Rosalynn and Jimmy Carter in my corner.

Back at home, I began my research to determine if surgery was the best option and, if so, where to have that surgery. For the next several days, I was either on my phone or on the Internet in my home office. I called a number of medical institutions, talked with fifteen or twenty doctors and researchers, ordered books and tapes, and had printouts of medical studies from on-line services scattered all over the floor. Dorothy started calling me "Dr. Jordan."

The choices became increasingly clear. For a relatively young man like myself with a medium-grade cancer that we hoped was confined, the choices were surgery or some form of radiation. While the studies that contrasted surgery versus radiation yielded comparable results for the first five to ten years, there was growing evidence that the surgery provides a better long-term cure rate.

After immersing myself in the subject, I became convinced that a lot of men who should have prostate surgery avoid it due to a general fear of the operation and the highly publicized risks of impotence and incontinence —

which are seldom explained or quantified and sometimes exaggerated. When I weighed my enormous obligations to my family against the possibility of a little physical inconvenience or some compromise in my own personal pleasure, there was really no decision to make. It was more important to be alive and to have at least the possibility of a long life with my wife and children.

As I told Dorothy, "I can't have sex if I am dead!"

The top name Dr. Hatcher had given me was Dr. Patrick Walsh, head of urology at Johns Hopkins. I was already aware of his international reputation; in fact, he had treated my friend Dick Riley — former governor of South Carolina and Secretary of Education in the Clinton Administration — who had been diagnosed with prostate cancer. (Dr. Walsh successfully removed his prostate, and Dick is enjoying good health today.)

Dr. Walsh had not only built a great urology program (rated number-one in recent years by *U.S. News & World Report*), he had pioneered a new surgical procedure that improved cure rates while preserving the nerves which control continence and potency. I located a tape of Walsh performing his surgery and watched it alone late one night.

I was all the more absorbed upon learning that the patient was a man my age with young children. Dr. Walsh, a slight figure in surgical garb, mask, and glasses, narrated as he worked: "I am making a midline incision," as his knife sliced quickly through the man's abdomen from the navel to the pubic area as if it were jelly. My pulse quickened. I wondered if I should watch this, but I was quickly riveted.

Walsh's movements were precise and sure, as he separated the muscles and then cut through the dorsal vein, tying it off and creating the "bloodless field." This was one of the critical features of the procedure that Walsh had developed, allowing the surgeon to see clearly the prostate gland, the nerve bundles, and the surrounding area.

The atmosphere in the operating room was businesslike. The only sounds were the occasional clink of instruments, the sucking sounds as an assistant struggled to keep the key areas dry with the suction, and Walsh's crisp directions: "Clamp, please . . . sponge stick, please . . . sharp right angle, please."

He paused occasionally to "teach," pointing out the rectum, the bladder neck, the urethra, and the nerve bundles that ran along the sides of the prostate.

Next, he cut through the urethra, then "eyeballed" the wafer-thin nerve bundles that run along the prostate. In this case, they appeared not to be affected by the cancer, and after a series of snips, he gently lifted both nerve bundles off the prostate gland itself. He then separated the prostate from the bladder neck, removing the gland. He then rebuilt the urinary tract, sewing the urethra directly to the bladder, installing the catheter and some temporary drainage tubes. After inspecting his work, he began to sew the man up.

After "closing," he pulled off his mask and cap, revealing kind eyes and a boyish face, and talked with passion about "his patients" and prostate cancer. Pat Walsh was a man on a mission: to defeat prostate cancer.

As I turned the VCR off, I realized for the first time that I had a layman's understanding of the prostate and the surgery to remove it. Pat Walsh was not only a great surgeon; he was a first-class teacher.

I went to bed 100 percent convinced that the "radical retropubic prostatectomy," created and performed by Dr. Patrick Walsh, was my best bet for being cured.

DR. PATRICK WALSH AND
JOHNS HOPKINS MEDICAL CENTER

I made the first trip to Johns Hopkins alone in early August.

It was a friendly place, and I could not help but contrast the campus and comfortable old buildings of Johns Hopkins with the National Cancer Institute, full of busy scientists, housed in tall and sterile white government "modules."

Pat Walsh flashed a smile and greeted me warmly. He worked quickly, his words and movements crisp and efficient as he checked my prostate, stepped into the lab for a quick look at my pathology slides, and returned with the verdict.

"Dr. Hatcher did a nice work-up, Mr. Jordan. You

have a significant amount of cancer in your prostate. In my opinion, you should have it removed. If you like, I'll be glad to take it out."

If you like . . . I wanted to hug him. I had expected to be handed off to one of his bright young associates. My goal had been merely to get into "his" program. It was a wonderful bonus to know that he would perform "his" surgery on me.

He talked for a couple of minutes about the operation, the likely outcome and the risks. Patrick Walsh oozed confidence. Here was a man at the top of his game. "You've got a problem . . . I'm going to fix it," was his attitude.

At one level, he was totally professional, cool, and a bit detached. Yet he was capable of shifting gears and talked with feeling about "my patients," and at one point held up his somewhat delicate hands, which he described as "the gift God has given me" to perform surgery.

When Dr. Walsh told me that I would have to wait five weeks to have my surgery, my heart sank. With my first cancer, I had received my diagnosis late one Friday afternoon and convinced my doctors at NCI to allow me to start my chemotherapy the next day, which happened to be my forty-first birthday. I had no intention of giving my body the weekend off so the cancer cells could multiply while I was eating birthday cake.

But this was different. Dr. Walsh explained that the needle biopsy irritates the prostate and that it was important for the prostate gland to return to a "normal condition" before he performed the delicate surgery.

He reassured me that waiting a few weeks with my medium-grade cancer was not of great concern. Easy for him to say.

When I started to push for an earlier date, Dr. Walsh cut me off, saying quietly, "After doing many, many of these procedures, I believe it's best to wait."

I dropped it. "We" had decided to wait.

It was not easy to tell Dr. Hatcher — himself a great surgeon and researcher — that I was going to Johns Hopkins. Dr. Hatcher had encouraged my aggressive attitude, performed a random biopsy when my ultrasound was normal, and actively supported my efforts to consider all my options. His reaction was gracious and generous. He described Dr. Walsh as a "great surgeon" and said I had made an excellent decision. The important lesson I learned from Paul Hatcher is that great doctors are not threatened by patients seeking second opinions or going other places for their surgery . . . they are too busy taking care of their own patients and making their own miracles.

The surgery would take Dorothy and me away from our family for at least a week. We could get away with telling little Kathleen and Alex that "Daddy has to go get his prostate fixed," but that would not satisfy Hamilton Jr., who had sensed something was wrong and was already asking questions. Should we tell him everything . . . or the bare minimum to protect him from unnecessary worry? Dorothy wanted to tell him everything. I was not sure.

When the moment of truth came, I chickened out,

As I walked on the path to the ruins, I made up my mind and dropped the pouch of salt on the hard ground. I did not turn my cloak inside out for I did not want to keep the wee banshee away. I wanted the message from my mother. I remembered her hair, soft brown and gently curling. Her face was shaped like a heart, except that her chin was round, rather than pointed. Her eyes were deep blue, and in summer months the slightest sprinkling of freckles danced across her nose and cheeks. I, too, sprouted a new crop of freckles each spring. *Kisses from the angels,* my mother called them. Her arms, before they became so thin, had held me softly as I drifted off to sleep. And she told me stories.

Not stories like my father would have told, not *bard* stories, but stories about when she was a girl like me and the things she discovered as she ventured out into the world.

I missed her so much.

And I missed Thomas, though I wished I didn't. He had been there with me, caring for my mother, helping me cook vegetable broths and oatcakes in hopes of making her strong.

Before the illness, she mothered him as well as me. 'Twould be strange to hear her words and not have Thomas there.

But he had made his choice. And so had I.

The late afternoon sun glinted off the Banshee's Tower. Soon, the sun would disappear, the sky would darken, and I would receive her message.

As I neared the top of the hill, the wind kicked up, as I had known that it would. The low moaning began, rising to a shrill shriek as gloom descended upon the ruins. I found the stone bench and sat on it. I would not be waiting long.

"Trrrriiiiinnkkeetttt," the wind called.

I did not reply. If the wee banshee was looking for me, she would find me easily out in the open. I tried to sit with my back straight, looking fearless. But there was a bone-deep chill in the wind and I clutched my mother's cloak tightly, though it was nearly useless against the icy gusts.

I hoped 'twould be the spirit of my mother that found me cowering in the wind. She would wrap me in a soft blanket, the one full of colors she had woven for me long ago. I would cry and she would tell me not to weep, that it rarely did anyone much good. And then she would impart her message.

It was, however, the wee banshee who came to me, her pale eyes alive with devilish joy. "Yoooooouuuu caaaaaaaame baaaaack." Her voice sailed on the wind.

"What is the message from my mother?" I asked. I had hoped to leave this place before the sun finished sinking in the sky. Perhaps I could catch up with Thomas in a day or two—if I decided to forgive him for deserting me.

"You have payment?" she whispered.

"Aye." I placed the bag with the harp on the ground in front of me.

She beckoned with fingers that looked far too long for a child's. I followed her carefully.

"Where is she? Where is my mother?"

The banshee did not answer, but continued on her path. I could do naught but follow, though the evening light vanished more with each step.

Gravel slipped beneath my shoes as she led me down a steep path on the other side of the hill.

"Wait! I cannot keep up!"

She floated faster and faster along the path and I started to run. Were I brave enough to look down to my left, I would have seen the pebbles skid out from under my shoes and fall hundreds of feet below, for on one edge of the path lay a cliff, on the other a wall of stone.

"Please, slow down!" I called, gasping for breath.

The wee banshee slowed and pointed over the cliff.

Did she want me to jump?

I shook my head, as no words would come. Thomas had been right. This fiendish child only sought my death, the chance to carry my soul off and cry most mournfully about it. Why hadn't I listened to him?

She pointed again as I clutched the rocky wall. I closed my eyes and bent my head. I would not look where she pointed, nor would I jump. But the wind was so strong, I could move neither forward nor back along the path.

I began to cry.

MESSAGE FROM BEYOND

——◆◆◆◆——

*T*rinket," a voice called. It was not the whiny cry of the wee banshee. It was a gentle voice, the most beautiful voice I had ever heard in my life.

It was *her.*

It was my mother.

I was afraid to open my eyes. What if she was not here with me? What if, in my moment of death, I was imagining that she was here? Would not everyone want their mother with them when facing something so frightening?

"Trinket."

Bravely, though I was sniffling, I opened my eyes and looked into the empty air above the cliff.

'Twas no longer empty.

She was more lovely than I remembered, her skin not as drawn as when I last saw her, although it was paler than the face of the moon. Her hair did not swirl in the wild wind, but hung silkily past her shoulders. She wore the dress they buried her in, the most gorgeous blue I had ever seen. The color of dawn.

I reached out my arms to pull her to me, but she put up her hand.

"Trinket, do not move."

I looked down. If I had taken but one more step, I would have joined my mother in death.

And when I stopped to think about it, perhaps it would not be so bad.

I could fly through the air in a dress of sky, by the side of my mother. I had no one else now. All it would take was one little step . . .

"Trinket, stop."

Her tone was sharp. I knew that tone. When I tried to take more than my share of oatcakes, she used that tone. When I would not go to my bed at night, she used that tone.

I learned early not to ignore it.

"Why?" I asked.

She smiled so sweetly, I thought my heart would break. "This is not your time, Trinket. But you already know that, don't you?"

I said nothing. The urge to run into my mother's arms was strong. It was all I could do to keep my feet planted on the ground.

"Trinket, you must listen to me."

I nodded. I had come to listen to her message. *But I wanted so much more.*

"There will be a time when you will need these words. I have risked much to see you, Trinket, as have you."

Her face was fading in the dusk.

"I'll not be allowed to come again, Trinket, so listen well."

My eyes filled with tears.

"Your heart, Trinket, keep it safe and strong. It will guide you on the right course."

I nodded.

"And, Trinket, do not judge by appearances. Evil may lurk in a harmless package. And something pure and good may reside under old, crabbed wrapping."

Her lips curved delicately and I sniffled. She faded even more, her body but the steam above a boiling kettle.

I wanted to smile in return, but I was confused. If you had one moment with the dead, what questions would you ask? What would you tell them?

"Mother, I love you."

"I know that, Trinket. Please forgive me for leaving you. *Forgive*."

"Mother, what about my father? Is he d-d-dead, too?" I choked out. "Is he with you?"

She was vanishing, and the small banshee drifted in between us, an endearingly innocent look on her face.

"Forgive."

"Stay . . . please . . ." I begged.

"Oh, my little Trinket," I could hear my mother's voice echo as she was lost to the mist. "I am with you more than you know."

I wiped my tears with my sleeve only to find the wee banshee there again in the space my mother had just vanished from. The wee banshee's long fingers opened and she held out her hand to me. So easy it would be to grasp it, to fall into the abyss and not feel this pain anymore.

I wanted my mother.

The banshee's outstretched hand slowly came closer.

"The harp," I said between sobs, pointing back to the tower where I had left the bag on the ground by the bench. "I offer it in exchange . . ." Paying the price was hard, but I had come prepared.

"I do not require the harp, Trinket," she said. Her voice was cheerful, almost kind. "I want *you*. Think of it. We could play all night, in the tower. We could comb our hair. We could fly on the wind."

Her bony finger beckoned and I watched as my own hand moved stealthily forward.

"You'll never hurt again," the banshee said. "You'll cry for the loss of others, but the pain will not be your own."

Sweet words. Never to feel my own pain again. The pain from a father who deserted me and a mother who died and abandoned me. Everyone left me. Even Thomas left.

Perhaps I drove them away.

"Yes, Trinket, you drove them away. They never cared for you," she crooned, her small face filled with compassion. "But I would not leave your side. We would stay young and ride the moon. We'd shriek at the world and watch as foolish mortals are carried off by Death."

Was I such a terrible person that no one ever wanted to stay with me?

"Your message has been delivered. Now 'tis time to pay," the wee banshee said. "The price is your life."

My hand was almost touching hers, but I could not reach her unless I took a step. I looked down. That one step would send me so far below that I could not see exactly where my bones would crash and break. Would they join others, there at the bottom of the cliff? Would my body lie next to the pub mistress's grandfather, and no one would ever know what happened to me?

Would I feel this searing hurt no longer?

"Trinket!" called a voice from the path above.

"Just one more step," the wee banshee whispered. "One more tiny step . . . no more pain . . . come, Trinket . . ." Her hand stretched out to me, just beyond my grasp.

"TRINKET!" Thomas shouted. "STEP BACK!"

The banshee grabbed at my wrist. Her nails scratched against my skin and I lost my balance.

THE BLUEBIRD

———◆◆◆———

*F*alling was not as peaceful as I thought it would be. It felt hard and rough and was over much too fast.

That is because I did not fall from the cliff.

Thomas had thrown himself at me and knocked me out of the banshee's grasp. She roared and wailed in despair. He landed on me and squashed me uncomfortably, but I would thank him later for it. Thomas had kept me alive.

He pulled on my arm, dragging my body upward, and forced me along the path. "Do not look back, whatever you do, do not look back." But I could not help it. Her eyes were fiery, like a demon's, and her face grimaced like a gargoyle. Thomas opened a small pouch of salt and flung it over his shoulder. Luckily, the wind did not blow the grains back at us, but carried them through the night, blasting the tiny specks against the thrashing, wailing form of the wee banshee. I could hear a *hiss* as the salt touched her skin.

Thomas pulled from his pocket my small silver mirror and flashed it at the wee banshee. Her moans and screams pierced the night.

My cloak whipped around and between us. Thomas batted it out of the way and clutched my hand, not letting go until we were far away from the top of the hill and the Banshee's Tower. All the way down the path, the wind did not let up, nor did the howling cease. We ran and ran as if Death itself was at our heels.

And it may have been.

When we got to the road that led back to Crossmaglin, Thomas took us in the other direction.

"Thomas, my things . . ." I sobbed, but my words were covered by the sound of feet on gravel. 'Twere the first words I had spoken in all the time it took us to reach the fork in the road. Nay, I had not spoken, but I was not silent. I cried all of the way, until there were no tears, only dry coughing sounds, and still I did not stop. Thomas said nothing but held my hand as we traveled, helping me along when the going became difficult.

There is a time to talk and a time to hold your tongue. Thankfully, Thomas knew the difference between the two.

At last we were so far away it seemed safe to stop and catch our breaths. I sat on a log and buried my face in my hands. "My harp," I said softly, thinking only I could hear. 'Twas selfish to be thinking of a mere instrument when my very life had just been saved. I knew it, but I could not help it.

"It's here. It's all here," Thomas said simply, patting the bag on his shoulder that I'd been too shaken to notice. "I found this inside, see?" He pulled the mirror from his pocket and placed it gently in the sack. "When I went back, the pub mistress told me you'd gone. She gave me some salt and asked if I had a mirror. I didn't, but I knew you did. And when I got to the ruin, I saw your bag on the ground by the bench."

I noticed then that all of Thomas's garments, every last one, were on backward and inside out.

"Do you suppose we banished her away from the tower?" he asked.

I shrugged. The wind around us was gentle now, like the breeze in the room after my mother had died.

As long as the wee banshee was nowhere near us, I did not care where she was.

"Thank you for coming back," I whispered, my voice hoarse from the tears.

"Ah, Trinket. You'd have done the same for me." He smiled a bit, grateful, perhaps, that I wasn't crying for the first time in a few hours.

———

Later, when we were miles from Crossmaglin and could no longer see the Banshee's Tower, I asked the question that had been rattling around in my brain.

"Thomas, how did you arrive at just the perfect moment? Had you been an instant later . . ."

"You know, Trinket, 'twas the strangest thing. I was already on my way along the path leading away from Crossmaglin, when a bird appeared. A beautiful bluebird. Well, I'd never seen such a bird before, and I've seen lots and lots of birds, and so I went to get a better look. Was flying all strange, it was, darting all around as if it were trying to get my attention. And I was afeared the poor thing was injured. So I ran to keep up, thinking maybe I could help it. 'Twas approaching twilight already, yet this bird fairly glowed. Never seen anything like it. I *had* to chase it. It stayed always just ahead of me. So there I was, running to catch a better look at the bluebird, and the next thing I knew, I nearly stumbled over the pub mistress. She handed me a bag of salt and . . . well . . ."

He did not go on with the story.

I did not blame him. But a warmth and a tingle went through me.

"Thomas, what color of blue was the bird?"

"The color of the sky at dawn."

THE THIRD SONG

The Bluebird Song

To fly in the sky
With thee, dear bird,
Betwixt the clouds
Of white.

A-floating, a-darting
Up high, dear bird,
From morn
Until twilight.

What wouldn't I give?
A treasure? A tune?
To fly with feathers
'Neath the cold, pale moon.

Like a mother who watches
Over her nest
And teaches the young
To fly.

Against the blanket
Of sparkling stars
'Neath the Mistress
Of the Night.

What wouldn't I give?
A treasure? A tune?
To fly with feathers
'Neath the cold, pale moon.

The Faerie Queen and the Gold Coin

ORLA

Each village has its own way about it. Some have a tragic sense to them and some can only be described as sleepy. Thomas and I like the happy villages the best, the ones where music can be found in the very sounds of bees buzzing or the mooing of cattle. The ones where laughter trickles from under the cottage doors like water over smooth rocks. Such a village was Ringford, where we met a girl who was born to dance. Perhaps the moon and stars twinkled in harmony the night she was born, or the ocean waves beat against the shore in the same rhythm as her little beating heart. Whatever the reason, the lass was born with dancing in her soul and she could do naught but move about, this way and that, every single minute of every single day.

Now, everyone knows how the faerie folk like their dancing. It's one of their favorite things, next to cake and revelry. And possibly romancing. But this tale is not about faerie romance. Or cake. 'Tis about dancing. And a bargain. And the girl who was born with the rhythm of the twinkling stars in her feet.

—

Thomas and I came upon the dancing girl's town after many days of walking. We were at the end of our rations and here was the fine-looking village of Ringford. We watched the townsfolk from behind a hedge, making sure the folks were friendly before revealing ourselves. Thomas and I had found that some people were kind and some were not, and the easiest way to tell was to watch how they treated their children. Villages where children were beaten were not places we stayed long, for where there was little tolerance for children, there was less for a young storyteller and her pig boy.

Instead of yelling at the dancing girl to be more helpful,

her family encouraged her, making the cutting of the turf a celebration.

"Dance, Orla, dance!"

Joyful voices frolicked through the breeze and to our ears, married with the sound of clapping. And then we saw Orla, dancing deftly in the peat bogs alongside her family as they worked. Tall and graceful, swift and strong, she was the best dancer Thomas and I had ever seen.

———

"If I were a true bard, I'd stay a whole week in a village just like this," I whispered to Thomas. It was impossible to say the word *bard* and not think of my father, but finding James the Bard became more of a foggy dream each day.

"I bet the Old Burned Man's been here. Maybe he's even here now." Thomas nudged me with his elbow. The more we searched for my father, the more we realized how difficult our task was. By this time, we were happy when we found *any* bard.

"Perhaps," I said, though I secretly doubted it. It seemed luck was never with us as we sought the Old Burned Man.

We had been fortunate enough to hear Bald Fergal tell tales the week before. His stories were mostly jolly and we'd giggled about them for days on the road. But when I had asked him about my father, he had supplied no information.

Thomas was about to laugh out loud at the scene the family created as they whooped and jigged on the turf when I poked him into silence. (Poking has its benefits.) Could he not see how amazing Orla was? Never before had I seen anyone dance so elegantly, yet with such power. Orla was a fine name for her, too. Her hair shone like gold and she carried herself like royalty. A golden princess, indeed.

We watched, spellbound, for a while. Then the bushes became too itchy and the family seemed kind enough, so Thomas and I came out and introduced ourselves. Orla's family, the McGills, offered us shelter and food, if we helped with the turf cutting. Naturally, we agreed. Thomas, of course, would rather have worked with the animals than alongside people, but he was learning to carry on a conversation quite well, as I made him practice when we traveled between towns. He'd developed a fine love of questions.

"Do you suppose 'twould be better to be a goat or a toad?" he might ask.

Or, "Why do we have five fingers and not seven? Then you could count the days of the week on one hand."

Or, "What if people got younger instead of older? Then I'd be bigger than you ... somehow ..."

That was what it was like to converse with Thomas. Though I hated to remind him, he already *was* growing bigger than me. His britches were no longer as saggy and his sleeves scarcely covered his wrists. If he kept up at this rate, we'd have to get him new clothing soon.

Perhaps if I worked more on my stories and songs, they'd be worthy of trade before long.

—

I practiced my harp that night by the fire as the McGill family sat around the old wooden table in their kitchen. Though I still got nervous when playing for folks, I found my fingers growing more sure of themselves each day.

"Do you play songs other than lullabies, though that is a lovely one," Orla asked as I strummed my father's lullaby, for

I played it every day. I had indeed picked up a few other tunes along the road. I nodded and Orla leaped from her chair with joy. "Will you play for me? I've never danced to harp music before."

" 'Twould be an honor, Miss Orla," I replied.

"Been a long time since we've seen a harper in these parts," said Orla's father. He was a tall man with a reddish beard and an easy smile.

"Long time, indeed," said Orla's mother. "Oh, but he could play. Long fingers he had," she said as she took one of my hands in her own. "Like yours."

"Was he called James the Bard?" I asked, hoping with all my heart to hear *yes* for once instead of *sorry, no* or *I don't remember.*

"Oh yes, lass. That was him. Not heard a harp like that for years. But your hands, child. Yes, I've seen hands like that strum a harp before."

I could not help but feel warmth travel from my heart to my fingertips. He might have once sat where I was now sitting. *His* blood made my fingers play more beautifully.

Orla's father nodded to me that it would be acceptable to

play a dancing song, so I played a lilting jig I had practiced in the evenings when Thomas and I camped. And though Orla was but a child, she danced more fair than any woman I had ever seen.

THE FAERIE QUEEN

'Twas my own fault that word of Orla's dancing skill made its way down to the faerie kingdom, for there was a faerie mound nearby. If you've not seen a faerie mound, I should tell you that 'tis not a sight you'll soon forget. Imagine a perfectly round hill, covered in grass that is both brighter and deeper green than any of the other grass around. And not a bush nor tree grows on this mound. Once a year, in the spring, a ring of flowers may sprout. Or it may not. Depending on the Faerie Queen's whim.

"If you see such a ring on the mound, do not attempt to pass through. Few have ever made it to the other side," Orla's mother told me as we sat around her table on our second morning there, eating fresh berries, cream, and bread. Her green eyes twinkled and her voice fairly sang. I liked how she spoke with her face as well as her voice and I told her so.

Her cheeks turned the color of strawberries and she said, "Well, I'm not so good as a proper teller."

"Have there been many tellers in these parts?" I asked, trying to summon enough bravery to bring the conversation around to my father once more.

She patted my hand as if she sensed the importance of my question. "If you are asking about that James the Bard, I've not heard of him being about for years. But the Old Burned Man comes from time to time. Ye'll have heard of him, no doubt."

Aye. I had.

Thomas's eyes lit up. "Did I not tell you, Trinket? I told you he came here." He smiled smugly.

He was becoming good at collecting gossip; his eavesdropping skills improved with each town we came upon.

"And Bald Fergal will be coming soon," Orla's mum said.

Aye. Bald Fergal. We had already heard *his* tales.

Thomas and I ate our midday meal by the faerie mound. He thought it would be exciting. I hoped there might be a story nearby. Instead, we both found it rather dull. No faerie ring to be seen.

We laid my cloak upon the ground and ate in silence, listening for faeries inside of the mound. I chewed my cheese slowly and frowned at Thomas as he made noise whilst peeling his egg. He dropped a bit of shell on the fine fabric my mother had woven and I glared at him until he picked it up and flicked it away. Finally, deciding there was nothing to hear, not even the buzzing of bees, we began to talk, though we should have known better.

"The girl, she can dance, no?" Thomas asked with his mouth full. Regardless of how many times I reminded him to chew and swallow before he spoke, he uttered whatever thought crossed his mind, the moment it crossed.

"Thomas, village folk would not want to see your food once it is inside of your mouth." *Especially boiled egg.*

"The way her feet move. Never have I seen a person move

their feet so fast." He stuffed the rest of the egg in his mouth, followed by a chunk of brown bread. "And she leaps so high, it's as if the sky holds its breath until she lands."

'Twas true. And the girl had rhythm in everything she did. The way she walked. The way she drew water from the well.

There was the crisp sound of a branch snapping, unusual because there were neither bushes nor trees nearby. Unfortunately, we kept up our conversation, going on and on about Orla, never suspecting that we had been overheard by curious faeries from the mound.

—

At first, we only noticed a few things going amiss. Like Orla's shoes being misplaced, or the fact that it took much too long to run a comb through her hair, so matted and knotted it was each morning. Or how the milk in Orla's cup would spoil before midday.

None of these minor catastrophes, however, had any effect on Orla's dancing.

'Twas Orla's duty to gather small, dry branches for kindling the fire. I accompanied her one day, for turf cutting was hard work and I preferred a good walk to a sore back. And with Thomas off investigating the sheep, I felt a bit lonely. Orla didn't talk much, but she twirled and leaped with her empty kindling basket, her feet barely touching the ground. I had to run to keep up.

"Which one of ye is Orla the Dancing Girl?" said a mysterious voice.

As if it wasn't obvious.

Orla turned around and found herself not a hand's length away from a most unusual creature. At first small of stature, the creature rose until she was tall enough to look the girl in the eye. Her hair was almost as fair as her skin but her eyes were of the black of a moonless night. Her clothing was sewn with a fine hand; I could tell as much, what with my mother being such a skilled weaver. The dress, of deepest rose, swirled delicately to the ground. Her cape was a rich emerald green. Afraid we were, but smart enough not to show it. Fear makes itself large if you let it out.

"I am," said Orla.

"I am the Faerie Queen, and I've come to make a wager with ye." She ignored me as if I weren't there at all.

"Nay, I'll not wager. Wagering brings nothing but shame to a family." Orla was bold to speak in such a way to a queen. "My great-grandfather warned me against making gambles from the day I could first take a step." And wise, too, for a girl so young. "Wealthy he once was, till he gambled it all away."

"Would this change your mind?" The Faerie Queen pointed to the ground at Orla's feet. Each pebble changed into a coin of gold. We gasped in unison as the path sparkled before us.

"Ahhhh," said Orla, bending to pick up one of the golden discs.

"Not so fast," laughed the queen, her voice echoing through the trees, the clouds, and the sky. "'Tis simple, you see, we will have a little competition between the two of us. A dancing competition."

Orla could not help but smile, for she knew no one could dance as fine as she.

I, on the other hand, felt frozen in place. I could not speak the words that formed on my tongue: *Orla, do not trust the Faerie Queen!* I had learned from my experiences with the wee banshee and the selkies that humans and magical beings often see things differently.

"Whoever wins gets the gold," the Faerie Queen continued. "Whoever loses never dances again."

Orla stopped smiling. "Never?"

"Never."

Orla, no! 'Twill break your own heart in two if you can never dance again. But I was frozen in my tracks. I could not even catch her eye. It was as if I wasn't even there at all.

Obviously, I had been bewitched.

The thought of being able to help her family and restore their wealth was too much for Orla. She balanced her weight from one leg to the other, back and forth, more and more quickly until . . .

" 'Tis a bargain!" cried the girl, and she held out her hand to clasp that of the Faerie Queen. As they shook, the sky clouded over and a crack of thunder filled the air. Then the Faerie Queen and the gold coins on the ground vanished in a blink.

"Orla, what have you done?" I whispered to the morning breeze when my voice finally returned to me. But Orla was no longer there. She was skipping and dancing merrily down the path, dreaming of the gold she would win for her family.

THE DANGERS OF GAMBLING

News of the contest spread quickly, through both the village and the faerie kingdom, like green over the hillside in the spring. The challenge would be danced at midnight under the full moon in five days' time. Orla practiced from sunup to sundown. Her family did not know what to think, but what was done was done. The best they could do was help Orla prepare for her challenge.

"We'll stay, then, to see it through?" Thomas asked me as I paused to adjust the tightness of the strings on my harp, then started plucking again.

I nodded. I hoped he did not mind too much, for we could not leave the family in their time of need. My harp playing was necessary for Orla's practicing. Since daybreak I'd been working hard to keep up with her feet as she created more and more intricate steps. My fingers flew over the strings until small blisters appeared under the skin. But if the blisters on her feet did not stop Orla from dancing (and I was certain her feet must be sore and swollen), then the small eruptions on my hand would not slow my strumming.

Thomas placed his hand next to mine, then turned it over, front to back. "Look here, Trinket, not a blister nor a cut." He took in the red bumps on my fingers. "Mayhap I've got the easier job this time!" He whistled as he trotted off to join the men for an *easy* day of work.

The day before the competition, Orla's great-grandfather called her to his bedside.

"Trinket, please come with me. Great-grandfather often frightens me. He never leaves his room nor gets out of bed," she said.

I had been most curious about the closed door at the back of the house. But this was not something you asked about in polite company. I was learning that hunting for stories required patience.

Usually, when a story lurked, it revealed itself in time.

His hair was white and sparse and even his wrinkles had wrinkles.

"It's been fifty years, fifty years, I tell ye," he croaked, "since I, myself, struck an ill-made bet with the faerie folk."

Orla gasped. "Is that how you lost all of your—"

"Aye. That was the gamble that ruined me."

"What was *your* wager?" asked Orla.

"Same as yours." Great-grandfather's voice was like slow steps on a gravel path. "Oh, aye. These feet that can no longer walk"—he lifted a threadbare blanket to reveal a pale, shriveled foot—"once danced the sharpest steps. The Faerie Queen challenged me. She cannot abide there being a better dancer than herself. Oh, it should have been easy for me to win. I was the most fleet of foot there was, but she was tricky. Faeries always are. She changed the rules at the last minute."

He sat up higher in his bed, leaning toward us, beckoning us closer with his finger. He looked to the left and to the right before he continued.

"You there, harp girl, make sure there's no eavesdropping faeries under the window. Orla, look ye well under the bed."

When we assured him that no one was listening in, he went on.

"She changed the rules. I was made to dance upon a gold coin and not fall off."

Orla's eyes were as large as goose eggs. *"What?"*

"Foolish and full of myself, I was. I took the wager, and increased it, betting all of my wealth, *my family's wealth*, against hers."

We held our breaths, though we knew how it turned out. We knew that he had not triumphed, for Orla's family was the poorest in Ringford. But still, it was painful to hear him say it.

"I lost. We became poor because of it. In shame, I left my village a pauper. I came to Ringford to better my lot, but . . ."

He reached his gnarled hand under his pillow and drew out a beautiful golden coin. "This is the coin from the bargain, the last gold this family has known. I was saving it for my burial so it wouldn't be a burden to the family." He grabbed Orla's hand and pressed the coin into her palm.

"I want ye to take it."

"I cannot." Orla shook her head as she tried to pull away from the old man.

"Ye must!" he commanded. "Worse than losing the family money was losing my dancing." His voice caught and I looked out the window awkwardly. I would have left altogether, but Orla was between me and the door. "Money is just for buying things." He sniffed. "Dancing is life itself. I'll not have ye meet the same fate."

I could hear Orla swallow. Her eyes glassed over, but she did not cry. The full weight of her bargain landed upon us both as we stood in her great-grandfather's bedroom. I felt the cold finger of fear tracing circles on my spine. I wondered if she felt it, too.

"Do not be afraid, child," the old man said gently. "You, harp girl, take her out to practice." He waved us off.

"That is what ye must do," he called after us. "Practice, practice, practice!"

A COIN AND A HOLE

———◆·⟨⟩·◆———

Outside, Orla tried without luck to balance her steps on the small circle of gold. Good as she was, she was not good enough to land each leap on the coin. Not only that, she practiced so hard that she wore holes in the soles of both of her shoes.

"These will need mending," she sighed as she unlaced the ghillies from her feet. "Have you a hand for sewing, Trinket?"

As if I could sew with my fingers so bruised and blistered from playing the harp hour after hour!

I shook my head. "I've no skill. And stitching through leather is no easy task. Have you a needle strong enough?"

"Nay," sighed Orla. "If I were to break one of mother's bone needles on my shoe, she'd be more angry with me than if I lost this match."

"Perhaps the cobbler?"

"'Tis worth a try," said Orla. "Mayhap he can help me."

The cobbler was not at his shop. As a matter of fact, the shops were all closed. The streets were deserted and our voices echoed in the emptiness. The excitement of the competition that night must have caused everyone to go home and rest up for the big event.

"I bet the Faerie Queen herself wears enchanted shoes made by leprechauns," Orla complained as we walked through the empty streets of the village. "And here I am, the afternoon of the match with nothing but ruined ghillies and a gold coin."

Orla was beginning to lose hope. I could not let that happen. There had to be a way to repair the shoes.

And there had to be a way to thwart the Faerie Queen.

If she was planning on changing the rules, we must plan as well.

Our steps echoed through the streets of the small village. The only torch still burning was at the blacksmith's shop. We had nothing to lose, so in we went.

The blacksmith's apprentice was a friendly young man with hair as dark as a crow's wing and eyes to match.

"Can you help me?" Orla asked as she slowly pulled the gold coin from her pocket. "I've holes in both of my shoes and this is all I have. I've been practicing my dancing on this coin, for that is what the Faerie Queen will ask of me. If I cannot do it, I must never dance again."

"Orla, ye wee fool," said the apprentice. "Why did ye go and do a crazy thing like that?" He looked at me accusingly, as if it had been my idea.

"The fault is my own," said Orla. "I was too proud of my dancing. And now I'll never get to dance—" A small sob escaped her.

"Now, don't despair." He took the gold coin from her and flipped it into the air. "'Tis about time someone beat the faerie folk at their own game." He winked at us both. "Give me the shoes."

Orla untied the laces and handed the ghillies over. The

smith began to measure the tips of the soles. *Was he planning on patching her shoes with iron?*

"Will it cost all of the gold?" Orla whispered. "My great-grandfather wanted me to practice dancing on the coin . . ."

"Nay, I'll not charge ye at all, Orla. 'Twould be accursed money if I did."

He flipped the coin back to Orla, who caught it with one hand. The sight of the coin twirling through the air gave me an idea.

"Orla, may I see the coin?" I asked.

It was not very large, but it was thick. If the fire was still hot enough, it just might work.

THE CHALLENGE

At supper, Orla hummed a reel quietly to herself as she sipped her soup and chewed her bread.

"Are ye not nervous, dearie?" asked her mother.

Orla simply smiled, tapping her feet under the table. Her mother moved her gaze in my direction.

"Trinket, has she been practicing too hard? She looks soft in the head this evening."

"Nay, she's been practicing a great deal, but not over much. She'll be ready."

I winked at Orla and she winked at me. We looked down at our bowls so as not to giggle. *Was this what it was like to have a sister?*

I heard a snort from Thomas. He gave me a *what have you gotten yourself into this time, Trinket?* look.

Orla's mother sighed and glanced up to the heavens, muttering something under her breath.

—

When the sun went down, people began to gather on the hillside. And by moonrise, the crowd covered all of the green. The faeries were in attendance as well. Oh yes, they can be invisible when they choose, but when they gather in such a great number, well, they sparkle and shimmer most visibly. The queen wanted them there, of course, to witness her victory over the mortal girl who was fool enough to bargain with the fey.

Thomas and Mr. McGill carried Great-grandfather, bed and all, out to witness the contest. He smiled, but his old eyes held the worry we all felt.

Just as the moon found its place in the center of the sky, the Faerie Queen arrived in a carriage drawn by six tiny white ponies. The wagon stopped in front of Orla and the queen stepped out. She pulled herself up to her full height and asked, "Are ye ready for the challenge?"

"Aye," Orla said, bending down to adjust a lace on her ghillie.

"And ye agree that the loser of the battle shall never dance again?"

Orla's father made a move as if to protest the terms, but though his lips formed words, no sound came out. Bewitched most likely, as I had been when we last met the Faerie Queen.

"Aye," said Orla, "and the winner shall have your gold?"

"Aye," laughed the Faerie Queen, and she clapped three times. Musicians appeared on either side of her, one with a flute and one with a fiddle. "You have your own musician, do ye not?" She pointed disdainfully at me, though I saw her look at my harp with envy. 'Twas, after all, a most unique harp.

"Trinket is the finest harper in the land," Orla bragged. I stood tall as those around, human and fey alike, whispered and mumbled.

"Indeed?" said the Faerie Queen. "Then 'tis only fair that she play for me as well as for you. I would not want anyone to say that the contest is not a fair one."

I swallowed hard.

"Of course, the harper must have some stake in this as

well." She turned her beautiful face. "The harp, of course, should you make a mistake in playing, will be forfeit," she said.

A boy's voice piped up from the crowd. "What does she get, then, if she plays without error?"

Thomas.

The queen glared at him, but quickly replaced her nasty look with a sweet smile. "She can have her choice of reward, of course."

I only nodded. I had no idea what I might ask for because I did not expect to be able to play without a slip. My hands shook, causing my harp to quiver, as the queen motioned for me to sit on the chair the McGills had brought for me from their house.

"So, we begin." The queen stood on one side of the wooden plank floor Orla's father had laid for the competition. Orla took her place opposite the queen. My fingers were poised over the harp strings.

"Oh wait, I forgot one small detail." *Ah, here it was.* She pulled from the pocket in her cape a gold coin. "All dancing must take place upon a gold coin. Each step, each leap, each twirl must land upon the gold!"

Orla's mother gasped and I thought she might faint, but Orla's father and Thomas fanned her with large leaves and held her upright. Murmurs, mumbles, and grumbles wove through the crowd, laced with the occasional cries of "Unfair!" and "Cheat!"

The queen might have expected to see Orla crumple in disappointment. If so, then she herself was the disappointed one.

"You first." There was the slightest bit of cheek in Orla's request. But perhaps I was the only one to notice.

The queen rose as Orla stepped back from the floor. The coin flipped into the air and landed smack in the middle of the planks. She snapped her fingers and I played.

The Faerie Queen began her dance. The village folk could not help but *ooh* and *aah* as she leaped gracefully about, the tip of her toe never touching anything but gold. My fingers raced along the strings, desperately trying to keep up with the queen's wickedly fast feet. My hands started to sweat, but never once did the queen look tired. Never once did she look anything but fresh and strong. And amazing. The villagers clapped as she finished her dance, pointed her toes one final time, and bowed.

She nodded her head the slightest bit in my direction. I had made no mistakes.

"Your turn." She looked Orla up and down, her mouth smiling, her eyes not. "I hope you enjoy your last dance ever." As Orla took her place on the dance floor, her eyes twinkled mischievously. She motioned for me to begin. The queen caught the glimmer. "Remember, you must dance upon a gold coin! Every step!"

ORLA'S GAMBLE

———◆◆◆◆◆———

*M*y fingers sprang to life again and I played. 'Twas harder this time, for I could feel fatigue rolling in like the fog on a fall evening. I'd no doubt the queen would count a fault against me even if I botched Orla's tunes instead of her own.

Not too fast, at first. *Give Orla time to ease in.*

Orla danced in a way that no one had ever seen before. Instead of leaping and prancing, as a lady should when she dances a reel, Orla's feet rallied and trebled, creating an intricate, pulsating beat. If you listened, you could hear her shoes click slightly each time she touched the wood. But the queen was too busy savoring her soon-to-be victory to listen. "Look how her feet do not even touch the gold!" she jeered. "She has lost the bargain already."

Orla's mother began to weep. She hid her head in her husband's red beard. *"Never even had a chance,"* she sobbed. Orla heard nothing but the music and continued to create the most amazing dance ever danced. My fingers, inspired by her feet, leaped over the strings, never missing a note. The villagers clapped in time with the tune.

"You're not following the rules!" the Faerie Queen shrieked.

Orla's feet hammered out a crisp rhythm, more musical, more graceful, and more entrancing than the Faerie Queen's performance. When she clicked her heels together for the last time, both faerie folk and townsfolk stood, clapping and yelling wildly. Orla pointed her toes and bowed regally.

"You lost! You lost!" cried the queen. "Now you'll never dance again! You stupid, foolish girl! You did not even try! It doesn't matter that your dancing was the finest, for even the fey cannot deny it." She gestured to the faeries on the hill, who were all leaping about and clicking their heels, imitating

Orla's spectacular performance. "But your foot never touched the gold!" she roared.

All were silent then.

Orla was out of breath and still smiling. She nodded at me to rise, which I did. "If you'll permit me, your highness." I bowed to the queen, then bent down and unlaced Orla's ghillie. I flipped the shoe over, revealing its sole. "You never said she had to dance on *that* particular coin." Nailed to the bottom of Orla's shoe with horseshoe nails was half of her great-grandfather's coin, pounded flat and covering the hole that had been there. The other half was nailed neatly to the shoe's mate.

"As you can see"—I held the shoes high, visible to all—"Orla completed all of her steps upon a coin of gold."

The queen was furious. Some even said they saw lightning behind her eyes, and many of the villagers, fearing her wrath, escaped down the hillside. Angry words in a language I did not understand spewed from her lips.

But she did not combust there, under the moon that night. Nay. She simply took in a deep breath and disregarded Orla altogether.

Instead, she turned to face me.

She tried to hide her ire, but faeries are of a passionate nature. I knew I would have to watch my step, and my words, very carefully.

"Come forward," she said, pointing to me. "Bring your harp."

I picked up my harp and held it close to me, lest she try to grab it away. I walked two paces forward, then stood my ground. If that was not close enough, then she could come to me.

"'Tis exquisite," she said. "Perhaps you would let me try?"

I knew I was foolish to refuse, but I could not bring myself to allow it. I wrapped my arms tighter around my harp and shook my head slightly.

"Very well," she said. "I did not expect that you would. We have other matters to discuss, do we not? Your payment. Have you thought about what you might ask of me? I could come back another day, when you have had time to consider your options."

I could see Orla's great-grandfather out in the crowd,

shaking his head. Yes, indeed she might come back... in a hundred years or so!

"I would prefer my reward now."

"Would you really?" Her voice, the quietest of whispers, was still so fierce that gooseflesh rose on my arm.

"Aye."

REWARD

*B*efore you think too hard about what you might have wished for yourself, consider my situation. I was but a young storytelling lass accompanied by a pig boy, traveling through the land, attempting to find my father and learn enough stories so I could make a living for myself one day.

'Twas a hard enough path I had chosen for myself.

I did not need an enemy.

"I would like . . ." My voice was small, even to my own ears. I cleared my throat and started again. "I *demand* as my reward . . ."

The heat from the queen's glare was burning my own eyes. I felt them water and blinked twice. Oh, she was angry, but smart as well. I was certain that, at this moment, she was in her mind thinking of the things I might ask for and finding a way to turn my request into a curse.

'Tis the way of the fey. They'll not be bested.

I turned from the queen and looked into the remaining audience. The faces lit by torchlight under the midnight sky were scary to behold. Too much shadow around the eyes, and the grins all appeared evil, villager and faerie alike.

"I demand that the Faerie Queen be released from her punishment of never dancing again."

There were a few gasps and shocked murmurs. I was not facing the queen now, for I was too frightened, but I could hear her sharp intake of breath, followed by a slow exhale.

"Turn around, harp girl."

Slowly I turned.

"Why?" Her black eyes narrowed as if trying to search inside my mind. Perhaps she gained entry, for in the next instant, she smiled softly. Her face was so luminous in that moment, outshining even the stars and the moon.

"I'll not be outdone, girl. Faeries do not like being in the debt of humans." She spoke so softly I was not certain if anyone heard but me. "For your troubles," she said as she raised her hand and flipped a gold coin in the air toward me. I was too shocked to catch it, and it clattered on the wooden dance floor at my feet. I reached down to retrieve it. 'Twas larger than a regular coin, with strange shapes on it, perhaps serpents, all interwoven with each other, with no beginning and no end. Faerie gold.

By the time I looked up again, the Faerie Queen, her carriage, the ponies, and all of the faeries in the audience had vanished in the night, leaving behind Orla's newly won gold in several sacks of fine, heavy brown velvet.

The people whooped and hollered, raising Orla over their heads and lugging her fortune back to the McGills' cottage.

As I watched the villagers disperse, a hand clamped around my hand that held the coin. 'Twas sweaty.

Thomas.

"My palms were wetter than a crying babe's cheek." He laughed, and I hugged him. Neither mother nor father had I, but I had Thomas. And I was glad for it.

—

A traveling bard cannot remain in one place forever. Though I liked Ringford well, 'twas time to journey on and find new yarns to spin and eager new ears to hear them. And I could not forget what had led me here in the first place—the search for my father.

The farewells the next morning were both sweet and sad. Orla hugged me like a sister and the McGills thanked me over and over again. And Orla's great-grandfather clutched my hand tightly as a tear rolled down his withered face. "She would have lost it all without you," he said. I decided not to mention that 'twas probably my own conversation with Thomas by the faerie mound that caused the challenge to be issued in the first place. Some tales are best left untold.

"Why did you not ask for riches?" Thomas asked as we left the town of Ringford. "Or food. This sack will not last forever."

The sack in question bulged at the seams. Orla's mum had loaded us up with more food than four fat men could eat in a month. A heavy bag, indeed. But Thomas did not mind carrying the extra weight. It was worth it.

"You could have asked for a magic sack that would have filled with food whenever it was empty."

"And take the chance that the food would be cursed? Take the chance that if you ate it, you'd be under an enchantment?"

I knew Thomas would have chanced such a thing, were he hungry enough. But now, on a full belly, he nodded. "Didn't think of that."

"But what about riches?" he continued. "Come on, Trink, did ye not think of wealth?"

"Probably cursed as well. And if not a curse from the Faerie Queen, than the curse of greed. Yes, Orla's family has wealth, but they must now be on guard for someone who might want to take it from them."

"You sound like a know-it-all, you *do* know that, do ye not?"

We walked in silence then, but for the sound of our steps as we traveled farther and farther from the village. Sure steps, strong steps. Steps that said with each crunch of gravel that there were more important things than wealth and food.

"You're not going to tell me why, are you?" Thomas was getting annoyed, which would make for a cranky next few hours.

I sighed. "Thomas, with my reward, I bought us freedom. Freedom from the faerie folk chasing us down to reclaim whatever it was I'd asked for. And the freedom to continue on our quest for stories."

He said nothing for a long time.

"*Your* quest, you know."

"Hmmm?"

"It's *your* quest for stories. I am only along for the food."

THE FOURTH SONG

The Faerie's Reel

*These are the words I sang in my head when Orla and the
Faerie Queen danced their reels. I found if
I concentrated on the words, I worried less about
my fingers slipping.*

Oh, she is fair and fleet of foot
When she spins,
When she spins.
Oh, she leaps o'er the dust and soot
And makes the laddies happy.

And nae mistakes does Lady make
When she twirls,

When she twirls.
She dances on a golden stake
And makes the laddies happy.

THE FIFTH TALE

A Pig Boy, a Ghost, and a Pooka

IN THE BUSHES

———◆◆◆◆◆———

'Twas late in the afternoon and the wind crackled between the trees, coaxing dead leaves to swirl devilishly through the air, into our eyes and our hair. It seemed like only days since we had danced under the late summer moon. But in truth, it had been weeks.

We wanted to reach the next village before nightfall. 'Twas rumored that the Old Burned Man had visited villages to the south. We still held out hopes of meeting up with him and hearing him weave tales, though he was proving to be more elusive than a butterfly on a winter's day.

We unrolled the map in the light of the dying sun. I wished, not for the first time, that we had been more orderly in our travels. I wished we had followed a more sensible trail. Instead, we had visited a hodgepodge collection of places. Up to the hills. Down to the coast. Back up the coast. Over to yon valley. Wherever we thought we might have a lead on a bard or a story of any kind, that is where we went. Or rather, that is where we attempted to go. Our latest stop had been the village of Moreglin, a tiny town with neither a teller nor tales. However, there were cows that needed tending, so Thomas and I lent a hand in exchange for food and shelter, as usual. How I wished I was brave enough to do my own telling and charge a fair price, instead of forever just practicing bits of songs and tales on folks. Oh, to sleep far away from the smell of cattle! Perhaps in the next village . . . except the next village was not there.

"Maybe they were wrong. Maybe the next village was more than three days away," I said.

"Then why did they not just say that? *The village is four days away.* How hard is that? If they'd told us right, we'd have the proper amount of food still." Thomas's complaint was punctuated with a loud growl from his stomach.

'Twas always food with Thomas.

"Perhaps we walked too slowly. They could have marked the days it would take a grown man, not a girl and a pig boy."

"Nay and nay again," Thomas argued. "If so, then why not just say, *It takes a grown man three days, but it will take you lot four*?

"And," he continued, "we've not been walking too slow. We've kept a steady pace." He kicked a rock, which traveled halfway up the hill we were approaching, then rolled back down to him. "If we cannot see the village of Agadhoe when we get to the top of this rise . . ." he said.

And yet, when we reached the top of the hill and looked down into the valley, no village lights greeted us in the twilight. Not a single torch.

I glanced at the map again, but it was no help at all.

We had not taken the wrong road. At least, I was fairly positive we had not.

Thomas muttered a word under his breath that I was certain his mother would have punished him for. I should have scolded him, 'twas my duty, being a year older and all, but I, too, was bothered by the lack of a town.

"I suppose we should make camp. I've still some bread left."

"Stale bread," Thomas said.

"And a few berries . . ."

"Mashed berries, probably rotting," Thomas said.

I gave him a look and began searching for a place to camp.

'Twas always a bit tricky, finding a camping spot. Not too close to the road, for there were stories of highwaymen that robbed and terrorized travelers at night. But close enough so that we could hear anyone approaching on the road and determine if they were friendly or not. Of course, there were times we traveled when there was no road at all . . . but those stories are not in this tale.

There we were at the top of the hill, out in the open. The nearest patch of trees and bushes was back behind us, still visible in the dusk, but it would take us several minutes to get to it.

"Those bushes are too far from the road."

"Thomas, just exactly what do you propose? It is near dark. It is getting colder by the minute. Unless you want to sleep right here in the middle of the hill, I suggest we start walking to yon bushes."

He gave a *humph* and followed me there.

Thomas whacked at the bushes with a big stick to make certain no small creatures already sheltered there.

"'Tis safe," he proclaimed. So there we slept.

IN WHICH OUR POSSESSIONS
ARE STOLEN

I heard hooves clopping down the path. I was dreaming of a man whose face I could not see, riding a horse against the moonlit sky. The sound grew louder and I could feel the ground vibrating against my back.

Thomas felt it, too, for he was shaking me awake. It was not a dream.

We scrambled to pull loose branches over us.

The clip-clopping slowed.

We held our breaths. I could see a horse-shaped shadow with a rider atop whose cape billowed in the wind.

"Stand and deliver," commanded a deep voice that echoed against the leaves and made them rustle.

We remained frozen.

He saw us, or heard us, or perhaps felt our presence. He called out again, "Stand and deliver!"

Thomas squeezed my arm and slowly released it, willing me to stay under the branches. He rose awkwardly, his hands in the air. "Sir, I have nothing but a stale piece of bread and some mashed berries," he said, sounding like a pitiful runaway boy.

Quite convincing. I was proud.

"Have it and welcome," Thomas continued, bending to reach for the crust of bread in his bag.

"Do not move, lad, not an inch nor a muscle." The outlaw's voice was harsh. I could see now that he had a large sword pointed right at Thomas, close enough to run him through. "And do not lie."

I could hear Thomas gulp as the blade moved closer to his throat.

"I'll have the bag. The one next to the lassie."

How he could have seen me, I know not, for I was completely hidden in the shadows of the bushes. At least, I thought I was.

"The bag, missy. Ye'll hand it to me, now."

Slowly I rose and stepped out from behind a branch, brushing leaves from my hair. The horse stood massive and mountainlike, and the rider's head reached the moon. A black mask covered most of his face, but peering out through two holes were a pair of eyes so dark and so cold they sent a new wave of shivers down my spine.

"I want the bag with the silver mirror, the harp, and the faerie coin."

The coin I did not care about, despite its obvious value. I had thought we might need it, or the mirror for that matter, to bargain with at some point. I had not expected the price to be our lives. But my harp. I did not want to lose my harp. With it, I was beginning to feel like a true bard. How could I be a bard without it? Perhaps if I fought. Or ran.

Thomas made the decision for me, choosing our lives over our possessions. He grabbed the bag from my hands and threw it up to the man.

"Sorry, Trinket," he said.

I said nothing.

I swallowed my anger and bit back my tears.

"Much obliged," the outlaw said, tipping his hat with a

flourish. Then he looked at me, cocking his head to one side, then the other. "Well, well, well." He chuckled. "How lucky I am to have stumbled upon you." I thought he would look the harp over, or make certain the coin was inside the bag, but he did neither. He continued to stare at me. Then, he reared his stallion and galloped off into the night.

He was gone faster than seemed possible.

THE GRAVEDIGGER

———————◆◆◆◆◆———————

*H*ow did he know what was in the bag?" I asked between sniffles as we waited for the sun to rise. I had tried not to cry too much, but being robbed was very frightening. And I knew it made Thomas feel better that he was not the only one to shed a tear. We'd found neither dreams nor sleep for the rest of the night.

"Followed us?"

"How could we not have seen? The countryside for the past few days has been open. There was nowhere to hide."

"Mayhap someone in the last town spoke of your harp. Ye did play it, after all."

"Mayhap . . . but I do not think . . ." My thoughts stopped as the sun finally burst over the horizon, so bright it made the insides of my eyelids turn red when I blinked.

"We'd best start looking for the village. Who knows how many days away it is," he said. I nodded, remembering that since my father's map was in my bag, the robber had that as well. I hoped we'd find a town soon.

Thomas led us to the top of the hill where, in the distance, we saw a most unusual sight.

The village of Agadhoe.

'Twas not there the night before, but now stood plain as day. Small thatched cottages sat clustered and golden in the morning light.

So confused we were, I did not even have time to cry about my harp or the map, not that there were many tears left.

We saw no people as we walked down the hill and into the town, which was unusual. In most places, many of the folks rise with the sun or before. There is always more work to do than there is daylight to do it in. But the streets were more silent than the inside of an egg before it hatches.

We went from house to house, knocking on doors, but

nobody ever answered. How utterly bizarre for a village to be completely deserted. Slowly and carefully, lest the highwayman be lurking, we continued on through the town. We saw not a soul.

At the far end there was a graveyard. Most villages that have a church also have a graveyard somewhere close by so that those who die can rest in holy ground. Near the gate to the graveyard was a small cottage with a sign on the door that read: Gravedigger.

I'd never met a gravedigger before.

I moved my hand to knock on the weathered door.

"What are ye doing?" Thomas grabbed my wrist.

"Knocking on the door, perchance it looks like something else?" We'd tried every other cottage in town without any luck. And this was the last in the village. Why not give it a knock?

Before Thomas could tell me why we should not knock on this door, it creaked open and an old man stood there, no taller than myself.

His head resembled a round, mossy stone, and he had a twitch in one eye. He looked us up and down. "Aye, ye'll do," he said. "Come on." And he grabbed the shovel that was leaning next to the door and motioned for Thomas and me to follow.

Thomas shook his head most emphatically. I grabbed his arm and yanked him along. I wanted to see what would happen. Would we be digging graves? I wondered.

"Excuse me, sir," I asked, struggling to keep up. For an old man, he was quite spry. "But if I may ask, where is everyone in the town?"

He stopped short and looked at us with his twitchy eye. Then he croaked, "Who wants to know?"

"I am Trinket," I said. "This is Thomas. We have traveled many days to find your village. We were set upon by a robber last night and have neither food nor money."

At the word *robber*, the eyebrow above the twitchy eye raised. The gravedigger looked around to the right, then the left, and asked me to describe the thief.

"Tall, on a horse bigger than a house. He wore a cape and . . ." Thomas had finally decided to enter the conversation. Unfortunately, we both realized that it had been too dark for any further description.

"But his eyes," I remembered. "When I looked him in the eye, it nearly froze my blood and bones."

"Humph," said the gravedigger. Then he turned and continued down the path through the headstones.

"Sir," I persisted, following. "We will gladly work in exchange for food."

"Will ye, then?" he asked, stopping in an open spot and handing the shovel to Thomas. "Dig then, boy. You, girl, you can clear the large rocks out of the way. It makes the digging go faster if the large rocks are gone."

He turned to leave us there to dig what could only be a grave. I tried once more. "Sir, where is everyone in the town of Agadhoe?"

"Do ye not know the day, girl? 'Tis Samhain. They'll be a-hiding in their houses, too afraid to walk the streets, too afraid to light a lamp, until the dead rest again. Tomorrow, most likely, or the next day."

Samhain. I'd heard of it, of course. The night when the dead visit the living. That was why there were no lights in the town below so it appeared as if there was no town at all. The townsfolk wanted to hide. They feared the return of their dead.

I wondered for a moment if *all* those who have passed return on Samhain, though I held little hope for seeing my mother again. Lucky I'd been able to receive her message in Crossmaglin. Had she more to tell me, she would have done so then.

She would not call upon me tonight.

Nay, if the entire town were concealing themselves, the spirits who walked tonight would not likely be gentle mothers paying loving visits to their children.

DIGGING

After the man went back to the cottage, Thomas threw the shovel on the ground. "I am not digging a stinking grave."

"What are we going to do then? I cannot believe you are not hungry." I did not want to dig a grave either, but we simply had to eat.

"I think the old man knows something about the robber," I continued. "Mayhap he will tell us what he knows if we ask him during the meal."

Thomas glared at me. "You're just trying to find another story, are ye not?"

"Aye, I suppose I shall need even more now that my harp is gone."

Perhaps it was cruel to use the loss of my harp to get my way. But it worked. Thomas began to dig.

And truly, what choice did we have?

—

Digging a grave is hard work. Morbid, too. It made me think about death. I didn't like to think about . . . about people I loved being buried in the ground. Better to think of my mother flying like a beautiful bluebird, across the sun, looking down at me from time to time. The grave made me think about my father, too. *Was he dead? Or was he still out there, somewhere?*

My search had still turned up no clues as to why he disappeared. And I knew he must have existed, because I existed. But there were few along the way who remembered him. I wondered if I would ever find an answer. However, I did not regret this quest. It had led me on many an adventure and given me my own set of stories.

Sometimes, when you search for one thing, you find something else.

I said a silent prayer for James the Bard, wherever he was.

We were starved when we finished digging what we thought was a respectable grave. It was past midday and the sun was getting lower, so we ran to the little cottage by the gate. A mess met us inside, with brown leaves and broken branches strewn about. Obviously, the gravedigger was not the tidiest housekeeper. Had I not known better, I would have thought the only inhabitants of the cottage of late had been mice and squirrels.

Nonetheless, the old man's stew smelled wonderful. A rich, brown broth with bits of turnip, parsnip, mutton, and the tiniest onions ever glistened in our bowls. And there were slices of apples and pears, warmed by the fire. I could not stop eating the sweet, tart wedges. I wanted to ask the gravedigger about the robber, but my mouth was too full, so the only sound during the meal was the slurping of stew and the clinking of spoons against the pottery.

"Thank you, sir," I said at last, mopping the remains of the stew with a crust of bread. " 'Twas the best meal we have had in many days."

He nodded, and then looked at Thomas with a wink. "I

expect you'll be needing all your strength tonight," he said as he ladled another helping in each of our bowls.

Thomas stopped chewing and looked at the man. His mouth was too full of apple to blurt out his question, so I helped him.

"What do you mean, exactly?"

The man sat back in his chair and lit his pipe from the fire. He did not even have to reach far, for the small table was next to the hearth.

"If ye are wanting to catch the Highwayman, it has to be tonight, else you'll never get your things back from him."

THE POOKA

———◆✦◆———

Thomas choked on his apple. I patted him on the back and handed him some cider. Neither of us had considered chasing after the outlaw.

"Here's what ye do," continued the old man, leaning toward us. "Ye've already dug the grave to trick the pooka. Once you've caught the pooka, he'll owe ye a favor. And pookas keep their word, they do. Ye'll ride the pooka out past the wall between the living and the other side and steal your wealth back from the Highwayman. Simple as pie." He chuckled to himself.

Thomas was the first to respond. He laughed out loud. "I

must tell you, old man, I didn't understand a word of what you just said. Not one word!"

However, I did understand. I had heard of the pooka, the enormous spirit horse that can speak to humans. There are tales of pookas carrying unsuspecting riders away, never to be seen again. My mother once tried to tell me one such tale (that she learned from my father), but I was too scared and I begged her not to finish. But I remembered that pookas, in addition to being large and terrifying, were surprisingly civil. They were also most easily bent to the will of humans on Samhain. There was, however, something in the gravedigger's instructions that did not make much sense . . . unless . . .

"Sir, the fact that we must cross the wall between the living and the other, does that mean that the outlaw is *dead*?"

"Nay. It means the Highwayman who robbed you was a ghostie."

Finally, Thomas stopped laughing.

Food remained in our bowls, but neither Thomas nor I had the stomach to eat it. The meal was finished.

"'Tis too dangerous," I said to Thomas that night as we walked back to the grave, remembering how close I'd come to following the banshee to the other side. The other side, I was convinced, did not play fair. "Perhaps if we wait . . ."

"Nay, it has to be tonight, or the wall will be too thick to pass through for another year." Thomas paused, then pressed on. "Do you not want your harp back?"

Of course I wanted my harp back. But if I had to choose between a harp and a pig boy . . . well, I would choose Thomas.

"You were the one who promised adventure would befall us if I agreed to accompany you on your quest for stories."

He had a point. But still, this was far too dangerous.

"Look, Trinket, you know the stories about Samhain. You've heard them since you were a babe, same as me. And if we get the help of a pooka—"

"*If* we find one," I interrupted.

"As I was saying, if we get the help of a pooka, I should be able to ride in and ride back out." He threw a crust of bread down in the grave, as the old gravedigger had instructed. I'd never seen Thomas so excited about anything.

"You've grown braver, I think, Thomas."

He paused, then looked me in the eye and said simply, "I had a good teacher."

The wind began to rise. We threw more and more crusts of bread down into the hole. 'Twas tradition to leave a feast for the pooka in the graveyard on Samhain, else ill luck was to follow for the year. At least that was what the old gravedigger told us. But when we searched again for the gravedigger, hoping he'd help us put together a feast, we could not find him. Perhaps he, too, feared the night of Samhain, like the other residents of Agadhoe, and was hidden inside one of the lifeless little cottages. Thus, our pitiful feast was leftover bread and apple slices.

We hoped it would be enough.

We heard a sound carried on the wind. Perhaps it was a large horse blowing gusts of air from his nostrils. We could not tell, however, if it was the pooka we were expecting, or the Highwayman atop his stallion, so we hid behind the nearest gravestone.

"Weeeeeeellll, what have we here?" said a surprisingly pleasant voice. "Crusts of bread? What kind of a feast for a pooka is that?" The voice changed from kind to perturbed.

'Twas not the outlaw, of course. 'Twas the pooka.

I chanced a peek. Deep gray, he was, with a mane the color of midnight and a tail to match. Quite handsome, but comical in the way his mouth moved when he spoke.

"And, putting the crusts down a hole? What way is that for folks to tell ye how much they appreciate ye? No way at all, I tell ye," he muttered, shaking his head back and forth.

"Mebbe something else is under the bread. Can't really tell from up here . . ." He leaned over the grave.

Before I could blink, Thomas jumped up and pushed the pooka from behind.

The horse wriggled and waggled and tried to keep his balance, but fell, as we had planned, into the grave.

"Och, now, why'd ye have to go and do a thing like that?" he whined.

Thomas and I peered down over the edge. The pooka sat with his legs crossed, nibbling on a crust.

"It's stale, ye know," he complained.

"Sorry," I said.

"Now that I've captured you, you have to honor me with a favor," said Thomas in his most commanding tone. Quite impressive for a pig boy, really.

"Perhaps I do not want to," said the pooka.

"Pardon me, sir pooka, but the custom says that you are to be most civil and agreeable when honored with a feast on Samhain." My voice sounded like I knew what I was talking about.

"Ye call this a feast?" he moaned. "It's more like table scraps a dog wouldn't eat, that's what it is. Now help me out of here."

"Very well, you have given us no choice but to leave you here." We turned our backs and took a few steps away.

"No! Wait!" cried the pooka. We glanced back over our shoulders. "I apologize. If you would assist me in my effort to get out of this . . . this . . . this whatever it is, I shall help you." His voice was most civil, now.

Not wanting to insult him by asking for his word of honor (as the custom says that pookas are most honorable creatures), we helped him out of the grave. 'Twas not easy, hefting a horse twice the size of a regular nag out of a hole in the ground. Thomas climbed down and leaned against the horse's huge rump with all his might.

"I beg your pardon!" the pooka cried.

"Forgive me . . . er, um, sir. It's just that if I don't push against your bum while Trinket pulls on your mane, we might never get you out." Thomas grunted between pushes.

I was already pulling on his mane, the coarse hairs cutting into my hand fiercely.

"Of all the indignities," the pooka muttered.

"You could help, sir," Thomas groaned. "Just place your forelegs on the edge and—there you go—now when I count to three—one, two, THREE!" Thomas cried, and with a final shove, the pooka stumbled up out of the grave. A sweaty Thomas emerged after him, breathing heavily. "I hope I never have to do that again."

"You are not the only one. I've probably got bruises all over me rump," said the pooka.

I quickly explained to him our situation.

"So," he began, taking a deep breath, still munching on bread crusts. "Ye want me to take ye through the wall between the living and the other so ye can find the Highwayman and steal back your harp, your mirror, and your gold coin? You're serious about this?"

We nodded.

"The Highwayman, nasty piece of work, he is. If he catches ye . . ." His voice trailed off.

Thomas said bravely, "Well, we just won't let him catch us. Are you fast?"

"Fast enough for you, laddie. Fast enough for you."

"Fast enough to carry the both of us?" I asked.

The pooka considered the situation before replying, "Aye."

TO THE OTHER SIDE

$\mathcal{N}$ay, Trinket, you're not coming—" Thomas began.

"Aye, Thomas, you'll not stop me, and we both know it. So we can stand around and argue, however I myself think that it is rude to quarrel in front of company." I nodded to the pooka, who winked back at me. "Or we can get this over with."

I handed a jug of water to Thomas. "Remember to drink up before we ride. There might not be time after."

Thomas glared but took several swigs from the jug. This was the part I was glad Thomas was willing to do. "Don't drink too much, though. It could be a bumpy ride." He did not laugh at my joke, but the pooka snorted. Bending down, the pooka allowed Thomas and me to climb on his broad back.

"You will not fall, for I will not let you. But hold tightly. I shall gallop faster than you have ever traveled. 'Twill feel like flying." The pooka seemed to be enjoying this. "And remember not to get down from my back while we are on the other side."

"Why not?" I asked.

"How can you not know this?" the pooka scolded. "If your feet touch the ground, you'll stay on the other side until next Samhain, plus one day more."

A year and a day with the dead? Perhaps it would not be so bad if I found my mother. She would not come to me, but if *I* found her . . .

"Do not think about it, Trinket," Thomas said. He knew me far too well. "There is a reason there's a wall between the living and the other, don't ye think?"

"Aye," said the pooka, "there's a reason indeed." And he left it at that.

True to his word, the pooka galloped faster than either Thomas or I could have imagined. The trees blurred into one long and eerie shadow that trailed after us. We traveled so fast that even the light of the moon could not catch up. Breathing was difficult, for the air was sucked out of our lungs as we rode faster and faster still. My mother's fine cloak flew behind me as if it had wings of its own. The pooka did not speak. With his head down, he raced against the night, speeding us toward the wall between the living and the other side.

I thought I would be able to tell when we passed through the wall. Perhaps there would be a sense of utmost despair. Perhaps it would be even darker. Perhaps there would be a tiredness in my bones that would compel me to seek eternal rest. Alas, I noticed no difference. The pooka whispered, "We are here. Do not get off my back."

He stopped. We listened to the silence, waiting for a clue as to which direction to pursue. I thought there would be the sound of wailing on the other side, like the wee banshee from

Crossmaglin. However, there was nothing but the faintest melody.

"Do you hear that?" I whispered in Thomas's ear. He shook his head. "'Tis my harp a-playing. I'm sure of it."

He whispered back, "Which way?"

I pointed to the left. Slowly and silently, we trod along. The pooka's hooves made no sound on the ground, if there was indeed ground under us. I could only see mist.

The tune became louder, proving we were going the right way. But no spirits did I see. Weren't there countless dead folk? I would have thought the other side quite crowded.

As if reading my mind, the pooka whispered, "The other side is vast. More so than you can imagine. And, of course, 'tis Samhain. Many souls have gone frolicking amongst the human folk."

"But not the Highwayman," Thomas said with a gulp.

"Nay, the Highwayman is a ghostie. He does not have to wait until Samhain, when the wall is at its thinnest, to travel betwixt the lands of the living and the dead. He can pass back and forth as he pleases." The pooka was most knowledgeable. I was glad we had him for our guide.

"Why, then, are not all of the dead folk ghosties? Wouldn't they like traveling back and forth of their own choice? I know I would." Thomas's voice was so quiet, only the pooka and I could hear.

"Would ye now? Ghosties are tortured souls who cannot rest. They long to feel blood rush through their veins again, to be alive. But they cannot return to life, nor can they feel comfort in death. 'Tis not a fate anyone would choose, lad. Like being more tired than ye can comprehend and not being able to sleep."

I felt a bit of pity for the Highwayman. Certainly, he had stolen from us, but an eternity of no rest sounded dreadful indeed.

The music was loud enough for me to discern the melody. And I recognized it.

Gooseflesh spread across my shoulders and down my arms. Thomas felt me shake off the chill.

"What is it?" he whispered.

"'Tis a song I know . . . a lullaby . . ." *My father's lullaby.*

And then, through the mist, I saw him.

THE HIGHWAYMAN

The Highwayman sat on a rock, playing my harp. His long fingers moved over the strings deftly. He finished the lullaby and began a sorrowful piece that broke my heart. I longed to get off the pooka and speak to him, but Thomas held my arm tightly.

Now what to do? Should we demand the harp back, or try to get close enough to grab it?

"You've come a long way to retrieve such a small treasure," the Highwayman said, turning slowly and facing us. "And on a pooka! 'Twould seem I underestimated you."

He rose, placing the harp on the rock, and took a step closer to us. Thomas clutched the pooka's mane even tighter.

The Highwayman smiled cruelly. "Your harp?" He addressed his question to me. "Come and get it." He stepped out of our way and bowed gallantly.

Ever so slowly, we moved toward the harp.

"Your eyes are familiar, girl." His voice was between a sneer and a whisper.

"Don't listen to him," warned the pooka. "I told you, he is evil."

"And the point of your chin," the Highwayman continued. "Aye, girl, I've seen it before. I knew when I first looked at you, I'd seen it. Somewhere . . ." His voice trailed off.

We were almost close enough. If I leaned far over and Thomas held me, I might be able to grasp the harp. If only we did not have to pass the Highwayman first.

"Who is it that you look like, dearie? Your mother? Or your father?"

I froze as the Highwayman chuckled. "Mayhap you do not know."

We inched forward, just past him, almost even with the harp.

Thomas pinched me hard. I'd have to grab it now, fast, or miss my chance altogether.

I reached out, the tips of my fingers touching the smooth white bone. The pooka moved us closer.

As I clasped the cold side of the harp and pulled it to me, the Highwayman's hand snaked out and jerked at the creature's mane. The pooka stumbled, nearly throwing me off. Had Thomas not been holding me so tightly, I would have fallen and I'd have been cursed to live a year and a day on the other side. Thomas dug his heels into the pooka's flanks and the creature reared back.

"A challenge it is, then!" The Highwayman laughed. He climbed upon his stallion, which had appeared from nowhere.

The pooka galloped hard and fast. I clutched the harp tightly with one hand and Thomas with the other, hoping we were going the right way, but at this point, any direction away from the Highwayman was a good one.

He was but a breath behind us. I could feel the stallion panting on the back of my neck.

"A gentleman of the road, I am," the Highwayman snickered. "Always willing to offer kindness to a fellow traveler." He reached out and caught a few strands of my hair and yanked. "Hmm, the father's hair or the mother's?"

I screamed, tempted to throw the harp back in his face. But that would not have stopped the Highwayman. He cared not for the harp.

He sought trophies of another kind.

We sped through the other side, the wind so harsh on our faces we were near blinded. I thought once or twice I felt a tug on my hair, but whether it was a strand caught in the branched fingers of a decrepit tree, or the Highwayman closing on us, I could not be sure.

I was far too afraid to look back, for if he were to catch us, I would not have his cold eyes be the last things I ever saw.

We crossed through the wall between the living and the other, but that did not stop the Highwayman. He was not as close to us now, but he didn't need to be. He could follow at his own pace and never tire. He was dead already.

But we were gasping for breath. Even the pooka was wheezing as we arrived at the gravedigger's cottage. "Hurry, Thomas, HURRY! You've got to do it now!" I cried, hoping he hadn't sweated off all of the water he'd drunk earlier.

A VISIT FROM THE QUEEN

———◆·✦·◆———

We got off the pooka and Thomas proceeded to relieve himself on the gatepost of the small house.

"The only way to keep a ghostie out of your house," the gravedigger had told us, "is to piss on the gatepost. They won't pass through. They cannot."

Thank goodness Thomas had no problem. Seemed like, in fact, he'd not relieved himself for days. I wanted to say, *That's quite enough, Thomas*, but preferred instead to look off into the distance. I caught the eye of the pooka, who was doing the same.

I did not see the Highwayman approach. But I could hear him circling.

"Ye'll be safe, if ye stay inside," the gravedigger had told us. But where was the old man now?

The door to the cottage was just large enough for the pooka to fit through, though Thomas had to push on the horse's large rump once again.

"Sorry," Thomas mumbled.

"Well, ye should be. Twice in one night. Now, close the door, will ye?" the pooka ordered. Thomas closed and bolted the door.

—

Through the window, we could see movement among the gravestones. Those from the other side, perhaps, paying a visit on Samhain. But nothing came near the house. We sat inside the cluttered, filthy cottage, a girl, a boy, and a pooka, trying to pass the time until daylight came, hoping the sun would keep the Highwayman away.

"They cannot go far, you know, ghosts and such," said the pooka. "A ghost cannot pass over water. Cross the stream half a day's walk east of the village and you'll be safe."

We heard clip-clopping again, louder, sending new waves of chills down my arms.

"Do you suppose . . ." Thomas began. "Ah, never mind."

"Go ahead. Ask me."

"Well, the Highwayman talked a lot about your folks . . . do you suppose . . ."

"Are you asking me if he knew my parents?"

"Or, maybe, could he *be* one of them . . . like your father, I mean? Think about it, Trinket. No one seems to know much about James the Bard. Mayhap your da became a robber—"

A loud growl interrupted us and we flew back to the window. The Highwayman stood at the gate, anger fairly spewing from him. But he was not alone.

I gasped as the familiar, terrifyingly beautiful form of the Faerie Queen emerged from the fog, cracking her whip overhead and driving her miniature ponies across the dry ground of the old graveyard.

"I'll have the coin," she said, her voice just as I remembered. She drew herself out of her carriage and up to the Highwayman's full height. Her pale hand gestured impatiently. "You should know better than to steal what the faerie folk have given, you foolish shade."

The Highwayman appeared as if he would refuse. But

then, all around the graveyard, spirits materialized from behind the headstones. Some young, some old, all as pale as the clouds at night. "Give it back," they whispered. "Give it back to the girl."

Whether 'twas a trick of the Faerie Queen, or the dead speaking for us, I did not know.

Slowly, Thomas and I walked onto the cottage porch. If the Highwayman had been able to venture past the gatepost, I was certain he would have done it by now.

Shaking with fury, the Highwayman gave the coin to the Faerie Queen. "It does not belong to me." She flipped it through the air and it clattered on the porch at my feet, just as it had after the contest in Ringford. "It belongs to the girl. Return all that is hers." She then turned to me. "You would do well not to lose a bargaining coin given by the folk. Prove yourself worthy, girl, for 'tis more valuable than you can imagine. I'll not help you retrieve it should you part ways with it again."

My sack flew through the air as the Highwayman glared at us one final time. Thomas raced through the doorway and caught the bag before it could fall to the ground and shatter the mirror. The Highwayman's eyes were no longer cold, but hot with rage, his mouth twisted in a sneer. *Was that the face of my father, hidden behind a thief's mask?* Then he turned and galloped off into the new light of dawn. The air was rent with the queen's laughter.

Naturally, the pooka was gone when we went inside, for 'twas daybreak and he was, after all, a creature of the night. And a magical one at that.

We wanted to say goodbye and thank you to the gravedigger, but he was still nowhere to be found and we were too anxious to get past the stream, half a day's walk from the village. And we'd no desire to bide with the folk in this town, who had cowered in their homes for the past two days and nights. Strangely, though, as we passed the farthest edge of the graveyard, we saw a weathered headstone with a small shovel leaned up against it.

HERE LIE THE BONES
OF OLD MACGREGOR
OF ALL HE WAS
THE BEST GRAVEDIGGER

That night, miles away, I felt for the bargaining coin deep inside the pocket of my britches. 'Twas warm from being so near my skin and I rubbed it twice for courage. Was I finally brave enough to speak aloud the thoughts that had crowded my head all day?

"Thomas," I said carefully, "what if that outlaw, what if he really *was* my father?" I swallowed, trying to sound like I didn't care as much as I did.

"What if he was?" asked Thomas. "Doesn't make you any different, does it? You're still Trinket no matter what."

I wanted to bury the bard's map in the dirt, for I'd follow its trail no longer. What if it had been drawn by the evil hand of the Highwayman? But Thomas would not let me.

"A map's a map, Trinket. We can still use it even if you don't like who made it."

Wise, wise Thomas.

"Still Trinket no matter what." I said those words over and over to myself for the rest of that night.

And many nights to follow.

If James the Bard was really James the Ghostly

Highwayman, then I wanted no part of him. And if he was not, sadly I was no closer to finding him. Though some folks remembered my father, no one had seen him for years. He was as good as dead.

Perhaps some truths are never meant to be uncovered.

THE FIFTH SONG

The Dangers of the Road

To tell the truth, this is not my favorite song, and
I cannot play it without getting a chill upon the back of
my neck. However, it is the duty of the teller to
warn the unsuspecting traveler, I think.

Go not, thou unsuspecting lad,
Oft through the blackened night,
For in the mists
And tree-claw limbs
There lurks a fearsome sight.

Hooves of fire,
Flanks of coal,

Only a moment
To forfeit thy soul.

And there, behind the callous swirls
Of danger and despair,
The clipping, clopping follows thee
Through empty evening air.

Hooves of fire,
Flanks of coal,
Look not upon him
Or forfeit thy soul.

The Old Burned Man and the Hound

CASTLE CHORES

Thomas and I were still determined to find and hear the Old Burned Man. Most villages considered it an honor when he paid a visit. No feast was too extravagant, no bed was too soft. He ofttimes visited castles or fine manor houses, and though it would take him a hundred days to tell all of his tales and sing all of his songs, he was not known for remaining long in one place. I could not even imagine what it would take to remember a hundred stories! I was still working on gathering and polishing seven.

I had become more courageous with my harp. Perhaps it was that I was tired of milking, drawing water, thatching roofs, and digging graves. Or perhaps, after being chased by creatures and beasties worse than Death itself, it seemed foolish to fear a quiet fire, shining eyes, and ears ready for the listening. In the last village we'd been to, a woman took one look at my harp and said to me, "Have ye songs to go with your harp? Or mayhap a story, lass?"

Aye. I liked how that sounded. The Story Lass.

—

But now we had finally arrived at a true castle, called Castlelow. It had received its name from being situated on a low, grassy meadow. The legend was that another castle, called Castlehigh, once sat at the top of the nearby hills, but now only ruins remained. 'Twas a good thing we chanced upon Castlelow, for each night as we camped, the sound of howling wolves grew louder. Never before had we heard such howling. Perhaps it was normal for this time of year, with winter approaching. Neither Thomas nor I were certain, though, for there were never wolves howling near our village on the coast. We were grateful to find the shelter of thick stone walls.

There are all manner of beings that live in a castle. Not

just kings and queens and lords and ladies. Not just servants down below or knights in the field. There are animals as well. Pigs, goats, and chickens running free through the castle yard and hounds, lying under the tables, waiting for crumbs to drop.

I'd met hounds before, of course. But a castle hound is a different breed from a village hound or a road hound. You can tell by the way he holds his head and the way he stands close to his master.

The way he'd give his life to protect him.

—

I was somewhat nervous, of course. Would Castlelow want to hear the tales of a traveling lass? Mayhap it would be better to do odd chores and such, taking the time to listen to the stories of the castle bard, if they had one.

I decided not to ask about my father here. He was the past. I had to focus on the future.

The Lord and Lady of Castlelow were kindly. They had a new babe, their first, a boy with sandy hair that stuck out from his head like the down of a newly hatched duck. I was assigned to help look after the child, which would allow me to practice my lullabies and perhaps a story or two. Thomas was assigned to the pigs, his first pigs in a long, long time. He was jubilant.

"Aw, Trinket, mayhap we can stay here a while. The food is plentiful and the straw is clean." He had a small piglet, pink and quite adorable, tucked under his arm. "And the work is not hard."

"Not like digging a grave." I laughed.

"Nay, not like digging a grave at all," he said.

True, we'd done much hard labor on our journey, slept on the ground, and gone hungry more oft than not. Life at the castle looked to be easy. My task was not difficult, either. I did the things the laddie's nurse would rather not do, which mostly consisted of dirty jobs like changing soggy clothes, feeding him gruel, and following him wherever he wanted to crawl. Unfortunately, the babe had a hard time getting to sleep and the nurse bade me stay with him in his nursery in the tower until he slumbered. I missed the storytelling for the first four nights we were there. 'Twas torturing me to be so close to a true bard and not be able to hear him, even if it wasn't the Old Burned Man, who was due to arrive any day, or so everyone said. Thomas had been luckier than I, for there was no need for a pig boy to lure the piglets into dreamland.

"They said if we were good and quiet and all, that we could come and listen," he told me the fifth morning of our stay. I could feel jealousy rising, and Thomas saw it in my face. "He wasn't near so good as you," he sputtered.

I only humphed.

"Trinket, they've seen your harp. They know you're a teller. Why do ye not just—"

"I am not ready for a castle, Thomas."

He walked off, but I was sure I heard him mumble, "Of all the things, never thought she was a chicken."

Thomas was right. I was being ridiculous.

One must be brave to tell stories.

I had met with creatures of unusual magic and lived to tell the tale. I had even escaped a deadly rider atop a phantom stallion and outwitted the powers of darkness.

Was I not brave?

FINN

I practiced, singing soft songs to the young babe each night with the lord's gigantic hound at my feet. He loved the songs, too. A larger dog I'd never seen in my life. Were he to stand on his hind legs, his head would have risen far above my own. His coat was the color of wheat in autumn. But the most amazing thing about him was that, for all of his enormous stature, he was gentler than the evening breeze. They called him Finn the Great. I thought of him as Finn the Oversized Kitten.

He watched over the babe each night while he slept. As I drifted off to sleep in my small closet of a room next to the nursery, I could see the hound lying still and protective on the floor at the foot of the boy's crib.

Perhaps I would have a dog of my own one day, I thought as I strummed and sang softly in the early morning before the babe awoke. A dog could watch over Thomas and me while we slept. What an odd family we would be. No parents, just a boy who tends pigs and a girl who tells tales.

There were worse families, I was certain. And yet—

The voice that interrupted my song was gravelly and rough. "I heard music on the stairs and followed it here. 'Tis a nice song. Is it yours?" 'Twas a damaged voice, but there was beauty in the ragged way he spoke.

I wish I could say that I answered, *Aye, sir, my own tune as well as my own words.* But when I turned to face him, I could not speak. His face was fiercely scarred and he wore a gray hood that covered his head. The scars were white and twisted his smile (I thought it was a smile) into a frightening skull-like grimace. I gasped and nodded stiffly. I could feel heat rush to my face. What horrible manners I possessed.

After all, exactly *what* had I expected him to look like? The Old Burned Man, for he could be no other, the bard I'd searched for, was standing *not halfway across the room*. The famed teller had finally arrived at the same place at the same time as Thomas and I. I should have been jumping with excitement. *He was here!* But all I felt was horror.

The Old Burned Man looked down.

I stammered, "Er, 'twas a song I wrote for my mother. She reminds me of a bluebird."

"She is blessed to have such a song written for her."

"She's dead."

There was silence, but it was not uncomfortable this time. 'Twas like he was offering a bit of silence in respect for my mother. That was nice.

"Well." He cleared his throat, which sounded painful. "The ones we love often leave us, don't they?"

"Aye."

"But my guess is they'd prefer not to, if given the choice."

His ruined eye winked at me, and I found myself smiling slightly at this gruesome-looking man.

"If given the choice," I repeated.

━

'Twas not simple to sneak down the stairs of the castle to hear the storytelling that night, but how could I miss my first chance to hear the Old Burned Man? As if the babe knew I needed him to sleep, and quickly at that, he refused to lie down for a long time. Even when he finally slumbered lightly, the quiet sound of my footsteps roused him and I had to start singing all over again. I found myself making up unpleasant words.

Go to sleep, little piglet,
Lest I roll ye in the mud
And make thee eat on worms and scraps
'Twill be for thy own good.

"Ye'll have to teach me that one. I might use it sometime," said Thomas with a snicker.

I carefully placed my harp on the cushion, tiptoed across the room, and whacked him hard in the gut.

"Oof."

"Shhhhhh." Most likely I should not have thumped him, but I was in a mood due to missing the very reason we had come this far.

Luck was with me, for the babe did not stir. "I got tired of waiting on the steps for you to come down," Thomas whispered. "He must be halfway through with the stories."

"Aw, Thomas, you didn't go and hear him without me? You waited?" I asked.

"Now, Trinket, how could I leave you with the wakeful babe and go listen to the Old Burned Man *and* live to tell the tale?" Thomas grabbed my hand and pulled me toward the stairs. Finn the dog opened one eye and watched us leave. Feeling the babe was in good hands, or paws, we continued on our way. I stumbled once on the hem of my dress, which I'd pulled from the bottom of my sack and worn for the evening. Finally hearing the Old Burned Man was worthy of my nice clothes.

'Twas not the Old Burned Man, though, but a string bean of a lad named Berthold.

Thomas rolled his eyes. "Not him again," he muttered.

"Where is the Old Burned Man?" Thomas whispered to a lady as we squeezed in beside her on the bench.

"Cough or fever," said the lady. Thomas groaned and was promptly shushed by the woman. "Now quiet down and give proper respect. Berthold is the nephew of—"

"Aye, I know. I heard him the other night," Thomas said, then mouthed the words *he's horrible* so that only I could see.

Berthold's voice quivered like a leaf on a branch. He kept clearing his throat and he forgot important parts of the story, so the ending made no sense. The crowd was beginning to get restless and the lord and lady looked annoyed.

"Is there not someone else who has a tale this night?" asked the lord. "Where is the girl who arrived but a week ago with a harp?"

I was determined to have courage this time. I raised my hand. "I am the Story Lass," I said.

"Well, go on, lass," said the lord, "give us a story."

I took my place on the three-legged bard's stool as Thomas raced up the stairs to get my harp. I felt in my pocket for the faerie gold, which I now carried with me always, and pulled it out. The coin felt heavy in my hand.

"A-hem." The lord cleared his throat. "Any time now, lass."

Whether I rubbed the coin for courage or for luck, I do not know. But I rubbed it thrice and placed it back in my pocket.

Then I began my tale.

My voice was timid at first, and I swallowed a couple of

times until I felt the shaking stop. *No better than Berthold.* I took a deep breath and calmed myself. Though 'twas my first castle, I hoped it would not be my last. This is what I had worked so hard for.

"The Story of the Gypsies and the Seer," I began again, "a tale of a princess with a rare gift and her father, who would stop at nothing to sell it."

With my words, I painted pictures of the places I had been. The exotic caravans of the Gypsy camp came alive in the great hall, so real, in fact, that I could smell the chicken coop and feel the silk of the tent under my fingers. The words were flowing from my lips now, into the ears and hearts of my audience. Their eyes shone with unshed tears at Feather's plight and they gasped when Lothar's men drew their swords. Best was the cheer at Feather's escape, and then the call from the crowd for another tale.

'Tis one thing to learn a story, word by word, to tell it the right way; 'tis another altogether to bring a tale to life, where moments before there was nothing but emptiness.

Thomas had placed my harp at my feet sometime during my tale, so quietly that I hadn't noticed. A hush filled the hall as I plucked the first note and sang the first song I had ever written myself.

The great hall of a castle is an amazing place to play a tune, for the notes echo and bounce between the old stone walls and out to the folks sitting on their carved benches, hoping to be whisked away to another place and time.

I have had many adventures. But this . . . this was the most magical.

For five nights they asked me for my stories. I sat on the bard's stool, rubbed my coin for luck, and told my tales: Gypsies, selkies, banshees, faeries, and pookas danced across my harp. Each yarn I spun was better than the last, each song sweeter.

Then, the Old Burned Man recovered.

IN WHICH I FINALLY HEAR
THE OLD BURNED MAN

❦

*T*he great hall was full, for Lord John had planned
a hunt and a banquet for the next day and had invited many
to the event. The room was overwarm and the air sticky, but
I did not care. We wedged ourselves through the crowd until
a lady in a dress of fine blue velvet tweaked my braid hard
and glared.

The Old Burned Man cleared his throat and spoke.

Perhaps it was because his voice was spoiled and the effort
to use it sounded painful, but I felt honored to be the recipient of his words. They sang in my mind, though the back of
my throat ached in sympathy. The spell he cast with his story

was more wondrous and mystical than I could have imagined, and that says a great deal coming from a lass who spends most of her time imagining.

The bench we sat on was hard and we were quite squished, but I did not care. The legend of a lady who tended swords for only the bravest knights and lived underwater in a lake that never froze over was both lovely and tragic.

I listened.

I dreamed.

Though his voice was ragged, his telling was far smoother and silkier than even Bald Fergal's. My heart soared at one moment with the magic of the story, then sank the next moment. I felt quite the fraud. My tales could not compare. I was no bard. What had made me think that I was?

And then the Old Burned Man pulled out his flute.

"I'll only do the one song tonight," he said, "for my throat's still a-paining me. 'Tis a lullaby I composed myself many years ago."

'Twas lilting and sadly sweet. But beautiful.

And all too familiar.

My blood stilled.

I knew the song.

And in my heart, I knew the player.

—

Thomas gulped, then he looked at me and his eyes grew wide. Did he, too, recognize the tune? His hand touched my sleeve, but I jerked my arm away and ran down the corridor and up the stairs. The tears on my cheeks were hot. I could not sniff them back no matter how hard I tried.

Finn raised his head when I stumbled into the room, saw it was me, and lay back down, his eyes still open. The dog watched me as I sobbed and grabbed my harp, clutching it so hard the strings bit into the flesh of my arms. But I did not care about the pain.

When you cry, your mind is a jumbled mess. Part of your brain is trying to make you stop crying and stop thinking about the things that are making you cry. *Hush, hush now, do not cause a scene.* The other part of your brain is lashing back, thinking thoughts so numerous and difficult that reason runs and hides for a while, until things die down.

Thomas was a reasonable fellow, and he did the same. I

heard his footsteps come up the stairs, pause, then go back down.

The only creature brave enough to offer comfort was Finn. He nuzzled his enormous head under my arm. My throat was too thick to even utter, "Not now, dog, go away." So I let him stay at my side as I sobbed, watching the tears splash on his golden coat. There was something terribly reassuring about the dog's presence.

I was glad to have such company.

I cried myself to sleep and the night was filled with dreams.

I dreamed that I saw my father and that he told me stories and kissed me goodbye and never came back.

I dreamed my father rode on a dark stallion, with a cape that flew behind him.

I dreamed my father smiled at me with a scarred and ruined face.

—

When I awoke, I was no longer overwhelmed with sadness.

I was confused.

How could a man that old, scarred, and hideous-looking possibly be my handsome father? How could he have been so heartless to have not returned if he was actually still alive? WHY?

And I was angry.

THE HUNT

*E*ven before the sun rose the nurse poked her head into my small closet room. "You're all red and blotchful. Been ye crying, girl?"

I sniffled and nodded, but quickly looked away. I did not want to speak of my suspicions.

"Never mind about it, girl, whatever it is, ye must get the babe dry and fresh. He needs to say goodbye to the lord. Off to the hunt, he is." The nurse tugged on my arms and pulled me up. "You're a weed of a girl, you know. I swear you've grown in the days since you have come here."

I only sniffed.

"'Tis a good thing you arrived when you did, what with the wolves in the forest and all. The pack's been a-howling each night. Had you met them on your journey, ye might not have made it here whole."

I swallowed, remembering the forlorn howls we had heard as we traveled. Sadly, it was more pleasant to think about being attacked by wolves than about having a father who stole for pleasure and laughed a dark laugh like the Highwayman. Or a hideous father who left you five years past and could have come back but chose not to.

"Seems foolish to go on a hunt for boars with wolves about, do ye not think?" the nurse continued, unaware that I was a poor contributor to the conversation. "I would think the wolves would have eaten the boars or scared them away. Alas."

"Aye. Alas," I offered.

"But if the lord says there shall be a hunt, then a hunt there shall be, I s'pose." She handed me a little gown of white lace with gold trim for the babe. "Dress him. Clean his wee face, too."

Finn the Great was at my side as I changed the babe from

his soggy clothes. The hound looked at the boy with deep, soulful eyes, perhaps thinking him a pup instead of a baby.

The wolves howled in the distance as I took the child down the stairs to see his father, who promptly kissed the boy's head and led his band of hunters out of the castle. Thomas was with them. 'Twas a boar hunt, after all, and a pig boy might be useful, for what were boars but meaner, more dangerous swine?

I was both glad and mad Thomas was gone. Glad, for I didn't want to speak with him about last night, and mad, for I did not want to spend the day alone with my thoughts.

After feeding the infant down in the kitchens and taking him to visit his lady mother until he became cranky, I sat him in his bed and began to play my harp for him. My fingers started to pluck a familiar tune and then stopped. I would not play my father's lullaby ever again.

Instead, I played the new tune I had composed for the selkie boy's song, and his eyes were closed before the last verse.

"You've a strong voice," a voice said, "for one so young."

The Old Burned Man stood in the doorway. I chanced a look at his scarred face. *Were those the eyes of my father behind his gargoyle's features?* I supposed they could be. They were similar to mine in color, but the shape wasn't right.

Nay. He could *not* be my father, James the Bard.

But then there was the lullaby.

My thoughts were muddled.

I had sought the Old Burned Man for such a long time, just to hear his stories, not thinking for a moment that he might be my father. He looked far too old, but perhaps he was younger and just horribly disfigured. What happened to him? I wondered, then shook my head. No, I would not pity him. It was his choice not to return.

Would I prefer that my father had died? Would I prefer him to be the Highwayman?

"I thank you, sir," I said, my voice hard like stone.

"You're a teller, too, then. I heard you the other night. Held them in your grasp, you did, lass. Where did you learn such skill? You are quite young, as I said."

Perhaps it is in my blood, I wanted to say, but I did not. I merely shrugged.

The silence was awkward.

I wanted him to leave, but then ... perhaps ... *Was I completely certain?*

I cleared my throat. "The song you played on your flute last night. 'Twas lovely. It was yours?"

He smiled, but it did not reach his eyes. "Just an old lullaby, written long ago, for a very special child." He sighed and looked off, his voice quiet. "Some say it has magic."

He had his secrets, too, then.

He asked to see my harp, so I showed him. "Unusual and fantastical," he told me.

The conversation continued in such a manner, stilted and uncomfortable. *Are you my father? If so, why did you leave us and never return?* The words screamed in my head.

But I could not make them come.

TRAGEDY

———◆❖◆———

After the Old Burned Man left me, the nurse reappeared and began tidying the room as the babe continued to doze. She took one look at my face and shooed me off. "We'll be fine here, lass. The hound can help amuse the boy when he wakes. Go try and shed whatever heavy weight you're carrying around. You'll do no one any good brooding about like that."

I grabbed my mother's cloak and set off, leaving through an old door at the bottom of the tower held ajar by a heavy rock. "'Tis cleaning day," I was told by a woman with a broom when I asked about the open door. "Got to sweep out the hall to make things nice for the banquet tonight." Ah yes. The banquet. In my dark mood, the thought of fine food made my stomach turn. I wandered under trees and down the green paths of the castle grounds, hoping that the farther away I was from the Old Burned Man, the clearer my thoughts would become.

Was I not happy, then, to have found the man I thought was my father? Truly, it was more likely that James the Bard was the Old Burned Man than the Highwayman. After all, the Old Burned Man was a teller. That was a clue right there.

But nay, I was not happy. All I felt was anger. When I set off on my quest for my father, I did not know what I would find. I hoped to hear of my father, of course. Had I expected to hear only of his death? Perhaps tragic, yet heroic. But that at least was an acceptable reason for him never to return.

If he was alive, he *would* have come back.

Should I tell him that my mother had died with a broken heart? Mayhap yes, if that would hurt him. Although the fact that he'd never returned showed his lack of care. It would not matter to him at all. And if *he* was not my father . . . well, those were thoughts I did not want, either. *How did the High-wayman know the lullaby?* I blocked this question from my mind.

I sat under the trees until the sun was low in the sky.

That was when screaming started.

"Wolves! A pack of wolves!" I heard someone cry. I dashed through the castle gardens toward the keep, bumping into a large figure wrapped in gray.

"Nay, lass," said the Old Burned Man, "'twill do you no good to run. Best to stay here and safe, until the guards round them up." He held me by my shoulders, the fine fabric of my mother's cloak in his scarred hands. I glanced to where his fingers softly touched the threads. *Did he remember when she made it?* I looked away.

"The wee lad might be afraid. I am going to him and you will not stop me," I said. "'Twould be sad, would it not, for the child to feel abandoned?"

His hands dropped in an instant, as if I had burned him myself, and I ran, red-faced, to Castlelow.

Had he noticed the cruelty of my words? The angry, beastly part of myself hoped so.

Up the stairs I climbed, taking two at a time when I could. I could tell he was panting and huffing behind me, but his legs must have been damaged as well, for he was not fast for a grown man.

I arrived in the babe's room to find the nurse wailing.

"He's dead! He's dead! I left him for but a moment alone with the hound. Just a moment! The beast!" she cried. Her arms were flailing and she clutched the hem of her dress against her face. Then she pushed past me and ran down the stairs. Finn was there, by the babe's bed, blood on his coat, blood on the floor. He looked at me and bared his teeth.

"The hound killed him! The hound killed my master's son!" The nurse's voice echoed eerily through the tower.

And truly, that is exactly how it appeared. Why Finn should attack the babe, I could not say. Had the howls of the wolves thrown him into a canine frenzy?

"There," said the Old Burned Man, "behind his left flank, the babe's arm . . . 'tis *moving*."

I gasped as my eyes followed where the Old Burned Man

pointed. The babe's chubby arm stuck out from behind the dog, and the fingers twitched. Most likely, the arm was still attached to the boy.

"We need to get the dog away from the baby! I think he's still alive!" I took a hasty step toward the hound and then stopped when he growled.

"Stay back, Trinket!" cried the Old Burned Man, pulling my shoulder.

Trinket? How did he know my name? Everyone except Thomas simply called me *girl*, or *Story Lass*.

I jerked away and cried, "The babe needs me!" I took another step forward. "Finn, be calm." I placed my hand palm up and moved closer.

Finn growled again, showing blood in his teeth. He lay on his side and his breathing was labored, but he glared at me in warning. The hand behind him moved again, followed by a soft cry.

I turned to the Old Burned Man. "See, the babe's alive. We just have to get to him!" I saw my harp on the bench by the door, the whiteness of the bone fairly glowing in the afternoon light. I slowly tiptoed over to it.

"Stop! Do not do this!" the Old Burned Man warned me. But I would not be stopped. I reached the creaky wooden bench and sat down to play. If my tunes could make selkies sleep and faeries dance, perhaps they would be able to calm a crazed hound.

LULLABY

———◆◆✦◆◆———

I don't know why, but I began to strum the song I had sworn but hours before to never play again. My traitorous fingers were plucking my father's lullaby, the most soothing, gentle song I knew. After a moment or two, my playing was joined by the sound of a flute, sweet, clear, and strong.

We played together as moment after moment drifted by. Finn stopped baring his teeth. Whether it was the tune that tamed him, or the fact that neither of us was approaching him, I do not know, but he relaxed. The Old Burned Man continued the melody as I put the harp down and rose.

When I got close enough, I could tell that Finn had been

hurt, very badly. The blood on his coat was his own. 'Twould have been impossible for a small child to inflict such damage upon a dog.

Finn's eyes softened and his head slumped down. "The hound is bleeding," I whispered. I knelt by the dog as the lullaby's final note faded into silence and the Old Burned Man crept around to the other side of Finn. There he found the babe, who was sobbing quietly, like a mewling kitten.

"He's unharmed." The Old Burned Man cuddled the child close to his chest. The babe's eyes were wide and his breathing strong. Placing the boy on the mattress, the bard continued to soothe him. "He's just scared. But look," he said, pointing to another furry mass on the far side of the child's bed.

"Where is the foul hound?" Lord John bellowed as he charged into the room, sword drawn. He pointed his weapon at Finn and cried in anguish, "You will die now, you filthy cur!" And he raised the sword over his head, ready to swipe at the back of Finn's bloodied neck.

"No!" I screamed with all my might. I stepped between the man and the beast, which was foolish, for Lord John was crazed. He only had eyes for the hound. Too late, I realized he would kill me in order to destroy the dog, if that's what he had to do. "No!" I cried again, cowering now, in a useless attempt to save myself from the blow.

"My Lord!" The Old Burned Man's ragged voice ripped through the air, louder than I'd ever heard him. He tried to grab Lord John's arms from behind.

"I'll have your head, man!" yelled Lord John. "The horrible beast attacked my son!"

"Nay! He did not attack! Finn did not attack the babe!" Breathlessly, I pointed behind the bed. "Can you not see?" I ran to the bed and held the child up.

The Old Burned Man did not let go of the lord. The two men struggled until finally, Lord John shifted his gaze from Finn to me and the babe.

"Look!" the Old Burned Man said, forcing Lord John's vision to the floor near the bed.

There, bleeding on the cold stones, was a large black wolf.

"What in . . ." the lord began, but did not finish as he realized what had happened. The hound had not attacked the child. The wolf had. He'd probably crept in through the open

tower door, though he must have been sly indeed to get inside the castle walls in the first place. And Finn had protected the babe from the wolf. The fury faded from the lord's eyes as his sword clattered to the ground.

He ran to me, gathered the lad in his arms, and sank to the floor, weeping.

Gradually at first, so stealthily that none of us noticed, the black wolf rose slowly, teeth bared, and emitted a low, demonic growl.

We all froze. I glanced at the Old Burned Man, whose intense gaze willed me not to move, not even to breathe.

Thomas skidded into the room. He ran past the lord and the bard, straight toward me, and unknowingly placed himself between Finn and the wolf.

"Trinket! What in the world . . . ?" Thomas gasped, bending down to the wounded dog. A snarl made him turn around.

He stepped back, but it was too late.

The wolf lunged at Thomas.

I screamed.

The wolf sank his claws into Thomas's shoulder and pulled him roughly to the ground. Thomas cried out as he went down, but when his head slammed against the floor, he fell silent.

Whether 'twas the shrieks of the quick battle or the unnatural quiet that followed that roused him, Finn, injured and bleeding though he was, sprang at the wolf. The wolf released his hold on Thomas and growled again, his dark eyes fairly screaming, *I have nothing to lose now, hound. My life is forfeit. But I'll not cross into death without taking a human child with me.*

But Finn, brave, strong Finn, could not be taken down. Their fight waged on, hound versus demon-wolf, creating a barrier between poor Thomas and myself.

"Thomas!" I cried.

But he did not answer. I could see naught but his still form on the ground, a puddle of red surrounding him.

I tried to go to him, but the firm hands of the Old Burned Man held me back.

"You can't help him if the wolf takes you as well."

The wolf latched onto Finn's throat, but in that instant, Lord John was there, still holding his babe in one arm and thrusting his sword into the wolf with the other.

"*Look away, my son,*" Lord John cried. He held the whimpering boy close, shielding his eyes from the grisly scene.

"Thomas!" I yelled, tears making it hard to see in front of me. I stumbled away from where Finn lay breathless beside the dead wolf.

Thomas was still. So still. I put my head down to feel his breath on my cheek.

So very faint. But there nonetheless. He lived.

The useless nurse returned with her lady, both gasping from running up the stairs.

"The babe!" cried the nurse, pointing to where Lord John stood with the child in his arms. Lord John's lips moved, as if he were praying silently. The lady let out a strangled cry and then dashed across the room to her husband and their babe.

"I'm so sorry, lass. I know he was your friend," the nurse panted as she approached Thomas and me, wiping her nose on her sleeve. "A pity to lose one so young and strong. Died like a hero, he did, trying to save the lord's son."

She reached for my arm.

"Go away!" I screamed, using every bit of my voice. *"He's not dead."*

But she was not to be stopped. "Mayhap not yet, but soon most likely. Wolf gashes are nasty and foul. Do ye not see all the blood on the floor?"

I held firm to Thomas, lest she try to wrestle me away. I would not leave him, and I would not let him leave me.

We had been through too much together.

"If you be so certain he is going to pass, then you best get the priest," said the Old Burned Man. The nurse nodded, then turned and ran back down the stairs, her footsteps and wheezing fading into nothing.

I cradled Thomas's body in my arms. He did not move.

"Trinket."

The voice was even rougher than usual, and right against my ear.

I did not answer.

"The bargaining coin. I know you have one. I saw you rubbing it before you told your tales." The Old Burned Man's hand was gentle on my shoulder and he patted my hair as if he were soothing a horse.

"Do ye have it still, the bargaining coin? The faerie gold?" he persisted.

I sniffled against Thomas and nodded.

"Place it on the floor, next to Thomas," he whispered. "Quickly, there is little time."

I released Thomas and reached in my pocket for the warm coin. I looked over to where Lord John and his lady were still sobbing over their son, planting kisses on all his fingers and toes. They noticed nothing in the room but the babe. Finn was panting and bleeding. The sword stuck out of the wolf and glinted in the last bits of afternoon sun that streamed through the castle window.

"Quickly, now," the Old Burned Man said. "Place it next to Thomas."

And so I looked into the gray eyes of my father, which shone silver with unshed tears, and set the gold coin next to Thomas's own head.

In a blink, the coin glimmered and was gone.

The blood vanished.

And Thomas's eyelids fluttered, just like they did in the mornings when he first awoke.

"What happened?" Thomas asked, his voice raspy and tired sounding.

Then he sat up. "The wolf! Finn!" he cried, and rushed over to where the hound lay suffering.

Thomas was just as skilled with dogs as with swine. Finn

let him examine his injuries and stroke his bloodied coat. "'Twill be all right, Sir Hound," Thomas murmured. "Ye've done well today. Your sire would be proud."

He knew not the danger he'd just been in. He did not even know that I had bargained his life back with the use of the coin the Faerie Queen had given me. I watched him tend the hound, as tears of gratefulness trailed down my cheeks.

When I turned around, I found the Old Burned Man staring at me.

He blinked twice, then cleared his throat and said, "You are brave, Story Lass."

"The coin," I said, "how did you know?"

"I thought all bards knew the tale of the bargaining coin," he said quietly.

I should have thanked him. I should have thrown myself at his feet and thanked him a thousand times for saving Thomas.

But I had no words.

In a bluster of robes and legs, the priest and nurse bolted into the room.

"Him!" the nurse cried, pointing to Thomas. Puzzlement filled her eyes as she took in the dead wolf, the injured dog,

and the quite lively boy. "He—there was blood—and he—"
she sputtered.

The priest, still breathing heavily from the run up the
stairway, walked over to Lord John and delivered a blessing
to the babe, just as if that was the reason he'd come.

Not to bless and comfort the dying at all.

—

I sighed. I did not want to talk with the Old Burned Man
about the things between us. I wanted only to leave this room.

Obviously, the Old Burned Man felt the same. He was no
longer there.

REMORSE

That night, there was a large banquet in the great hall celebrating the hunt, the safety of Lord John's son, and the bravery of Finn the Great.

Finn, his body striped by bandages, gnawed happily on an enormous joint of meat. I was presented with a beautiful case for my harp, crafted from the softest leather. Thomas received a pup that Finn had sired, and although it would be one more mouth to feed on the road, the protection he would offer would be quite worth it, we thought. Thomas promptly named him Pig.

The Old Burned Man was absent from the fine banquet table.

"Ah, yes, our storyteller, our Old Burned Man. Where is he? We've a token for him as well." Lord John raised an elegant pillow upon which was a golden cup. Next to him, the puffy-eyed lady held the boy upon her lap. "The life of my son is beyond price," she began, "however, we ask for the Old Burned Man to come forward and accept—"

"He's gone," interrupted the nurse. "He's a-packed and left from the castle."

I should not have been surprised. But I was. I thought perhaps he would seek me out.

But he did not.

However, 'twas not a helpless child who he left this time.

—

Thomas, Pig, and I took our leave from Castlelow the next morning. It still amazed me that Thomas bore neither scratch nor bruise nor memory of his encounter with the wolf. But I would spin it into a fine tale for him on the road. He'd be proud.

It would not be hard to catch up to the Old Burned Man, for his pace was never quick. Though I felt like I did not want to see him again, I *would* know the truth I had sought for so long.

And James the Bard alone could tell me the story.

THE SIXTH SONG

Hound Victorious

*This song sounds best if there is a drummer in the audience
who agrees to strike the beat, strong and true. If no drum
can be found, spoons from the kitchen tapped against the
wooden benches work almost as well.*

*Oh, thee, my hound,
From heaven thou come'st,
Where birds and angels
Sing.*

*Soft and sweet,
They bring thee down
In honey'ed arms to
Dream.*

Valiant and brave,
A babe's life to save,
Valiant and brave,
Ta-roo.

We honor thee, Finn,
Of the wheaten coat.
Of the lion heart
So true.

A nobler beast
Ne'er did roam,
To fight
The wolven doom.

Valiant and brave,
A babe's life to save,
Valiant and brave,
Ta-rooo.

THE LAST TALE

The
Storyteller
and the
Truth

THE OLD BURNED MAN SPEAKS

*I*t took us only a day to follow his path and find him. He was sitting by his campfire, silhouetted against the last of the daylight.

"You've come for the tale, then, Trinket?" he asked without looking up.

"I've come for the truth."

The Old Burned Man cleared his throat. His voice scattered against the clear evening air like a jar of pebbles that had been dropped.

Stories are like stars. They shine brightly for us in times of darkness. Some of them draw our attention and hold

it. Some we forget, but these are no less beautiful simply because our careless minds cannot hold on to them all.

But then there are stories that burn inside of us, waiting for the right moment to be told. My dear Trinket, this story has burned inside of me for a long, long time. Finally, it can be told.

The Old Burned Man cleared his throat once again and continued.

I loved your mother. Of all the things I will tell you, this is the most important. I loved her like the sun loves the moon or a moth loves a flame. She was the best person I ever knew. Lovely Mairi-Blue-Eyes.

And I loved you, too, Trinket, with your sparkling raindrop eyes.

You must believe that I wanted to come back to you. Sometimes I think about how different all of our lives might have been had I not taken to the road to begin with. But that was my calling. 'Tis the way of a bard. This is something I think you understand, now.

I left, that early spring day, prepared to travel and tell my stories until the appearance of winter's first frost. I would have come home, bearing a small bag bursting with gold and perhaps some thread in exquisite colors for your mother to weave into fine things. But, as you know, life does not often go as planned, and the road is fraught with adventure.

The ruined eye winked.

I spent my days away from you doing what I do best, telling tales and playing songs on my harp. Yes, I had a harp once, but my fingers are now too scarred and clumsy to pluck the notes. And my voice too withered to sing the songs. A flute works best for me now.

I met Gypsies along the way and stayed with a caravan many weeks. They offered me beautiful silk, in a lovely shade of blue I thought your mother would like, if I stayed and told my stories. I sang a song to the Gypsy King's daughter every night to lull her to sleep. She was a smallish girl plagued by bad dreams. The king wanted me to stay forever, until I refused to play for his daughter a special lullaby she'd heard me practice. I'd created that song for only one child. You.

I met all manner of creatures on my journey. I played sleeping songs for the seal people, told ancient tales to a wandering clan of banshees, and strummed jigs and reels for dancing faeries. And though I knew hundreds of tales already, I gathered a hundred more as I traveled. Some from folk in rare and unusual places, some from my own experiences. Yes, there were many of those.

But none of those tales are the one you want to hear, are they? You want the story, the reason I never went back to the small cottage by the sea. Very well. But I warn you, 'tis a frightening tale, where all is not as it seems. And in truth, dear Trinket, I did go back to the cottage, not once but several times.

SO PERFECT A DAY

———◆◆◆◆◆———

$\mathcal{M}$ost accounts of a terrifying nature begin at night. This one does not. This one begins on the most gorgeous day you could imagine. The trees were turning and the air was filled with the scent of dry leaves. The sun was not too hot nor the breeze too cool. 'Twas a perfect day.

I was walking between villages, making my way to a castle whose name I cannot remember. 'Twas taking longer to get to the next village than I had been told it would. But I had an apple in my pocket and a bit of cheese and a crust of brown bread. And, as I said, the day was beautiful and golden.

Through the forest came the sound of hooves pounding against the soft ground. I could feel the vibrations under my feet, traveling up through my legs. Around the bend galloped the largest horse I'd ever seen. Atop him was a gent in fine clothes and a flowing black cape.

"Good day, good sir," I said. 'Twas not unusual to meet others along the road. I'd found that being friendly to fellow travelers was the best course. However, I was no fool. I kept in my bag a large, heavy rock. Already, the rock was in my hand, hidden behind my own gray cloak.

The stranger swept down from his horse and brandished his sword. "'Twill be a good day, indeed, sir, when you give over your purse." He smiled with his mouth, but his eyes held menace.

I hurled my rock, but the stone hit the ground behind the man. The rock had gone right through him.

I gasped as he laughed and said, "I should run you through!"

Being a bard, naturally I'd heard tales of those who, though death had visited them, chose not to pass on. I'd even told stories of those who remained in the world of the living as shadows of their former selves. Ghosts. But I'd never met one on the road.

Until now.

Perhaps his sword is but an illusion as well, I thought, though the sound of it slicing through the air above my head was real enough, as was the feel of cold steel when he held it against my throat.

"Your purse, good sir," he said through closed teeth.

"I have no money."

"You'd prefer to forfeit your life, then?"

"Nay. I do not wish to die."

"Then convince me, good sir. What reason have I to let you live?"

What reason, indeed? I swallowed and thought of you and your mother. I would use whatever method I could to stay alive, to see you again. And I had but one weapon. My words.

"Do ye not become bored, sir, from time to time?" I asked.

His dark eyebrows rose in question. "What are you about?"

"I, sir, have a gift worth more than sacks full of gold." Strangely, my fear made me brave. Perhaps you have felt this along the road as well. "A gift so fine that even the wealthiest lords pay handsomely for it."

He rolled his eyes in disbelief, but allowed me to continue, which I took as a good sign.

"The chance to experience great adventure."

"I am a gentleman of the road. I've plenty of adventure, sir."

His voice was mocking, but I was glad for each second I managed to distract him from killing me.

I looked from side to side, as if I was imparting a sacred secret, which indeed I was. "I offer the chance to feel alive again."

This gave the Highwayman pause.

"'Tis not possible to cross back into the living and remain," he said at last. "I have tried."

"Nay, I am not offering life, I am but a poor bard. I could not possess a secret so amazing and majestic."

"Then what do you offer, sir?" The sword lowered slightly, then poised over my heart.

"Feeling. I offer feeling. Would you not like to feel as if your heart were racing, as if your blood were once again thrumming through you?"

"You talk circles, sir, and I grow tired. State your intentions or meet my sword." The tip of his sword pressed against my chest.

What had I to bargain with but my craft? And truly, I could weave a story like no other in those days. My voice was smoother than the velvet on a king's robe. With but a whisper, I could send chills up any spine.

Were my stories fascinating enough, and could I tell them well enough, to win my life back from a ghost?

I would find out.

A YEAR AND A DAY

I should have known better. I should have known not to expect one who steals from others to honor his word. And these were his words: "I shall keep you with me, sir, until I feel what you say I will feel." He flicked at the edge of my cloak with the tip of his sword. "Or until I grow tired of you and kill you." He laughed without humor.

He pulled me up onto the back of his horse and we rode faster than I could imagine riding to a place I had never seen before. The trees were cold and dead, although winter's chill had not yet touched the land. There were mists and the sky was neither dark nor light. I got down off of the horse—

The Old Burned Man noted my gasp, but continued.

—and sat upon the large rock. The Highwayman smirked and commanded me to begin.

So I did.

I began with a rollicking tale of betrayal, heroic triumph, and a magical coin. 'Twas one of the old tales, from when the land was young. The kind of tale that sings in the veins, for even though parts of it are impossible to believe, every word rings true.

He feigned boredom, at first. But he could not maintain his pretense for long. When a story decides to claim you, it takes both your heart and soul during the listening.

"Too bad *you* did not possess such a bargaining coin," he jested. "Mayhap you could have bargained yourself a better deal."

I remained silent, letting the story have its final

moment. Like a song, a story needs that one last note, as it flies off on the wings of the world.

"Or perhaps *I* could have used a coin such as that ... to barter my way back ..."

He was thoughtful then.

A good tale always makes one thoughtful afterward.

Next he asked me to play my harp, which I did most willingly. I played lullabies guaranteed to calm and relax the fiercest of beasts. Perchance, he would doze ... but even I should have known that 'tis impossible to lull a ghost to sleep. For those who do not join the dead, those who stay in the shadows in between, never rest.

After that, one story per day was all that I would grant him, thinking each day he would release me.

But he did not.

He could not. I should have remembered from the old tales what happens to those who travel through magical boundaries. When I'd stepped off the horse and touched my foot to the ground, I had committed to spending—

"A year and a day."

—

Yes, a year and a day on the other side.

Truly I had hundreds of stories. And I told one each day, to save myself from being run through ... but sometimes ...

The withered voice cracked.

Sometimes, when I felt I could go on no more, when the loneliness and longing for you got to be too much, I would tell tales that made you and your mother come alive in my heart.

I told stories of you, Trinket, and of my memories of your sweet face and clear gray eyes. I told tales of your mother's beauty and the way her laugh made the flowers in my heart bloom.

And in desperation, I played for him the lullaby I had composed for you. Yes, the one I played for you, and only you, when you were a babe. It became his favorite and he demanded it after each tale. And so, to stay alive, I played.

You may ask what else I did on the other side. The

truth? I cannot remember. Perhaps time moved differently, for the year passed more quickly than a leaf falls to the ground. I am certain that I met other souls, there on the other side, but I can recall neither their names nor their faces.

I was true to my word. The Highwayman *felt* for the first time since his foul life had been cut short by the hangman's noose, years and years before. He laughed at the escapades of a luckless prince. His eyes glistened with unshed tears when the last of the great warriors was betrayed by a friend and killed. The thief, however, was not true to his word.

"The souls here are restless," I said to him before one telling, for it was not unusual for us to converse before or after the story.

"'Tis the eve of Samhain, sir. Only natural they should be excited."

"Samhain? Already?"

"Aye." He sat polishing his sword, though it never grew dull, so there was not much point.

"Then—" I began.

"Nay, I have not yet tired of your tales, sir." He kept

polishing. He liked the way the sword flashed with the light of the moon. "You shall stay."

But I was determined not to.

There were few who were willing to help a mortal soul lost on the other side. Fewer still willing to cross a shade as cunning and ruthless as the Highwayman. However, luck was with me when I met the ghost of a gravedigger the next day.

"Ye don't belong here," said he. His hair, what was left of it, was long and white, and he walked stooped over, leaning on an ancient shovel.

"Nay, I don't. I'd very much like to go back. 'Tis Samhain, after all. Isn't the wall between the living and the dead at its thinnest?" I asked, even though I knew this to be true from the tales I'd told.

He handed me the shovel and said, "Ye'll do."

The Old Burned Man nodded as if to say, Aye, 'tis true.

And so, a year and a day after the Highwayman captured me, I dug a grave, captured a pooka, and rode him back across to the other side, to the land of the living.

THE WRATH OF THE HIGHWAYMAN

The Highwayman was angry, though, for he had been deprived of his prized entertainment. If I had crossed a stream or lake before he caught up with me, things might have been different.

But I did not.

Soon after the pooka let me off, I was walking through a village, down deserted streets where not a sign of life could be seen or heard. But there was light. On the outside of each house a torch burned fair and bright, perhaps to keep the ghosties away. On a night like Samhain, the torchlight was not enough.

I could hear the clip-clopping of his horse's hooves, not behind me but as if he was next to me, or on a nearby street.

I tried to hide in a doorway, but I could not flatten myself enough. The clip-clopping echoed between the buildings, louder and louder still. The Highwayman was advancing. I started banging on the door.

"Let me in! Please! I beg you!" I shrieked. I am not proud of the fear I felt nor of the way I screamed. I could hear stirring in the house, and the door opened but a crack. Staring up at me, through the narrowest of slivers, was a clear gray eye.

He paused and stared off, then gazed into a different set of clear gray eyes.

"Mum," said a tiny voice, "there's a man here at the door. Sore a-feared he looks. Should we let him in then?"

"Please," I begged. "He comes for me. The Highwayman comes!"

"That's exactly the reason we shan't let you in!" cried

a stern voice on the other side of the door, which was being pushed against me hard. "Ye think I'm a fool?"

I gave a shove and tumbled into the house and closed the door behind me. The wood was rough and my hand was filled with splinters from all my banging.

"How dare ye bring the wrath of the other side down upon my wee home!" yelled a woman with her hair stretched back so tight as to pull her eyes apart. "What are ye thinking? Me here with only me daughter." She probably would have sobbed had she not been so angry with me.

And I didn't blame her. What *had* I been thinking, bringing the horrible Highwayman to the doorstep of a mother and her lass? I thought of another mother and lass left home alone.

Another lass with cool gray eyes.

The Highwayman laughed, the sound harsh and cruel. The mother and her child huddled close together, and I crouched behind the door, cursing myself for involving this innocent family in my struggle with the dark side.

We heard a crash, as if something had been thrown

upon the roof of the cottage. Then smoke, light at first, but quickly growing thicker and darker, engulfed the room. The thatch on the roof must have been dry, for it erupted in flames like a bonfire. I heard the girl cry and the mother yelling at the girl to stay close, but I couldn't see anything in the dense black smoke.

There were screams, naturally. And I am certain some of them were mine. I only knew that I had to get the woman and child out of the house before it was too late. I grabbed them to me, though my own cloak was ablaze, and somehow found a way out of the fiery cottage.

He was silent for a long time, and his eyes filled with unshed tears.

The next thing I knew, I was wrapped in bandages, feeling like I was still aflame. I could barely see and my skin was red, blistered, and painful, indeed.

The woman and the girl with gray eyes had been saved from the fire. I had rescued them, though 'twas my own fault their cottage was burned by the vengeful

Highwayman. Lesser folk would have turned me out, injured or not. But the woman was a healer. And so she practiced her remedies and potions upon my hideous burns.

They looked after me, filling my dry mouth with cool water and restorative broth, keeping my bandages fresh and applying ointment as I would let them. 'Twas sore painful, to be true.

My harp was destroyed in the blaze, as were my hopes of seeing you again.

But time heals. If it does nothing else, time does that.

Slowly, the anger I felt at being horribly disfigured, and their anger at me for causing the roof of their cottage to be torched, melted away as a cautious friendship grew. I told them about you, you know. They did not understand why I could not someday go back to you.

But I could not.

I left your mother and you a whole man. A handsome man. How was I to return, a shell of my former self?

Thus, I stayed in the strange village, hidden from view, as the healing ointments and remedies gradually did their work. Until one day the girl woke afrightened in the night and asked me to tell her a nice tale to help her sleep.

And so the stories came to me, again.

I had no harp, but the woman carved me a flute and I told stories and played. Although my body would forever be scarred, my heart was healing.

I no longer possessed the handsome looks of a young man, but instead a destroyed face and ruined white hair. So, I called myself the Old Burned Man and took to the road once more. My fame as a teller grew. Far more fame than I had ever known as my former self. Perhaps folks were intrigued by my scarred face and body. I know not, but with that fame, I gained courage.

Mayhap enough courage to go back.

RETURN

❖◆❖

The woman and child begged me not to
return to you and your mother. True, once they had
encouraged such a reunion, but we had grown fond of
each other and they feared losing my company, and
quite possibly my purse, for many a lord paid amply
for my tales. My guilt would not allow me to keep
much for myself, so the woman and child were well
cared for. But I had to go back. I had to.

And so I returned to that little cottage by the sea and
watched from afar, too self-conscious to show my hideous
face. I kept hidden behind my gray cloak and watched.

Oh, your mother was so beautiful!

Mairi-Blue-Eyes tended the sheep and sheared their wool. She carded the wool in the evening whilst sitting on a stool outside the cottage. The sunlight caught the gold in her hair as she smiled. And you, Trinket, you played at her feet, or danced. Or sang. Even then, you had a voice that carried on the wind, true and sure.

As I watched, I felt a tear on my cheek. *She* no longer *needed* me. *You* no longer *needed* me.

The Old Burned Man put up his hand. He did not wish to be interrupted.

It had been more than three years since I'd seen either of you. Much of a year spent tale-telling, one year spent on the other side, and over a year spent healing from my wounds, for I even had to learn to walk again! And I realized that your lives had gone on during that time. Mayhap you would not even remember—

Again the hand went up.

⚊

Whether it was the wrong decision or not, it was the one I made. I would not be a burden to your mother nor an embarrassment to my child. I had left the village a strapping, handsome man. James the Bard. Now I was so scarred and twisted, folks thought I was aged. And pitiful.

I journeyed from then on. Village to castle. Castle to Gypsy camp. Gypsy camp to manor house, and all sorts of dwellings in between. The stories were my life now, even though I could not help myself from looking in on you, and you'd blush if you knew how I swelled with pride at how you grew. Tall, strong, and filled with such promise.

I left things from time to time, on the back step, small bags of gold and such. Once I left a small silver mirror given to me by a princess who liked my tales. Mayhap you remember it?

An ever-so-slight nod.

Now the story becomes even more tragic, for a chance encounter with the Faerie Queen convinced me of my selfishness.

"Do you really believe," she said after listening to a story. (For the faerie folk are always around when there is a tale to be told. Watch for the way the light moves in the corners of the room, or the way the trees sway just so. That is them.) "Do you really believe that your wife and child only loved your looks? Are you foolish enough to think they would not care for you? The true you that lurks beneath the damage?"

At least, I think she said these words to me. I'd fallen asleep after telling the tale, near a perfectly round mound, dotted with the most lovely flowers. I awoke after dreaming of you and your mother and hearing the Faerie Queen's words. I knew then that I would return. However, I was struck ill, which happens often. My throat never healed well and I spend many weeks each year nursing myself through fever. By the time I went to visit you again, your mother had died and you were gone.

If I live to be one hundred, I will never forgive myself for not taking the risk sooner that she would reject me, just to see her alive once more.

⊷

There was silence for a long time. What words could be left? At length, he cleared his throat and continued.

> Then I heard of a girl with a white harp, a Story Lass, traveling with a grubby boy, and I thought, Could it be her? Could it be Trinket?

The words were but whispers.

> So I began to follow your trail, though illness and my scarred legs made me too slow to catch up to you, until you came to Castlelow.
>
> And now you know, daughter, what became of your father.
>
> Now you know.
>
> Most stories have only one ending, but at this moment, this particular story has two. Two possible endings.

James the Bard stood, bowed slightly, and excused himself.

THE FIRST ENDING

I looked over to where the Old Burned Man was resting. He'd spilled his heart out, that much was true. Admitting to low feelings such as cowardice and vanity was most likely difficult. Cowardice, as he was not brave enough to return to my mother and me in time. Vanity, in assuming that we would reject him based upon his appearance.

It had taken courage, yes, to confess these things.

But perhaps it was a case of far too little, far too late.

Did he not remember my mother had died? Could he have saved her from the illness had he been there?

We would never know.

Therein lay the poison. We would *never* know.

It no longer bothered me to look at his scars, for they were as much a part of him as his eyes or his nose. No, it was not his physical appearance that bothered me. I could not look at him because he angered me still. Still.

I would not look at him because that would mean forgiving him. Forgiving him for abandoning me.

I motioned to Thomas to gather our things.

"Why, Trinket, we just got—"

I silenced him with a glare.

I felt the Old Burned Man's gaze and eventually returned it. I glanced at him with as little emotion as possible, then looked away, as if he were something insignificant, like an earthworm or a small beetle crawling among the dried grass.

From the corner of my eye, I saw him nod in understanding.

The Old Burned Man bent down and petted Thomas's pup. Thomas clasped hands with the Old Burned Man, as grown men do, then walked over to stand beside me.

I turned in the direction of the road.

I did not wave.

I did not look back.

THE SECOND ENDING

⬥━◆━◆━⬥

*T*he second ending, were I to choose it, would be more difficult.

I let the silence settle around me, comforting like the cloak my mother had made for me. Thomas knew better than to disturb my thoughts, and the Old Burned Man, well, he was intelligent in the ways of people.

The question was, could I forgive him?

Could I?

I knew in my heart it was the right thing to do. I knew I *should.*

But could I?

Would I always, when I looked upon his scars, feel my

blood seethe beneath the surface? Would I blame him for the death of my mother? Not that he could have prevented her illness, but perhaps he could have been there. He could have been there for me.

And I would not have been so alone.

Is there anything worse than being alone?

There was a time when I thought not. But now I was uncertain. I had managed fine with just myself and Thomas. Now we even had Pig. We had made our own family. And a person didn't need much if they had someone as loyal as Thomas by their side.

I did not need a father.

But did I, perhaps, still *want* a father? Not an imaginary one who lived on pirate ships or lulled dragons to sleep. But a real father. A damaged, disfigured, and remorseful man who somehow still managed to touch my soul with his words and touch my heart with his own.

I could not imagine what it cost him to tell me his tale.

Perhaps, one day, I could tell him mine.

—

I readied my sack, but I did not leave.

We had food aplenty that night. The Old Burned Man taught Thomas how to set a snare and he'd captured a fine rabbit, which they roasted on a stick over the fire. 'Twas tasty, and it is always easier to think when your belly isn't growling. I watched the Old Burned Man eat carefully, out of the corner of my eye. He handed little bits of food to Pig and laughed as the pup stood on his hind legs, trying to get the morsels.

"Look, he's a dancer," he said.

And then he smiled.

The Old Burned Man's smile reached all the way to his eyes. Eyes that were silver gray, just like mine. And when he smiled, he didn't look like a gruesome, scarred man.

He looked like my father.

James the Bard.

In that instant, the tiniest sliver of memory came to me and I saw him kissing my mother goodbye. I felt him pat me on the head.

He could feel that I was staring at him and he turned toward me.

"Where is it you'll be traveling to, then, Trinket?" he asked quietly.

"I do not know, I'll have to look at the old map—"

His eyes grew wide and he interrupted me.

"The map? You have my map?"

"Aye," I said. "You left it." I took the leather canister from my bag and placed it in his hands.

"I always wondered where it was. Thought I'd lost it along the road somewhere. And here *you* had it." He unrolled the map with care and pointed to a place east of Castlelow. "We are here." He paused for a moment, then added, "The question is: Where next?"

There was something in his voice that just might have been hope.

"I am not yet certain," I said, making up my mind at last. "I have many more stories to learn . . . Father."

THE SEVENTH SONG

Of Baubles and Trinkets

My father's lullaby

A chest of gold,
For thee, my sweet,
A chest of jewels
To lay at thy feet.

For no other lass
In all the land
Can tame the world
With but her hand.

Thy eyes like drops
Of crystal rain,

I know thy heart
But not thy name.

So take my gifts,
But darling dear,
And come with me,
There's naught to fear.

And I shall give thee,
My one true love,
The blessings of
The morning dove.

And in return,
For days long gone,
The nightingale
Will sing her song.

There is no trinket,
Bauble, nor pearl
Can match the grace
Of thee, sweet girl.

AND SO . . .

———◆━◆×◆━◆———

$\int$easons change.

So must we.

That which we hold on to so tightly eventually withers in our hands, and it is time to let go.

Time to let the winds carry the pieces away. For mayhap the small pieces are seeds. Seeds that will find a new, fertile ground somewhere to take root and sprout.

I took the small handful of seeds I had been clutching and cast them to the winds. Some took to the air; some fell in the nearby grass.

And one fell by my foot.

Only to be spirited away by a small bluebird.

"Do not judge by appearances," my mother had told me on the mountain overlooking Crossmaglin, "for something pure and good may reside under old, crabbed wrapping."

And so I was learning to see past the scars and sadness of my father and into his mending heart.

"Forgive." Her words drifted around me as she became a part of the evening sky.

And so I would learn to.

—

"Come now, Trinket," said Thomas.

"Aye," said my father. "Your harp is itching to be played again, and I know of a village not too far, just o'er the hills. They are soon to celebrate the marriage of their lord to a mysterious lass. Some say she's a Gypsy."

"Aye," I said, repeating it in just the way my father had said it. "'Tis time."

—

It took us three days to travel to the wedding of Feather and Lothar. Three days of getting used to a different rhythm on our journeys, for there were three of us now, instead of two, although Thomas would claim there were four. He counted Pig as a person.

Banners of crimson and gold were displayed up and down the narrow streets of Foresthill. This marriage was more a festival than a solemn ceremony.

And when I finally got to see Feather, she looked truly happy.

"Little Trinket, you have grown much," she said, taking me by the hands and twirling me around.

I stepped back. She was right. I had grown. No longer was I timid Trinket, the girl who searched for a father. Now I was Trinket the Story Lass. I had learned from a Gypsy girl to follow the calling in my blood and make my own future. I had been to the isle of the seal people and earned my harp. I had followed a young banshee to hear words from my dead mother. I had played music for the Faerie Queen and won a reward. I had traveled through the wall between the living and the dead with the help of a pooka. I had saved the lives of a loyal hound and my best friend.

And I had found my father.

"Trinket, will you play your harp for the wedding and tell us a tale?" Feather asked me. I looked at my father, and he nodded.

So I sat and strummed my harp. The notes rose up from my heart, out through the air, and into the coolness of the evening as a smile played upon Feather's lips.

I smiled back and cleared my throat, for now I did indeed have a tale or two for her.

For that is what I do.

That is who I am:

Trinket the Story Lass.

AUTHOR'S NOTE

I drew heavily from Celtic folklore (Irish, Scottish, and Welsh) when creating Trinket's stories, attempting to weave in bits of magic from the tales I heard as a child, researched as a grownup, and told to audiences myself as a professional storyteller. A good *seanachai* (Gaelic for storyteller) always flavors a story upon the retelling with a bit of her own soul.

The Gypsies and the Seer. Often I have wondered about seeing into the future. If I could, would I want to know what my future held? Those born with "the sight" appear often in folklore, and in ancient times, many a king had his own personal fortune-teller. The seventh daughter of a seventh daughter (or the seventh son of a seventh son) is said to be gifted with "the sight" in many cultures.

The Harp of Bone and Hair. Harps made from bones and hair have appeared in folktales all over the world. More often than not, the bones used are human. However, there is an old tale of a babe stolen by faeries and a mother who bargains with a harp made from a sea creature's bones, which is the basis for this story. Famed storyteller Sorche Nic Leodhas collected a version of this tale, called "The Stolen Bairn and the Sidhe." Of course, because of my fascination with seals, selkies found their way into the mix in my version. Selkies, the seal people, are common in Irish and Scottish folklore, and are often called roans or silkies.

The Wee Banshee of Crossmaglin. When I first researched banshees (back when I was about Trinket's age), I remember wondering if they were always ladies, or if there were ever child banshees. I could find no evidence of banshee children, but then, maybe those who know did not survive to tell the tale. I named my village Crossmaglin, which is similar to the real village of Crossmaglen in Ireland, because I love how that name sounds. However, my imaginary village with its Banshee's Tower bears no resemblance to the real town of Cross-maglen.

The Faerie Queen and the Gold Coin. I knew a former Irish priest who, when my daughters were first learning Irish dance, claimed that the best Irish dancers could complete their steps on the face of a penny, or so his old aunt had told him. I later learned that in truth, dancers would often pound large horse nails into the bottoms of their shoes to create sound when they danced, or even the occasional coin. Perhaps Orla was the first. As for the faerie folk, they have always been known as fine dancers and dangerous competitors. Irish poet and playwright W. B. Yeats collected many stories about the faeries.

A Pig Boy, a Ghost, and a Pooka. Oftentimes stories get jumbled up in the telling, where elements from one tale meld into the next. The term "highwayman" wasn't really in favor until the eighteenth century, although robbery along the road has been a danger since the creation of roads. There is a famous poem, "The Highwayman" by Alfred Noyes, which is hauntingly lovely, though the highwayman in my story is far less noble. As for the pooka, he is perhaps the most misunderstood creature of Celtic folklore. A shape-shifter who can be a wolf or an eagle, he is most often known as a horse who can talk with humans. Whether his intention be good or foul depends upon the story (and the pooka). In some places, the *pooka's share* is still left out for him on Samhain (the ancient name for the holiday we call Halloween). I visited a graveyard in the west of Ireland called Aghadoe, and though no ghosts came out to haunt me, the image of the graveyard with its crumbling headstones still does. So I rearranged the letters a bit and made Agadhoe the name of my town.

The Old Burned Man and the Hound. There is an ancient Welsh tale called "BeddGelert," about a brave hound that protects a royal babe but is killed by the king, who unfortunately misunderstands the situation. There is even a monument to this dog in Snowdon, Wales. I always hoped they got the story wrong, and that the brave dog lived. The great thing about being a storyteller is you can create a better ending.

The Storyteller and the Truth. *A year and a day* is a magical unit of time. Some legends hold that marriages can be dissolved after a year and a day or that perhaps the dead can return in special circumstances, but only for this length of time.

As with all tales, the true meaning of each story is for the listener to determine. And though I enjoy researching folktales, I do not claim to be a folklorist. Just a simple storyteller with a desire to pass along the magic of stories, hoping they'll reside in your hearts and minds for more than just a year and a day.

ACKNOWLEDGMENTS

Above all else, two very extraordinary people are responsible for Trinket getting the opportunity to tell her tales. Joanna Stamfel-Volpe, my amazing agent, who e-mailed me before she was even done reading the story to let me know how much she was enjoying it and how beautiful she found it. That e-mail changed everything for me. And Beth Potter, my brilliant editor, who loved the story as much as I did and helped me weave the words even more tightly so that they would hold together, true and strong.

Thank you to teachers/writers Nancy Villalobos and Chris Kopp, who read each of Trinket's tales, one by one, as I slowly finished them, and always seemed eager to read another. And faraway thanks to friends Holly Pence and Kathy Duddy, whose long-distance support is worth more to me than a thousand gold coins.

I could not be more pleased with the work done by the copy editors, the art directors, the amazing Dan Craig, and everyone at FSG Macmillan. I appreciate you so much.

Special thanks to my parents, John and Nancy Moore, and the rest of my wonderful family in New Mexico: John Moore III, Tammi Moore, Hope Moore, Jacob Moore, Jim Daniels, Elora Daniels, and Mia Daniels. My sister, Susan Moore Daniels, plays the harp so beautifully that I am certain her strumming echoed in my brain as I wrote this book. My nephew John Moore IV composed a hauntingly beautiful version of "Trinket's Lullaby" that makes me tear up whenever I listen to it. I am not sure what I did to be part of such a wonderful crew, but I am thankful for them.

To the dancers of the Comerford Irish Dance School and their director, Tony Comerford: thank you for several years of amazing rhythms and the inspiration I've gained from watching your feet fly.

To the students and staff of Jefferson Elementary: every day you give me hope for the future of our world. And, kids, I never get tired of you asking for more stories. Never.

And finally, to my husband, Sean: you put up with a lot while I was working on this book and it is only because of your support that I was able to finish it at all. And to my beautiful daughters, Noel, Isabelle, and Caledonia: you are my muses. My stories are always for you, first and foremost. So is my advice: never be afraid to live your dreams and tell your tales. I love you.